CHANGE OF HEART

"Look at me, damn it!" Jake insisted, shaking China. His fingers tightened in her hair, and he pulled her head back. She could hear his breath coming as fast as hers, harsh and shaky, ruffling the fine strands of hair on her forehead.

As soon as their eyes met, his lips came down on hers, while his arm pulled her closer. She braced for violence, but instead his touch was fevered, soft and urgent. Beneath this tender assault she wavered. Her hands slid from the wall of his chest to loop around his neck, and she was kissing him back.

"Jake, please—we can't do this," she said. "I'm angry at you. I don't like you."

He held her more tightly, and put swift, light kisses on her temple and her throat, then buried his lips against her breast. "I'm going to change your mind," he whispered.

Heaven help her, she knew he already had. . . .

ANNOUNCING THE

TOPAZ FREQUENT READERS CLUB
COMMEMORATING TOPAZ'S
1 YEAR ANNIVERSARY!

THE MORE YOU BUY, THE MORE YOU GET

Redeem coupons found here and in the back of all new Topaz titles for FREE Topaz gifts:

Send in:

 2 coupons for a free TOPAZ novel (choose from the list below);

☐ **THE KISSING BANDIT**, Margaret Brownley
☐ **BY LOVE UNVEILED**, Deborah Martin
☐ **TOUCH THE DAWN**, Chelley Kitzmiller
☐ **WILD EMBRACE**, Cassie Edwards

 4 coupons for an "I Love the Topaz Man" on-board sign

 6 coupons for a TOPAZ compact mirror

 8 coupons for a Topaz Man T-shirt

Just fill out this certificate and send with original sales receipts to:

TOPAZ FREQUENT READERS CLUB-1ST ANNIVERSARY
Penguin USA • Mass Market Promotion; Dept. H.U.G.
375 Hudson St., NY, NY 10014

Name_____

Address_____

City_____State_____Zip_____

Offer expires 5/31/1995

This certificate must accompany your request. No duplicates accepted. Void where prohibited, taxed or restricted. Allow 4-6 weeks for receipt of merchandise. Offer good only in U.S., its territories, and Canada.

A LIGHT
FOR MY LOVE

by

Alexis Harrington

A TOPAZ BOOK

TOPAZ
Published by the Penguin Group
Penguin Books USA Inc., 375 Hudson Street,
New York, New York 10014, U.S.A.
Penguin Books Ltd, 27 Wrights Lane,
London W8 5TZ, England
Penguin Books Australia Ltd, Ringwood,
Victoria, Australia
Penguin Books Canada Ltd, 10 Alcorn Avenue,
Toronto, Ontario, Canada M4V 3B2
Penguin Books (N.Z.) Ltd, 182–190 Wairau Road,
Auckland 10, New Zealand

Penguin Books Ltd, Registered Offices:
Harmondsworth, Middlesex, England

First published by Topaz, an imprint of Dutton Signet,
a division of Penguin Books USA Inc.

First Printing, February, 1995
10 9 8 7 6 5 4 3 2 1

 Topaz is a trademark of Dutton Signet,
a division of Penguin Books USA Inc.

Printed in the United States of America

For my mother, Nikki Harrington—
You were right, Mom.
I *could* achieve whatever I wanted.

And for my grandmother, Mary John—
Yaya, I wish you were here to see this.
But maybe you're watching over me after all.

For nuts-and-bolts support,
my thanks to Janet Brayson, Catherine Anderson,
Muriel Jensen, Stella Cameron,
and Katherine K. Brown.

To KMC and MEM, my special thanks
for inspiring Jake and China.

Author's Note

This is a work of fiction. While I used some of the locations, names, facts and events from late nineteenth-century Astoria, I omitted or changed others for the sake of this story of China Sullivan and Jake Chastaine.

I would like to acknowledge Captain George Flavel (1823–93), his great-granddaughter, Miss Patricia J. Flavel, and the Clatsop County Historical Society for providing inspiration for China's lovely red-roofed home.

Prologue

China Sullivan ran down the street in the fog-shrouded dawn. She could feel her heart pounding against her breastbone. Hurry, she told herself, every second counted.

Headed for the wharf, she clutched a letter in her hand. It was a poorly spelled, masculine scrawl of words that would profoundly affect at least three lives if she could not reach its writer in time. What she would say she wasn't sure, but she had to try. She tightened her cloak against the chill mist, fear and fury impelling her toward the waterfront.

Something had awakened her with a start just a half hour earlier. She realized now it had been the sound of the front door closing. On the pillow next to her she'd found this accursed letter from her older brother, Quinn. At the bottom of the page she'd also found Jake Chastaine's scribbled signature. A rough, brawling fisherman's son from down the hill, he was Quinn's best friend, but China detested him. She was mildly surprised that Jake could even write, considering that (it seemed to her) he'd skipped more days of school than he'd attended.

The letter contained Quinn's good-bye to her, saying that he and Jake would be leaving on this morning's tide, shipping out on the *Pacific Star*, a full-rigger bound for Canton. The journey would take more than a year.

She had scrambled into her clothes and run downstairs and out the door.

Now she dashed past the tidy, gracious homes in her neighborhood, past maple and walnut trees, shed of their leaves. A hollow reverberation sounded beneath her shoes on the sidewalk, and her breath came in harsh gasps, creating vaporous clouds. Dodging a puddle in the muddy street, she agonized over this turn of events. Quinn was really, truly going. How could he simply leave? she wondered. Didn't he realize that without him in their tiny, parentless family, she'd have to raise their younger brother, Ryan, practically by herself? Aunt Gert was a dear soul but so giddy-brained, with her collection of people's calling cards. China had long ago assumed responsibility for running the house and directing the help. She had tried every argument on Quinn. Some of their encounters ended in disgracefully raised voices and slamming doors. But in the end he could only give her a bored look and keep repeating the same answer. He had to go—if he didn't, he was going to bust. He was almost twenty and he hated the soft life they had in this big house, he said. He wanted adventure, he wanted to see the world with Jake.

Jake, she thought venomously. It was at his feet that China laid the blame for Quinn's ideas. He had far too much influence on her brother. In fact, many people fell prey to his indefinable magnetism—even Aunt Gert adored him. But China wasn't so gullible.

Even his name irritated her. John Jacob Chastaine. Trust that a swaggerer like him would be named after the town's famous and affluent founder, John Jacob Astor.

She paused on the corner, breathless, holding her side, to let Mr. Gerding's milk wagon pass. The driver gave her a startled look, as if wondering why a well-bred young woman was out at this hour of the morning. She had Jake to thank for that too. She lifted her hem and hurried across the street, which was slick with fallen leaves.

When it had occurred to her that Jake might be the only one who could talk sense into her brother, in desperation she'd sought him out. And she *was* desperate. Nothing short of this calamity could have made her want to spend more than two minutes with Jake. He was not the kind of boy her mother had raised her children to associate with. And where had the meeting with him gotten her? China's face burned when she thought of that discussion in the parlor alcove yesterday afternoon.

"Jake, the family needs Quinn. There are just the four of us, counting Aunt Gert. The Captain is never home. You're the one person who can make him see that he has to stay in Astoria."

Jake Chastaine stood at one of the long windows with his shoulder slouching against the frame. China turned a displeased eye on his dungarees and work shirt. The gentlemen in her circle wouldn't dream of appearing in a lady's parlor dressed like that. But Jake was no gentleman.

At twenty-one years old, he was tall, muscular, and long-legged, having skipped altogether the awkward, lanky phase other boys went through. Although he was certainly not the type of man who appealed to China, even she had to admit that he was good-looking, in a rough, earthy way. Quinn had mentioned once or twice that Jake turned female heads wherever he went. Well, Althea Lambert could probably vouch for that.

There was an offhand self-assurance about Jake that had always annoyed China. A boy who had grown up on the docks had no reason to exhibit such insolent confidence. Was she the only one who saw through the veneer of his lazy charm to his barely suppressed, reckless danger? That Quinn had brought him home all those years ago—well, there was just no accounting for it.

Jake pushed aside the lace curtain and looked out at the masts lined up at the wharf in the Columbia River as though he hadn't heard a word she'd said about Quinn. He thrust a hand through his sandy hair, finally directing his gaze at the well-furnished parlor.

"The Captain gave you a nice house, China," he said, gesturing at the room. "I grew up poor, in the row houses on Tenth Street." He gave a dry, humorless chuckle and turning back to her, fixed her with a stare. "But you know that. I don't want to spend the next fifty years working on a fishing boat like my pop." He looked absently at the scars left on his hands by fishhooks and heavy nets. "There has to be something better and I'm going to get it."

China raised one brow and gave him a skeptical look. She wondered if that was what he was telling Althea as well. China knew a lady shouldn't even acknowledge such tawdry gossip, but the whispers were flying around town about the ship chandler's daughter. Althea was saying that Jake Chastaine had gotten her in trouble, then refused to marry her. That scandal alone had given China more than adequate reason to bar him from the house. But Aunt Gert had reported that Jake swore Althea's claim was nothing but a jealous lie, and Gert had sided with him.

He narrowed his eyes briefly as he glared at her full in the face. Then, as if seeing her thoughts, he said, "I'm not the man who got Althea Lambert pregnant."

China blinked at the blunt term—no one of her acquaintance ever said that word. *Expecting*, or *in the family way*, or *enciente*, those were words they used.

"If she really is pregnant," he added as a cynical afterthought.

Caught in his unwavering gaze, for an instant China almost believed him. Then she pushed away the thought. Of course he denied responsibility—China wouldn't have expected more from him.

"The reason I'm going is because I want a better life than I grew up with," he continued. "If Quinn wants to come along, I can't stop him. He's old enough to make his own decisions."

China supposed she couldn't fault him for wanting to improve his lot. But Quinn had a decent life right here and now. Her brow wrinkled as she grew impatient. "My father is never home in this nice house he gave us, Jake. I'm eighteen and I can count on my ten fingers the number of times I've seen him. I hardly know him, and Ryan—he's only ten. He thinks the Captain is an exciting stranger who comes to visit." China was grateful that Zachary Stowe, her most ardent suitor, had no interest in a career at sea. Being a sailor's daughter had been hard enough. To be a sailor's wife was unthinkable. "We're all the family we have, the four of us. If my mother were still alive . . ." Her voice trailed off, then she repeated, "Quinn will listen to you. If he's really your friend, tell him to stay home."

He shook his head with finality. "He made this choice himself. I have my own plans. I need to prove—" He shrugged his shoulders and jammed his hands into the pockets of his dungarees. "Look, it's his decision."

Jake was every bit as stubborn and unreasonable as Quinn. China cast about in her mind, trying to think of a way to move him from his resolution. Then an idea struck her. It was disagreeable at best, but she didn't know what else to do. "Maybe if *you* stayed in town, Quinn would too."

He looked at her and carefully searched her face. For the briefest moment, she saw something in his clear green eyes that was so intense, so painful to look upon, that she could only stare, unable to identify it. Then it vanished and his expression became—well, suggestive was the only way she could describe it. Even if Althea Lambert was lying about Jake—and in China's mind, that was unlikely—she hadn't created his reputation. He'd done that himself, and it was firmly established. Suddenly China hoped that Aunt Gert was still close by in the back parlor down the hall and not in some far-off corner upstairs.

He gave her a slow smile. "And maybe there's another reason you want me to stay. One that has nothing to do with Quinn."

China felt a blush heat her cheeks and ears. "If

you're implying that *you* interest me in some way—" she began indignantly, putting special distaste in "you."

It seemed to do the trick. The smile faded and he flinched as though she had rapped his knuckles with a ruler. When he spoke, his words were hostile, but at least he returned to the subject at hand. "Damn it, China, I'm not Quinn's father. He's going to do what he wants. And maybe he should."

"Then there's no point in continuing this conversation, is there?" she said icily, anxious to end the meeting. "But know this, Jake: if you take Quinn with you, you will never again be welcome in this house as long as I live in it."

Jake glanced out the window once more, as though there were something fascinating to see beyond the glass. Suddenly he turned to face her and walked to the dark brocade settee where she sat. For a horrible moment she thought he was going to sit beside her, and she gathered her full pink muslin skirts to rise in retreat.

Instead he stunned her by dropping to one knee in front of her. He reached out and rubbed one of her black curls between his fingers. She sucked in her breath and pulled back. She'd never been this close to him; he certainly had never touched her. His eyelashes were uncommonly long, she thought irrelevantly, and he smelled of the ocean.

He gave her another long, searching look. "I'll *never* be welcome?"

She shook her head, wary at his closeness.

In a low, intimate voice he said, "Then here's something to remember me by," and he covered her mouth with a hot, voluptuous kiss. His mouth on hers was evocative and demanding, as though he was trying to bend her to his will. His touch made her insides feel shivery in a way that she'd never known. China was so completely shocked, she couldn't speak. Then he jumped to his feet and strode from the alcove. An instant later, she heard the front door slam.

All through the night she'd been tortured by the thought that her first kiss, an important event in a young woman's life, had come from that uneducated, impudent son of a fisherman. And what was even worse, for an instant she'd almost liked it. Almost.

Now, in the cold dawn, China hurried down the wharf, her feet pounding on the weathered boards. She had to step carefully to avoid the gaps left by missing planks, through which she could see the oily river water eddying far below. Held in place by the thinning fog, the pungent odors of creosote, rotting sawdust from the sawmills, and refuse from the slaughterhouse and seventeen fish canneries slapped her in the face.

The docks were alive, swarming with horses and wagons and shouting, swearing longshoremen rolling barrels, filling cargo nets. China hung back for a moment. This was no place for an unescorted woman. But then she thought of her mission again and hurried on.

Only a few ships were in port this morning. She peered at their names as she passed them. Where was the *Pacific Star*? Suddenly she heard the deep-chested bawl of a horn and looked through the lifting mist to see the huge barkentine being towed downriver by a tugboat. Indistinct figures moved on the deck.

Too late. Oh, God, she was too late.

"Wait!" she yelled at the top of her voice. She

jumped up and down, waving the letter like a flag. "Quinn, don't go! Quinn! Come back." But the river was wide and her words were lost under the noise of the tug's steam engine and the screeching gulls hovering over the docks.

She stood like a statue on the planking and didn't try to stop the tears that blurred her vision as she watched that ship carry away her brother and the man who had convinced him to go. For no matter what he said, China would always blame Jake for this. The vessel would continue its westerly course down the last seven miles of the Columbia River and then it would cross the bar into the Pacific Ocean. After that, any fate could befall her brother—disease, accidents, drowning were all common to sailors. It was entirely possible that she would never lay eyes on Quinn Sullivan again.

China took bitter pleasure in knowing that Jake Chastaine faced the same risks.

Chapter One

Astoria, Oregon
January 1888

Jake Chastaine stood on the dock in the waning daylight, the long shadow of a main mast falling across his shoulder and over the planking. He glanced back at the tall ship behind him, a graceful barkentine named the *Katherine Kirkland*. Then he pushed his hands into his back pockets and took a deep breath as he scanned the town laid out before him.

The steep streets looked the same, reminiscent of San Francisco's. More homes had been built, but up behind them lush forests still rimmed the town, dropping back to Saddle Mountain to the southeast. From the crown of those high-hilled streets, he knew, a person could watch fog creep in from the Pacific Ocean. It stole up the Columbia River and spread out over Young's Bay, cloaking in soft gray mists the tall ships anchored at the wharf.

Or if the weather was clear, the bones of the *Desdemona* showed themselves. They rose from the sandbar named for her, the first ship to run aground there in 1857.

On the west end of town, sitting proudly on its own block, was the biggest house in Astoria. It was an impressive structure, with red shingles and three-story turret, and within its sturdy walls lived a sea captain's beautiful black-haired daughter.

Every night a hall window on the second floor glowed with a lamp that burned for all the men gone to sea and all the souls lost forever to its dark, icy depths.

Jake lifted his eyes to the faraway red roof on the hillside. He'd faced a lot of uncertainties since the long-ago day he sailed from Astoria. But he knew that lamp was still—and would always be—there in the window. Nothing would change that.

After all, it had burned in his heart, kindled by hope, consumed by futility, for half of his life.

Jake paused just inside the door of the Blue Mermaid, taking in the chaos before him.

The noisy, hot saloon was in the heart of Astoria's toughest district, aptly known as Swill Town. The dirty windows were steamed over, and the place was jammed with seamen, loggers, and fishermen. A nickelodeon played in the corner. Dancing to its tinny melody, a nearly comatose sailor shuffled around the floor with a bored-looking saloon girl. He held a gin bottle by the neck while his head sagged on the girl's powdered-white chest. Kerosene lamps hung from the ceiling, their smoky flames adding to the haze. There were so many spittoons placed around the floor, a person had to walk carefully to avoid stepping into one. Like most of the buildings on the waterfront, this one was built on pilings over the Columbia River, and the stench of low tide drifted up through the floor. Added to that were the

smells of fish, beer, and whiskey, all overlaid with
a trace of opium smoke.

Jake smiled. The Blue Mermaid was like any of
the other fifty such establishments in Swill
Town—dirty, crude, and raw. But to him it felt
like home.

"By God, I don't believe my eyes! Jacob
Chastaine!"

Jake turned to see Pug Jennings vault over the
bar, an amazing feat for a man of Pug's short stat-
ure. He plowed through the crowd, and when he
reached Jake, he gave him a hug that crushed the
breath right out of him. The saloon owner stood
not one inch over five feet, but in his compact
body he had the strength of a bear. Any patron
foolish enough to challenge him came to regret it
when he found himself on his duff in the street,
his broken nose bleeding into his lap.

"Lemme look at you," Pug said in his gravelly
voice. His entire face lit up with an ecstatic smile
as he held Jake back at arm's length. "By God,
Jake Chastaine," he repeated. "I can't believe it's
you. You sure got big since you've been gone. But
I knew you. I'd know you anywhere. When did
you get in?"

Jake laughed with honest pleasure. Here, at
least, someone was glad to see him. Even if it
was Pug Jennings, and even if this was the Blue
Mermaid. Thank God, it looked the same, right
down to the painting of a coy nude that hung on
the back wall. "Early this morning. It's good to
see you, Pug. I wasn't sure you'd still be here after
all this time."

"Of course I'm here. Where would I go?" he
questioned, waving Jake toward the counter. "I'll
buy you a drink." The little man returned to his

post behind the crowded bar, playfully slapping one of the saloon girls on the rump as she passed. He stepped up on an eight-inch riser that ran behind the bar and brought him up closer to Jake's height.

Jake let his gaze wander around the place, recalling the many times he'd sat on the end bar stool when he was a kid, drinking root beer and hiding from the truant officer. No one had thought to search for a youngster in a dockside saloon. Pug hadn't nagged him much about skipping school. It had been plain that he took for granted that Jake would end up a fisherman like his father, Ethan Chastaine.

"Hey, you gob!" Pug snapped at a sailor passed out with his head on the scarred oak. He reached over and shoved the man's arm until he stirred. "Go sleep it off somewhere else and make some room here." The sailor dutifully roused himself and staggered to the door.

Pug set two glasses on the bar, then unlocked a cabinet and produced a dark bottle. "This calls for the good stuff."

Jake chuckled again, taking the vacated space at the counter. He remembered "the good stuff." On his fifteenth birthday Pug had declared him a man and bought him his first scotch right here. Quinn's aunt Gert had thrown a fit when she found out about it.

Pug poured them each a hefty measure, then raised his glass to Jake's. "To bowlegged women."

"To bowlegged women," Jake repeated, clinking his glass to Pug's.

The little man leaned a beefy arm on the counter. "How is that you're home after all this time?"

That was a good question, Jake thought. Since the morning he left, he'd wondered if he'd ever see Astoria again. After all, he'd had no reason to come back, even though his memory had turned toward this town nearly every day for the past seven years.

Then, five months ago, in a New Orleans saloon a lot like this one, a small miracle had occurred. And it had changed everything—his status, his future, his possibilities. He'd had to return.

Jake took a big swallow of the smoky, peat-flavored whiskey. "That big barkentine tied up at Monroe's?"

Pug nodded. "I saw her. She looks like a real lady."

"She is," Jake agreed. He put his elbows on the bar and leaned forward. "But she needs some work, so I brought her to Monroe. Then I'll be looking for a cargo for her." Jake smiled with a sense of quiet exaltation. "She came to me thanks to the owner's folly and a pair of threes."

Jake almost laughed at the bartender's amazed expression.

"You mean she's yours? And you won her in a poker game?"

"She's mine, all right, Pug. Every inch of her canvas."

Pug slammed the flat of his hand down on the bar, his face split with an incredulous grin. "Well, I'll be damned for a one-eyed dog! She's really yours? What's her name?"

"The *Katherine Kirkland*."

Obviously impressed, Pug straightened his stained white apron and backed up to salute him. "So it's *Captain* Jake, is it? And a tycoon, too?

I'm surprised you'd want to come back to the old Blue Mermaid."

"Come on, Pug," Jake mumbled, slightly embarrassed. I'm not any different. And I'm sure as hell not a tycoon."

Pug punched him in the shoulder, his smile undimmed. "I'll bet your old man is proud of you. What did he say?"

Jake looked away and drained his glass. "I haven't seen him."

"You probably will while you're in port. You might even catch him in here—the rheumatism keeps Ethan on shore most of the time now." Pug poured them both another drink.

Jake sipped this one more slowly. With his stomach empty, that first shot had gone straight to his head. "Things weren't so good between Pop and me before I left. You know that."

"Yeah, I know," Pug said. "He didn't like the company you were keeping, hanging around up at Brody Sullivan's house, if I recollect."

Jake took another drink of scotch. "That and some other things."

Pug glanced at him, then pushed a bar rag down a short length of countertop between them. "He meant well, but you and him were too much alike to keep from butting heads. To him, your being friends with Quinn was bad enough, but wanting to leave Astoria . . ." Pug shook his head, letting the sentence hang unfinished.

Jake wasn't comfortable with this topic. He and Pop were *nothing* alike. A familiar pain, a dull anguish he had believed healed long ago, suddenly rose in his chest. His thoughts turned down old paths he'd rather they not take. Especially when he thought of the reason that had driven him to leave Astoria in the first place. The echo of arguments and accusations rang through his memory: Pop's voice raised in fury, Jake's own voice shouting back, an image of his father's set, angry face.

Changing the subject, Jake said, "Can a man still buy a meal in here? I haven't eaten since daybreak."

Pug's face took on the expression of a concerned hen. "Anything you want, we can cook it for you. You want oysters? We got oysters. Steak? Fish? Ham? The food isn't fancy, but it's good."

"A steak would be fine. I haven't had one in weeks."

"You got it, and all the trimmings." Pug turned toward the kitchen door. "Jimmy!" he shouted.

No one appeared.

Pug shouted for his cook again. "Jimmy, damn it!" He turned to Jake. "He's a nice kid and a good cook. Came from Athens by way of a Lisbon steamer. But he hasn't got much English, and I don't know any Greek except for swear words." After a third try, Pug went to the kitchen himself, yelling to Jimmy in his limited Greek.

Jake grinned, recognizing every curse. He'd worked with a few Greek sailors himself. Good old Pug—except for some gray hair he hadn't changed one bit, and Jake was glad for that.

He nursed his drink while he waited for his dinner, drawing solace from the fuzzy, relaxed comfort the whisky gave him. That made it easier to push thoughts about Pop to the corner of his mind for the time being.

But the chief cause of their old arguments— well, *she* was as clear in his thoughts as ever. How would she view him now? If China Sullivan saw him today, captain and owner of his own ship, would she still look down her nose at him? Or would she instead see him for the man he'd become?

Now and then he glanced at the mirror on the back bar, casually watching the people behind him and next to him. He listened, too, to bits of conversation going on around him. It was a habit he had acquired over the years—never letting down his guard, especially while he was in a waterfront saloon.

After a few moments he became aware of two men to his right. Something about them seemed off kilter. They wore expensive suits. That alone caught his attention. A dive like the Blue Mermaid didn't attract the upper crust, but that description didn't fit these two, either. They were a little too rough.

"Well, I'd feel better if Williams was out of the picture. He's getting to be a goddamned pain in the ass," the younger of the pair complained. "Every time I turn around, there he is, stirring up a ruckus. Last week he stood outside Maggie Riley's saloon, handing out leaflets and ranting like a preacher at a revival meeting. He went on and on about the 'poor sailor' being a victim of 'the new slavery.' He's like John Brown back from the grave. The *Astorian* even ran an item about it."

The other man nodded, holding a match to his cigar. The end of the Havana glowed like a hot coal. "I didn't pay him much mind when he started this a couple of years ago. But he's a persuasive firebrand, and people are beginning to listen to him." He let out a huff of laughter and a cloud of smoke. "It's a good thing city hall doesn't."

The first man went on. "But up till now he's always worked alone. Lately I've heard a rumor that he has a partner helping him, maybe financing him. We don't need that."

"Larry, you worry like an old lady. I've heard that rumor too. But at fifty or sixty dollars a head, there are too many people making too much money for that Williams character to be real trouble for business." The man shrugged. "Anyway, maybe we can find out who his partner is. Who knows—with a couple of double eagles in the right hands, we could teach them both a lesson."

Jake continued to sip his whisky, elbows on the bar and shoulders hunched, giving no appearance of eavesdropping. He knew the "business" of these two businessmen. They were crimps, shanghaiers. They took blood money from captains, the fifty or sixty dollars mentioned, to find crewmen for outbound deep-sea vessels. That usually involved getting a man drunk, drugging him, or somehow tricking him aboard a ship. Most captains got their money back by deducting it from the sailor's pay. Jake saw it as a regrettable but necessary part of sea trade. He knew it was also very profitable for men like those next to him, as well as bartenders, boardinghouse landlords, and brothel owners. Captains who resisted working with the crimps could get the holy hell beaten out of them or find their vessels damaged. The crimps sure wouldn't let some crusader—or his sidekick—get in their way. It wouldn't matter how zealous this Williams was. To these people, he was only a fly speck.

Just then he saw Pug coming toward him, a big platter in his hands. Jake's last thought about Williams was that he'd probably get his name in the newspaper one more time: when the police fished his gray, water-bloated corpse out of the river.

"Please be careful with that," China Sullivan appealed. "It—it's been in my family for a long time." With no little trepidation she watched as the two sturdy Jesperson brothers maneuvered her mother's elegant sideboard down the hall toward the front door. She knew that the draymen were more accustomed to loading barrels of flour and lard for Landers Bakery than moving fine furniture. As they passed her, red-faced and sweating from their efforts, she stretched out a light hand to touch the beeswaxed cherry wood one last time.

She followed them as far as the porch, watching anxiously as they ferried the heavy piece down the steps. When it listed sharply to the left, China's breath caught on the lump in her throat.

A muffled but audible curse rose from the general vicinity of the sideboard. "I told you we should have brought Lucas to help!" Rogan Jesperson grunted at his brother.

They righted their burden after a brief, grappling struggle, and continued to the waiting dray. With considerable effort they hoisted it onto the back of the wagon. Their horse, as sturdy as the brothers, stood like a granite sculpture in the traces while the wagon pitched under the weight of the sideboard.

China waited until Rogan covered it with a tarp, and then allowed herself a shaky sigh, feeling her eyes begin to burn. She was being ridiculous, she knew, but telling herself that didn't seem to help.

The drayman climbed the stairs again to China's porch, his auburn head a bit of color under the slate gray sky. "Ma'am," he huffed, "if you'll just sign here—" He held out a receipt book and pencil while dragging his forearm across his wide brow.

China hesitated a moment, then took the pencil into icy fingers. In complying with his request, she signed away one more piece of the life she'd grown up with.

"You'll try to avoid the bigger ruts in the street?" China asked hopefully as she scratched her name on the slip.

A look of mild horror crossed Jesperson's broad face as he took the book back and poked the pencil behind his ear. "Mrs. Landers would have our hides if we damaged this sideboard before she even got it into her house. Don't you worry, ma'am, we'll give it a real smooth ride." He handed her the receipt.

China only nodded, afraid that hearing her own increasingly constricted voice would make her break down all together. This was just business, she kept reminding herself. She had no way to pay her long-delinquent bill at Landers Bakery, and this was the agreement she and Sam Landers had arrived at. In exchange for the cherry sideboard his wife had admired, the debt would be forgiven, and she would even have a credit balance. The fact that Mrs. Landers had first seen the piece as a dinner guest at her parents' table was something China would have to disregard. Those days of comfort and security were gone forever—she'd so taken for granted that her future held both—and she was in no position to entertain the luxury of embarrassment. There were mouths to feed in this house.

Rogan Jesperson returned to his wagon, and

China went back into the house, unwilling and unable to watch them leave. She should be used to this by now, she supposed. But if she was forced to sell or trade away too many more of their furnishings, the family would be sitting on packing crates brought down from the attic.

As she looked down the hall toward the kitchen, she saw the bright rectangles of unfaded wallpaper, ghosts that marked the places where pictures used to hang. And as she saw those, her mind automatically took a right turn into the back parlor and relived the afternoon six months ago when she'd sold the red turkey carpet. She'd half hoped that she'd find money hidden under it when it was rolled up. But there had been nothing beneath except bare hardwood floor.

If only Quinn were here, she pondered, as she did at least once a day. He would have made all the difference. She wouldn't have been reduced to these penurious circumstances. Or suffered the humiliating experience of having shop owners call at the front door to collect on the bills she'd incurred to support the household. He would have prevented all of this.

But Quinn wasn't here. And, as always, when she thought of why, Jake Chastaine's rough good looks rose in her mind's eye to irritate her. Still, she reflected on her way to the kitchen, she'd made a certain peace with herself about the matter. After all, Quinn might someday find his way back to Astoria.

Jake Chastaine? She knew she was rid of him for good.

"You have to say yes. China will be so happy to see you."

Like hell she will, Jake thought. He eyed Gert
Farrell dubiously. He'd just stepped out of A. V.
Allen's store when he'd seen Gert, the woman
who'd been more of a mother to him than his own
had. After the excitement of reunion, Gert had
begun pressing him to come back to the house.
Pride prevented him from pointing out that China
had banished him from the Sullivan home long
ago.

He lifted his voice slightly to be heard over a
beer wagon that rumbled past, letting his eyes rest
unseeing on the gold-leaf lettering painted on its
dark side. "I wouldn't be too sure about that . . .
besides, I've got a lot of things I need to take care
of and I don't want to be a bother."

"Stuff and nonsense," she snorted, not letting
him wiggle free of the invitation. "That house got
to be so big and empty, we rented out a couple of
rooms. You're family—you wouldn't be any more
bother than our other guests."

Jake brought his gaze back to her, puzzled. The
Sullivans were renting rooms? He supposed that
might make things more businesslike if he stayed
there. He discarded the idea, shaking his head.
"No, it wouldn't be—"

Gert drew herself up slightly and fixed him
with a determined look. "You said yourself you
hate living in a hotel. You used to like staying
with us. You spent enough time there when you
were a boy."

Oh, goddamn it, Jake swore to himself. He felt
powerless against her barrage of guilt-provoking
arguments. He *did* hate hotels. He'd spent last
night at the Occident, and even though it was a
nice place, he'd lain awake, listening to every foot-
fall in the hallway, every key in every lock on the

floor. Still, he knew in his bones that it would be a mistake to give in to Gert. He wanted to see China, to talk to her, but not under these circumstances. So he wondered where his next words came from.

"All right, I'll come, but only if you let me pay you."

Gert glanced behind her at the grocer's door, then turned back to look at him. Her blue eyes twinkled. "It's a deal."

"Aunt Gert, is that you?" China called from the kitchen. She cocked her head, her scrub brush halted in mid-stroke as she listened to the sounds of indistinct voices and muffled footsteps in the entry. The clean, damp smell of the wooden flooring drifted up to her nose. "Aunt Gert?"

When she got no answer, China threw the brush in the bucket of soapy water and rose from her knees. She pushed a wet hand at loose curls that straggled from her hairline. Susan Price must have wandered away and left the front door open again. China glanced out the window at the monotonous drizzle falling from a leaden sky. The cold dampness would seep into the house faster than the furnace could keep up. She'd have to make a point of watching Susan more carefully. The poor soul was becoming more absentminded and vague every day.

China was about to step into the hall when her great aunt appeared in the doorway, carrying two plucked chickens.

"Well, there you are," China said. "I thought I heard someone. Where are the groceries?"

"A. V. Allen's is sending their delivery boy with them. And you'll never guess what," Aunt Gert

said, carefully making her way to the table on a
dry path across the floor.

"What?" China responded warily. "Is Mr. Allen
complaining about our bill?" She felt terrible that
she'd been able to pay so little on their account.
Thus far Mr. Allen had been very kind about letting her charge, though not all of her other creditors were so patient.

"No, no," Aunt Gert replied, putting the chickens on the table. She pulled off her gloves and
removed her hat, revealing snowy hair pulled into
a tidy knot. "Maybe that's because I told him
we've rented another room."

"Not yet we haven't. You probably shouldn't
have said that." China wished they could avoid
taking in another boarder, but there was no helping it. She couldn't bring herself to ask for more
rent from old Captain Meredith and Mrs. Price.
She charged them less than they would have paid
anywhere else in town, but their circumstances
were even worse than hers.

China began to walk around Aunt Gert, but the
older woman blocked her way, her expression triumphant. "But that's my news, dear. I found another paying guest while I was out. He's in the
foyer."

"Aunt Gert! Without asking me? Without an in-
terview?" China was aghast. She was accustomed
to handling all of the family business, including
the boarders, and she was very particular. "How
could you rent a room to a total stranger you met
on the street? We might be murdered in our
beds!" She loved her mother's aunt with all her
heart, but Aunt Gert could be as trying as a child.

"That's just it. He's not a stranger and he paid
me, *three months* in advance. Now how do you

like that?" Gert folded her arms over her chest, her smile smug.

"Who is it?" China asked, her misgivings continuing to grow.

Aunt Gert only gave her that same pleased grin. "Go see for yourself."

"Oh, God," China moaned as she pushed past her aunt, rolling down her sleeves. Certain that no good could possibly come from this, she hurried toward the front door, trying to tuck up her straying hair, her stride purposeful. She couldn't imagine who Aunt Gert had dragged home—not one of their acquaintances needed a room in a boardinghouse. "We'll just have to return the money."

"China, wait a minute—"

China rounded the corner and saw a tall, wide-shouldered figure standing in the entry, his back to her. He wore a pea coat and faded dungarees. A sea bag was on the floor next to him, propped against his long leg. Just as she suspected, this was no one she knew.

"Good afternoon, I'm China Sullivan," she said, fumbling with her cuff buttons. "I own this house and I understand—"

The man turned to face her, and every word she was about to say left her brain. She could only stare at him.

"Hello, China," he replied. His voice was rich and seasoned, like polished mahogany. He considered her for a long moment, his gaze appreciative, his smile tentative.

No, it couldn't be him, her stunned mind insisted. Not after all these years. Every emotion she'd ever felt crowded together, electrified by a sense of shock.

He was bronzed and blonded by seven years

of punishing storms, equatorial suns, and wind-whipped saltwater. His sea green eyes were more vivid than ever, and even his brows and lashes were tipped with golden frost. He was so stunningly handsome, even if he'd been a stranger, his face alone would have made China pause but—

"Jake?" she managed in a bare whisper, her hand at her throat. "Jake Chastaine?" She'd supposed he must be dead. As much as she'd disliked him, she'd found no pleasure in the idea, after all. But now here he stood, not ten feet from her, a full-grown man. And a memory of that afternoon in the alcove, including the kiss, came rushing back as though it were yesterday.

"Isn't this a happy coincidence?" Aunt Gert chirped, joining them. "You see? I told you we knew him. I was just going into A. V. Allen's when we ran into each other. He had a room at the Occident, but we can hardly let him stay there, not when he has us." She turned to China and gripped her wrist. "Heavens above, child. You look like you've seen a spirit. Are you all right?"

"I'm fine," China breathed unsteadily, trying to comprehend the reality of the big man standing in her entry hall. His eyes swept over her, taking in her faded skirt, wet at the knees, and her plain blouse, unbuttoned at the neck. She knew she looked like a scullery maid. "I'm fine."

Studying China, Jake swallowed and tried to decide if he agreed. The pampered, baby-doll prettiness that had made her name so fitting was gone. She was a woman now. She was thinner than he remembered, the hollow in her throat more noticeable, her jaw a bit sharper, her cheekbones better defined.

At the same time he couldn't help but recognize

how the curves of her body had ripened, giving her fuller breasts and rounding her hips. Her skin looked creamy white and marble smooth in contrast with her black hair, and her blue eyes glimmered like dark sapphires. Even dressed like a scrub woman, in that old skirt and blouse, the grace of her upbringing shone through. And she fixed him with a look that could have crumbled stone.

"You didn't say what brings you back to town, Jake," Gert went on.

He dragged his eyes away from China. "I decided to come home for a while. I'm doing some business here, and I had to bring my ship into dry dock."

"Why, Jake," Aunt Gert exclaimed, beaming, "are you a captain now?"

He looked at China again, nodding. "I own the *Katherine Kirkland*. Her home port is San Francisco." His gaze lingered on China's face. "She's beautiful."

China closed her collar, feeling uneasy. His scent, an evocative combination of salt and fresh air, drifted to her. It was a scent she remembered very well. Why was he here now, after all this time? she fretted. Over the years she'd tried so hard to temper the fury she felt toward him for taking Quinn away with him. Now it was back with a vengeance.

"It's interesting that you still think of Astoria as home," China sniped, regaining her voice. She made a fussy show of adjusting her cuffs. "Let's see, how long has it been since you left?" She knew that it had been precisely seven years and three months.

Barely conscious of it, Jake leaned backward a

bit. China's voice and words were as sharp as obsidian. Although he ignored her barb, his tone acquired a slightly defensive edge. "Mrs. Farrell told me you're renting rooms now."

China heard the question buried under his remark. How had the wealthy Sullivan family been reduced to taking in boarders? She glared at the older woman.

"When was I ever 'Mrs. Farrell' to you, Jake?" Gert scolded affectionately, obviously missing the tension of the conversation. "I was your Aunt Gert as much as my niece's children's. You might be all grown up now, but haven't I known you since you were just a pup? Before you were Captain Chastaine?"

China nearly scowled at her aunt.

Jake's frown relaxed into a sheepish smile, and tipping his blond head, he looked at the oval rug under his feet. "Yes, Aunt Gert."

China barely refrained from rolling her eyes.

"All right, then. I'll let you two work out the details. I need to put a couple of chickens in the oven for dinner."

"*One* chicken, Aunt Gert. There is nothing to work out," China jumped in, anxious to put an end to this right now. "We don't have a room available."

"China," Gert murmured. "Where are your manners?"

"I'm sure Jake understands," she replied, directing a cold glare at him. "Give him back his money, Aunt Gert."

In turn, Jake gave China a hard, intimidating look that almost made her back down. He still had a sense of reckless danger that made a person think twice about crossing him. Finally he released her from his gaze. His frown returning, he bent to lift his heavy bag to his shoulder. "I'd better go back to the hotel, Aunt Gert."

Panic crossed the woman's face.

"What's the matter?" China asked.

"Jake, please—don't go," Gert urged. "Just excuse us a moment." She gave China a meaningful look.

Jake straightened and put down the bag. He nodded, turning to look out the window in the front door, as China and Aunt Gert retired to the kitchen.

He had navigated ships through furious storms, confronted men who would have slashed his throat for the gold in his back molars, and worked in gale-blown rigging a hundred feet above a rolling deck. But he'd never been as scared as he was just now, facing China Sullivan in the foyer after all this time. His stomach in knots, it had taken every ounce of courage he had to climb those front steps. As it turned out, his fear had been justified.

But he'd be damned if he was going to let her see it.

When China and Aunt Gert reached the kitchen, China closed the door.

"What's wrong?" she whispered impatiently.

Aunt Gert clasped her hands together, lacing and unlacing her fingers. "China, we have to let Jake stay, at least for two months."

China shrugged irritably. "Why? Let him go to a hotel—let *him* worry about it. We don't owe him a thing."

"Yes we do. Nearly all the money he gave me is gone. I paid our bill at Allen's Grocery. Mr. Allen was going to cut off our credit."

China gaped at her aunt. This situation was growing worse by the minute. She massaged her temples as she looked at the rain snaking down the windows in thin rivulets. "But—but Jake can't stay here. He just can't!"

"I don't know what else we can do," Aunt Gert said. "Anyway, that little spat between you two happened years ago. I'd think you'd have put it behind you by now."

It was all China could do to keep her voice down. "Little spat? You know I never liked him. That nasty business with Althea Lambert was a terrible scandal. And what about Quinn? Am I supposed to forget that Jake coaxed him to desert the family? Quinn wouldn't have left if Jake hadn't talked him into it, and we wouldn't be in this fix."

"Your brother was a determined, stubborn mule. Jake couldn't have talked him into or out of anything. As for Althea, I never believed her story for a minute. I don't think she was even expecting. As soon as Jake was gone, so was the baby."

"Well, she had a miscarriage. Aunt Gert, why on earth would a girl make up something like that? Her reputation was ruined, and she had to move to Portland. All because of Jake Chastaine." China would never understand Gert's blind loyalty to him.

"Althea was jealous and determined to marry him. When all her coquetry didn't work, she tried to trap him. There *are* women like that, you know," Aunt Gert replied.

"I suppose Jake told you that?" China demanded.

"Yes, and I believed him. He was no angel, but

he was never a liar. Anyway, at least we *know* Jake. He paid in advance, and we can use the money. The boy from Allen's is going to be here any minute with our order." She opened the bread box and looked inside. "I can't understand why our food doesn't go farther—sometimes it seems like we're feeding an army instead of four people. I could have sworn there were two loaves left after dinner last night. This morning I only found one." She closed the box again.

"I wish we could have discussed this first," China complained, sidestepping Gert's remark about the bread. Her aunt was right about one thing. There was nothing else they could do now that most of Jake's money had been spent. China would have to let him stay, for a while anyhow. But she didn't have to make it pleasant for him. And despite whatever saintly notions Gert might have of him, China certainly wasn't going to put him in easy proximity of her own bedroom. She wouldn't rest a minute.

"All right, we'll rent a room to him," China huffed, lifting a key from a row of hooks next to the back door. "But we're going to put the rest of his money away and not spend it. I want him out of here as soon as possible."

China walked back to the foyer where Jake waited. At her approach he turned to face her. She swore he was taller than when he'd left and he'd definitely filled out. He blocked out most of the light coming through the front door window. He was still slender, but his shoulders were bigger and there was just more of him. Not much of the rowdy boy she'd known remained in this man's muscular form. But in his eyes—those green eyes—she saw a fleeting expression so familiar, she had to look away for an instant.

"This isn't a good idea, China," he said, his words cool. "I don't want to cause you any trouble, so I'll be on my way."

"No, it *isn't* a good idea," she agreed bluntly. "The day before you left Astoria I told you not to come back to this house again. But Aunt Gert acted in my stead, so I'll honor the agreement she made with you. Now, come on. I'll show you your room." She turned on her heel and marched back down the hall, not bothering to see if he followed.

She finally heard his tread behind her as she led him through the butler's pantry to the back stairs. She was very aware of him then, as though he generated heat and light, and she strove to stay far ahead of him as they climbed the circular staircase. She stopped a moment at the linen closet on the second floor to collect bedding and towels. Then, never once looking at Jake, she continued to the third story, where the attic and two servants' rooms were located. Thin gray daylight from the small windows revealed a couple of battered chairs, picture frames, a birdcage, toys, and assorted boxes and trunks. She continued down a narrow passageway, finally stopping at a pair of doors.

She pushed open the door to one of the little bedrooms and let Jake go in first. It was a wood-walled enclosure, as plain as a monk's cell, painted white and sparsely furnished with a bed, a washstand, a spindle-back chair, and a four-drawer chest, all made of pine. An oil lamp was set on the chest. The window had no curtain and not even a rag rug decorated the painted floor. Being directly under the eaves, the ceiling angled down sharply. The room had the smell of an old closet, long ignored.

"This is what I have," China said, waiting for him to object. They stopped just inside the door, and she could see this was the only place in the small room where he'd be able to stand completely upright. "The other room is just like this, but it doesn't have a window."

He dropped his sea bag on the floor and looked around the stark quarters, then at her. "China, does the captain know you've had to turn this place into a boardinghouse?"

"I'm surprised Aunt Gert didn't tell you," she said coldly, struggling against rising humiliation. "Three months after you left, I learned my father was washed overboard in the North Atlantic. He'd made several bad investments and he died without a dime." She gained a measure of satisfaction from his stunned expression, and deliberately paused a beat before adding, "We've done our best to get by, but of course, it would have helped if my brother was here."

He hunched his shoulders, jamming his hands into his pockets as he glanced at the dark floor. With that single mannerism, one that he'd had since childhood and one which had always annoyed China, she felt propelled back in time.

He looked up at her again. "I'm sorry to hear about it." He started to reach for her elbow. "Can I help with—"

To cut off his question, and before he could touch her, she pulled away. She didn't want his hand on her arm, and she certainly didn't want his hypocritical sympathy.

Taking a step back, she recited the rules of the house. "Meals are at eight, one, and six. If you're not on time for them, we won't wait and you'll go without. You get clean bed linen and towels once a week." She dumped the sheets and blankets into his arms. "You're responsible for making your own bed, and you can use the bathroom on the second floor. We have two other guests in the house—you'll meet them at dinner."

"Are you sure you want me in the house? Maybe you'd rather give me a stall in the carriage house," he fired back, his expression stony.

The carriage house. China froze, a flutter of caution rippling through her. "Do you want this room or not? It doesn't make any difference to me. I can rent it to anyone."

After an uncomfortable moment he grumbled, "Yeah, I'll take it."

China quietly released the breath she held. "Then you'll follow the rules. Here's a key to the back door, but at ten-thirty I latch the night locks. If you're out past that time, you'll sleep somewhere else. All right?"

"I suppose I can remember all that," he snapped. He took the key she held out to him while trying to keep his grip on the bedding.

"Fine, then." She turned to leave, then stopped, her hand on the doorknob. Keeping her back to him, she asked, more quietly, "Do you know where Quinn is?"

"Not for sure," Jake replied, plainly surprised that she didn't know either. "I lost track of him a couple of years ago. I thought he must have written to you."

She looked at him over her shoulder. "He never has." She nearly ran from the room to get away from the questions lurking behind his green eyes.

*   *   *

Jake listened to the sound of China's footsteps hurrying down the back stairs. He made his way to the bed, careful to duck as he went, and sat heavily on the bare mattress. The bedsprings screeched under his weight and he sighed, resting his chin on the bundle in his arms.

He felt like a dog trapped on the wrong side of a fence. He knew he wasn't supposed to be here, and China hadn't forgotten that either. Of course, she'd been shocked to see him, but he'd hoped she might not be so mad about it. After all, they were adults now. But she was still as high and mighty and stuck up as she'd been when he left. That intense rush of emotion he'd felt when he first caught sight of her in the hallway, that was just a reasonable reaction to seeing a familiar face after so long.

He shifted on the bed and looked out the small window to the street below. What, he wondered, had transpired between China and her aunt that made her change her mind about renting a room to him? And such a room, he thought, looking around again. The door, apparently not hung correctly, began to close. Why had he agreed to stay here and *pay* to be treated like gutter slime? Okay, maybe he felt a little guilty, and goddamn it, guilt was a bad reason to do anything.

He'd paid his best crewmen two months' wages to stay around Astoria until the ship was ready to sail again. They were probably getting drunk in the saloons, Jake assumed a bit wistfully, and visiting the girls who worked upstairs. He shifted to move away from a bedspring that was poking him through the thin mattress. He knew they were having more fun than he was.

The Occident was beginning to seem like paradise compared to this. Better still, he wished he was back aboard the *Katherine Kirkland* in his own quarters, somewhere on the ocean. They were no bigger, but they were captain's quarters, not servants'.

He thought about what he'd found, coming back to this house. The captain was dead? The family broke? He didn't see Quinn as often as he would have liked—they'd been on opposite sides of the world since their voyage to Canton—and now he realized that China's brother was as ignorant about all this as he'd been. He didn't know his father had died, or that his sister was renting out rooms. What else had happened to China, to the rest of the family? She hadn't let him ask, and he supposed he had no right to.

He knew time could change a lot of things, but China was the most changed of all. Her soft girl-ishness was completely gone. She'd grown more beautiful than he'd ever envisioned, but in a cold, untouchable way.

He put the sheets down and flopped back on the too-soft mattress, feeling morose. As a young-ster, the only sense of family he'd ever known he'd found here. He hadn't expected to come back and find everything to be the same after all these years.

But he hadn't expected everything to be differ-ent, either.

After she finished the kitchen floor, China went directly to her bedroom at the end of the hall and closed the door. She sank to the little sofa in front of the cold fireplace. Her legs felt like rubber and her hands trembled so, she could barely pull the handkerchief from her pocket. She twisted the square of linen, nervously tying the corners in knots.

Captain Jake Chastaine, she sneered to herself, the brawling fisherman's son, the one who'd convinced her brother to abandon his family and sail around the globe. How dare he come here? she marveled. Oh, and he was proud of that title, wasn't he, *Captain* Chastaine?

For the first few months they'd been gone, she'd let herself hope that Quinn would come home. He'd have his adventure and then return. She'd worried and fretted, wondering if Quinn was safe, thinking she'd forgive him—and even Jake—for anything, just to have the family together again. But when the months rolled into years, she'd begun the struggle to put them both out of her mind. The pain she'd felt eventually healed, but had left a scar in her heart.

Now instead of getting Quinn back, Jake was here, and she felt that scar begin to ache again. He looked so different. He was still able to charm Aunt Gert, too. He'd actually blushed when Gert had reminded him that she was still his aunt. But there was something more to him that maturity alone hadn't given him. It was hard for her to put a finger on. It was the air of experience he had about him, an authority, a seasoning that could only come from the kind of work he'd done and the places he'd seen. It should have come as no surprise to her that he was more attractive and compelling than before. Still, after all his misdeeds and escapades, she thought it only fair he should be weathered and coarse and ugly.

She rose from the sofa and went to her cheval glass. Putting a hand to her cheek, she knew she, too, looked different from the eighteen-year-old girl Jake had last seen. Her face had lost its gentle roundness, and she felt as though every trial of the last seven years must be written there.

Well, she thought, a pretty face could hide a disloyal heart the same as a tired one. More easily, in fact. That made her remember Jake's remark about the carriage house. She was almost certain he didn't know anything. He'd been gone a long time, and she and Dalton Williams were very careful to keep that secret. Even Aunt Gert didn't know about the carriage house.

She wandered to the window and looked out at the Columbia River, moving in its relentless path toward the open sea. That sea had taken so much from her—Quinn, her father. Even Ryan.

Quinn. In all these years she hadn't had one word from him. Not a letter or a wire. She struggled against the hurt that rose from this thought. It was Jake's fault, she reminded herself. Jake was the one who'd dreamed up the idea of going to sea.

China stayed in her room, looking at the river from her alcove, until her own gloom touched the January day and evening settled in. She thought of sneaking down to the kitchen to bring dinner up here, but that would be a cowardly thing to do and her pride wouldn't permit it. So a few minutes before six, she changed her clothes to go downstairs. As she stood before her mirror repinning her hair, she wondered how in the world she'd be able to sit at the same table with Jake, three meals a day, for the next two months.

Jake woke suddenly, his eyes snapping open to darkness. He jerked up to his elbows in a middling panic. Had he slept through his watch? That was impossible—the second mate would have come to wake him. No, wait, he was the captain now. Captains didn't stand watches. Automatically his mind turned to estimating the *Katherine*'s location. He always had an approximate idea of where his ship was, no matter which ocean she sailed, even during a storm. Now he came up with a blank. Expecting to feel a slight rolling under him, to hear creaking timbers, the very silence and stillness of his bed added to his groggy confusion. Then he saw a square of feeble moonlight on the wall next to him and remembered where he was.

He sat up and rummaged in his coat for a match, striking it with his thumbnail to read his mariner's pocket watch. It would be just his luck to be late for dinner and give China another reason to level that frosty sapphire glare on him. Before he could open its gold case, the watch chimed six bells. Great, he thought dourly, seven o'clock straight up. God forbid that she'd bother to get him. It wouldn't have inconvenienced her to send Ryan up here to knock on the door. The fuse on his temper began to shorten.

He shook the match out and huddled deeper into his coat to ward off the chill. It looked like he'd have to buy a meal from one of the saloons downtown. While he was at it, he'd get a stiff drink, too. He'd need it to stay warm in this cupboard.

His mind made up, he stood without thinking and banged his head on the low ceiling over him. "Son of a bitch!" he swore loudly, stooping and rubbing his scalp. Lighting another match, he held it cupped in his hand and went to the door. He yanked it open, nearly pulling off the knob. As he stalked through the black passageway to the stairs, he resolved to get *several* stiff drinks.

But before he did anything else, before another minute passed, he was going to find Miss China Sullivan and demand a room on the second floor.

"Don't worry about the dishes, Aunt Gert," China called from the kitchen. "I'll wash them. You go on to St. Mary's." She ran hot water in the sink, clanking the cooking spoons and silver noisily. Then she found a tray in the butler's pantry in the hall and brought it to the table to put a napkin on it. From a pot on the stove she ladled leftover chowder into a bowl. All the while she listened tensely to hear the front door close.

Aunt Gert was due at St. Mary's Church on the next block to play piano for the benefit musicale rehearsal. She'd been pressed into service by Sister Theresa after the nun had broken her finger playing baseball with her geography students on a rare sunny day. Gert would be busy all week with the practice, and the timing couldn't be better.

"I should be back by about nine, dear," Gert replied, coming to the doorway while she buttoned her cloak. "That is, if there are no more arguments about the program. Last night Mrs. Rand got into a huff about having to perform first. I'm taking Susan with me. It will do her good to get out among people."

China glanced at the tray, then walked toward Gert, barely resisting the urge to take her aunt's arm and escort her to the foyer. "Have a good time."

Gert sniffed. "I don't know about that. If the church didn't need a new roof, I'm not sure I would be so eager to do this. I'd rather stay here

and work on my cards." Gert's collection of calling cards had grown to imposing proportions, and
she endlessly sorted and arranged and rearranged
them. "Oh, that's good, China," she said, nodding
at the chowder, "I'm glad to see you're fixing
something for Jake. I wish he could have come to
dinner, but I put some roast chicken and dressing
on a plate for him. It's in the oven."

"Um, well, I suppose you don't want to keep
Sister Theresa waiting," China prompted again,
growing nervous.

Aunt Gert turned toward the front door. "No,
no. Patience is certainly not one of her virtues. By
the way, did you give Jake your father's old room?
He'd probably be comfortable there."

"*I* would not be comfortable with him there!"
China exclaimed, stiffening her back slightly. Indeed, she thought it was a perfectly dreadful idea.
That room was directly across the hall from her
own and much too close. With his reputation, she
wanted Jake as far away from her as possible. "I
put him upstairs."

"Yes, dear," Gert went on, "but in which
room?"

"He chose the one with the window," China
declared, her tone defiant.

"You mean in the servants' quarters?" Gert's
voice dropped as though she spoke of the ante-
room to hell. "But China, it's so plain and bare
up there. And there's no heat on the third floor—
you wouldn't even let Casey sleep in those
rooms." Casey had been their elderly dog. They'd
buried him next to the gazebo a year ago.

"Casey was old and sick," China said. "Jake is
anything but. He'll manage. Don't worry about it,

Aunt Gert." She stressed the last sentence, meaning to convey that the subject was closed.

"Well, dear, it doesn't seem right . . ."

China listened to Gert's voice and footsteps trail off and held her breath until she heard the front door open and close again. Letting out a sigh, she went back to her task.

She looked at the chowder in its plain white bowl. Soup wasn't much of a dinner for a big man used to big meals. After a second's hesitation she went to the oven and pulled out the warm plate Aunt Gert had left there for Jake.

She glanced over her shoulder now and then, half expecting to see him. She didn't know why he hadn't come downstairs for dinner, and she supposed she should have gone to get him. After all, the money he'd paid secured him a place at the table. But, blast it, she'd told him what time dinner was served. She herself had been so edgy, her food had sat untouched. The shock of seeing him again, combined with the anticipation of having to sit across the table from him, took her appetite. When he didn't appear, she was relieved.

Just as she was filling a coffee cup to complete the meal, she heard footfalls pounding down the back stairs. Alert to the sound, she lifted her head. Jake. She knew it was him—no one else in the house used that staircase. Quickly she grabbed her old shawl from its hook next to the back door and threw it over her head and shoulders.

The steps grew closer.

She snatched up the tray and—silver, there was no silver. Her heart beating fast, she put the tray on the table again. Then she rushed to the china cabinet and jerked open a drawer to pluck out a fork, knife, and spoon.

Footsteps sounded in the hall.

Hurry, she told herself. She had to be outside before Jake saw her. She pulled open the back door and rushed into the foggy winter night.

Jake arrived in the kitchen just in time to see an indistinct female figure run past the window through the misty light that reached the walk. The blue gingham curtain on the back door pane still swung gently on its rod. He walked to the door and opened it, but couldn't see much besides the vague shape of her skirt moving across the yard toward the carriage house. He closed the door again and scanned the room. The smell of food lingered in the air, but there was none to be seen.

His stomach growled, and Jake, his appetite raging and his patience gone, strode down the hallway. He looked in the dining room, the library, and the front and back parlors. He found no one except an old man dozing in a chair by the fire in the back parlor. One of the boarders, Jake assumed. He retraced his steps to the kitchen, but China wasn't there. No one was there.

Baffled, but by far more irritable and hungry, Jake walked back to the front door and let himself out. His boots carried him down the path to the sidewalk. He glanced back at the big house. Jake had few regrets in his life. He hoped that returning to Astoria wouldn't prove to be one of them.

Chapter Two

China stood before a lamp set on a small cherry table at the second-floor hall window. Given the elegance of most of the other furniture in the house, this serviceable lamp was plain to the point of homeliness. Lacking even a hint of decoration, its chimney and base were clear glass, showing its wide ribbon of wick floating in the kerosene. She had others that were much prettier and more delicate of craftsmanship, made of milk glass and hand-painted with roses and forget-me-nots. But to China, no other lamp burned as bright, no other was as necessary. She patted her apron pocket to make sure she had matches, and heard the clock downstairs mark the quarter hour. Fifteen past ten. Usually she lit the wick right after sunset, but so much had happened today, she hadn't been able to get to it. Now it was late and everyone in the house had settled down for the night.

Everyone except Jake.

She extended her hands to lift the lamp's chimney, then paused. Pulling aside the lace curtain, she tried to see down to the street, looking for an approaching figure. The gas streetlight on the corner was a watery yellow orb in the mist, seemingly suspended high above the sidewalk with no post. She couldn't see anything except black night and the rain that had fallen steadily since morning.

Jake wasn't home. She knew because she'd crept up to the attic a few moments earlier to check. She hadn't heard anything of him since he'd come pounding downstairs just after dinner, and she assumed he'd gone out. Slinking along the passageway like a thief, a skill at which she was becoming quite adept, she'd seen no band of light under his closed door. She'd knocked once, sharply, then swung the door open and found the room empty. She hadn't stayed there long—what if he'd walked in and found her? He might think she wanted to talk to him or something. Besides, the room was uncomfortably chilly. But she'd been there long enough to glimpse his sea bag propped against the wall, and his chronometer and octant on the dresser, so she knew he'd be back.

Well, he'd better step lively, she told herself. If he thought she was joking about locking him out at ten-thirty, he was in for a surprise. She *would* lock him out and not feel a moment's remorse. At least she told herself she wouldn't.

As she pondered this, she heard footsteps on the back stairs up to the attic and knew her threat wouldn't be tested tonight.

A whisper of relief brushed her. Not because she cared what happened to him, she told herself. Certainly not. Jake Chastaine could sleep in the gutter for all she cared. Forcing herself back to the task at hand, she removed the lamp chimney and struck a match on the matchbox.

"For all men gone to sea, living and lost," she intoned, touching the match to the wick. "May you find the way back to your home port." She replaced the chimney and light filled the end of the hall. Continuing the tradition her mother had begun as a seafarer's bride, China said this blessing every evening.

For all *men gone to sea* . . .

For her father, for her brothers. But never for Jake Chastaine. He was the only one who had found his way back, she reflected again, and still her mind could barely comprehend it. She'd seen him, infuriatingly handsome, taller than ever, vaguely threatening. She'd talked to him and heard his voice, full and mature.

As she headed back downstairs to lock the doors, she knew that though she had to let him sleep in her house, she would never forgive him for what he'd done.

"Captain Olin Meredith, this is Jake Chastaine. He'll be staying with us while his ship is in dry dock." China introduced the two men, nearly shouting at the old sailor, whose hearing had faded.

She made an effort to ignore the way Jake looked this dark, rainy morning as he stood at the mantel in the dining room, his back to the fire. The various shades of blond in his hair shone under the gaslight of the chandelier. He wore an oatmeal-colored wool sweater that revealed the stretch of his shoulders. The sleeves were pushed up on his forearms, which were dusted with sun-bleached hair. His dark blue wool pants fit close against his flat belly and long legs. When China lifted her eyes to his face, she realized he'd caught her staring, and heat rose to her cheeks. He gave her a long, steady look before turning his attention to the captain. She quickly turned her gaze to the tablecloth.

Captain Meredith appraised Jake from under bushy white brows. The captain's face was florid and leathery, his hands as gnarled as driftwood. The ever present meerschaum pipe clamped between his teeth was unlit, in compliance with China's ban on smoking in the house.

"What're you sailing, lad? Not one of those goddamn steamships, I hope." Captain Meredith couldn't hear himself any better than he could hear others, so his voice boomed across the room.

"No, sir. She's a barkentine, built in Maine, home port in San Francisco," Jake answered in a voice trained to carry.

"You her master? There's a good lad. By God, I'm glad to have a man to talk to. These women just don't appreciate an exciting story. I remember when I was about your age, let's see, I was sailing on the *Black Pearl* out of Portsmouth. Or maybe it was the *James Wright* out of Boston. Aye, those were the days. We were on the west coast of Africa, working our way toward Good Hope. No, come to think of it, it might have been the east coast. Anyway, a squall came up out of nowhere, howling like the devil's own whore from hell—"

China winced at the language, but left the dining room with a malicious smile when she saw the look on Jake's face: that of a man who realizes he's trapped and is helpless to do anything about it.

She crossed the hall to the kitchen to help Aunt Gert serve. There she found Susan Price, their other boarder, slicing bread at the table.

"Susan, you know we love your help, but really, you don't have to work," China said.

Susan was just a few years older than China and her complete opposite. Hardly bigger than a child, she was plain-faced, fragile, and fair-haired, with a temperament to match. Her husband had been killed at sea two years earlier, when he fell from a yardarm into the churning ocean. Months had passed before the news of his death reached her, and when she came to live at China's house, she was hollow-eyed, detached, and of severely limited means. She had a talent for millinery fashion and earned extra money making hats for Aunt Gert's friends.

"Oh, but I don't mind," she said in her small voice. "Edwin loves my cooking. He always wants seconds." Edwin Price was Susan's late husband.

Aunt Gert looked up at her from the other side of the table, then exchanged glances with China. This had happened a couple of times now—Susan referring to Edwin as though he were still alive.

"Well, we're glad for the extra hands. Come and hold the platter while I spoon up these eggs," China urged from the stove. The woman complied and watched China slide her cooking spoon under the fried eggs as Aunt Gert scooped mush into a tureen.

"I wish we had some bacon to go with this. What will Jake think of plain old oatmeal and eggs for breakfast?" By way of explanation, Gert turned to Susan and added, "We have another guest staying with us, Susan. An old friend of the family."

"Jake isn't going to starve, Aunt Gert," China said. "We've gotten along all right on this food. It certainly is good enough for him."

"I still think bacon or sausage would have been nice," Gert complained. She paused and gazed at the floor a moment, as though trying to harness a memory. "I was just thinking about the first time Jake came to the house. Let's see, I guess he was around fourteen years old." She let out a wry chuckle as she resumed scraping the sides of the mush pot with a wooden spoon. "He brought Quinn home after giving him a prize-winning shiner. Those two boys, both of them were proud and brash. Quinn was a roughneck, but Jake, he was just as tough, growing up on the docks the way he did, and big for his age. I never knew who started the fight—one of them said something the other didn't like and the fists started flying. But for all that he was a bad boy, Jake had a kind heart in him. I knew it right off." Gert laughed again. "Jake tried to pretend that he was just delivering a troublesome smart aleck, but I could see he was really worried about Quinn. And Quinn was so mad that he had gotten beat! Remember, China?"

China rapped the big spoon on the edge of the pan. "Oh, I suppose."

Did she remember? How could she forget that clear summer morning? She and Gert had been right here in this kitchen, helping Edna, their cook, bake cakes for the parish bazaar. A tall, dangerous-looking boy with dirty blond hair had come through the back door, pushing her brother ahead of him. They'd both been a horrifying mess— filthy, scraped, and bloodied—and still as wary of each other as two gamecocks. Jake might have won the fight, but Quinn had given nearly as good as he got. Jake sported a purpling bruise over his cheekbone, and his right hand was a shambles of raw, bleeding flesh, torn across the knuckles. He looked down at it and pulled out his shirttail to wrap it up. One of his sleeves flapped at the shoulder where it had been ripped away, and both boys had obviously rolled around in the dust.

Aunt Gert laughed about it now, but at the time she'd been so agitated she was nearly useless. China, often the one to take charge despite her youth, had found a piece of beefsteak for Quinn's eye while he slouched in a chair at the table, scowling at Jake.

China hadn't meant to stare at Jake. But she had never been that close to a boy from "down the hill," as she and her friends had referred to the people living near the docks. He was so different from anyone she knew, so fascinating and scary. His clothes were old and worn and poorly mended. And she didn't like him. Not because he was poor. She knew her own father had had modest beginnings. No, she disliked Jake because he was tough and dirty and looked like nothing but trouble. Still, she'd supposed she should see to him.

But when she approached him and tried to look at his hand, which by that time had blood-soaked his shirttail, he backed away, nearly snarling at her.

"Don't touch me," he snapped. "I don't need your help."

"Fine, then," she replied, surprised by his raging hostility. "Your mother can take care of it." His face went oddly blank at her remark. Later she learned that his mother was dead.

Jake wouldn't come into the kitchen but lingered by the back door, his sea green eyes flashing. His stance was rigid, hostile, and too cocky by half to suit China. Yet when he'd looked at her again, for just an instant she thought she saw something else in those eyes. Something that stopped her in her tracks and made her feel pity for him, although she couldn't imagine why. He was the one who'd hit her brother.

He shifted his glare to Quinn. "I don't want to have to whip you again, and you know I can do it. So don't come down to Tenth Street looking for trouble."

Then, bleeding and scraped as he was, he turned and was gone.

But in the way of boys and youth, the argument was forgotten, and China had seen Jake back at the house a week later. And he and Quinn had begun a friendship that would take them around the world together.

Even at fifteen or sixteen, Jake had sometimes been known to get roaring drunk on a Saturday night, after having spent the week working on his father's fishing boat. On those occasions he would participate in spectacular fights. China had never understood why he bothered to attend mass the next morning. She'd see him sitting in a back pew, fidgeting uncomfortably in the ill-fitting, old-fashioned dress clothes he wore, his thick hair combed flat to his head with water. She was certain she felt his eyes drilling into the back of her head. It was a scandal, the way he looked, his face bruised and puffy. She had never shared Aunt Gert's view that it was repentance and Jake's basically good heart that brought him to Father Gibney. Jake had never been repentant a minute in his life, for anything. She'd seen it in his swagger, in the way she caught him looking at her when she suddenly turned in his direction.

China dragged herself to the present. Now that he was grown, he'd given her no reason to change her mind about him. Oh, true, some of that cockiness he'd had seemed to be gone—now he was commanding in a way that gave her the impression he expected to be obeyed.

Gert, China, and Susan crossed the hall to the dining room, bearing the breakfast dishes. China could hear Captain Meredith still taking advantage of the audience he'd found in Jake.

"In ribbons was her tops'il and I thought Davy Jones would have us sure, that blackest of black nights—"

"If you two will take your places, we'll eat breakfast," Aunt Gert said. She put the mush on the table, then pointed to a chair directly across from Susan's. "Jake, you can sit there."

Grateful for the reprieve, Jake stood behind his chair, waiting for the others. The old captain told a good story, but there was no stopping him.

Jake flexed his shoulders, trying to work the ache out of his back. Sleeping on the lumpy, sagging bed in that cold room had told on him. He'd already had a knot on his head before he hit it on the ceiling again this morning. During the long night he'd been wakened by the clatter of rain pelting the roof just a couple of feet over him. The sound usually had a sedating effect on him, but this had been so close it made a noise like gravel hitting the shingles.

His gaze was pulled to China as she moved around the table, pouring coffee from a flowered porcelain pot. She was tidier than when he'd seen her yesterday. Now a fringe of inky curls framed her face while the rest of her hair was pulled into a soft knot on the crown of her head, revealing her long, creamy neck. Her small sapphire earrings matched her eyes. She'd abandoned the silly, frilly gowns he remembered for a high-necked white lawn blouse with leg-of-mutton sleeves and a skirt of deep burgundy. When she got to his cup, he caught the subtle fragrance of her perfume, of dark spice and wood, unlike the lavender and rosewater other women wore. Their eyes met for an instant before she moved to the next cup. She stood so close, he could see her black, silky lashes.

Overall, she looked softer and more approachable than she had yesterday. He was glad, since he planned to ask for a room on the second floor. Maybe she would be easier to deal with now—

"Well, sit down, Jake," she ordered, moving away.

He briefly gripped the back of his chair with tight hands. Then he stepped forward and held Aunt Gert's chair.

"Thank you, Jake," Aunt Gert replied, clearly approving.

Jake was introduced to Susan, who stared at him across the table with haunted, searching eyes, as though trying to place him.

To escape the uncomfortable scrutiny, he let his own gaze wander. The dining room was as he remembered, with pale yellow walls and a fire blazing on the hearth. The first time he'd eaten in this room was when Quinn had invited him to dinner. He was afraid to sit on the fine brocade chair in his dirty dungarees and old work shirt, but Aunt Gert had welcomed him and set a place for him with the rest of the family. For the first time in his life, he felt it most keenly that he was just a kid from the waterfront, especially with Quinn's snooty little sister staring at him from the other end of the table. He was terrified he'd spill something or break something or make a mistake. To hide his nervousness, he kept his eyes on his plate, looking up only now and then at a painting on the opposite wall. It was a picture of one of Captain Sullivan's early vessels, the *Joyce P. Frankenberg*, a square-rigger under full sail in choppy seas. He searched for that painting now, but he didn't find it. Then he realized the floor was bare and the massive sideboard that had stood against one wall was gone, too.

China tried to pretend that this breakfast was no different from any other, but she wasn't having much success. She was painfully aware of the extra person sitting at the table. Though she refused to let herself look at Jake, that blond head of his shone like a beacon, and time and again he appeared in her peripheral vision. Feeling no more appetite than she had the night before, she pushed her cooling food around on her plate with her fork. Only a bite or two actually went into her mouth. Her mush, for which she had no particular fondness anyway, congealed in its bowl. She was glad Aunt Gert kept the conversation going because she could think of nothing to say.

"Jake, tell us about the *Katherine Kirkland*," Gert urged, pouring a drizzle of cream over her mush from a silver creamer. "It's uncommon for a man your age to own a ship. How did you come into the money to buy her?"

China flinched at the bald question, and directed the slightest frown at her aunt. Gert could be artlessly blunt sometimes, and she was getting worse. She claimed that her nearly sixty years gave her the right to be frank. Still, although loath to admit it to herself, China was curious about the same thing: had Jake done so very well after leaving Astoria?

Each person at the table except China, but especially Susan Price, leaned a bit in Jake's direction, forks stilled. Old Captain Meredith cocked an ear toward him, waiting for his reply.

Jake sipped his coffee, the dainty porcelain cup looking out of place in his grip. "I didn't buy her. I was the ship's mate and I won her in a poker game from the man I sailed under."

"Eh?" came Captain Meredith's blaring inquiry. He wiped his nose on the napkin tucked into his shirt collar, and his white brows drew together as he demanded, "Who'd be daft enough to wager a ship in a card game? That's like wagering your own mother!"

"Yes, it is. But the master who bet her said she'd lost her luck."

The air filled with a confusion of voices, all speaking at once.

"Lost her luck! Jake, dear, have you lost your *mind*?"

"Aye, that master wasn't daft, but you must be. I'm surprised you made it all the way to Astoria on that doomed ship."

"Sell her—you must sell her. There's terrible danger—"

China said nothing, thinking that this was so typical of Jake. Bold and audacious, he thought he could lead anyone, conquer anything. But this was serious. Loss of luck was the worst thing that could happen to a vessel, even worse than sinking. A drowning, the voice of a ghost, any odd occurrence could jinx a ship. Once it occurred, ill fate would hound her to the day she sailed to the scrap yard, and until then she would lose lives, money, and time. No captain or buyer would knowingly enter into an alliance with a jinxed ship. This was just another example of Jake's recklessness.

Jake glanced down the table at China. She remained silent, offering no advice, not looking at him. She jabbed idly at her eggs. Judging by her expression, he wasn't even sure she was listening.

Jake shook his head and put a spoonful of sugar in his coffee. "I've navigated the *Katherine* for four years. She was stubborn and slow and plagued with all kinds of accidents. But she hasn't lost her luck. It was that captain who was unlucky. He was a foolhardy tyrant who was too fond of Russian vodka, and he sacrificed crewmen's lives and his ship's grace because of it. He stayed in Charleston after the card game, and once he was ashore, she never gave me another moment's worry. I sailed her around the Horn to get here. She has the manners of a lady, and she responds like a new bride."

China's head came up at this remark.

Captain Meredith nodded approvingly, then posed in a hopeful tone, "Will you at least rename her? To trick the bad spirits who've taken note of her?"

"No. It's said she was named for a woman with rare beauty and a very kind heart." He looked at China again, then added, "No man could ask for more."

China focused her attention on her plate, her mouth tight at his allusion. Jake Chastaine was in no position to discuss kindness. If he'd had a kind heart, he would have left Quinn in Astoria. Ignore him, she told herself. Just eat your toast and ignore him.

"I was hoping to see Ryan. He must be nearly grown by now," Jake went on, gesturing at an empty chair. "Has he already left for school?"

A vast, yawning silence fell around the table, and no one rushed to fill it. The hiss of the gas chandelier overhead suddenly seemed very loud. Only two people looked at him: Susan Price, with her vague, troubled gaze, and China, her face paled to snow and her eyes glinting back at him with blue frost. Aunt Gert studiously folded her napkin, and Captain Meredith continued spooning up his mush, apparently deaf to Jake's inquiry. No one spoke, and Jake began to wonder why asking such a simple question made him feel as though he were sitting there in his drawers.

China swallowed convulsively, and the toast went down her throat in a dry, choking lump. Reaching for her tepid coffee, she took a drink. She struggled to keep her voice steady. "The sea got both of my brothers—Quinn and Ryan."

The feeble remainder of her appetite gone, she stood and began clearing the table, avoiding Jake's dumbfounded gaze. She hadn't considered that he might ask about Ryan. Her younger brother's absence was such a painful subject, it was never discussed in the house.

Gert and Susan also stood, and Captain Meredith started as China lifted his nearly finished breakfast away from him. "Say, missy, I'm not done with that," he complained.

"It's time for your medicine, Cap," China replied distractedly, leaving with the plate. She reached for the tureen with the mush in it. "Come out to the kitchen and get it."

"Fussing females," Captain Meredith groused, yanking off his napkin and flinging it on the table. "Never let a man have a moment's peace—"

China stepped into the hall, the other two women close behind her.

"China, wait a minute," she heard Jake call. "I'd like to talk to you."

She turned reluctantly and let him catch up with her. A slight frown formed between his gold-laced brows, and China detected his salt-air scent again. Its effect alarmed her; how strongly it drew her, how it made her notice the curve of his mouth. She retreated a pace.

Jake began, "The room in the attic—"

China braced herself, waiting for him to ask for his money back.

At the end of the hall, Susan Price stared at Jake one last time before sliding into the kitchen.

He waited until she was gone, then observed in a lowered voice, "That Mrs. Price, I get the feeling her hatch isn't battened."

"She's a good example of what happens to a woman who spends her life waiting for a man who'll never return from a voyage," China responded tartly, then turned and strode away before he could say anything more.

Captain Meredith hobbled past him, grumbling under his breath about bossy women, and Jake was left standing there, dispensed with, having never gotten the chance to talk about moving out of the attic.

Jake looked up and down the empty hall as he pushed up his sleeves. After a moment he muttered a curse himself and went to get his coat.

There was a far less complicated lady waiting for him at the repair yard. A lady with better manners and a very kind heart.

Chapter Three

"She looks sound enough, Jake, but for that bottom," Monroe Tewey observed. He shifted the toothpick in the corner of his mouth while his experienced eyes ran the length of the *Katherine Kirkland*'s starboard hull.

Jake stood on the busy dock, bareheaded under a soaking rain. The river was slate gray, mirroring the color of the sky. It had always bothered him to see a ship out of the water once it had been launched. He knew it was necessary, but a vessel on groundways, exposed and somehow vulnerable, felt unnatural to him, like a dog with wings or a sunrise in the west. Still, he was glad to have Monroe doing the work—he ran one of the best repair yards on the West Coast.

Monroe gestured at the tenacious forest of goose barnacles clinging to the ship's hull. Tangled in them were snarls of seaweed and other ocean flotsam. "When was she scraped last?"

Jake hated to admit it, but the evidence of her neglect was there for all to see. "It's been way too long. I was the mate, but her last captain wouldn't spend the money to take her in." He stressed the point. The mate was responsible for seeing to a ship's maintenance, along with countless other duties, and he didn't want anyone to think that he had personally allowed the *Katherine* to deteriorate. "He didn't care that it slowed her down."

Monroe's toothpick darted back and forth with a sucking noise as he shook his head disapprovingly. "You should think about coppering her hull. It would help keep the worms off her. It'd cut down on leaks, too. A wooden ship begins sinking the day she's launched, you know."

Yes, he knew. But copper was expensive and Jake wasn't ready to make that investment without committed cargo. "Not this time, but if I make a decent run during the next year, I'll bring her back to have it done," he said, swiping at a raindrop on his forehead. "For now, we'll just tar and caulk her. And I need to replace a few blocks, check her lines, varnish her. Take a look at her rudder, too."

Monroe nodded and walked away to schedule the work.

Jake crossed under the bowsprit and glanced up at the figurehead. It was a beautifully carved woman with wheat gold hair, blushing cheeks, and huge blue eyes. Her arms were outstretched, as if to embrace the sea ahead of her and guide the ship through the waves. Her white robes draped as though windblown, but, in keeping with nautical custom, she was bare-breasted due to the belief that such display had the power to quiet storms.

His gaze climbed, following the rigging to the mastheads. They rose to such a dizzying height, they seemed to scrape the bellies of the heavy gray clouds overhead. The ship was a beauty, all right, with flowing lines and graceful curves, and after sailing her for four years, he knew every inch of her.

Since that sultry night in Charleston, he had marveled again and again at his incredible good luck—and profound idiocy—to have wagered everything he owned on a pair of threes and won. He'd wanted this ship. His hands had itched to take her wheel without the bloodshot, beady-eyed stare of Captain Josiah Marshall on the back of his neck. The only thing Jake had had going for him in that card game, besides rock-steady nerves, was a clear head. Captain Marshall had possessed neither. Marshall had bid "good riddance to the bitch" as he signed his ownership over to Jake with a vodka-palsied signature, vowing that Jake would never know a moment's peace as her captain.

Jake had left Charleston the very next morning with only one thought on his mind: he would set sail back to Astoria, triumphant. He'd stopped for nothing, knowing there would be plenty of time to see to the ship's repair after he got there.

Marshall had been wrong. Jake knew as much contentment as any man could who wandered the world. The *Katherine Kirkland* had asked nothing of him but reasonable care and a sure hand on the wheel. In return, she lulled him to sleep in his bunk on calm seas and offered cover during storms. If she hadn't satisfied his every desire, she came close, and that was about all a person could expect in life.

He started to walk back down the dock and caught the pungent odor of the salmon cannery up ahead on his right. A young man stood at the edge of the dock, wearily dumping barrels of chum into the river while gulls hovered overhead and dove into the water in pursuit of the fish remains. A half-dozen skinny wharf cats twined around his legs seductively, meowing and spitting at each other in competition for the scraps.

That easily could have been him mucking out a cannery in rubber boots and a butcher's apron, Jake thought. It probably would have been, too, considering the sparks that flew between Pop and him. He would have had to find other work away from the fishing boat, and for someone like him there weren't many options. Fishing and the ocean were the only two things he'd known, so he probably would have taken a job at one of the salmon packers. And once the smell of fish got on a person, nothing could budge it. It clung to hands, clothes, and dreams. Jake had grown up with enough people who labored in the canneries to know that. The work he'd done over the past several years had been just as hard, at times more dangerous by a hundredfold. But he knew he'd had the better life.

He turned to look at the *Katherine* one more time. Pride rose in him. He was certain he'd made the right decision in leaving Astoria all those years ago, although he hadn't expected to be gone so long. This ship epitomized recognition, success, respect—the attainment of everything he'd only dreamed of so long ago. Well, almost everything.

China stood on the back porch and peeked through the window in the kitchen door, hoping to sneak in unnoticed. It would be impossible to explain to anyone what she was doing outside in the rain with a cold, untouched meal in her hands. Seeing no one, she balanced the tray against her hip and turned the knob to let herself back in. She set the tray on the table and considered the soup and sandwich on the plate in front of her. Leaning forward a bit, she looked through the window toward the carriage house to see if—

"I guess I almost owed you an apology."

China spun around, her breath caught in her chest. Jake stood in the doorway to the hall. His hair was wet and curling at the ends, and the smell of his rain-soaked wool coat drifted to her. He sent her a hard look.

"Wh-what?" she stammered. Again she was struck by the sheer presence of him. It gave her a funny feeling in her chest, a perplexing combination of apprehension and warmth. She was unaccustomed to having to look that high to see a person's face.

"I was just about to light into you for cheating me out of another meal that I paid for. I see I was wrong."

She felt certain he hadn't seen her come in, that he couldn't know she'd been outside. But when she touched a hand to her hair she realized it was damp too, and she saw rain spots on her skirt. Of all the luck, she stewed. None of this appeared to be lost on Jake—his gaze swept over her. She knew she must look harried and suspicious. Just one minute more and she'd have been upstairs or in the parlor, or anyplace else. There was nothing to do but to face him down.

"Yes, you *were* wrong. I put this aside for you," she fibbed and retreated to the shelter of self-righteousness. "Of course, the soup is cold now, since lunchtime is at one." She looked at the clock. "Not one forty-five."

Jake maintained his steady scrutiny. It was plain to him that she was up to something, there was no doubt about it. She looked worried, guilty. He took off his coat and hung it up to dry on one of the hooks next to the stove.

"Maybe I should buy the food. That way I might get to eat even if I'm not able to keep to your schedule."

China felt her face flush. "We went over that yesterday. As a *boarder* in this house, you're welcome to join us at mealtimes. But this isn't a restaurant—you can't come in and order something whenever you like."

When he walked to the back door and opened it, China almost bit her tongue to keep from objecting. She watched in an agony of suspense while he glanced around the yard, then leaned over the porch to ruffle the rain out of his hair. After he closed the door, he pushed up his sweater sleeves again and came to the table.

Pulling out a chair, he said, "Since you've gone to so much trouble to keep this lunch for me, I'd be a real ingrate not to eat it, even if it is cold." He bent another hard green look on her.

China fidgeted, not entirely comfortable with her story about the sandwich. Still, it was only a white lie, not a really bad one.

Jake sat down in front of the tray and pulled out the damp napkin from under the silver. "I'd almost forgotten how much it rains here," he continued. "I thought I'd drown standing out on that dock today." He glanced at her damp hem and then up at her face. "I guess you already know how wet it is out there."

Defensiveness climbed higher in China and tightened her jaw. It was bad enough that he was here at all, bad enough that for some reason, she had to struggle to keep her eyes off him whenever he was nearby. Nobody else in the house had been so nosy about her comings and goings—not until he got here. She kept her back to him while she rearranged the butter, milk, and cheese in the icebox. At least he couldn't read her eyes. "Yes, well, it does rain a lot here in January," she babbled inanely.

What was she hiding? Jake puzzled. He knew this food wasn't for him. Even if he hadn't seen her from the dining room window, crossing the yard with the tray in her hands, he would have doubted her story. She could barely tolerate being in the same room with him. She wouldn't have gone to any trouble for him. It was as if she were protecting someone. He shouldn't care. There'd never been anything between them, apparently not even friendship. But more than idle curiosity made him wonder why she was sneaking around.

He took a bite of the unappetizing sandwich and put it back on the plate. "This sandwich tastes like you used it to soak up a leak in the roof. The bread is soggy."

China's head came up and she turned to look at him, strangely stung by his criticism. "I'm sure this isn't the worst thing you've ever eaten."

"That's true," he agreed, lifting the bread to pick out the chicken underneath. "One time I lived on hardtack for two weeks when my ship was caught in the doldrums off the Canaries."

China clenched her teeth for an instant before answering. Why was she letting him vex her? "This isn't a hotel. You knew that before you came here."

"Which brings me to what I wanted to talk with you about this morning."

This abrupt shift caught China off guard. If he mentioned Ryan again—

"I want a room on the second floor. If I'm supposed to act like the other boarders, I should have a room like the other boarders."

"Except, as I told you, there is no other room available on the second floor."

"Come on, China," he snapped, and put a hand flat to his chest. "This is Jake Chastaine you're talking to. I *know* this house. I stayed here dozens of times when I was a kid. There are more than four bedrooms upstairs."

China held her ground. "If you think back to just a few years ago, you might remember that you were banished from this house altogether."

He pushed away the sandwich plate disgustedly and rose to his feet. "Aunt Gert invited me here. I'm her guest, not yours."

He towered over her, and she felt his impatience. She hated being alone with him, but it kept occurring. Showing far more bravado than she felt, she insisted, "But I'm in charge of all our business matters, and I have the final word."

He pushed past her and reached for his wet coat. He jammed his arms into the sleeves, then gave her another hard, long look. "I'll be back in time for dinner, China, and I'd better get something more appetizing than a leftover soggy sandwich, or I'm going to start charging *you* for the meals I have to buy."

He strode to the back door, flung it open, and walked out without bothering to close it.

Late in the afternoon, Jake sat at the library table in the back parlor, making necessary adjustments to the ship's clock. The distant sound of the side door closing broke his concentration, and he looked up from his work on the chronometer. He usually had the ability to shut out all distractions when he needed to. Not today. He was tense and restless—he swore he could feel his own hair growing. He stood and wandered to the tall windows in the back parlor, trying to stretch his spine as he went. It still felt like a corkscrew. He wasn't looking forward to spending another night on that lumpy mattress in the attic, but he'd gotten nowhere with China. She was determined to keep him up there. The idea of a room at the Occident Hotel was sounding better all the time.

From deep within a leather chair near the fireplace, Captain Meredith's wheezy snores trespassed on Jake's thoughts. He was beginning to yearn for the anonymity to be found in the long, carpeted halls of a hotel, for the impersonal solitude of a hotel dining room. Those were the very qualities about hotels that he'd always disliked. But he wasn't about to spend two months in that cubbyhole upstairs.

Jake rested his chin on the top of the window sash and gripped each side of the frame in his hands. A sigh escaped him, momentarily fogging the glass. Maybe he'd been a fool to think he could come back here. He shouldn't have let Aunt Gert talk him into it. He hadn't forgotten that China had banished him from this house, and she hadn't forgotten it either. This afternoon she'd tossed it in his face like a custard pie. Her youthful, white-hot anger had cooled and hardened into bitterness.

His mood matched the dark, brooding weather. He stared out at the parklike yard that stretched between the house and the next street. At least the rain was beginning to let up. A long, narrow band of late-day sun brightened the western horizon where the clouds had lifted.

Then a sudden flash of movement and color caught his eye, and Jake watched as China darted across the yard. His eyes narrowed. He saw her long black hair hanging free, and the tails of her wool shawl streaming behind her as she ran. Her maroon skirt billowed in the winter wind. Through the glass he heard her light steps on the flat stones of the path. What the hell was she up to? he wondered once more. Then he had his answer. She flew toward the carriage house. There a medium-built man in seaman's dungarees and pea coat stood waiting for her. The sailor reached out to grip her wrist, and China, with a furtive backward glance over her shoulder, hurried them inside. Even from where he stood, Jake sensed the powerful urgency between them.

Jake stepped back from the window, recoiling as though he'd been slapped. He wasn't sure what he'd seen, but he sure knew what it looked like, what it *felt* like.

An intense emotion, one he didn't want to consider very carefully, knifed through him, painful and swift. He took a deep breath and tried to smother the feeling, along with the impulse to storm outside and drag China into the house. Had anyone else seen her? He looked around at Captain Meredith, but the old man slept on, oblivious. Aunt Gert sat at the desk, deep in concentration, sorting and arranging what looked like some little cards, and he'd last seen Susan Price in the sewing room upstairs.

All the pieces of China's puzzling behavior—the sneaking around, the lying, taking trays of food outside—began to fall into place, and Jake didn't like the picture it created. He didn't like it at all.

But it gave him an infallible means by which to get what he wanted, and he planned to use it.

It was just after five, and dusk was upon her when China glanced up through the kitchen window a half-hour later. Good, she thought; Aunt Gert must be in another room. From where China stood, she could see no one in the kitchen. She climbed the porch stairs and turned the doorknob. Before she was inside she recognized the delicious aroma of ham baking in the oven. Chicken last night, and now ham. They so rarely could afford good meals anymore, the meat seemed like a dangerous extravagance to her. She'd have to talk to Aunt Gert about this. China suspected that her aunt was cooking with Jake in mind, rather than economy.

Despite what Jake had said at lunch, China hoped he would eat dinner someplace else again tonight. She didn't have much appetite when he was around, and the combination of lack of food, her own anxiety, and hard work had her energy flagging. She pushed open the door and pulled off her shawl to hang it by the stove.

"Hello, China."

China swallowed a shriek and whirled to see Jake sitting at the table. He slouched low in the chair, with one foot crossed over his knee. His eyes were as cold as jade. She had the awful feeling that she was being called to task. He'd changed to a plain white shirt with a band collar, and it was unbuttoned to his sternum. A small medal on a gold chain hung around his neck, half hidden by the folds of his shirt, and her eyes were drawn to it. In her confusion, her gaze moved on to the dark blond hair revealed on his chest, and she felt her cheeks grow warm.

"Jake," she acknowledged and closed the door behind her, showing more calm than she felt. Blast it, she thought. She hadn't realized till this second that someone had closed the curtains on the kitchen door. And the big window was too high above the path for her to see anyone who was sitting in the kitchen. If she'd known he was there, she'd have gone through the side door and right up the stairs to her room.

"Nice evening, isn't it?" he remarked, lazily pushing himself upright and unhooking his ankle. "Has the rain stopped?"

"Why are you always sneaking up on me?" she snapped, the level of her words rising on fear and anger.

His shrug was casual, but his green eyes bored into her. "I suppose it could seem that way—to a person with something to hide."

Panic began inching its way into China's heart, but she tried to show only annoyance. "I can't imagine what you mean." She turned to walk away and would have left the kitchen to escape him and his questions, but the next thing he said stopped her dead in the doorway.

"You might as well give up the game, China."

She heard the chair legs slide over the flooring as he pushed himself to his feet. He crossed the room and stood right behind her, nearly touching, but not. She sensed him there—she could feel the heat of his body, almost like an electrical charge. She took a step forward to put some distance between them.

"I saw you with him. And I know *everything*."

Oh, God, China thought, lacing her cold hands

tightly in front of her. She'd tried so hard to be careful, to stay away from the carriage house. But in the last few days that had been impossible. She turned and faced him.

"I guess you've developed a taste for the working class," Jake said, irony in his voice. He reached out to tweak a lock of her loose hair. "I imagine there are people who'd be interested in hearing all about what keeps you so busy out there." He tipped his head in the direction of the carriage house and gave her a shrewd look. "And I'll be happy to tell anyone who'll listen, starting with Aunt Gert, if you don't let me move to a room on the second floor."

China could hardly believe what she was hearing. She tried to think of some way to throw him off, but the only defense she could formulate lay in denial and feigned ignorance. "I repeat," she said firmly, "I don't know what you're talking about. But whatever it is, I guess I shouldn't be surprised that you'd stoop to blackmail to get your way."

Jake leaned a little closer. She should no longer find him attractive, not after all the problems he had created, especially given the horrible things he was saying. How could she even notice his lean jawline or the curve of his mouth, turned down in a humorless smile? For the briefest instant, he gazed back at her with an odd yearning expression that caught at her heart. Then a frown darkened his face, and he crossed his arms over his chest as he considered her.

"My using blackmail isn't any worse than a man who's low enough to risk a lady's reputation by meeting her for a tryst in a stable."

"What!" she choked, inflamed by his outrageous insinuation.

"But I guess he's done me a favor. He's made it possible for me to move out of that closet you gave me to sleep in."

"Just what are you implying?" China demanded. She knew exactly what he meant. There was an angry, ominous glint in his eyes that should have frightened her. Instead, it nipped at her own temper.

"Shall we go upstairs? I'd like to choose my room and get moved in before dinner."

Jake strode from the kitchen and down the hall to the back stairs, taking the steps two at a time. It was all China could do to keep up, encumbered by her full skirts on the narrow, circular staircase.

"Jake! Stop it!" she commanded breathlessly, but he ignored her and charged ahead. Her eyes were fixed on the broad stretch of his shoulders, which the white shirt only accentuated.

"Let's see." He flung open the door to the guest room where he'd often spent the night years earlier. "I remember this room—"

The gaslight from the hall threw a shaft of light across the bare floor and up the empty wall. Except for a small table near the closet, the dark, shuttered room held no furniture. Only the lace curtains still hung at the windows.

"Hmm, what did you do? Burn everything after I left?" he asked with vague amusement.

"You have no right—" she snapped, but he moved on to the next door as though she hadn't spoken.

Down the hall he went, opening another room and finding it the same as the first: empty of furniture, rugs, and pictures. China hurried after him, pulling on his arm, but there was no stopping him.

After he pushed on the door to Quinn's bare room, China exclaimed, "*John Jacob Chastaine!* That is *enough!*"

That stopped him. Some of the fury and spark that had sent Jake charging up the stairs fizzled away. He knew that the nameless emotion, the one he refused to identify, had fueled his anger. He'd seen the guilty flush in her cheeks when she faced him in the kitchen, and his imagination filled in the rest. Now he stood before the last empty room he'd opened, feeling a little stupid over the way he'd acted. He forced himself to look at China and tried not to wince. Though slender and pale, she seemed to tower over him like a raven-haired avenging angel. Her face was paper-white, but she held her chin high and her dark blue eyes pierced him like harpoons. He could hear the breath rushing in and out of her lungs.

"How dare you," China began, her voice low, shaking with rage and humiliation. "How dare you come back here and demand to be treated like an honored guest? Prying into things that are none of your business? Making filthy insinuations?" Her hands closed into fists at her sides. "Did you think you could just drop in after all these years, after—*everything*, and think nothing would be different, that I'd welcome you as if nothing had happened? Did you really think that, Jake?"

"No, I didn't think that," he muttered impatiently, jamming his hands into his back pockets. "What I really expected—"

"That's good, because hardly anything is the same," she continued, interrupting him. "These rooms are empty because I've had to sell the furniture and rugs and paintings. I saw you looking for my father's picture of the *Joyce P. Frankenberg* in the dining room. Well, it's gone too. I even had to sell most of my mother's jewelry to support Aunt Gert and the others here. The only thing of value that we have left is this house." China permitted herself a brittle, acerbic smile. "You finally have more money than I do. If I remember correctly, that was one of your goals."

It had never been one of his goals, but he wasn't going to debate the issue. "You're not responsible for old man Meredith and Mrs. Price," he pointed out, reaching forward to close Quinn's door.

China pushed his hand aside and shut the door herself. "They are family, Jake. They live under this roof and I take care of them."

Jake had nearly forgotten how important family had always been to China. With her mother dead and the Captain always gone, she'd struggled to keep her brothers and aunt together. That part of her was the same—except now both of her parents were dead, her brothers were gone to sea, and her "family" composed mostly of strangers.

"I'm surprised you didn't get married," he said, picking up his earlier thought. "That's what I *expected*. I thought Zach Stowe would be your husband and you'd have a couple of children by now."

"Husband." China felt her breath leave her. His remark made a ragged cut, like a piece of broken glass. China drew herself a little taller, though she felt a scarlet flush creeping up her face. "It would seem I lost my marriageability along with my money."

For the second time in as many days, Jake's conscience jabbed at him, and he didn't like it one bit. He felt like he was eight years old again and had just been caught stealing that pocketknife from the hardware store. He wished he could turn back the clock a few days and be magically transported to the deck of the *Katherine Kirkland* in the middle of the Pacific. He'd know nothing about China's circumstances, and she wouldn't have had the opportunity to put him in the attic. And he wouldn't have seen her with the sailor who took her by the hand as she led them away from prying eyes.

"And that sailor I saw out in the yard? I suppose he's *family* too?" he snapped sarcastically. He knew he was overstepping his bounds again, but he couldn't forestall the remark.

China felt certain that if this conversation went on much longer, she would burst a blood vessel. It was supposed to remain a secret, for the sake and safety of so many. But Jake had goaded her with his vile accusations, and she was not a very good martyr. She would tell him what he'd seen. Oh, she thought with relish, it would be a pleasure, a *joy* to prove him wrong. She shot a quick, cautious glance to the end of the hall. She saw no one.

"This is really none of your concern," she began in a furious whisper, drawing herself up stiffly, "but for your information, that man is the voice of the mute, speaking for those who are not heard. He's working to defend and protect scores of subjugated men taken against their will from their families."

Jake lifted his brows at this flowery speech and at the worshipful zeal in China's words. She sounded like a convert to some religion, coached to repeat its doctrine, but it told him nothing.

"You mean defend them in court? I haven't met many lawyers, but I never saw one dressed like a common seaman."

"Shhhh!" She held a finger to her mouth, which was pressed into a tight line, then looked up and down the hall again. She shook her head, frowning irritably. "He's not a lawyer. Dalton founded the Sailors Protective League."

"And he comes to see you about donations for its library, right?" Jake scoffed. He found himself whispering back.

China gave him a pained look. Of all the things she'd worried about when she and Dalton began using the carriage house, the one that had never occurred to her was how it might appear to someone else if they were seen out there together.

She searched for a good description of the man. "Dalton Williams is—is a hero," she extolled, "working to end shanghaiing in Astoria and Portland. He tries to save men who've been drugged in crooked boardinghouses and saloons, to be kidnapped by the crimps—" here she turned another icy glare on him—"and sold to captains like cattle. He's trying to establish a safe boardinghouse for seamen, but till he can I'm helping him by letting him board men out back who are too sick or injured to go home or to take care of themselves."

An alarm bell sounded in Jake's mind. Dalton Williams, he pondered. Why did that name sound familiar to him? Then he thought back to the night he had stood at Pug's bar in the Blue Mermaid. Suddenly he felt the blood drain out of his face. China was the accomplice those two snake-oil salesmen had speculated about. The one they thought to be rid of for twenty dollars.

"You're working with Williams?" he asked incredulously.

China smiled with fierce pride, lifting her chin. "Yes. I see you've heard of him."

"Heard of him! Jesus Christ, China, his name is poison in Swill Town. He's a target—he's got a big bull's-eye on his forehead, and it's suspected that someone is working with him." Jake went on to tell her what he'd overheard. "So far, I don't think anyone knows you're the one helping him, but you've got to get out of this, now, before someone figures out what you're doing. You're mixed up in dangerous business."

She shook her head. "I don't care. This is too important to give up and Dalton needs me."

Jake ran a hand through his hair. *"Dalton,"* he blasted, "is either a fool or a lunatic to involve you in this scheme. And I know better than you the kind of people involved with crimping."

"Yes, I'm sure you do, since you've probably done business with them!" China replied heatedly, emotion driving her own words far above a whisper. "Well, Dalton knows, too. He was shanghaied from Astoria a few years ago with other men, some of them really only boys—"

"You're right," Jake interrupted. "I've paid blood money a few times under captain's orders, and I might have to again. But I've always made sure the men got decent wages and were treated well. It's not a great system, but it's an unavoidable part of deep-sea merchant sailing. I don't know why I have to tell you that. You grew up in this town—your father bought crewmen himself."

"Let's leave the Captain out of this, shall we? I don't need your permission to help Dalton and I'm not asking for it. There is no excuse at all for what the crimps do. Stealing men off the street, men who've never been on a ship in their lives. For heaven's sake, they take men from their farms and out of the woods. They even tried to shanghai Reverend Grannis right out of his church last year. If he didn't have some skill with his fists—" She stopped, seeing Susan poke her head out of the sewing room at the end of the hall.

Following China's glance, Jake stared at the woman until she retreated, softly closing the door again behind her. Sighing, he turned back to face China. "Look, you're in deep water with this, but I guess you're going to do what you want. You Sullivans are a stubborn lot, and I've got my own business to attend to. Like I said the other day, I shouldn't have come here."

China took a deep breath and briefly pressed her hand to her forehead, struggling to regain her composure. Those were the truest words he'd spoken so far. Her life wasn't easy, but she'd had far better control of it before Jake Chastaine came back. Despite all the promises she'd made to herself to ignore him, it just wasn't working. It was her fervent wish that she could show him the front door and throw his things out after him. But she was in no position to do that. She'd have to tolerate him.

The anger drained out of his voice, replaced by a hint of weariness. "I'll get my gear and go to the Occident. Just give me back two months' rent. You keep the other one for your trouble."

China gaped at him. "You mean you're leaving?"

He gave her a faint smile that didn't reach his eyes. "Yes. Isn't that a relief?"

"Well—no, yes—" She groaned inwardly, thinking about that old saying, Be careful what you wish for . . . you may get it. She would be thrilled beyond measure to see Jake move to a hotel. Unfortunately, even less than the one month's rent he referred to was left of what he'd paid them. She couldn't return his money—she didn't have it. And now that she'd blurted out all that information about the carriage house and the league, she'd given him a powerful weapon to use against her if he chose to. She should have just kept her mouth shut and let him think the worst of her. Her mind began whirling. Maybe she could sell another few pieces of furniture or the rest of the jewelry to get the money—

"I'll be ready to go in a few minutes. Don't set a place for me at the table. I won't be staying for dinner." He stepped past her and strode down the hall toward the back stairs, his boot steps muffled on the runner.

Oh, no, China fretted. He meant to leave *right now*. She had to do something. "Jake, wait a minute," she called.

He stopped in a shadow and turned to look at her. Beyond the reach of the gaslight, his eyes shone with a hint of danger.

"Maybe we can come to a compromise," she said, walking toward him with dragging steps and forcing a tight, conciliatory smile. "I'm sor— Well, I don't want to see us part with hard feelings." This was so galling she thought she might choke on the words.

Jake raised his brows again at her sudden change of tune. "No hard feelings, China. Just give me back my money and I'll be on my way." He watched her as she stood in front of him, nervously turning her ring on her finger. She was still worried, he suspected, and probably more so now that she'd told him about Williams, and that was why she was trying to placate him. Well, too bad, let her worry. Her scheme with the carriage house was none of his concern. If she was determined to continue, he couldn't stop her. The less he knew about it, the better. "I don't want to be here any more than you want me to stay. I can't keep to your schedule and I'm just upsetting your routine."

"You mean about meals? From now on, we'll put a plate in the warmer for you if you're not home on time." China was not good at this kind of game, but she didn't know what else to do. She couldn't tell what he was thinking—his expression revealed nothing more than a slight frown. She hoped he wouldn't make her beg him to change his mind.

He seemed to consider her offer, then shook his head. "Naw, I want to sleep in a real bedroom, not in an attic." He turned to go.

Oh, damn him, she thought. She was going to have to give him everything he wanted. And that was the last thing *she* wanted. "Jake, wait," she called after him again. He stopped and shot her an impatient look. "Um, my father's room still has furniture in it." She gestured awkwardly behind her. "Y-You could stay there."

"Oh?" he replied softly. He gave her a knowing look. He took two steps closer. "I thought you didn't have any place for me down here."

"Well, it wasn't clean," she improvised. "But if you can wait until after dinner, I'll make the bed and dust the room."

Jake suddenly found circumstances to be completely reversed. Instead of being elbowed out the door, the high and mighty Miss Sullivan was asking him to stay. "Oh, I don't know," he pondered. "If I go to the Occident, I'll get maid service. They'll lay the fire, they'll make my bed every day."

"Well, we don't have a staff here anymore," China replied, "but I—I suppose I could clean the room and make the bed."

Jake rubbed the back of his neck, apparently giving the matter great thought. "At the Occident, I can get something to eat whenever I want. They'll even bring it to my room."

China tightened her jaw until her head began to ache. Surely hell must be something like this, she simmered. She wanted to shout, Then go to the damned Occident, damn you! But she knew she couldn't. He stared at her, waiting for her response. "I guess I could—" she began, then he cut in.

"But as you pointed out, this isn't a hotel." After a moment, he tipped his head and said, "All right, I'll stay. For the time being, anyhow."

Afraid of what she'd say if she spoke, China led the way to the end of the hall and opened the door directly across from hers. After lighting the gas fixture just inside, she waved Jake into the room. It held a massive bed and other furniture, a fireplace, and a corner sink, and a red oriental carpet covered the floor.

Jake walked through the room, nodding his approval. Then he looked across the hall toward her bedroom. "Isn't that your door?"

China straightened her spine and, trying to hide her anxiety, glanced at the cold fireplace. "Yes, it is." Oh, how would she manage? She didn't want him in the house at all, and now he'd maneuvered his way down from the servants' quarters to this room directly across from hers. That meant he'd be here, just a few feet away, all during the night. Althea Lambert and her ruined reputation came to mind again. She had to stop thinking about it or she'd go crazy.

Her eyes still on the mantel, she said, "I'll get the bedding and do the dusting after dinner, if that's all right."

"That will be fine. Thanks, China."

His voice had taken on a low, resonant quality that made her look up. Expecting to find a smug grin on his face, she was unprepared for the fleeting haunted expression she'd seen only a few times before. It disappeared so quickly, she wondered if she'd imagined it—and hoped she had. Something about it stung her heart, and that was the last thing she wanted.

China turned and left the room without a backward glance.

Chapter Four

China paused on the landing to look at the watch pinned to her blouse, then hurried up the stairs to the second floor. It was already past seven, and she still had to comb her hair and wash her face before she met Dalton. Sending Aunt Gert on her way to St. Mary's had taken some doing, but at last the front door had closed.

China slowed as she approached Jake's room. The door was open, and she could see the yellow-orange gleam of flames from the hearth reflecting dully on the margin of hardwood floor not covered by the runner.

He'd wasted no time moving in and making himself at home last night, once she'd made the bed and dusted the furniture. He'd simply given her that cocky grin, told her good night, and shut the door in her face. She hadn't spoken to him since. That made mealtimes stiff, uncomfortable affairs, but only for her. Jake got on famously with the rest of the family, and they didn't seem to notice her pique. God, he was infuriating!

Even when she'd told her aunt about his outrageous behavior over this room (carefully omitting just how he had gained the upper hand), Gert had merely given her a satisfied smile and said, "Well, dear, I told you he should have had your father's room from the beginning.''

This morning, after Jake had gone out to do whatever it was that kept him busy, China had dutifully, if grudgingly, gone to his room to make his bed. She stood by the mattress, looking at the rumpled sheets he'd so recently left, and the depressions in the pillows where his head had lain. Obviously he wasn't used to sharing a bed, she thought. And for the life of her, she didn't understand why that notion made her hands damp and her heart feel like a landed fish flopping around in her chest.

Now she stole a glance at Jake from the doorway. Full of Aunt Gert's thrifty biscuits and gravy, he slouched low in a deep chair and dozed in front of the fireplace, like the lord of the manor. His shirttails were pulled out, the shirt buttons open down to his navel. In the low firelight, his bare skin was the fair copper color of a new penny, frosted by hair that gleamed falsely red. China's eyes went directly to his coyly displayed chest like a pair of arrows, and a shiver fluttered through her. What was the matter with her? she wondered. After all, he was just a man, not to mention the most irritating one she'd ever known. She'd been tending men in various states of undress for nearly two years for the league and had long since gotten over any girlish timidity about the job. Impatiently glancing away, she noticed that a book lay open and facedown on the floor next to him. She couldn't read its title from where she stood, not even when she came a step closer and craned her neck. But she assumed it was some hack-written dime novel that had captured his attention. She'd never known him to pick up any book willingly, much less one that was worthwhile.

Curious in spite of herself, she remained just inside the doorway, considering him. Sleep smoothed his face, and the glow of the fire highlighted his pale hair and cast shadows under his lowered eyelashes. She had to admit he didn't have the look of a man baseborn. The bones in his face were fine but sturdy, his forehead wide. His nose was long and straight, properly positioned above a full, strong mouth. He was clean-shaven, which was unusual given that most men wore either moustaches or full beards, and his hair was longer than current fashion dictated.

She glanced at his hand where it rested on his flat stomach, rising and falling with his slow, even breathing. It wasn't a grubby-looking paw. His fingers were long, the palm wide at their base.

She jumped when he shifted in the chair and snuffled, stretching his stocking feet toward the fire. But he didn't wake up and only settled deeper into the cushions. In China's opinion, he looked altogether too comfortable and relaxed. She was anything but, seeing him thus, and she didn't like the jittery feeling it gave her in her chest. He might have had the decency to close his door if he wanted to sit there half naked. Then she wouldn't have to look at him that way.

Backing away, she went to her own room, her face unaccountably hot. A few moments later, after lighting the lamp in the hall window, she was on her way out and saw that he still dozed in boneless contentment. Reaching for the doorknob, she yanked hard and let the door close with a bang. She hoped it woke him.

China herself had hardly slept at all last night.

Exhaustion would claim her soon if she didn't get more rest. It felt strange enough to have that room in use again after all these years. But every time she'd begun to drift off, she would remember that it was Jake sleeping over there, and she'd curse the bad luck that had brought him back to Astoria to upset her life. Now as she wrapped herself in her shawl to go outside, the image of him asleep in that chair crept into her mind again and it rankled. He was the reason she had to go to the carriage house to wait and worry.

A fine drizzle began to fall as she crossed the dark yard, made even darker by the towering black fir trees that blocked out the night sky. Walking as quickly as her limited vision would permit, she reached the carriage house, on the opposite diagonal corner of the property. China had sent a message to Dalton this morning to let him know she needed to talk with him. It was a two-word note she knew he'd understand; she'd used it before. It said simply "carriage house." There was no sign of him yet, so she let herself in with the key in her pocket.

The apartment was plain, almost rustic, with raw wood walls and flooring, a table and two chairs, a narrow bed, and a couple of other pieces of furniture. The quarters had two windows with heavy shades, one that looked back at the house and another that faced the street.

With a slightly trembling hand she struck a match to light the old oil lamp that sat on the table. Once more she looked at her watch. It was almost seven-thirty. There was no fire in the stove, and the room's cold dampness penetrated her shawl, but she didn't plan to be out here very long this evening. Just long enough to explain what she'd done. And what would Dalton say about it? Would he be disappointed in her? Angry?

Trying to warm herself, she began pacing the length of the floor. In the silence she could hear her skirt and petticoats rustling softly around her legs. Now and then she went to the street-side window and lifted the shade, looking for Dalton. But there was nothing to see except darkness and her own transparent reflection in the rain-streaked glass.

She'd spent many anxious hours in this room, sitting by the bed while feeding and tending injured men who had been snatched from the hands of crimpers. Dalton had devised a system of signaling her by putting the oil lamp in the window to let her know when he'd brought someone here. The strain of keeping this secret and worrying over each man stolen from his family, his job, his freedom, sometimes made China wonder how long she'd be able to keep this up. Just sneaking out of the house under the noses of three people taxed her ingenuity. Four people now, she reminded herself.

Fortunately, Sister Theresa was still not satisfied with the progress of the St. Mary's musicale performers, and that kept Aunt Gert busy. Susan Price was upstairs in the sewing room working on a hat, China thought. Captain Meredith sat in his usual spot in the back parlor. And Jake—she knew where he was.

She stopped pacing and settled into a straight-backed chair at the scarred drop-leaf table. When it was quiet like this, and especially when she was tired, her thoughts tended to wander back to the days before her father had died, before Quinn and Ryan were gone. There had been two horses in the stable next door then, a carriage for the carriage house, and a driver who lived in this unadorned apartment. They'd had a staff to do the cooking and cleaning that now fell to China and Aunt Gert.

China had had three beaux, Zachary Stowe among them, who escorted her to dances and Sunday socials. All of them had been well-groomed, polite, educated young men with promising futures. All of them had been the complete opposite of Jake.

When Zachary had asked for her hand, she'd accepted. It hadn't been a love match, though it was a well-advised one. But then she lost her money, her social position went with it, and that changed everything.

Zachary had eloped with Camella Hooper a month later. Camella's father owned two lumber mills.

Most of the people China had grown up with and had believed to be her friends began to leave her out of their plans and lives when word got around that the Captain had died broke. At first, she was bewildered, then devastated. Popular as a girl, she was astonished to discover how shallow those relationships were. She felt betrayed and retreated into what remained of her family, Aunt Gert and Ryan.

After that, any chance for China to marry was lost. Now she was caught between two lives: the privileged, comfortable existence she'd once known, and this one of pinching pennies and stalling creditors. All she had left was this house, and her pride.

That wasn't so bad, she supposed, except—except, oh, sometimes she craved the intimacy of spirit she had imagined marriage brought. Now and then she wished there was someone with whom she could close her door and shut out responsibility and the rest of the world. A companion to talk with, a shoulder to rest her head on when she was tired, a hand to hold. Someone to care for rather than to take care of. To answer the odd quickening she sometimes felt pulsing through her body.

She usually tried not to dwell on what she didn't have, and most often succeeded. Then last night Jake had asked why she wasn't married. Given the circumstances, it was enough that they still had a decent roof over their heads and food to eat. She couldn't afford to wish that her heart be satisfied as well.

China was jerked from her gray thoughts by two short knocks on the door. She flew to answer it, responding first with two more short knocks, then opened the door.

"I hope I haven't kept you waiting too long," Dalton said, his expression grim. He strode in, bringing the clean scent of rain with him. After one last quick look outside, he closed the door behind him.

Even though she had known him for two years, a tremor of awe rushed through China. When Dalton Williams walked into a room, the air sizzled with a dynamic force. He was not a physically imposing man, nor was he typically attractive. His face reflected his humble background, far more so than did Jake's, China thought. Of medium build, he presented no illusion of strength. He walked with a marked rolling gait that bespoke twenty years spent at sea—over half his life. But his appearance was deceptive; she'd seen him carry unconscious men into this room, a few of whom had outweighed him by a third. And he radiated a fierce intensity that burned like hellfire in his sharp cobalt eyes. In front of an audience, he was a fiery and surprisingly eloquent speaker. It gave him a charismatic aura of power that alternately drew people to listen and made them back away in fear. It was his profound, single-minded dedication to the abolishment of shanghaiing that had won China's respect and her loyalty to his cause.

He sprawled in the chair she had recently occupied and rubbed his face with his hands, then pushed his brown hair off his forehead. She could see something was wrong. "I almost had someone to bring with me, but I wasn't fast enough. I guess another farm boy is going to see the world after all." Defeat hung around him like a nimbus.

"What happened?" she asked quietly, taking the other chair.

He sat forward and put his elbows on his knees. "I was in the Salty Dog and I saw the bartender put the drops in a beer." Knockout drops were one of the common methods of dispatching a man to a waiting ship. "It was crowded in there, and the light wasn't too good. I tried to keep track of that beer mug, but it ended up on a tray with a lot of others, and I couldn't tell who got it. I kept walking around the saloon. I could only hope to be nearby when the poor bast— uh, pour soul passed out. In a few minutes, there was a commotion in the corner and a big husky plowboy went crashing over a table. Like a broken mainmast, he went down. I was on the far side of the place, and he was hustled off to the back room by two crimpers before I could get to him." He straightened and shook his head. "Damn."

China shared Dalton's regret. Somewhere, at this moment, or perhaps tomorrow, a woman—his mother, his sister, maybe a sweetheart or a wife—would be watching the road for that young man. They wouldn't know what had happened to him, only that he didn't come home. It might be years before he could make his way back. It might be never.

"I know you did your best," she said. "There's only you doing this work. You can't be everywhere at once."

He looked at the wall, as though reliving the scene at the Salty Dog. Frustration laced his words. "Except I was *there*. Right there. I could have saved him." He held out an open hand, then closed it into a fist. "He just slipped away from me."

"But Dalton, if you could have saved him, you would have," she reasoned. "It wasn't possible this time. It's not as though you didn't try."

He glanced back at her and finally nodded with weary acceptance. "I know you're right. But, God, it gets to me sometimes. If people would just listen, if the captains would stop doing business with those scurvy sons of bi— I mean those devils—" Dalton often struggled with his colorful vocabulary when he talked to China—"crimping would end next week." He let out a sigh, then almost magically his moment of discouragement disappeared and he was all business again. "Well, I know you didn't send for me to listen to this. What's the matter?"

China folded her hands in her lap so tightly her knuckles turned white. She took a deep breath and confessed what she'd revealed to Jake.

"I'm sorry, Dalton," China said. "I know I

shouldn't have told Jake about this, but he saw us out here and, well, he insinuated that you and I— that we—" She came to an embarrassed halt, unable to repeat what Jake had meant. Glancing at the window shade, she let her forefinger run along the sill. "He thought you and I were meeting for a rendezvous." Her face burned with a blush. She hoped he wouldn't realize how easily she'd given away their secret. She lifted her eyes to meet his. "I know I should have let him believe whatever he wanted and kept quiet about this."

Dalton tipped his chair back against the plain pine wall and stared at her, saying nothing, his expression deadly serious. She saw the effect of her words written on his face, and she quailed. A crease formed between his brows.

If only he'd speak, she thought.

"Myself, I've never cared what people say about me," he said slowly. "I guess I can't expect you to let someone insult your reputation for the league. But then, Chastaine must not be much of a man if he talks to a lady that way, especially when he's sleeping under her roof." He let the chair drop to the floor. "I take it he's not a friend to our cause."

China released the breath she'd held. Tightening her wool shawl against the damp chill in the unheated room, she shook her head. "Not really. He admits that crimping isn't a good practice, but he says it's necessary."

"If he's not a friend, then he's an enemy." Dalton saw everything as black or white. With him there were no gray areas, no vacillation. He drummed his fingers on the table, apparently pondering the possible consequences of the situation. "He could make trouble for us. This," he said, gesturing at the apartment, "isn't safe to use anymore. But I suppose it had to end sometime."

"Are you any closer to finding a good spot for a boardinghouse?"

"Maybe. About seven blocks over, there's a big, run-down place. The old man who owned it died years ago, and it's been standing empty all this time. The owner's son would rather have sold the house—it needs more work than he wants to pay for. But he said he'd let us have it for cheap rent if we'll fix it up. So I signed the lease." Dalton shrugged. "The tricky part is raising enough money for the repairs. It's in pretty bad shape."

Money, China thought. Everything, it seemed, always came back to money. "I wish I could spare something, but I just don't have it."

He waved away the suggestion and leaned toward her. "I know that, China. You've done enough already. Just housing and feeding these men, seeing to their injuries and sickness—I couldn't put a value on that."

They sat in silence for a few moments. Then a notion struck her. "Maybe we can ask for donations—you know, create a boardinghouse fund, like a charity. There are a lot of people who agree with you and the work you're doing. You could ask for contributions from businesses and the sailors themselves. After all, this is for their benefit."

The league had received donations all along, but sporadically, the way a street beggar collected pennies. The money paid some of the printing costs for the leaflets Dalton distributed, but not much more. A concerted effort, China thought. That was what they needed.

Dalton grinned suddenly and stood. He didn't smile often, and she was glad that he harbored no anger toward her for talking to Jake. "Good idea, China. That's why I need you—for your good ideas and your brave heart. And you have been brave." He put out his hand as though to touch her arm, then apparently thought better of it.

"I'd best be going. Until that house is ready, I'll still have to bring men here. We'll just be as careful as we've always been."

They parted outside the door. Dalton slipped away again into the misty night, and China made her way back to the kitchen. Thankfully, no one was present when she came in; she was relieved that her absence had gone unnoticed. She removed her shawl and hung it by the stove. Then, remembering that she'd forgotten to give Captain Meredith his medicine, she picked up a blue tonic bottle. She left the kitchen and stopped in the hall to pluck a spoon from a drawer in the china cabinet, then went in search of the old man.

Half a minute later, Jake walked in through the same kitchen door and quietly closed it behind him. He was cold, damp, and cross, but glad that he hadn't had to spend another second in the rain waiting for China to come out of that goddamned carriage house.

Late the next morning, China vigorously pushed the carpet sweeper across the hall runner near the front door. Navigating the awkward contraption into the front parlor, she ran it over the deep pile of a blue Persian carpet, one of the few in the house that she'd not yet sold. Finally stopping to rest, she brushed off her skirt and sank into a velvet armchair by the cold fireplace. She rested her elbows on the chair arms and glanced around the elegant room. The front parlor didn't see much use anymore—after all, except for one or two of Aunt Gert's friends, they never had company these days. That was just as well. She'd had to sell several pieces of furniture from this room, too, and now it had an empty look about it. No matter how artfully she tried to arrange the remaining pieces, the room was simply too big for its contents.

Still, China wasn't sorry that she'd decided to keep this house. It was her anchor, an enduring constant in a life that had changed so drastically she barely recognized it anymore. But it was a big house and a lot of work to maintain. The sweeping, mopping, and dusting never ended.

Once she'd had only to direct a capable staff to do both the heavy cleaning and the daily work. Young as she'd been, she possessed a natural skill for running a large house. She dressed in pastel ruffles and flounces and sat at her writing desk in the back parlor answering correspondence, paying bills, or planning teas and luncheons. Sometimes she did needlework, as did all the proper young ladies in her circle, embroidering linens with snowy monograms and delicate floral sprays for her burgeoning hope chest.

Now everyone in the house used the sheets and towels—and Cap wiped his nose on the napkins—that she'd so meticulously stitched and crocheted edgings for, once intended for a different future. Money was too scarce to let perfectly good linens sit yellowing on a shelf, layered with lavender sachet and old dreams.

China let her hand drift to a small potpourri box that sat on the cherry table next to her. It was an exquisite piece, one of her most prized possessions, made of fine gold filigree and topped with a delicate porcelain lid. It still contained the remnants of dried rosebuds and leaves, their colors faded by time. She held the box to her nose and, closing her eyes, inhaled the ghost of fragrance that remained.

Her reverie was interrupted when, from down the hall, she heard the back door open and close. That made her look up, since she was the only one who usually came and went through the back.

She heard the sound of heavy boots moving around the kitchen floor and knew it was Jake. He'd been here scarcely a week, but she was learning to recognize the sound of his footsteps. That realization made her distinctly uncomfortable. She listened, baffled, as he pulled open cupboard doors and what sounded like the door to the pantry, muttering to himself all the while. Seconds later, she heard him bearing down the hall in her direction.

"I hope your boots are clean," she called sternly.

He came to the door and looked in. "Of course they are. I wasn't born under a rock, you know." He gave her an even look and took two steps forward to stand just inside the door. He carried a long, bulky package wrapped in paper and string. "I guess this means you're talking to me again."

"I wouldn't count on it if I were you," she said coolly.

The first thing she noticed was his heavy blond hair, as bright as a candle flame. Why on earth did he have to be so attractive? she fumed again.

From her seated position, it was hard to ignore his long legs. His dungarees, though loose in the leg, fit indecently snug against his narrow hips, across his belly, and— Realizing where her eyes and thoughts had turned, China drew a swift breath and quickly glanced upward. The black sweater he wore accentuated his golden coloring and green eyes. He walked toward her, straight-backed, broad-chested and long of bone, with just a touch of a seaman's gait. With him, he brought his scent of fresh air and salt and rain. It was as if she stood in a soft breeze coming through an open window. Suddenly she felt a yearning, a frightening urge to rise from her chair and walk into his arms, to bury her face against that chest.

God, she must be losing her mind to think something like that! This was Jake Chastaine, a man she'd sworn would never set foot in this house again. Not only had he wormed his way back into her home to sleep in the room across from hers, here she was, imagining his arms around her.

Jake dropped to the settee opposite her chair and laid the long package across his knees, wrapping a big hand around the shank of it. It was amazing to her that with little exception, he always seemed to be comfortable in whatever environment he found himself. He could walk into her formal parlor, dressed in work clothes, and sit down as though he were wearing a suit. He nodded at the potpourri box where China's fingers still rested.

"That's an interesting box," he remarked.

Relenting a bit, she said, "It really is beautiful." Glad for the diversion, she picked it up and held it out on her open palm. "I think it came from France."

Jake appraised the container without touching it, his face blank. "Probably. Did the Captain bring it to you?"

"Oh, no. I didn't know who gave it to me, at first. A young boy delivered it one day. It's been years ago now. It came with an anonymous note and just my name written on the outside of the package."

"A secret admirer, huh?" he asked with a hint of ridicule for such romantic nonsense. "What did the note say?"

China hesitated, a trifle embarrassed, not wanting to repeat the words aloud. "Well—uh—it was just a personal message. Every Tuesday for the next few weeks, a dozen roses were delivered, with a note that said I should save the petals and dry them for this box. It was a rather expensive gift. I asked the boy who brought them who hired him, but he said the man had sworn him to secrecy." She sniffed again at its faint perfume.

Jake rolled his eyes with a derisive snort. "Jesus, what a gutless sap he must have been to hire a kid to be his messenger. If he was going to go all moony like that, he should have just brought the thing himself."

"I know you think it was foolish and sentimental. But I was quite . . . charmed." The memory made her smile.

He watched her for a moment, then sat back and laughed, crossing his arms over his wide chest. "It *is* silly. What's the point of giving someone a present if they don't even know who it came from?"

"That's the romantic part of it, Jake. But I don't suppose it's something that would interest you."

"Not really. I prefer a more direct approach. Did you ever find out who was behind it?" His expression was suddenly hard.

"Yes, finally." Direct approach, indeed. China

privately congratulated herself for refraining from the mention of Althea Lambert.

Jake's brows rose while he waited for her to fill in the rest. "And?"

"Oh, it took some checking, but Zachary eventually admitted to sending the box and the flowers."

"Zach Stowe? It figures," Jake hooted. He seemed angry. "I remember him. His chief talent was his ability to balance a cup and saucer and cake plate on his lap during those dumb tea parties you used to have here. There's a useful skill."

It wasn't the slur on Zachary that she minded. After all, he'd shown his true colors when the Captain died. And in the deepest corner of her heart, China had always harbored a slight doubt as to Zachary's responsibility for the gift, though she'd never known why. What bothered her was Jake's attack on the small ceremonies of life that she'd once held dear. Those "dumb tea parties," as he referred to them, were gone forever, and so were the people who had attended them. But she clung to the remembrance of them, just as she sheltered her memories of her parents and brothers. Of course, though Jake had spent a lot of time in this house, she would never have accepted him to participate in her social functions even if he'd expressed the slightest interest, which he hadn't. He and Quinn had been too busy terrorizing the town with their escapades. Jake certainly hadn't developed an appreciation for the social skills necessary for fine living.

"Well, what's so wonderful about someone who can tie a sheet bend knot?" she challenged.

Jake smiled with amusement and tipped his head, as if to compliment the fact that she actually knew what a sheet bend knot was. He let his eyes drop pointedly to the soft curve of her breasts and linger there, then drift down to her hips. It felt like they left burning trails on her body, as surely as if he'd touched her with his fingertips, and she shifted against the velvet upholstery. He brought his gaze up to her face again, which now felt as hot as a stove lid.

"There's a lot more to be said for a man able to tie a decent knot," he said softly. "You can be sure he's good with his hands."

China pressed her mouth into a tight line, unable to think of a suitable reply to his crude allusion. It suddenly came back to her that just a few feet away was the alcove where Jake had kissed her that dreadful day when she was sixteen. The memory of his mouth on hers, consuming and demanding, returned with surprising clarity. Her face burned hotter, and she twiddled with a pleat in her skirt. "I really don't care to hear—"

"I slept much better last night," he continued, obviously enjoying her uneasiness. Indolently, he stretched his spine, arching his back enough to strain the knit stitches in his sweater. "That big bed is a lot more comfortable."

"I'm *so* glad." Her words were laced with sarcasm, but she glanced down at her lap to escape the look she saw in his eyes. She couldn't define it, but no man had ever directed such a look at her before. At least, no nice man.

"Here," he said abruptly, putting the string-tied package in her lap. "Maybe you can make this fit in the icebox. I didn't know what to do with it."

"What is it?" China asked, thrown off guard. He was as slippery as grease when it came to changing subjects. Not that she was sorry to leave the discussion of knots and men's hands and big beds.

"It's a leg of lamb. Aunt Gert can fix it for dinner."

"Leg of lamb—where did it come from?" she asked, holding the paper-wrapped roast as though it were diseased.

"It followed me home," he quipped. "Where do people usually buy meat? I got it at the butcher shop."

China scowled. Now he was acting as though she and everyone else in the house were charity cases. Noble Captain Chastaine, bringing food to the needy. Pride pulled her chin up, and made her sit taut and tall.

"We don't need your help, Jake. And I don't want it." She would have stood to leave, but his eyes bored into her and kept her in the chair.

"That isn't why I got it. If I'd said I'd like to have lamb for dinner, you would have reminded me that this isn't a restaurant. So I bought the roast myself."

He made a reasonable argument, but she wasn't willing to concede. She held out the leg of lamb in mute refusal.

He leaned forward and pushed the roast back into her arms. "It would be a shame if this went to waste, wouldn't it?" he asked, his voice lowered. "Just accept it, China."

The intensity in his eyes and the tone in his voice made it impossible for her to argue further with him. He was a natural-born leader—even as a youngster, hadn't he led a pack of street urchins, *and* Quinn, like the Pied Piper? He was always in command of himself and usually those around him, excepting China. But this felt different. For an instant, she was capable only of looking up into his face to study the gilt-edged brows, the straight nose, the full mouth, as though he'd willed her to do little else.

Perhaps, she considered tentatively, just perhaps the lamb was an apology for his rudeness two nights ago. She supposed it would be graceless not to accept it. Her arms closed around the package. Finally, she broke away with an impatient huff and stood up, stepping around him to take the roast to the kitchen and grabbing the sweeper handle on her way out.

Jake turned to watch her walk away, her hips swaying gently as she pushed the sweeper ahead of her. A long black curl that had escaped its pins hung down her back. She held her chin so high, he wondered how she could see to keep the sweeper headed in a straight line.

He took a deep breath and swallowed, then stood to go upstairs.

Jake got his leg of lamb for dinner that evening, and even produced a bottle of wine to go with it. To China's infinite irritation, this served only to elevate his standing with the rest of the family.

"Here, Missy, let's be having some more of that roast down here," Captain Meredith bellowed, gesturing at the lamb with his fork. Directing his bushy brows at Jake, he added, "By God, lad, we've eaten better in the week since you got here than ever before. Chicken, ham, and now this." He turned knowing raisin eyes on China and cackled, "I guess having a good-looking young buck around makes the lady of the house want to fatten him up."

This drew a quiet, tittering laugh from Susan

Price, who, China noticed, cast oddly pleased, sidelong glances at Jake from over the rim of her wineglass. Susan's was a strange, aloof personality most of the time anyway, but when she was around Jake, her behavior was always peculiar.

China, however, didn't find Cap's remark amusing and refused to rise to his bait. He was like a crotchety grandfather or a toothless uncle who thought nothing of heckling a person to the point of excruciating embarrassment with baldly put questions and bad jokes. Any sign of weakness would only encourage him.

Jake avoided the looks Susan sent him and instead caught China's rather tart smile as she passed the meat platter down to the old captain.

They lingered at the table afterward, enjoying the last of the burgundy and a peach cobbler Gert had baked. All the elements—the wine, the food, a lively, snapping fire in the fireplace, this familiar dining room—made a warm, comfortable blend, and Jake knew a mellow pleasure. Slouching back in his chair, he turned his wineglass by its stem. Again and again he caught himself studying China, the way her thick black lashes framed those sapphire eyes, her small, smooth hands, the curve of her ear, the delicate coral color of her mouth. And he almost wished again that things had been different, that he hadn't needed to leave Astoria.

For while he'd gained a lot in the last few years, he knew he'd lost something as well.

Chapter Five

China dallied on the sidewalk in front of Otto Herrmann's door, asking herself one last time if she had made the right decision. She'd lain awake half of last night, staring at the eerie shadows of bare-limbed trees on her bedroom wall and struggling with this same question. It seemed to have only one answer, but she'd not arrived at it easily. She looked up at the watchmaker's sign again, and through the single plate-glass window. At least he had no other customers right now. Taking a deep breath, China adjusted her dark blue wrap and, her mind made up, walked into the shop.

It was a tiny place, lined with glass display cases containing rings set with precious stones, brooches, wedding bands, gold bracelets, watches, and every manner of necklaces and chains, all reposing on black velvet beds that made them sparkle like a night sky.

"Ah, Fräulein Sullivan, how good to see you again," Otto Herrmann greeted her, glancing up from his bench behind the back display counter. He was a courtly, pleasant-looking gentleman in his forties, but the jeweler's loupe at his eye gave his face a strange, deformed appearance until he removed it. Spread before him were the intricate internal workings of someone's watch. To China, they appeared hopelessly complex and minuscule. She couldn't imagine how he would put them back in the empty gold case and have the thing actually tell time again.

He rose from the task and stood across the counter from her. "To what do I owe this pleasure?" he asked. A discernable Austrian accent clung to his speech despite his twenty years in America. "Perhaps you wish to treat yourself with a small adornment, yes? Or you've a timepiece needing repair?"

"You have such beautiful things, Mr. Herrmann," she said. "That is especially lovely." She gently tapped the top of the glass case with her gloved finger to indicate a small cameo brooch within.

He reached down to slide open the door. "Yes, I've just received it. It would look very nice as a collar pin." He handed the cameo to her.

China took it in her palm, and admired the carved female profile. Then, remembering why she was here, she hastily handed it back. "But in fact, well, I—" she broke off uncomfortably. God, this was so awkward, she thought. Although she had faith in the man's discretion, she hated being in the position of requiring it. She glanced up at his kind face, but his green eyes and fair Teutonic coloring suddenly reminded her of a certain young blond sea captain, and she dropped her gaze, flustered. This was not going well. Forcing herself to remember her objective, China cleared her throat and began again.

"A year ago you purchased several pieces of jewelry from me, ones that had belonged to my mother."

He nodded. "An emerald necklace with matching earrings, and some rings."

China put her bag on the glass countertop and removed a quilted white satin pouch. "Yes, well, I find it necessary, um, that is, I could be persuaded to also part with this garnet pendant and garnet bracelet." She withdrew the jewelry from the satin. The necklace was a circle of red stones, like gleaming blood drops suspended at intervals by short lengths of gold chain. The pendant consisted of a large stone surrounded by tiny white diamonds. The companion bracelet contained alternating garnets and diamonds.

The watchmaker put on his loupe again and took the pendant from her outstretched hand, carrying it to the window, where feeble winter sunlight filtered through the glass. He studied it carefully for several minutes, back and front, praising it with wordless sounds of appreciation. In turn, he looked at the bracelet as well.

"They are exquisite pieces," Mr. Herrmann said finally, removing the loupe again and examining the jewelry with his own eyes. "The stones are of high quality, nearly flawless. They are matched well for color—one stone is almost indistinguishable from the next. The design is a bit dated, yes, but not so much."

China began to breathe a little easier. She trusted him and knew he was bound to propose a fair price. She began visualizing which debts to pay first, and wondering if there would be something left to donate to the league's boardinghouse.

He walked back to her and returned the pieces to their satin pouch. "It is with great regret that I must decline your offer, Fräulein."

China's heart plummeted with disappointment

and embarrassment. Her hands clenched inside her gloves. After agonizing over this decision, it had never occurred to her that Mr. Herrmann might refuse her.

He pointed to the glass case behind China. "You see, Fräulein, I have yet to sell the emeralds I bought from you last year." China turned and saw her mother's necklace and earrings artfully displayed. "They, too, are lovely pieces, but quite dear, and if I cannot interest a buyer soon, I may be forced to the unfortunate task of removing the stones to put them into smaller, shall we say, more attractively priced, settings."

China tucked the satin pouch into her bag again. Discouraged and vaguely depressed by his last statement, she felt as though a weight had descended on her chest. Which was worse she couldn't say: knowing that a stranger wore her mother's jewelry or hearing that it would be cannibalized and made into something else. It seemed like a defilement of her mother's memory. She pictured the empty settings, like eyeless sockets, plucked clean of their green gems one by one as the need arose, and she was horrified to feel tears gather behind her lids. She quickly blinked them away, ordering herself to maintain her dignity. She abhorred females who wept publicly; she considered it the height of manipulative bad manners. So well had China trained herself that now she never really cried, in public or in private, no matter how much she sometimes wanted to.

"Of course, Mr. Herrmann. I certainly understand." Anxious to leave while her shaky composure was intact, she lifted her face to give him a bland, concealing smile and tugged at the hems of her gloves.

The watchmaker looked carefully at her expression, and his voice dropped to a consoling murmur, empathy lacing his words. "Ach, Fräulein, I am sorry. I know that fate is not always so kind to us. She likes to plague us the way a cat worries a little mouse. While I cannot purchase your beautiful garnets, perhaps—" He hesitated here, poised on the edge of delicacy, and though they were alone, he whispered. "Might a loan be of any help?"

China felt here eyes widen before she dropped them to the drawstrings on her bag. Her humiliation was complete. She knew he hadn't intended it, but Mr. Herrmann's offer was salt to her already lacerated pride. Terrified that she would begin weeping, she was overwhelmed with a frantic, desperate need to get away from his kind concern. She backed away, unable to look at him, and ignored his question.

"I apologize for taking your time, Mr. Herrmann. Please give my regards to your family, won't you?" She rushed out of the shop and hurried down the sidewalk toward home.

Troubled and despondent, she wouldn't have noticed anything or anyone on the other side of the street. But from the corner of her eye she caught sight of a bright blond head, one that towered far above his companion's and everyone else's on the sidewalk. She saw Jake standing outside the druggist's, deep in earnest conversation with a woman who clutched his arm. He wore a jacket and tie, as though dressed for an appointment. China slowed her pace and moved a bit closer to the storefronts, her curiosity roused.

The woman wore only a shawl over her shabby dress to protect her against the winter afternoon.

Her hair, falling from its loose knot in limp, mousy hanks, blew around her thin shoulders. Even from this distance, China could see that despite her careworn, slatternly appearance, she probably was no older than herself. She beamed up at Jake with what China recognized as an inviting smile. He lowered his head, apparently to listen to some murmured comment, then reached into his pocket and produced a gold coin. He pressed it into the woman's hand. She threw her arms around his neck and, to China's horrified astonishment, kissed him full on the mouth.

China turned away and hurried down the street. She didn't look back, and she didn't slow her steps until she was on her own porch.

In the foyer of James O. Hawthorn and Company, Jake shifted in the hard oak chair where he'd already spent the better part of ninety minutes. Glancing up at the wall clock, he saw that it was getting close to six, and gave vent to a loud sigh. If not for the clock, he would have sworn he'd been there three times as long. He had never been good at sitting patiently. As a kid, the punishment he hated most of all was when his father had made him go to mass. That usually happened after the truant officer visited Pop or after Jake was caught for some prank. Sitting here like this reminded him of those infrequent but interminable Sunday mornings. Fidgeting on a hard pew at the back of the church, he would listen impatiently for the benediction but hear only the ring of the censer and Father Gibney's droning Latin.

Jake leveled an unwavering gaze on the determinedly oblivious clerk who sat at a desk, involved in some clerkly task, behind a low gated fence of turned spindles. A brass nameplate on the desk identified the skinny man as Dexter Morrison. Behind Morrison was a door with frosted glass in the top panel, upon which was painted the name "James Hawthorn." Jake had watched men come and go from that office for the last hour and a half and now, he knew, Hawthorn was alone.

Dexter Morrison's lofty attitude was somewhat undermined by the faint but very detectable smell of fish that pervaded the office. Well, canneries didn't smell like French perfume. Jake couldn't see much of the clerk beyond the top of his dark head and very prominent nose. The scratching of his pen grated on Jake's ears and nerves. Finally he stood and walked to the fence.

"Look—" Jake read the nameplate again, "—Dexter, does Mr. Hawthorn know I'm waiting to talk with him?"

Morrison looked over his spectacles at Jake with small, close-set eyes and a supercilious air. His large nostrils flared disdainfully above a pair of rubbery lips that just barely covered his considerable overbite. The man's weak chin must have been tucked into his shirt collar, because Jake sure as hell couldn't see it.

"I told you, sir, this is a busy cannery and Mr. Hawthorn has been in several meetings this afternoon. And as I also told you, without an appointment he probably will not see you. *You* chose to wait."

At the end of what had been a frustrating day, Jake was in serious danger of losing his patience. He shifted his weight to one hip, resisting the urge to pull at the throttling tie around his neck. The occasions in his life when he'd had to wear anything dressier than dungarees were few, and this time wasn't any more fun than the others. But if he was going to call on businessmen to secure cargo for the *Katherine Kirkland,* he supposed he'd have to get used to stiff collars, boiled shirts, neckties, and flimsy wool jackets. Of course, if he couldn't get in to see anyone, it didn't matter what he wore.

Jake decided to try the persuasive approach. He put both hands on the fence railing and leaned toward the desk. "Come on, Dexter. The day is almost over, and I've been waiting a long time. Go see if Mr. Hawthorn can give me a few minutes, okay?"

Morrison pursed those rubber lips and put down his pen, obviously discommoded. "I will try, but I can't make any promises. Who did you say you are?" The man's Adam's apple protruded so alarmingly, Jake thought it looked like bones.

Jake gave him his name again.

Morrison stood, went to Hawthorn's door, and tapped quietly. A muffled voice invited him in, and the clerk stepped into the office.

The door was left ajar, and at first Jake could make nothing of the murmuring he heard. But slowly the door began to swing open, as though on a draft.

"... remember him—nothing but a trouble-making wharf rat as a boy, hanging around saloons, getting into fights, womanizing. I doubt that he's any better now. Get rid of him, Dexter. I don't have time for—"

Jake felt a flush surge up his neck and face, and he gripped the fence rail so tightly that a joint in the wood creaked in his hand. He turned on his heel and strode toward the door, rage and injured pride boiling like lava in the pit of his stomach. He stepped out into the waning daylight and thundered down the wharf's wooden planking. A film of sweat broke out on his face and body, making his shirt feel like a steam cabinet, closed at the neck. With fierce impatience, he reached up, viciously jerked loose his tie, and flung it into the river with all the strength in his arm. It bobbed on the dark surface with the current and caught on a piling. Fumbling to open his collar, he yanked on the button too hard and it shot off the shirt like a bullet.

Goddamn that arrogant bastard and his arrogant, toadying clerk! He'd like to see that bony-assed little bootlick haul sheets in a hard blow off the Cape. Or climb a hundred feet to the masthead and secure the skysail while the deck was pitching under him like a fifty-dollar whore. He'd be shark bait before he could blink his beady eyes. Well, at least he had deprived Dexter Morrison the pleasure of throwing him out of the fishy offices of James O. Hawthorn and Company.

Jake continued down the long dock, his hands in his pockets, trying to walk off his consuming fury. He had set out this morning wearing this uncomfortable getup, ready to set Astoria on its ear. After all, he wasn't that hooligan who had left here in 1880. No, sir. That was all over. He owned a ship now.

But apparently Astoria wasn't ready to give up its long-held memory of Jake Chastaine, the rake-hell, the guttersnipe. He'd been trying to arrange meetings with businessmen for days now, and none of them would see him. They were busy, or not in, or just on their way out. Then, of course, there was James Hawthorn, who may have expressed the true attitudes of all of them.

Jake wandered along the waterfront, sidestepping coils of rope and crates, dunnage and barrels, and fishing nets spread to dry. The chill air smelled sharply of wood smoke, fish, and river. A gray-striped cat with a salmon tail clamped in her teeth hurried past him and darted into a small hole in one of the warehouse doors. He'd spent a lot of time down here as a kid, eluding the efforts of many people to civilize him. A few of them, like Aunt Gert and Father Gibney at St. Mary's, had been well intentioned and saw him as a motherless stray, running wild on the docks. Others, like some of his teachers, had merely been offended by him and sought to bend him to their will or break him in the trying.

Then there'd been Pop and his gloomy admonitions to accept the life he had and settle down to it. "Remember where you come from and find yourself some fisherman's daughter or farmer's girl to put in your bed."

Despite his reputation, which was only further inflated by that incident with Althea Lambert, Jake had known few women in Astoria. And they'd mostly been girls who worked above the Blue Mermaid and had taken him into their beds when business was slow.

Oh, yeah, this town had had quite an opinion of him. And now, even though he was a grown man of twenty-eight with his own ship, Jake was still found to be lacking. He could have all the money in the world, but he still wouldn't be good enough.

He looked up and realized where his thoughts

and steps had taken him, as he stared at the row houses on Tenth Street.

It was a working-class neighborhood that bred large families, where children and dogs ran together in packs and weary mothers never took off their aprons except to go to church on Sundays. It was hardest on the women, life in this place.

That had been emphasized for him this morning when he ran into Belinda McGowen outside the druggist's shop. She was tired and aged beyond her years. Not very well herself, she'd had to stay home from her job at the cannery to care for her sick baby. Roddy McGowen, her husband and one of Jake's boyhood friends, was on a ship somewhere between Astoria and the Orient. The crimps had gotten him, she said, one night when he was on his way home. The five dollars Jake gave her would buy medicine and groceries for a week. She didn't want to take the money, but it was easy to get lost in the small world on Tenth Street, and they both knew it.

It was a place where the sons of fishermen became fishermen themselves and daughters went to work in the canneries, packing their fathers' catches.

In this place where Jake grew up, men met head-on the challenges of raging gales and an uncertain life, but they couldn't reveal their hearts to tell their women they loved them.

The sun was a smoky orange ball on the western horizon as Jake walked past the shabby little dwellings. It shimmered on the river and made the shadows long. He heard a woman calling her children to dinner at the far end of the street and the cry of a loon as it winged across the darkening sky toward the marshes around Young's Bay.

Without deliberate effort, Jake was drawn to a house at the end of the row. A deep sigh rose in his chest as he stood before the place. It looked pretty much the same as he remembered: the siding weathered to silver gray, drizzled with rusty vertical stripes running from each nail. The windows, one on either side of the door, were covered by cracked green shades pulled nearly to the sills. They made Jake think of a face near death, its eyes not quite closed.

He climbed the one step to the front stoop of the shanty where he'd been born. An old rocker took up half of the small porch, and for the space of a heartbeat he thought of a rustle of skirts, a hint of honeysuckle, and wheat gold hair. His mother had sometimes sat out here, even on cold, gray days, and rocked in that chair, watching the river flow past with wistful eyes. The memory was so faded, it was almost as insubstantial as the mist. After all, he'd been just six years old the last time he'd laid eyes on her.

He raised a closed fist to knock on the door but then stopped, his hand an inch from the wood. A confusion of feelings bumped around inside him. Despite old differences between them, and wounds still not quite healed, he felt honor-bound to visit his father. If what Pug had told him was true, Pop probably could use a little help. But Jake didn't know if his father would take anything from him. In fact, he wasn't really sure what kind of reception he'd get.

He wanted to show his father that he'd proven him wrong, that the son for whom he'd predicted mediocrity had succeeded. But the events of the afternoon had left Jake a bit less certain of that. He'd won his ship from a captain who wagered her because she'd lost her luck. That wasn't much to brag about. The men whose shipping business he wanted wouldn't give him the time of day. And China, well—China . . .

He took a swift, deep breath and knocked on the door. Several moments passed and no one answered. He knocked again. He was about to turn and leave when he detected a sound. Leaning his head closer, he heard slow, unsteady footsteps on the floor inside, followed by a fumbling at the doorknob. The door opened, and Jake was confronted by a bent, aged man who stared back at him. His hair was as silvery as the boards on the house, as was the stubble of his day-old beard. His shoulders sagged and he hunched forward. The deep lines in his face reminded Jake of furrows the ocean sometimes left in the sand at low tide. A medicinal smell drifted from inside the little house.

"Who are you? What do you want?" the old man grumbled crossly.

Jake swallowed. "Pop, it's me. It's Jake."

Ethan Chastaine squinted at him suspiciously, looking him up and down. Finally the light of recognition dawned in his father's faded eyes, and a hint of gladness crossed his face. He opened the door wide. "Jacob?"

Jake nodded, unable to speak. He wasn't prepared for the flood of emotion that washed through him. For just that moment, he forgot the friction and animosity that had driven a wedge between them. He only remembered that this man was his father—his blood. Instinctively, without thinking, Jake reached for Ethan to embrace him. But the older man pulled back stiffly, reducing the hug to a clasping of arms.

In this dour place, men didn't show affection either. Not for the first time, Jake felt the lack.

Ethan pushed Jake back to look at him, like a grandfather trying to read a newspaper without his glasses. Jake thought he saw a trace of wetness in the old man's eyes before he turned away.

"You'd best come inside," Ethan said, his gruffness returning as he stepped aside to let Jake in. He pulled a big handkerchief from his back pocket and blew his nose. "I heard you was back. I hardly knew you."

Jake might have said the same thing. When he left Astoria, Pop's hair had been lightly scattered with gray, and he'd been as tall as his son. Jake followed him as he shuffled his way back to a chair by the stove in the corner of the front room. His father had become an old man. How could someone have changed so drastically in so few years?

"It's good to be back, Pop. It's good to see you."

Jake glanced around. A quick inspection revealed a small sitting room that was drearily familiar, having long been in want of a woman's touch. The wood walls were dingy, the paint faded to a neutral absence of color. A stack of what must have been a year's worth of newspapers sat in the corner by the door. Liniment of varying brands and in a rainbow of different bottles sat on a tray on a bureau, the way liquors were kept in some homes. Under the bottles was a dresser scarf that Jake was certain hadn't been moved since he left. It was one his mother had made.

Ethan tipped his head back to look up at him. "By God, you grew up tall. Sit down here so I can talk to you without sprainin' my neck."

Jake dragged a low stool over and sat in front of him. Unbuttoning his own jacket, he pushed his hands into his pockets. "How have you been? Pug Jennings said you don't get out on the boat too much these days."

"My joints just give up," Ethan said with impatient disgust, gingerly putting one hand on each knee. "Some days, it's all I can do to get out of bed."

"Did you go see Doc Tuttle?"

"Bah, what do I need with a doctor?" Ethan groused. "They can't do no good till the time comes to declare a body dead. Any fool can do that, and do it for free."

Jake shrugged. "He might be able to help you."

Ethan waved off the idea. Any lingering trace of sentimentality disappeared beneath his scornful resentment. "Help! It would have been a sight more help if you'd been around these last years instead of gallivantin' around the world. Your place was here. But oh, no, you had big plans. You wanted that—"

Jake interrupted with a sigh. "Come on, Pop. Let's not start in already."

Ethan nodded his angry acquiescence, then narrowed his eyes and leaned forward. "I hear you came in with that full-rigger I saw down at Monroe's yard."

Jake couldn't completely suppress his smile. Despite the way he'd acquired the ship, pride rose in him. "She's a rare beauty, isn't she?"

Ethan shrugged negligently. "Eh, she's not bad. First mate isn't a bad job. It isn't the same as bein' captain, though, is it?"

Apparently the full story hadn't reached Pop, Jake thought, and his grin widened. "I *was* her mate for four years—we sailed around the world twice. I'm her captain now."

Ethan lifted a gray brow, seemingly taken aback. "You've done well, then, since you left."

"I can't complain much."

The older man sat back in his chair and eyed him speculatively. "Well, still, there's lots of men your age what are captains. The owners, now, they're the important ones. Bein' the captain, you'll have to answer to them. They're the only ones who make any real money."

Jake's buoyancy faded. He'd been down this road with Pop more times than he could count. The path of this track was carefully mapped with verbal snares and pitfalls from which it seldom deviated.

Of course there was to be no outright joy in telling his father about his success. Pop wouldn't permit it.

Skipping a step in his needling, Ethan advanced to what could have been the finishing blow. "That is, they make money if there aren't too many shareholders." His eyes gleamed with a satisfied expression.

"I own the *Katherine Kirkland*, Pop, anchor, mast, and wheel. I'm her only shareholder—she's all mine," Jake said.

Ethan stared at him from under a frown, momentarily vanquished. He shifted in his chair, then shook a finger at him. "Well, don't get too far ahead of yourself. You could lose everything tomorrow. Your mama may have named you for a rich man, but fate can be a cruel bitch, you know."

Jake's insides clenched. God, how many times had he heard that? he wondered. *Your mama may have named you for a rich man, but—* A thousand times, maybe a million.

It had prefaced reprimands. *—But don't think I can't take a strap to your backside.*

It had been stuck on the front end of admonitions. *—But you're not one of the Astors, you're still a fisherman's son.*

Jake knew it was too much to hope that his father would be glad for what he'd accomplished. Despite all the changes, in some ways it seemed as though he had never left. Apparently Ethan felt the same. His attitudes and gibes were frozen in time. Jake could feel an argument brewing, and he knew if he didn't get out of here now it was going to erupt like a storm in the Atlantic. And after the day he'd had, he just wasn't up to a verbal battle with Pop. He unfolded his long frame and rose from the low stool.

"You're goin' already?" Ethan asked. "You just got here."

Jake reached into his front pocket and pulled out a ten-dollar gold piece. He extended the coin. "I promised I'd be on time for dinner where I'm staying. It kind of throws things off when I'm late." He'd already missed dinner, but it was as good an excuse as any.

Ethan glanced at the money, then up at his son. "And where might that be?"

Jake hesitated. If he made up something or skirted the question, he knew his father would find out anyway. "I'm staying at the Sullivans."

Ethan's scowl turned black and he pushed away Jake's hand. "Still tryin' to rub elbows with them, huh? Well, they're broke. All they got left is that house." A humorless cackle escaped him. "Important Captain Brody Sullivan, gone to the bottom a poor man, leaving his daughter to rent out rooms."

Unable to resist any longer, Jake retorted sharply, "Yeah, fate can be a cruel bitch, can't she?" Squeezing the gold coin till the edges dug into his palm, he turned and crossed the small room in two angry strides, meaning to leave without further comment beyond slamming the door behind him. A lot of their quarrels had ended that way.

But he lost his resolve when he glanced back over his shoulder and saw his father, shrunken and rumpled, still sitting in that chair, watching him in silence, his hands on his aching knees again.

"I'll stop back in a couple of days, Pop," Jake relented in a murmur.

Ethan nodded once.

Jake placed the ten dollars on the little table next to him and quietly closed the door.

Out on the street, he pulled in a deep breath, trying to dispel the smell of liniment that lingered at the back of his throat. The sun was just about gone, its last red streaks muted by the gathering mist. Lights glowed along the waterfront, and from downriver he heard the distant clang of a buoy.

Jake turned up the hill toward the house on Eighth Street. A chill, damp wind kicked up, slicing through his light wool jacket, and shivering, he leaned his shoulder into the gusts. Darkened storefronts of businesses, closed for the evening, gave way to the fenced yards of pleasant, well-tended homes, their windows radiant with the mellow light of supper lamps.

He searched his mind for some reason that returning to Astoria hadn't been a complete mistake. He couldn't think of even one. He no longer fit in the world where he'd grown up, yet the life he aspired to remained a closed door to him. In so many ways, this town now felt as alien as a village in the Peruvian jungles. In fact, there were seaports on the other side of the world that were more welcoming.

Jake trudged along under black, leafless tree branches, his head down, feeling morose, listening to the sound of his boots hitting the planks in the walk. If he couldn't get a decent cargo for his ship, the *Katherine Kirkland* could quickly change from the best opportunity of his life into just another liability. He'd already advanced his crew two months' pay to wait for her refitting. He had to earn that money back somehow. If he couldn't do it for himself, who did he know in this town that could help him make the connections he needed?

And he thought of her, as he often did, whether or not he wanted to. Hair as black as onyx, dark blue eyes, skin like cream and pink rosebuds, and soft, full curves that begged a man's touch.

China Sullivan, with a dignity she maintained even when pushing a carpet sweeper and a haughty pride that was as touchy as a blind rattlesnake.

Her life was infinitely better than Belinda McGowen's. Yet within her own world, her situation was nearly as dire. For just an instant, he pictured China penniless and exhausted, with a sick, colicky baby in her arms and dark circles beneath her eyes, and it shook him to his bones.

She may have lost her wealth, but she was still better connected than he was. She could probably arrange introductions to the men he wanted to do business with. If she'd do it. If he could swallow his own pride to ask her. But why should she? he scoffed to himself. For old times' sake? Not likely. He'd have to offer something in return, something so tempting it would be difficult for her to refuse him. Money.

Deep in thought, he didn't realize he'd reached Eighth Street until the big Sullivan house loomed directly ahead of him. Its windows glowed softly like those of its neighbors, but a single light shining from the hall window on the second floor reached out to him. He stopped in his tracks to look up at it, and a shaky sigh rose from deep within him. He'd been so preoccupied with other things since he arrived, he hadn't noticed that light glowing in the window.

For all men gone to sea . . .

He was well acquainted with China's tradition of the lamp. He homed in on that light as though he were bringing in a ship on a storm-ravaged night. Here, at last, was one good thing that hadn't changed.

Jake crossed the street to go get his dinner from the oven, a faint smile on his face and the germ of an idea in his mind.

China sat with one foot tucked under her on the sofa in the back parlor. Susan sat next to her, and China, her own mending forgotten in her lap, watched in fascination as the woman attached a cluster of tiny cream satin roses to the jade green hat she was making. One of the ladies in Aunt Gert's musicale group had ordered it. With a froth of cream tulle and a wide ribbon of jade grosgrain, it would be a lovely, feminine confection. Susan's needle flashed in and out, making stitches so tiny, even under full lamplight, they disappeared as soon as she pulled her thread taut.

China stood to sweep a hot cinder from the tiled hearth back into the fireplace with the hearth broom. "Susan, you've got such a talent for this, I'll bet if you talked to some of the dressmakers in town, they'd send their customers to you to make their hats. You could earn some real money. Who knows, you might even be able to open your own shop someday."

China was grimly amused by her own remark. Having handled the family's finances since her early teens, she'd never been a spendthrift, but she'd never had to worry about money or how it was made. It had simply always been there. Now she thought about it every day, although she hoped that experiences like the one in Mr. Herrmann's shop wouldn't happen on a daily basis. She replaced the broom and, tightening her shawl, sat beside Susan again.

"Oh, it would cost a lot to open a shop," Susan replied in her small voice. She leaned closer to the lamp on the table next to her to snip a thread with a pair of tiny gold scissors that hung from a chain around her neck. "And I don't suppose Edwin would approve of that anyway. Women in business, you know."

China looked from the hat to Susan's pale, plain face, pointed down at her work. Was she making another of those odd references to her husband? China wondered. She sympathized with Susan's loneliness and loss, but the woman's hours of near silence and her long walks worried China.

"Would he have minded your success?" China questioned subtly, trying to determine if Susan spoke of Edwin in the past or Edwin in the present.

"No, not success, but leaving the protection of home to achieve it. That he won't like." Susan's silver thimble gleamed like a shiny dime as she turned the hat.

It was a troubling answer, and China glanced at Aunt Gert, who sat at a small marble-topped table, to see if she'd noticed Susan's response. But Gert, her box of calling cards before her, wasn't listening. Her white head bent, she muttered to no one in particular, while from the stack of many dozens she withdrew a gaudily ornate card, over-burdened with scrolls, flowers, hearts, cherubs, *and* birds.

"I guess I'd better move Mrs. McIntyre to the deceased group." Mrs. McIntyre's funeral had taken place the week before. "God rest her soul, this thing was always a problem. I never knew where to put it before—with the bird group or the flower group."

Death, apparently, was a great equalizer. Once a card was relegated to the "deceased group," it didn't matter if it held birds, flowers, or flying elephants. China had never understood why calling cards, including those of strangers, held such appeal for her aunt. But Gert spent a lot of time on them, arranging and sorting them, to what end China couldn't guess.

Sometimes, when she'd sat up all night in the carriage house or when sleep eluded her but she still had to preside at the breakfast table and face a day full of work, she resented those silly cards. She could always think of half a dozen tasks more urgent than sorting pieces of paper according to what flower was printed on them. Then, she would feel guilty, knowing that her impatience was childish and uncharitable. After all, her aunt was nearly sixty and entitled not only to China's respect but to an easier life as well. It was only that she got so tired sometimes, of the work, of the responsibility.

Just then, as eight low-throated chimes sounded from the grandfather clock in the hall, she heard the back door open and close. So, Jake was finally home. He'd missed dinner again, probably having spent the afternoon with that draggle-tailed woman she'd seen him with earlier. But to keep her part of their new agreement, China had been obliged to put a plate in the oven for him. The food would be dried out, but she couldn't help that. If he was late, he'd have to take what he got. She heard his footfalls on the hall runner and listened tensely to determine where he was going. Realizing that her hand was clenched damply in her skirt, she forced herself to relax. Why did he have that effect on her, making her feel breathless and jumpy, as though she were waiting for a suitor? Or an executioner? Perhaps because lately she'd found her eyes straying to him, drawn to his rough handsomeness and tall, wide-shouldered frame. Or sometimes she'd realized she was listening for the sound of his rich, mellow voice. She'd even caught herself idly wondering what it would be like to touch his hand, his shoulder. She couldn't imagine what prompted those thoughts, but they had to stop. She had to try harder to *make* them stop. She didn't like Jake Chastaine, and that made her embarrassing daydreams even more unseemly.

His steps grew closer, and she saw that Susan

had put her work down and lifted her vacant eyes with a kind of expectant, puzzled expression.

Jake appeared in the doorway, nearly filling it, and China forgot about Susan. He wore his good white shirt and a suit, something China had not seen on him since those long ago Sundays at mass. He greeted Aunt Gert and Susan before turning his attention to China.

"Could I see you in the kitchen for a minute?" he asked her.

What was it now? she wondered suspiciously. Whatever he wanted, it couldn't be good—it hadn't been yet. Every time he asked to talk to her, he had a demand, or a complaint, or an insult. Or he threatened her somehow in ways that made her uncomfortable to contemplate. She didn't want to go into the kitchen and be alone with him.

When she didn't move, he glanced at Susan, who continued to stare at him. He looked at China again and raised his brows. "Please?"

With more than a little reluctance, China rose from the sofa and approached him. His face was pink with the cold night and she could feel it, even smell it, radiating from his clothes. He stood aside and let her lead the way back to the kitchen. When they got there, she turned to look at him, prepared for some new grievance.

He walked to the stove and stood close to its heat, letting the warmth sink into his legs, holding his big hands out over the still-hot surface. "God, it's a raw night out there."

"I saved your dinner," she began defensively. She took up a dishtowel and pulled his plate out of the warmer. As she expected, the hot oven hadn't been very kind to the salmon fillet and rice she'd set aside nearly two hours ago. Holding it out with wary regard, she added, "It looked better than this when I put it in here."

He glanced at the dinner with only minor interest. "I know, China, I know. It doesn't matter, this is fine." He moved to the table and pulled out a chair, motioning her to sit.

She put the plate at the table setting she'd left for him, and after pouring him a cup of coffee, she hovered uncertainly behind the chair. He obviously had something on his mind. In the brighter light of the kitchen, she could see he was bothered about something, preoccupied. His eyes looked tired and he slumped into the chair opposite her. The wind had blown his long hair into unruly wheat-colored snags.

He picked up the fork next to his plate, stared at the dry rice and shriveled fish, its edges the color of coral, and put his fork down again.

China felt a treacherous moment of regret. Expecting him to gripe about the food, she spoke first. "Jake, it really did taste good when it was fresh. But it sat too long."

Again, he shrugged it off. "It's not so bad. Hell, I've gotten by on far worse." He paused, as though trying to decide something, and then went on. "For the first month after Quinn and I signed on the *Pacific Star*, I lived on ship's biscuit soaked in watered-down tea."

"Good heavens, why? Didn't they take on provisions before she sailed?" She arched her brow and gave him a knowing look. "Or were you being punished?"

A thin smile dashed across his features, then disappeared. "No, I wasn't being punished. There was good food and a lot of it. But I couldn't eat. I was seasick day and night for four weeks. I couldn't keep anything down and I lost thirty pounds. When I started puking blood, the captain said I'd never get my sea legs. By then, we were on the west coast of southern Mexico. He wanted to put me ashore and leave me there. Quinn talked him out of it."

China winced slightly. The torturous sea-sickness he described happened to unseasoned landlubbers, sailors who weren't used to the constant rise and fall, and the rolling, sometimes heavy, swells of the open ocean. "But you did have your sea legs. You grew up on the water, working on your father's boat all those years."

"I know. I couldn't understand it either." He retrieved the fork and took a tentative stab at the fused grains of rice. "Sometimes I worried that I'd die." The half-smile returned. "Most of the time I was afraid I wouldn't."

If she'd heard about this at the time it happened, she would have relished the news. That kind of green-faced agony was something she'd have wished on him for the turmoil he'd caused in her family. But now it gave her no joy. In fact, she felt an alarming urge to reach over and smooth his wind-wild blond hair.

Ruthlessly, she pushed down the compassion fighting its way to the surface of her feelings. If Jake was trying to make her feel sorry for him, it just wasn't going to work. She responded with deliberate coolness. "I see you recovered. Is that what you wanted to tell me?"

Jake glanced up sharply. China remained standing next to the table, stiff and aloof, gripping the back of the chair. He didn't know why he'd told her the story, and now he wished he hadn't. He had never let anyone know about that first month, which had seemed more like a year. Aside from feeling too sick to live, and having the daylights scared out of him when he saw that blood, it was one of the very few times in his life over which he had no control, and he hated it. He was accustomed to thinking, doing, and deciding for himself. Even if some of his actions hadn't always been the wisest, at least he'd been the master of his own fate.

But for those few weeks he hadn't been the master of anything, and he wasn't now, and that brought him back to his reason for asking for this meeting.

"I wanted to talk to you because I have a business proposition for you," he said, and indicated the chair again.

China stared at him in amazement and fumbled with the button on her collar. "Business proposition! Really, Jake, if you're looking for a loan from me—I mean, you can't be serious."

He erupted into roaring laughter—snorted, was what China thought indignantly, failing to see the joke. Her face grew warm as he sat there shaking his head, his teeth white behind his smile. He put the fork down again and pushed away the dried-up dinner.

Propping his elbows on the table, he leaned his chin on one hand and looked up at her. "I don't want to borrow money. China, please, sit down so we can talk about this."

Cautiously curious, she replied, "Well, maybe for a minute." She slid into the chair opposite him, but couldn't relax.

He lifted the coffee cup to his mouth and considered her over its rim. With the cup poised like that, covering most of his lower face, her attention was drawn to his dark, uncommonly long lashes, the green eyes, the gold-frosted brows. She glanced away, breaking the contact. He took a sip and settled back.

"You've lived in Astoria all your life. You know a lot of people here."

She nodded and shrugged. "So do you."

"Not the kind I'm thinking of, China," he said drily. "Saloon girls and fishermen aren't likely shipping customers. I want to talk with the men who own the canneries and the lumber mills and the flour mill. The *Katherine* needs a cargo and that's where you can help."

Surprised by his suggestion, she steepled her hand over her chest. "*Me?* I don't know anything about the details of shipping. What could I do?"

He broke off a little corner of the salmon and popped it into his mouth. "I'd like you arrange a business dinner for me, here. I'll give you a list of names. You send the invitations, organize the evening, and act as my hostess."

China couldn't believe what she was hearing. His plan was out of the question, and he must be out of his mind if he thought she'd agree to it. "Jake, the rent you're paying wouldn't begin to cover the expense of something like that."

He swallowed another bite of fish. "I'll pay all the expenses. It won't cost you anything. In fact, you'll make money."

She eyed him suspiciously. "How?"

He cut off a chunk of rice with the side of his fork. "For every deal I make with your help, I'll pay you a percentage."

China's will to refuse shifted a bit on its foundations. She pulled her shawl closer. "Well, but—"

"But what?"

She didn't need a list to know precisely which people Jake should meet. They'd been friends of her parents, and the children of those friends. She'd been to their homes many times in the past, and they'd visited here. But that had been long ago, when she'd moved in their social circle and had lovely clothes, good food, and enough furniture to fill all the rooms. She wasn't eager to have the pillars of the community in her house now, poking their inquisitive, assessing noses into her privation. And, she suspected, providing she agreed to Jake's scheme, curiosity would be the chief reason they would accept her invitation—*if* they accepted.

"But there isn't enough furniture left in the front parlor or the dining room," she asserted.

He dismissed the problem. "We'll figure out something, maybe move some in from the back parlor. I'll take care of that." He picked a bone out of the salmon and took another bite. He sat there, chewing the fish and looking at her, as though formulating the reply to her next objection.

China made a face. Damn him. As usual, he had an answer for everything. But her next objection was one she couldn't give voice to. If she agreed to his proposition, it would mean spending entirely too much time with him, and that was something she did not want to do. She'd never wanted to lay eyes on Jake Chastaine again. She reviewed his shortcomings: he was the man who had urged her brother to abandon his family. He was a rakehell with a taste for whiskey and a reputation with women. Despite Aunt Gert's defense of him, China still believed Jake was responsible for Althea Lambert's ruin. He'd been too much of a libertine to be innocent. And since he'd returned, she had no idea what he did with his time on those nights when he came home late, but she could certainly guess.

And worst of all, he was too attractive for her own good.

But the more she tried to distance herself from Jake, the narrower the gap became. Now here he sat, eating in her kitchen and suggesting a business arrangement. He might gain a lot from this, but what would she really be getting?

Then she remembered standing in Mr. Herrmann's shop, trying to sell her mother's garnets. And being refused. Money. Everything always came back to money, she reminded herself again. She needed it and the Sailors Protective League needed it for its boarding house. She laced her fingers together tightly on the table and took a deep breath.

China looked up at Jake and found him watching her, waiting, his face carefully blank.

"Well?" he asked softly. "Will you do it, China?"

No, no, say no, tell him you can't—you won't— "Yes. I'll do it." God in heaven, had she really said that? She'd given him the answer he wanted, as if powerless to do otherwise. Jake looked as surprised as she felt. But now that the words were out, she couldn't retract them.

He bolted the rest of his awful dinner and wiped his mouth on the napkin. "Hmh, guhd," he replied around the last of the rice, and swallowed. "Then we'd better shake on it. This is business, after all." He stood and came to her side of the table. He rubbed his right hand briskly on the leg of his pants and extended it to her. "My hands are still cold," he explained.

But his hand wasn't cold. And as soon as they touched, a loud spark fired between them from the static he'd created, making her jump back.

"Oops, sorry," he said, and pushed his hand toward her again.

Hesitantly, she put her hand in his and watched his long fingers curve around hers. She noticed odd little details—the gold hair on the back of his wrist, the angry-looking scar that ran between the first and second joints of his thumb. He pumped her hand a couple of times, his grip warm and sure and firm. But when he should have let go, he didn't. Instead, he brought his other hand up to completely enclose her own. Startled by the contact, she looked into his face. His eyes on hers were searching and intent, and she saw a low flame burning in them that was distinctly unbusinesslike. She was swamped with a sudden longing to lean against his wide chest and feel his arms enclose her, while his hand cradled her head against his shoulder. She suspected that she might come to regret this agreement.

With no small effort, China escaped his warm grasp. "We can talk about the details tomorrow," she said and rose from her chair. She walked out of the kitchen to go back to the parlor, her head high, her pace dignified.

But in her heart she was running like a rabbit, running from the spark he'd just ignited within her.

Chapter Six

Late that night, Jake sat at the desk in his room making a list of the people he wanted China to invite to dinner. He decided to start with three names to keep the evening manageable, both for himself and for China. He hated asking for her help. It made him feel like a beggar. *Please, Miss Sullivan, ma'am.* But he wasn't having any luck on his own, and he was out of ideas.

Huh, he'd have bet anything that she'd intended to refuse his proposition. She'd worn a stubborn, superior face while he talked. He got the feeling she saved that look just for him. Fully expecting her to say no, he'd tried to appear indifferent while he waited for her answer, but his heart was pounding in his chest. He didn't want her to realize that he was placing his entire future in her hands. Then when she agreed, he wasn't certain he'd heard her correctly.

He studied his broad pen strokes under the harsh lamplight. There was a lot riding on this piece of paper and ink, but there was nothing more he could do until morning. He laid the pen aside and turned down the lamp. Yawning, he rubbed his eyes with the heels of his hands. When he took out his watch and opened it, it chimed one bell—midnight straight up. This had been a long, tough day. He felt as wrung out as he did after facing down a hurricane at sea. But it was ending a lot better than it had started.

He stood and stretched his back, pulling his shoulders first to the right, then to the left, trying to ease the stiffness in his tired muscles. The fire had burned down and he went to the fireplace, pulling off his shirt over his head, to stir the remaining low red embers. This was a night for warm quilts and a warm bed.

The wind wailed against this corner of the house, making the walls creak. There was only one sound in the world more lonely, Jake thought, and that was the low moaning of a foghorn. He'd listened to that most of his growing-up years, lying in the dark in the same run-down house on the Columbia River he'd visited this afternoon. Lying in the dark, surrounded by the damp and the smell of the river, trying to escape the sound of Pop's snoring in the other room by imagining a better future, a nice home, maybe even a wife. Jake shook himself from his reverie. He had the *Katherine Kirkland*, and she was his focus now.

He turned to glance at the huge bed behind him, and like a reflex reaction, China's face came to his mind again. She was so goddamned prickly, she was almost impossible to talk to. Before he'd left Astoria, she'd regarded him only with long-suffering exasperation—when she wasn't ignoring him.

For his own part, he had harbored confused feelings for her: lust, anger, longing.

Since then, he'd lost himself in the bodies of vague, unmemorable women in ports around the world. He sought them out on nights that were too long, when sleeping alone had seemed unbearable. He paid to lie with them, fostering the thin hope that satisfying his body might also fill the aching loneliness he sometimes felt. More often than not, the scheme failed. Maybe because he always made a special point of avoiding any woman with black hair . . .

But during the past seven years he'd just about convinced himself that what he had felt for China Sullivan was nothing more than a lowborn boy's fascination with a beautiful, unattainable princess. Sure, he'd taken it hard when she rejected him that day in the alcove—to a kid every one of life's bumps was a soul-wrenching catastrophe. Now that he was grown, he'd acquired a much cooler head, thank God, and a clearer view of things.

But tonight in the kitchen, when she'd lifted her face to his, it had taken every bit of willpower he owned to resist lowering his mouth to her moist coral lips. Her faint scent of warm spice had drifted to him, nearly making him forget time and place, and who they were. Luckily, he remembered before he did something really stupid, and settled for holding her hand between both of his own. As soon as he had a cargo for his ship, he'd be leaving Astoria. He wasn't sure when he'd return. Or if he even wanted to. He didn't need to drag more memories of China Sullivan with him.

He sat on the edge of the mattress and kicked off his boots and socks, then shed his pants, throwing them over a chair. He climbed into bed and shivered. Jesus, it was a bitter night. The sheets were icy on his long, bare frame, and he felt goose bumps rise all over his body. He lay back against a pillow with his hands clasped behind his head, and for a long time he watched the tall, flickering shadows the firelight cast on the walls. Outside, the wind moaned with a desolate voice.

When the faint tolling of the clock downstairs marked the passage of a half hour, Jake sighed and rolled over. He burrowed into the cold bedding, seeking comfort and finding none. At length, he wrapped both arms around his other pillow and hugged it to his chest, waiting for sleep to come.

Some nights were just too long.

The following morning after breakfast, Jake and China agreed to hold their dinner party on a Saturday evening two weeks hence. Or rather, China insisted on two weeks and Jake conceded with irritable impatience. It would give her time, just barely, to handle all the details she knew must be seen to for the kind of evening he had in mind.

"Jake, think about what's involved. A dinner party doesn't happen just like that," she said, snapping her fingers. She watched as he paced back and forth past the fireplace in the dining room, his hands clasped behind his back. With his blond head bent and his eyes on the floor, the roll in his walk was very obvious. She had no trouble envisioning him on the deck of a ship, easily keeping his balance by adjusting his long-legged stride.

"I don't need to think about what's involved," he carped, throwing his arms wide. "That's your job. I just don't understand what could take so long."

Truthfully, Jake knew he was in strange territory with this stuff. The detailed habits and requirements of the upper class had never particularly interested him. He'd always lived by a more basic set of rules: eat when you're hungry, work when you're supposed to, and sleep when you're tired. Life wasn't always that simple, but enjoying himself had never been as complex as these people seemed to make it.

Once again, he had no control, and he didn't like the helpless feeling that gave him. He hadn't gotten more than three hours' sleep last night; his thoughts had careened around in his head like a ship with an unmanned helm, plaguing him with the events of yesterday—Belinda McGowen, sickly and indigent; Dexter Morrison and his condescending arrogance; Pop, still looking for a fight after all this time; and China, with her small white hand tucked into his for the space of a handshake.

He glanced at her now as she sat at the table with paper, pen and ink, and ill-disguised exasperation. The tight, high collar of her blouse was buttoned securely, like a fortress against all intruders, and it gave her neck a long, swanlike appearance. Seeing her like that, prissy and cool, made him think of the manifold times he'd been in trouble at school, facing a critical teacher who fixed him with a baleful, angry stare. The salient difference, of course, was the rush of desire for China whipping through him—the urge to pull her into his arms to see if she felt softer than she looked, to sink both hands into her heavy jet curls and pull her head back to make her look at him, *see him* as more than the poor boy she had, by turns, disregarded and disdained. Then, while her face was upturned to his, he'd cover her soft lips with his own in a kiss that would melt her iciness and make her ask him for more—

"Are you listening to me?" China rattled her sheet of paper, yanking him back to the matter of the moment.

Jake pulled in a deep breath and strode away from the fireplace, suddenly too warm. He harnessed his thoughts to listen as she continued reading from the list she'd created while they talked.

"The invitations must be written and sent, the house needs to be cleaned, the menu planned, the food ordered. I'll have to hire Mr. Frederickson to tune the piano—"

Jake halted and glanced up. "Tune the piano? What the hell for?"

China wondered why he looked so furious. His face was flushed and damp, his brows lowered. "Music, of course. I'll have to play for the guests. Certainly the ladies will expect it. Mr. Frederickson doesn't charge much, Jake."

"It isn't the money I'm worried about. But Jesus, China, this isn't one of your tea parties. It's business. Next I suppose you're going to tell me I'll have to learn to balance saucers and cake plates on my knees." He squinted at her suspiciously. "And what ladies do you mean?"

"Well, the wives. You can't send invitations to a formal dinner like this and not include these men's wives. Not only would it be rude, it would be improper."

"So now I have to worry about entertaining the wives? Forget it." With a scowl, Jake flopped his big body into the chair opposite her and crossed his arms over his chest. China thought he looked like a youngster who'd been told he'd have to spend the day visiting some musty, ancient relative instead of playing ball.

Her exasperation increased incrementally. She let a small frown develop between her brows, and she folded her hands on the tabletop.

"You asked for my help, because, among other

things, I know what it takes to make this kind of function successful." She sat taller in the chair, and her chin lifted slightly as she looked at him. "By all means, if you feel that I'm not doing as you'd like, perhaps you should offer your 'business proposition' to someone who shares your philosophy." She sent him a look of imperious dignity. "Whatever that may be."

He continued to glare at her for a silent, tense moment, then she saw a glimmer of concession. Finally he looked away. He had no other options, and they both well knew it.

"Get the damned piano tuner, then. We wouldn't want the ladies to be unhappy," he grumbled and rose from the chair to begin pacing again. "What else has to be done?"

She continued down the list, talking about hiring help to cook and serve—she could hardly expect Aunt Gert to do that, getting the table linens sorted out, the silver polished. "You need a haircut, and you have to buy a good suit and allow time for the tailoring. You can see we'll need every day of those two weeks."

"You should have a new dress, too, probably," he said, turning to her. "Get one made for yourself and buy all the under—well, whatever else you need that goes with it." She thought he actually blushed. "Have the bills sent to me."

China gaped at him in horror. In truth, she'd been wondering what she would wear. Everything she owned was threadbare or hopelessly out of date. But Jake's suggestion was outrageous.

"You *cannot* buy a dress for me!" she exclaimed. She gripped the pen so hard her fingertips turned white. Seeing his stupefied expression, she continued hotly, "Don't you dare stand there and pretend you don't know how improper it is to buy such personal things for a lady. Like I was a—a strumpet, a kept woman?" Remembering that frowzy female she'd seen him with yesterday, she quivered with insult, and she threw it right back at him. "I realize the women you consort with don't care if people think that about them, or mind if men give them money, but I certainly do!"

Jake's face clouded over with a dark expression, and China felt a sudden tremor of fear lurch through her. He walked around to her side of the table, his eyes like green fire. She jumped to her feet, keeping the chair between them. He towered over her with wide shoulders and muscled forearms that flexed visibly below his rolled-up sleeves.

Jake let his gaze rake her plain, dark gray skirt and dull cream blouse. Her breath caught in her chest. The slow up-and-down look he gave her was more insulting than any she'd ever known.

"What are you talking about?"

"I saw you yesterday outside the druggist's," she replied, not totally unaware of the shrewish tone creeping into her own voice. "You gave that woman money and she threw herself into your arms."

"You mean Belinda? She—"

"Oh, is that her name?" China went on, astounded by her own behavior but unable to stop. "And she kissed you too, right there on the street in plain sight! Heaven only knows what else she gave you in exchange for that money."

"And it's none of your concern." He didn't raise his voice. In fact, it was a low, ominous rumble, issued from a tight jaw. "You're only a business partner, China. And our deal doesn't have anything to do with ladies or—what was it you said? Strumpets? And it doesn't have anything to do with who I give money to or why. Paying for your gown is no different to me than paying for the piano tuner. I expect you to get a dress, because I expect you to look good that night. But if you think your reputation will be ruined, then consider it a loan. I'll give you cash for the dressmaker so there's no bill to send. You can pay me back later." His expression stony, he leaned closer so that his face was within inches of her own. Then he reached out and held her chin between his thumb and forefinger. "Do you want to sign a note for it?"

She refused to respond, and she wasn't about to blink. She pulled her head back like a turtle to get away from his grip, but he held fast. The smell of him—soap, salt air, and that vague male scent that was all his own—surrounded her. His little gold medallion glimmered dully against his chest where his shirt fell open. Her cheeks blazed as though she'd leaned over a hot stove.

He released her chin. "I guess you don't. Now you get started on that long list of yours. You've only got two weeks." Then he turned and left the dining room.

China watched him go, her heart pumping double-quick with fear and indignity from the stinging reprimand, and with faint disillusionment. She felt for the back of her chair with a cold, shaking hand, as reaction set in. Pulling it close, she sank into it.

. . . *Only business partners.* Of course they were only business partners. Why, then, did she feel so snubbed and humiliated by the reminder?

She'd made a horrible mistake, agreeing to help

him, although she hadn't expected to feel the regret so soon. She yearned to fling their damned arrangement back in his face and order him out of the house. That—that womanizer. But she didn't have the freedom to do that. Her mind came back to the boardinghouse Dalton had found. There were a number of complications that entangled her with Jake, and a number of opportunities, whether she liked it or not. She glanced down at her cuff, already turned once and now slightly worn.

Shakily, she rose to her feet, resolute of purpose. She had a chance to do some real good, both for the family and for the Sailors Protective League, and if going forward with this meant she had to acquire the appropriate costume, then by God, that's what she'd do. As long as he made good on his end of their bargain, Jake Chastaine could go to hell for all she cared.

Well, it sounded good to tell herself she believed that.

China sent out invitations to the three names on Jake's list. They went to a cannery owner, a lumberman, and the owner of the flour mill. None of them were men that Jake had already spoken with or tried to meet. She privately expected to receive only letters of regret, but when the first acceptance came back three days later, China went to the dressmaker's to order her gown.

Jake and China kept a wary distance from each other, and neither of them mentioned the scene in the dining room again. But she couldn't forget what she'd seen outside the druggist's, no matter how often she told herself that, as he'd said, it was none of her business. Still, after their argument, Jake was home on time for dinner almost every night. The only reason for that, she supposed, was that eating the dried-up salmon had cured him of being late.

Just as China had predicted, the time flew. As the second and third acceptances arrived the project gained momentum and she became increasingly fussy in her preparations. She hired a cook and a serving maid from the Astor House Hotel, sent the table linens to the laundry, and worked with Aunt Gert and Susan Price to polish the silver flatware, candlesticks, and serving pieces. She ordered flowers for the centerpiece, placed an exacting order with Mr. Nyberg at Alderbrook Meat Market for a *very lean* sirloin of beef, and brought in Mr. Frederickson to tune the piano in the front parlor. In between, she returned to the dressmaker's for three fittings.

Jake made good on his offer to help solve the furniture dilemma in the front parlor. He spent most of a day sweating and swearing, with dwindling patience, while she directed him in moving the best remaining pieces in from the back parlor. It took some artful arranging to give the room a graceful appearance, and China appraised it from every possible angle. When she took off her shoes and climbed to the marble-topped library table for a higher view, Jake irritably threatened to quit. Despite her preoccupation with the task, it was impossible for her not to notice the sinew and muscle flexing under the fabric of his shirt and the way its buttons strained across his chest. And though she would happily have chosen death rather than admit it, she knew she'd made him push that love seat around one more time than was necessary, just to watch.

At the outset Jake gave her cash to pay with, since her own credit was shaky and not many were inclined to believe that Jake Chastaine should have credit at all. After a while, though, China's repeat business and the quality of her orders sweetened up the merchants somewhat and they began sending the bills to Jake in care of the Sullivan house.

Once things started falling into place, China began to relax—a little. All the while, she felt Jake's eyes following her and the proceedings with proprietary interest. To her secret amazement, all of the invitations had been accepted. Regardless of the circumstances, she had to admit that it was great fun to organize a party again, and to have enough money to do it justice. Maybe, just maybe, if everything went well, this might be a way to regain the social standing she'd lost when the Captain had died. She'd tried not to miss this part of her old life, but the truth was she did miss it dreadfully.

After losing his temper with China that morning in the dining room, Jake decided he'd be better off to stay out of the way. For the most part, he kept to the male-dominated territories of the Blue Mermaid and Monroe's repair yard, where he oversaw the caulking of the *Katherine*. When China showed him the last letter of acceptance, he breathed a relieved sigh. His plan could work, he just knew it could.

Once or twice he had the opportunity to see China haggle with the baker and the wine merchant to get exactly what she wanted, and at pretty much the price she wanted. She was thrifty and imaginative, and despite their differences,

Jake was not unhappy with the job she was doing for him.

Now if only she wouldn't look at him the way a butcher eyed a Christmas turkey . . .

"There you go, dear, that's the last of the hooks," Aunt Gert said. China stood in front of her cheval glass and could see Gert looking over her shoulder at the reflection there. "And, my, my, but don't you look beautiful." Her aunt shook her head with appreciative wonder and beamed. It was good to see the smile. Gert had been grumbling all afternoon about "those strangers" in her kitchen, the people China had hired to cook. "I wish your mother could see you."

"Maybe it's just as well that she can't," China said. Her new gown was made of midnight blue moire taffeta, cut low over the bosom, with enormous puffed sleeves lined with stiff tulle to keep their shape. The bodice hugged her ribs, requiring a tight corset that pushed up her breasts. The effect gave her a long, narrow waist that seemed no bigger than an afterthought. Styles had changed considerably since she'd last bought a dress gown. In the dressmaker's mirror, China had thought only that she looked fashionable. But now, before her own mirror, she saw the swell of her bosom above the décolletage and wondered if she'd chosen well. The bustle cascading over her bottom had more fabric in it than the bodice of the dress did.

"Is it—do you think it's, maybe, you know, a little too much? I mean, not enough?" she murmured uncertainly, putting her hand over her cleavage. China gripped the edges of the neckline and tugged upward, but it didn't budge. She had no jewelry to wear at her neck, and she wasn't sure that would have been a good idea anyway. There was no point in drawing attention to her chest. "Maybe I ought to loosen the stays a little."

"I don't think you can. The waist on this dress is pretty small," her aunt replied, assessing the form-fitting bodice. "Stop worrying. It's lovely on you. I don't know any other woman who could wear that shade of blue. It goes with your eyes."

The gown's color wasn't the issue, but there was nothing to do except wear it. The guests would be arriving in just an hour, and she had no alternatives anyway. China dropped her hands to her sides and took a slow, tentative breath, then let it out. Inside the white-satin-and-whalebone cage of her corset, there wasn't much room for air.

"I haven't worn stays drawn this tight in years. I hope I don't faint."

Gert chuckled with a wicked sparkle in her pale eyes. "I hope *Jake* doesn't faint when he sees you."

China frowned slightly, discomfited by the reference to Jake. She'd already thought about what his reaction might be, and that was unnerving enough. She walked to her dressing table. Picking up her perfume bottle, she touched the stopper to her throat and wrists. "Never mind about Jake. But do see that Cap gets his medicine, will you? I'll be down in a minute to make sure everything is on schedule."

Gert agreed and went to check on Captain Meredith, leaving China alone to collect herself. She went to the chair and perched on its edge, careful of her bustle, to slip on her shoes. She extended her leg to examine the hosiery. Silk stockings— she hadn't had silk stockings in ever so long. But she'd done what Jake had suggested: she not only bought the dress, she got everything that went under it as well.

She returned to her mirror and raised a hand to poke at her high-swept hair, then took another look at the gown. It irked her that Jake's money had paid for it, and even though she'd selected the design, she imagined that it was the kind of dress he would choose for a woman if given the chance. Realizing that only made her more determined to pay him back as soon as possible.

Her hands trembled slightly, and her face, though pale, flamed with heat over her cheeks. Jake wasn't the only one to whom this evening was important. She had worried over every detail twice, once in her role as Jake's business partner and once as herself. Picking up her sapphire earrings from her dressing table, she slipped the wires into her ears. She walked to her door and paused to smooth her hands over her skirt. Well, this was it . . . She turned the knob and stepped into the hall.

At that precise moment, Jake's door opened and he stood framed in the doorway, tall and broad, wearing a black suit that had been well tailored to fit his wide shoulders. Being blond, he looked very good in black and, to China's dismay, even more strikingly handsome than usual. His hair was brushed back from his face. She'd told him to cut it, but it appeared that he'd done no more than have it trimmed. He was phenomenally stubborn. China was surprised to see that his tie was expertly knotted over the collar button of his crisp white shirt. She'd expected him to have trouble with it. But hadn't he said something about the advantage of a man's being able to tie a good knot? Oh, yes . . . Without thinking, she glanced down at his large hands, then back up the length of his torso to the clean lines of his newly shaved face. He caught the trail of her gaze, and a knowing expression crossed his features. Her throat constricted, suddenly dry as chalk.

Jake stared at her intently, his mouth open slightly. He closed it, then he advanced one step toward her, and another. She let him take her hands and hold them wide. Her heart pounded inside her stays.

"Beautiful," he murmured on a breath. His voice was so quiet she barely caught the word. His eyes swept over her, resting briefly on her bosom, then rose to her lips. He didn't leer at her. No, the look he gave her was grounded in many thousands of years of instinct—primitive, territorial, possessive. She stared back, spellbound. He freed one of her hands to slide his own hand to the small of her back, drawing her closer. Power and authority emanated from him. China found it confusing yet oddly familiar, as though she needed to submit to him somehow. She could smell him—soap, fresh air, male scent; she could feel his breath fan her cheeks and eyelashes. His golden head slowly lowered to hers, angling to the right as his lips neared her own, and his eyes began to close and—

China came to her senses in time to wrench herself away before his mouth could claim hers, to escape the feel of his hands on her. She jumped back, her pulse thundering in her head. They eyed each other, the air so charged between them that it fairly crackled.

"Nice dress," he said finally, riveting her with a hot green gaze. His jaw was tight, and a trace of anger streaked his words. "Where's the rest of it?"

She resisted the self-conscious urge to put her hand up to her cleavage again. Instead, she pulled herself to her full height and took a deep breath. The effect was startling. "My business partner told me to buy a gown," she replied tartly. The memory of the insulting reprimand he'd dealt her that one morning in the dining room was clear in her mind. "I am supposed to 'look good' tonight. Apparently, I've succeeded."

Jake's brows lowered as he glared at her, but he said nothing.

"I—I'm going to the kitchen to check on dinner and make sure the family eats first."

He nodded shortly.

Jake stood in the hall and watched her walk away, her nose up, her hips swaying under the swish and rustle of her skirts, the music of femininity. He released his fists and let out a long breath. His momentary loss of sanity shook him. He'd almost kissed her, and he would have, too, if she hadn't suddenly yanked away from him like he was street sweepings.

He looked down at the expensive suit, and again he was swamped by a sense of futility. He could have a promising future, dress the part, and move in her circle, even if temporarily, but she still regarded him as someone who wasn't fit to enter the house through the front door. And if she wouldn't accept him, how would she convince their dinner guests to accept him?

He was trying not to notice her, but she made it difficult to ignore her. Damn her and that dress. How the hell was he supposed to sit at the same table with *that* all evening and concentrate on business? Or on anything else besides her tiny waist, or the swell of her breasts, or her long, slender neck rising above her nearly bare white shoulders? Her dark, smoky fragrance lingered like a whisper around him, while a series of jumbled images rippled across his imagination. He could almost feel his mouth buried against her throat, her soft flesh under him, his hands around her bottom as he pulled her tightly to him—

Jesus, Chastaine, stop torturing yourself, he ordered, lacing his hands through his hair. As it was, he'd lost every battle trying to keep her out of his thoughts, and now he was losing the war. Seeing her like that, as radiant as a blue star, as beautiful and sleek as a clipper ship, he figured he might as well give up the fight. But he knew he couldn't. If they were going to work together, he'd have to quell the smoldering heat she kindled in him. Sure, and while he was at it, maybe he could make the Columbia River flow east instead of west.

Sighing, Jake followed China's scent down the hall to the stairs.

"China, I can't tell you how delightful it is to see you again. And looking so lovely, too," Julia Stanhope gushed from her place next to Jake at the other end of the table. She poked a big piece of rare beef into her mouth. "We'd all wondered why you dropped out of sight. Of course, we'd heard amazing rumors, but, *ma chère*, they are so unreliable, and it's somewhat unkind to put much stock in gossip." The toothy grin on her equine face created the illusion of a smiling horse. Her rose silk dress, overloaded with frills and furbelows, didn't help dispel the image, nor did her heavy lower lip, which gapped away from her bottom teeth.

China thought the woman's words might have sounded less insincere if she had been looking at her while she spoke, instead of eyeing Jake as though he were a rich, tender morsel on a dessert cart.

"Well, after I lost my father, I withdrew from social occasions for several years," China replied, giving the answer she'd formulated last night while drying her hair in front of her fireplace. She'd known that someone was bound to ask; the only mystery had lain in who it would be. She swallowed hard to avoid choking on the next words. "But Captain Chastaine is an old family friend, and since he's back in town on business, it seemed like a good reason to celebrate." In a lightning-quick glance at Jake, she saw a pair of gold-laced brows lift imperceptibly before she looked away again to her dinner.

Julia was a tiresome, pretentious woman. Her husband was Emory Stanhope, the short, bullet-shaped man who sat on China's left. Emory's very prosperous lumber mill financed her trips to the East Coast and Europe, her expensive, if garish, dresses, and a grand home. But he was old enough to be her father, and she had an unashamed eye for young, attractive men, which he apparently chose to ignore.

"Daddy," she addressed her husband, reminding everyone of their age difference, "isn't China's table every bit as lovely as the Raymonds' was last week?"

Emory agreed, smearing a big lump of butter on a flaky roll. "Reminds me of the old days when Captain Sullivan was in port, China. Your mama threw some pretty fancy parties, too."

China glanced around the table, laden with

food, snowy linen, glowing candles, and flowers, and she was flattered by the comparison. Except for a couple of awkward questions, the evening was proceeding very nicely. Her gown, it turned out, wasn't so scandalous after all—the other ladies wore similarly cut necklines.

Jake, she noticed, was managing surprisingly well at the other end of the table, certainly better than she'd expected. For someone she remembered to be an insolent smart aleck in his youth, he was doing a passable job of making conversation and fielding questions about himself. She was very conscious of him sitting in that far chair. He looked relaxed and at ease, but even seated, he was taller than anyone present. Now and then their eyes would link, and every time they did, his gaze made her feel as though they were alone in the room. She tried hard not to think about that scene upstairs earlier this evening, when he'd put his hand on her back to pull her to him, the curve of his mouth as he lowered his face to hers, those long lashes drifting closed. She clenched her napkin in her lap. It was very distressing.

Above the general murmur of conversation, she heard his rich, smooth voice politely responding to a question. The guests were also fascinated by the blond newcomer—fortunately, some of them were new to Astoria themselves, having arrived in just the last few years, and not a one of them seemed to remember him from the old days. He replied with truthful answers that carefully avoided jogging anyone's memory of a wild rowdy who gambled, wenched, and got a girl in trouble.

The aroma of the expertly prepared meal, gracefully served by silent, competent help, wafted through the dining room. The air was filled with the sounds of lively conversation and the clink of silverware on dishes. China viewed the delicious food with a little regret; she was too nervous and her corset was too tight to allow her to take more than dainty tastes of the beef and parsleyed potatoes. So far, her strategy had succeeded. She glanced anxiously at the clock on the mantel. Seven-thirty. Now, if the next part of the night went as well, it would be a total triumph. Jake was bound to be angry about the after-dinner guest she planned; she could only hope that he was smart enough to avoid creating a scene. The prospect of being the object of his cold green glare was daunting. Still, everything was running so smoothly to this point . . .

Then, just as dessert was being served, Lavinia Buchanan spoke up. She motioned the white-aproned serving girl to put an extra dollop of whipped cream on her chocolate cake as she said, "It's wonderful to see you looking so well, China. Here you'd been in mourning for your father, and I—" Her voice dropped to an astounded, distressed whisper, as though she reported news of an appalling fall from grace. "I'd heard that you're actually operating a *boardinghouse* here. Well, I suppose I should have questioned the story. Still, I wish you'd made an effort to stay in touch so that we'd have known what happened to you."

China felt a blush rise from her chin to her hairline, and she briefly bit down on the tines of the fork in her mouth to stifle the blunt reply that popped into her head. For an instant the candles were not as bright, the crystal less sparkling. All these years, she'd been regarded by most of her former friends and acquaintances as a social leper, ignored and avoided, through no fault or choice of her own. If Lavinia knew tonight that all that stood between China and her exile was a sirloin of beef and a blue moire dress, both paid for by the guest of honor, it wouldn't stop her from shoveling chocolate cake into her mouth. No, indeed. She would accept China's hospitality, then bear the juicy tale straight to those who now carefully averted their eyes when they saw China at the grocer's, or the dry goods store, to avoid speaking to her. She concealed the bitter hurt brought on by the thought. She sensed Jake's gaze on her, but she didn't look at him, afraid of what she'd see there. And much as she longed to, she knew she couldn't respond in kind to Lavinia's bad manners. Instead, she gave her a cool smile. "I've been kept rather busy with ... the house and a couple of pet charities. But there are no boarders here, Lavinia, only family. And Captain Chastaine."

Lavinia returned the half-smile and gave her a smug, unconvinced look.

At the other end of the table, Julia Stanhope leaned toward Jake and burbled, "I'm sure I should know you, Captain. Are you of the Boston Chastaines?"

Jake shook his head and turned the stem of his wineglass in his big hand. "Not that I know of, Mrs. Stanhope. My family is pretty much from the West Coast."

"I beg your pardon, Captain Chastaine," Peter Hollis broke in. About China's age, he managed his father's cannery. "Did you say that you grew up in Astoria? We must have run into each other at some point, but I can't place you."

China looked up, alert at the question, formulating a diversionary remark in her mind. Of course Peter would think he should know him. Dressed as he was, Jake looked every inch the gentleman.

Jake laid his fork on his plate and took a big swallow of burgundy, stalling while an answer came to him. What could he tell Hollis? That they'd never met before because while Hollis had probably been doing things like learning to waltz and going to Sunday socials, he'd been ditching school, working on Pop's fishing boat, and hanging around the Blue Mermaid? He carefully set his wineglass down.

"Well, I've been away at sea for a long time, seven years. I came back just a few weeks ago to bring my ship into dry dock and to develop new business."

China let her breath out.

"Say, is that your barkentine at Tewey's?" Douglas Buchanan asked. "I saw her on my way to the grain office last week. By God, she's a good-looking ship."

Grateful for the appropriate turn of conversation, Jake couldn't help but smile. "She's trim and fast. As soon as she's back in the water, I'll be sailing her to the Far East. I've got cargo space for lumber, wheat, flour, other goods."

Buchanan, a middle-aged man with carrot-colored hair, was apparently more polite than his wife. "If you have time in the next few days, I'd like to arrange a meeting with you. The world is hungry for American grain, and I'm interested in pursuing—"

"Oh, dear" Julia sighed with great exaggeration and rolled her eyes at Jake. "I do hope you gentlemen aren't going to spend *all* of dinner discussing business."

"Julia," Emory Stanhope murmured.

Ignoring her husband, she leaned closer to Jake's shoulder. "My, to think you've sailed the whole world. You know, my sister and I traveled all of Europe three years ago. We even went as far as Turkey."

Jake squelched his escalating irritation at having this woman flirting with him. She was like a fat, lazy fly droning around him, begging for the mortal swat of a rolled-up newspaper. But he hadn't yet secured a meeting with her husband, so he had to endure her. He straightened away from the big-toothed mouth murmuring to him. "Really? As far east as Turkey? Did you see the Dardanelles?"

Obviously warming to the attention, Julia put her heavily ringed hand on the arm of his chair. Jake fought the urge to bring his elbow down on it, halfway expecting to feel her chubby fingers in his lap any minute, fondling him beneath the tablecloth. "See them! Why, my dear, they invited my sister and I to dine with them three different times."

Jake dug his fingers into the upholstery next to his thigh and sucked in a deep breath, struggling against the pressure of laughter that filled his chest like an overinflated balloon. He'd known his share of pompous name-droppers, but he'd never met one who claimed to have had dinner with a waterway. He sneaked a glance at China, who was staring at Julia with her napkin pressed hard to her mouth. She looked away as soon as their eyes met, seemingly overpowered by a coughing fit. Elizabeth Hollis, Peter's pleasant, timid wife, blushed furiously at Julia's error and concentrated her attention on her plate.

Jake had no sooner regained control of his own breathing than he heard a familiar blare.

"Say, Missy! I'd have a word with you, if you don't mind!" Conversation ceased, conquered by the bellowing, and all heads swiveled to face its source. Captain Meredith came to the double doors of the dining room and fixed China with a stern look. His ever-present pipe clamped in his teeth, he wore a bulky sweater, and his bushy white brows were lowered like thunderclouds.

Susan Price appeared behind him, tugging on the old man's arm and urgently whispering something to him, probably trying to get him to come away. But he couldn't hear her in any case, and irritably shook her off.

"Stop fussing with me, girl."

Jake began to rise, but Cap ordered him back into his chair. "Not you, lad, although I daresay you had a hand in this, too."

China put her napkin on her chair and excused herself, feeling all eyes on her as she crossed the room in silence so profound that her taffeta skirts whooshed like ten pairs of brand-new dungarees.

Cap launched into his cantankerous complaint as she drew near. "A man works hard all of his life and, goddamn it, if he can't live in his own house, he ought to be able to sit in his own chair without it being stolen right out from under his ass—"

China winced and grasped him by the arm, pulling him into the hall and closing the dining room doors behind her. She'd long ago grown accustomed to his rough speech, but the dinner guests didn't need to hear him. The chair to which he referred was the leather wingback where he dozed every night by the fireplace. It had been her father's, and Cap had claimed it. Everyone knew it was his, and none of the family sat in it but him.

Susan Price stood by, wringing her hands helplessly. Her eyes were huge, and the color drained out of her already pale face. "I tried to stop him, but when we went to the back parlor after dinner, he saw his chair was missing and, well—" Susan gestured toward Cap.

"It's all right, Susan. Cap, please don't be upset," China began, facing him.

The old man bawled on, his craggy face as creased and weathered as a walnut shell. His pipe bobbed up and down with each angry word. "Upset! Where do I find my favorite chair? In that fancy parlor you don't let anyone sit in, so I guess I can bid it a fare-thee-well, now can't I?" He bent a severe look on her, waving a gnarled hand at her gown. "And what the hell kind of dress is that for a decent woman to wear? Your titties will be falling out of that thing like peaches from a leaky bushel basket."

"Cap!" China gasped at the vulgar rebuke, accentuating the reason for his objection to the dress. Susan uttered a little shriek, then clapped her hand over her mouth.

Her nerves already on edge, China was in no mood for his tantrum. "Just you never mind about my gown. As for your chair, we only borrowed it for this evening. You knew that—Jake explained that to you, didn't he?" He'd said he would; if he hadn't, she'd brain him.

At this question, Cap's jaw dropped and his petulance evaporated, replaced by guilty chagrin. He scratched his scalp through his thin white hair.

"Well, by God, I guess he did. I suppose I must have forgotten about it."

She pursed her mouth and gave him a look as stern as he'd given her earlier, but said nothing.

He patted her hand clumsily. "You won't hold it against me, will you, Missy? You can't blame a man for getting old and forgetful." He glanced away, his blue eyes faded. "At least I hope you don't, because there's not a damned thing I can do about it."

His expression was contrite, but it was his words that made her eyes sting suddenly. She couldn't be angry with him. She clasped his frail arm inside the heavy sweater. "Don't worry about it, Cap. It's all right. Now why don't you go with Susan to the back parlor? You can sit on the sofa just for tonight, can't you? I promise Jake will put your chair back before he goes to bed."

"Aye, girl." He turned to leave, then stopped to give her gown another once-over and shook his head. "I'll tell you something, though. If I was your father, I'd blister your fanny for wearing a dress like that. I don't care if you're a grown woman. You wouldn't sit down for a week." He grinned at her then, his pipe shifting in his teeth. "But if I was forty years younger, I'd give that young buck in there a good run for his money. And I'd win." He tipped her a wink.

China laughed in genuine amusement and fondness. Cap was a dear old devil. She watched Susan lead him away, then turned back to the dining room. Taking a deep breath, she touched a hand to her hair and pulled open the doors.

The low murmuring ceased, and again she was the focus of all eyes. "Well!" she said brightly, trying to camouflage the awkwardness she felt. "If everyone has finished, shall we retire to the parlor?"

There was a lot of shuffling and scraping of chair legs on the bare hardwood floor as the guests hauled themselves to their feet. Jake walked over to her and took her elbow.

"Is everything okay?" he asked in a casual but confidential tone.

"Yes," she replied, acutely conscious of his warm hand on her arm. "Cap was being, well, Cap. He was upset about his chair."

Jake flashed her a crooked grin. "It sounded like he was more upset about peaches in a bushel basket." He squeezed her elbow before releasing it, then walked past her to the hallway.

That boor! China fumed, wishing she could have kicked his shins. She followed his broad-shouldered back with her eyes, boiling with outrage and embarrassment. God, did that mean everyone had heard Cap's scolding?

"China, whoever was that musty old crosspatch who came to the door? Is he one of your paying guests?" Lavinia Buchanan asked as she brushed crumbs from her black silk lap.

The insult was unmistakable. "Captain Meredith is a member of the family," she replied tightly.

"Mon Dieu," China heard Julia Stanhope's affected murmur behind her. "If I had family like that, I'd lock him in the cellar."

Chapter Seven

The evening wore on in the firelit front parlor, with brandy and port for all. After China played several piano selections, the men convened around the mantel to discuss business, while the ladies gathered on her assembled brocade love seats and chairs to engage in lighter conversation.

For China, the fine glow that had embraced her earlier in the evening had dimmed just a bit, although she wasn't certain why. Sipping her wine, she felt oddly disconnected, a foreign observer outside the group. Though lacking the lively exchanges about literature and music that she'd so enjoyed, the discourse among these women was typical of what she remembered from parties long past: which debutantes had become engaged and which of those matches were ill-advised, the suspiciously frequent number of trips made to Portland by the mayor's sister-in-law ("Well, you know it must have something to do with a man"), the gruesome, whispered details of Mrs. Warner's *eighth* lying-in, the outrageous price of Swiss chocolate.

Although she nodded and made appropriate responses, with dull surprise China realized how insignificant it all seemed to her now, and how frivolous and cruel these women could be. After losing the captain and her brothers, after tending men in the carriage house who'd been drugged and beaten in saloons and dark, fetid alleys, she could hardly care about the best way to remove a wine stain from a velvet ball gown.

Was this how she'd been discussed after being ostracized? Probably, she thought, based on Lavinia Buchanan's report of what she'd heard.

China still yearned for the ceremonies and celebrations of life—an elegant table with fine china and silver, good food, and beautiful clothes. But at this moment the table in her mind's eye stood with only two place settings because there was no one in this room she'd care to share it with except . . . Resolutely, she pushed the thought from her mind.

Jake nursed his first brandy, while the men around him partook more freely. The heat from the fireplace made him wish he could loosen his tie and open his collar, but he knew it would be at least a couple of hours before he could get out of these uncomfortable clothes. Still, the expense and preparation for this party had proven worthwhile. He had meetings scheduled with two of the three men, Emory Stanhope excepted, who was becoming soddenly drunk. Jake glanced across the room at the knot of women and decided that if he were married to Julia Stanhope, he'd probably be drunk a lot of the time himself.

His gaze drifted a bit to the left, where, cool and lovely and slightly remote, China perched on a chair. She was a charming and gracious hostess, there was no question about that. To the casual observer she appeared to be listening to Julia's affected bleating, but Jake sensed her thoughts were on something else entirely. What she saw in those women, he couldn't guess. Hollis's wife seemed all right, but those other two—though their clothes were nicer, they had fewer manners than some of the saloon girls he'd known in his time.

Their husbands were a little better, but still caught up in the snares of social position and rank. He couldn't imagine sitting down to have a beer and swap stories with any of them. They were all too stiff and self-important for that kind of informality. But that wasn't why they were here, anyway.

Watching China, he saw the way her hand curved around her wineglass and imagined it lying palm up in his own while he lifted it to his mouth and pressed a kiss into its warm softness. Just then she turned her sapphire eyes on him and laid her open hand on her lap, as though she shared the same thought.

"Still with us, Chastaine?" Peter Hollis nudged him.

With effort Jake pulled his attention back to the group. "Sorry, what did you say?"

"We were discussing the new president, Benjamin Harrison. He's promised to impose a tariff to protect American manufacturing interests against foreign imports. Do you think you'll be affected by that?"

Stanhope broke in, his voice overloud and somewhat blurry around the edges. Perspiration gleamed on his forehead and upper lip. "By God, I don't give a damn what he does. It's good enough to have a Republican back in the White House after Cleveland."

One of the things Jake had learned from his father was to avoid discussing religion or politics.

Pop hadn't told him that outright. Instead he'd set the example by getting into roaring arguments with the patrons at the Blue Mermaid and the neighbors on Tenth Street, haranguing people until they began to avoid him.

Jake resisted the urge to put two fingers inside his collar to ease the tightness. "Since I've spent so much time out of the country the last few years, I really haven't followed politics here."

"Just as well, Chastaine, just as well," Stanhope said over a soft belch, and looked at his wife. "Time, politicians, and the ladies have turned my hair gray. Gr-granted, the ladies were a good deal more fun."

China's head came up at the burst of laughter that rose from the men's group. Jake seemed to be having a good time, she thought grumpily, at least more so than she was. Lavinia had wrested the conversation away from Julia, and now China and Elizabeth Hollis were hostages of a monologue that might very well have no end.

At that moment the front doorbell rang, and she jumped as though she'd been prodded with a hot wire. Oh, God, she'd almost forgotten. Although uncertain about the wisdom of the plan she'd devised, she was grateful to escape Lavinia's domination, and she rose from her chair.

"Well, who in the world could that be at this hour?" Lavinia demanded, apparently quite annoyed at being interrupted. She read the clock on the library table. "It's nine-thirty."

China's gaze slid nervously to Jake, who sent her a quizzical look. She quickly looked away. "Please do continue, Lavinia. I'll see to it." She rose from her chair and left the parlor, her hands pressed to her skirts to muffle their rustling.

Through the glass in the double front doors she saw the silhouette of a man's shoulders. She reached for the knob and turned it to let Dalton Williams in.

"Dalton," she murmured. "How good to see you."

"Hello, China." After a stunned, admiring glimpse at her gown, he gave her a brief smile. "You look—very nice."

"Thank you. I'm glad you were able to come by," she replied.

Another burst of laughter came from the front parlor. "Does Chastaine know?" he asked.

She shook her head. "It didn't seem like a good idea to tell him."

Dalton remained right next to the door, looking decidedly uncomfortable, which was unusual for him. He'd been in the house only one other time, and that had been the first day she ever laid eyes on him. In the two years since, they'd always met in the carriage house. The lifestyle of the privileged was even more alien to him than it was to Jake. He lived in a furnished room over Columbia Cigar and Tobacco Store, which, of course, China had never seen. But in a rare moment of self-disclosure Dalton had once told her that he'd never known his father and that his consumptive mother, to support herself and her son, had done "whatever she had to" until her death at age twenty-four, leaving behind nine-year-old Dalton. After three years of living in the streets and at the back doors of restaurant kitchens in New York, he'd gone to sea as a cabin boy.

Tonight he wore a tired-looking dark suit that China was sure he'd either borrowed or bought secondhand for this occasion. She couldn't expect a man whose chief activities took him into saloons, brothels, and alleys to own formal evening clothes. But still, his attire tonight was a noticeable step up from his typical uniform of pea coat and dungarees. His fine, unruly brown hair was sternly repressed with hair tonic, and his tie, China noted wryly, was knotted correctly.

"Shall we meet the other guests?" she asked.

"All right," he said. He looked around the hall with a wide-eyed glance, and she heard him take a deep, steadying breath as she led him into the front parlor. From the corner of her eye, she saw Jake stiffen as soon as they set foot in the room. Oh, please don't let him make a scene, she prayed. Everyone else was alert at their entrance—Dalton electrified a room with his presence.

Jake stepped forward, suddenly seeming even taller than usual, his thick, pale hair reflecting the firelight. His eyes were as dark as emeralds, fixed on Dalton, his expression blank.

"China," he said, his voice smooth and controlled, "who is your guest?"

An icy lump formed in the pit of her stomach. She'd thought her plan brilliant when she conceived of it. Now she wasn't so sure. "Captain Jake Chastaine, this is Dalton Williams," she said, going through the motions of proper etiquette even though, in fact, she knew each man recognized the other. A tense, silent moment followed. Neither offered a handshake.

The two glared at each other with barely disguised hostility, and she pulled Dalton away to meet the rest of the group.

She hurriedly introduced him to the others, who surveyed him with mystification until China added, "Dalton oversees one of the charities I've been busy with."

"Really? Well, I'm involved with a few charities myself," Julia beamed. "Mostly I've been working with St. Mary's Hospital Committee"—here her horse grin turned into a bit of a scowl—"although those blasted nuns are so bossy, it's a trial." She leaned forward and remarked confidentially, "They're Catholic, you know."

China briefly seized her upper lip between her teeth. Dalton gave the woman an assessing look but merely nodded.

Peter Hollis, regarding him with a speculative expression, said, "I know you from somewhere, Mr. Williams. Have we met before?"

"Not formally. But I've stood on the sidewalk outside your office once or twice, Mr. Hollis, distributing information about the shanghaiing that goes on in Astoria and Portland."

A collective "ah" of recognition sounded within the group as most of them made the association between Dalton Williams and the Sailors Protective League.

From the corner of her eye, China saw Jake go to the brandy decanter and pour a large measure for himself. His knuckles were white as he gripped the container. His fury was palpable; she almost expected to hear the sound of the glass shattering in his grip. He bolted the brandy and coughed once from its searing heat, then poured another drink while he leveled an ice-cold glare at her.

Emory Stanhope, dozing in the blue velvet chair near the fire, roused himself from his partially anesthetized state to comment. "Oh, yes, bad business, that shanghaiing. Bad. Sn-snatch law-abiding citizens right off the street."

Dalton raised his piercing cobalt eyes from Stanhope and settled them briefly, evenly, on Jake, who clenched his right hand into a fist at his side. Then he let his gaze sweep the room to rest on each face.

"Yes, that's true. Honest citizens are being taken, but so are men who make their living by sea trade." His voice rose and deepened a bit. "Imagine renting a room in a boardinghouse, then being drugged or hit over the head and sold by the landlord to a sea captain waiting in the harbor."

Douglas Buchanan shook his head skeptically. "I don't know, Williams. From what I've seen, it's my impression that a lot of sailors are their own worst enemies, going into the saloons and, if the ladies will pardon me, brothels on Astor Street, where they know it's dangerous. I don't mean to say that crimping is right, but—if I put my hand in that fireplace," he said, pointing to the roaring blaze, "I know I'd be burned. And knowing that, if I put my hand in anyway ... ?" He let the question hang.

Dalton Williams nodded, walking around to a point in the room that allowed him to face everyone present. "What you say is often the case. But not always. The night I was shanghaied from Astoria, I wasn't in a saloon or with a—I was staying at the Sailors' Home on Third Street. For those of you who don't know it, Jim Turk owns that boardinghouse." James Turk was a notorious crimp. "So one of the goals of the Sailors Protective League is to establish a safe boardinghouse, not like the ones owned by Turk or the Grant family. A place where a man can get a clean room and a decent meal without having to worry about waking up ten miles from shore on an outbound ship."

Peter Hollis looked a bit pinched. "Don't you feel that it's risky taking on a man like Jim Turk? I mean, it's said he shanghaied his own son."

Dalton lifted his face slightly, then continued with the passion of a true believer. "I can only say what I tell everyone else. No other American adult suffers the complete lack of legal rights that a seaman does. There is no justice for him—no Emancipation Proclamation or Bill of Rights. But there will be. There *must* be. Sailors cannot be slaves any longer." His voice sounded like low, rolling thunder, echoing against the ceiling of heaven. He held his audience's rapt attention as he addressed them, his features animated as though lit by a fire within.

Dalton leaned forward just a bit, his resonant words gathering energy and power, like the climax of a storm.

"To abduct a man against his will, sell him like livestock, strip away his dignity, and force him to work for almost no wages, ladies and gentlemen, that is slavery, and it must stop. Because until it does, no man is safe in Astoria—not plowboys or bankers, seamen or schoolteachers, your husbands or your sons. If it means that I challenge Turk or the Grant brothers or Paddy Lynch, then, by God, so be it. I won't rest until the evil of shanghaiing has ended."

A hush fell upon the room, and chills flew up China's arms and down her back. This wasn't the first time she'd heard Dalton speak, but it was always thrilling. Even when addressing a larger group, he had the ability to make each person feel as though he spoke only to the individual. The guests sat mesmerized. Then the applause began.

Finally, Julia Stanhope spoke, her equine face beatific. "Mr. Williams, I assume you will accept donations for this cause. Certainly Mr. Stanhope will write you a check immediately." Then she turned admiring eyes on Jake. "And you, Captain Chastaine, what a courageous thing to do, to support the Sailors Protective League. I've heard that captains who resist buying crewmen from the crimps risk great danger, both to themselves and their vessels. I applaud you, gentlemen."

China stole a peek at Jake and saw him exchange a long, glittering, look with Dalton. She hoped no one else noticed the perceptible animosity between the two men. But as a general murmur reflecting Julia's sentiments went around the room, Jake's thinly concealed wrath changed to bafflement and then to uneasy, tacit acceptance of their praise. The men standing near him shook his hand and clapped him on the back. China began to breathe a bit easier.

Over the course of the next hour, Dalton answered their questions and discussed plans for the boardinghouse, carefully omitting China's very direct involvement in activities to date. Every man present gave him a donation, and the evening broke up shortly thereafter.

He was the last to leave, and he and China stood at the door, exuberant over the tidy sum he'd collected. She hoped this made up for revealing the carriage house to Jake. "You were wonderful, Dalton," she whispered, mindful of Jake still in the parlor. "I think you really made them understand how important this is."

Impulsively he leaned forward and pecked her cheek. She smelled the faint scent of bay rum. "I have a good assistant." He glanced beyond her shoulder, as though looking for Jake as well. "Will you be all right after I leave tonight? I can talk to Chastaine if you think it will help."

"No, we'd better leave it alone. Don't worry, I can handle Jake." She spoke with more confidence than she felt.

He looked at her for a long moment. "You're quite a woman, China." Then he opened the front door and disappeared into the misty night. The compliment, coming from someone she so admired, gave her enormous pleasure. Jake might pick at her and find fault with her, but at least Dalton, champion of the oppressed, acknowledged her value.

Though Jake remained in the parlor, he was very aware of the whispered conversation taking place at the front door. He couldn't hear what was being said, but the intimate nature of it, hushed and taking place in a darkened entryway, rankled him. He reached up and loosened his constricting tie.

That jack-tar Williams was an expert at manipulating a crowd, that was certain, Jake thought, leaning against the mantel. His own guests, the ones *he'd* wanted to meet, had made a big fuss over Williams, like he was some kind of celebrity. With more than a little resentment, he remembered China staring at Williams with glowing exaltation. He had no doubt that she was helping him with his campaign, but Jake couldn't help but wonder if that was the extent of their relationship. She gazed at the man a bit too ardently for a co-conspirator. Oh, he'd like to have him under his command for a week, even a day. He'd have him on his hands and knees, holystoning the decks until they were whiter than snow, and then he'd make him do it again.

After closing the door behind him, China called good night to Jake with every intention of scurrying upstairs to her room. She didn't want to be alone with him, for more than one reason. But she'd taken only two steps toward her goal when she heard him summon her from the parlor doorway. Hang it all, couldn't he allow her an easy escape? She'd done everything he'd asked of her. She turned to look at him.

"China, let me pour you a nightcap," he said, dim yellow light framing his broad silhouette. He had turned down the lamps, and the room glowed with the low flames on the hearth. His tie was unknotted and hung on either side of his open shirt collar. He didn't seem angry, but she could read nothing in his expression. She only felt his gaze drift over her lightly, from breasts to hips.

She hesitated. "Really, it's late and I'm tired—"

He held out his hand. "Just for a minute."

He ushered her into the room and went to the brandy decanter to pour each of them a drink. Then with his large, warm hand on her back, he steered her to the settee in the semi-darkness of the alcove. She sat stiffly amid her puff of taffeta moire, one hand clenched in her lap, waiting for his tirade to commence.

He remained standing as he clinked his glass to hers. "Here's to the night's success. You did a good job, China, and I appreciate it." He took a swallow of his drink and leaned against one of the tall window frames.

That surprised her. Breathing a bit easier, she

sipped the brandy and kept her eyes trained on his shoulder. It was less distracting than looking at his handsome face, which was beginning to haunt her thoughts almost constantly. "I'm glad it went well," she said, and then more to herself, "except maybe for Cap's contribution."

She thought that would make him smile, but Jake directed a frown at her. "You'll never know how close it came to ending not well at all. When I saw Dalton Williams walk into this room, and you leading him, I had to stop myself from beating the holy hell out of him. And you," he emphasized by leaning toward her, "narrowly escaped being locked in that room in the attic."

China flinched at the sudden anger in his voice and looked at the distance from the alcove to the door. "Apparently you forget yourself, Captain Chastaine," she replied sharply, mustering a facade of courage. "This is my home and I can invite to it whomever I please."

"When I'm paying the bills, I expect to know who's been invited to my dinners, *Miss Sullivan*."

"And if I'd told you in advance, would you have agreed to let Dalton come?" she demanded. "I hardly think so." She made a haughty show of gathering her skirts in preparation to rise and leave.

Humorless, incredulous laughter escaped him, as though she'd asked an asinine question. He reached over and put his hand on her arm, indicating that she would stay and listen. "You're right, I would've said no. I asked you to arrange this dinner because nobody would—because I wanted to make business contacts. I need cargo for the *Katherine Kirkland*, China, or she'll turn into a financial anchor chain around my neck. What if

having Williams come here and make his speech
had offended those people tonight? They all assumed I agree with him. What if all the planning
and spending and—" he gripped his jacket lapel
and shook it "—and dressing up had gone for
nothing because of him? Did you think about
that?"

Even in the low light, she saw his tight jaw, his
rigid posture, his eyes blazing. And she felt an
embarrassing, culpable stupidity crowd her in the
little alcove. No, she'd never considered that she
might jeopardize Jake's business opportunities.
She'd merely thought of the captive audience and
a clever chance to gather donations for the league.

She had to look away from the flame in his eyes,
so she drank her brandy. "Well, no, I guess I
didn't think about it," she mumbled, toying with
the braid on the arm of the settee. Then she continued with more assurance, "But everyone was
impressed with Dalton. And that only helped you
even more."

"Yeah, everyone came out of it lucky," he replied grimly. He rubbed the back of his neck, then
pushed her skirts out of the way and flopped on
the settee next to her, startling her. "So think
about this: one of those people, Douglas Buchanan
or Peter Hollis or whoever, is going to repeat what
he saw here tonight. In fact, one of them might
even have a direct connection to the crimps here
or in Portland. And, with gossip traveling the way
it does, eventually the wrong person will learn
that you're working with Dalton Williams. You'll
make powerful enemies among people who can
do you real harm. If they didn't know who you
were before, they will now." He shook his head.
"Christ, he even named some of them."

The brandy, taken on a nearly empty stomach, had loosened China's tired muscles and given her a careless, relaxed confidence. It was almost comfortable to have Jake sitting so close that his thigh bumped hers. Almost.

"Pfft, so what? What are they going to do, shanghai *me*?" I rather doubt it. No one knows about the carriage house. And I don't care if everyone knows I'm working on the boardinghouse. Lots of people are involved in charities. Besides, whether you like him or not, you heard Dalton tonight. Everything he said is true, and you know it."

For a woman reared in a genteel family, she was as stubborn as a salt-rusted hinge, Jake thought. Headstrong, too. That soft, protected upbringing, in its own way, had left her defenseless. China hadn't seen much of the scummy underside of life beyond taking care of a few sailors. She didn't know anything of the inhabitants who peopled that dark underside, or of the malevolence that drove them. And she apparently didn't believe him, either.

He took a drink from his glass, appreciative of the mellow feeling that spread through his limbs. He sighed and considered her, stately and breathtaking in that damned dress. A rumble of laughter rolled out of him.

That made China look at him, but he was concealed by lacy shadows the curtains made and she couldn't see much except the gleam of his white teeth.

"You're just as muleheaded as you were seven years ago. I remember you sitting right here in this alcove, insisting on having your own way."

She was disconcerted by the abrupt shift in the

conversation. There were things about that day she'd tried not to recall, but one thing in particular she'd been unable to forget. The memory of his kiss had developed a life of its own that she could not conquer. She attempted to move away from him, but the settee wasn't very long.

Glancing at her skirt, she retorted, "Perhaps not quite so muleheaded, Jake. After all, I swore you'd never set foot in this house again. But you're here, just the same."

He drained his glass and set it on the table next to him. "Still, I didn't expect to ever see you again. So I left you something to remember me by." Oh, hadn't he, she thought.

He reached over and lifted her hand from her lap. He held it open, palm up, in his own. She was transfixed.

"I wanted to take my belt off and strap you, I was so angry. I thought you were a spoiled, snotty brat who'd had an easy life." He paused, then added, "I didn't know then what would happen to all of us."

She couldn't see his face, just his blond head bent over her hand. He held her fingers open with his own, then raised her hand to his mouth as though he would drink from it. The startling feel of his lips on her palm, soft and warm, made her suck in a breath. He kept his face turned down to her hand and murmured, "I also thought you were the most beautiful girl I'd ever seen. And since I couldn't strap you, I kissed you instead."

That voice, she thought, with a kind of dreamy anguish. It was how warmed honey would sound if it could speak—rich, lulling, so hard to resist.

She knew she shouldn't let him do this, lean toward her, take her face in his hands. But she *was* letting him do it. She smelled brandy and soap and Jake, all jumbled together. And just like she had upstairs earlier this evening, she watched his lips near hers, slowly, and his eyes drift closed. This time she didn't pull away, because, God help her, she wanted him to kiss her. She wanted it very much.

Jake wondered vaguely if he'd lost his mind, giving in to the soft temptation of her and the darkened, intimate alcove. It would bring more trouble than good. But she was here and he wanted to hold her, he wanted to touch his fingertips to her cheek ... he just wanted her. He slid his hand to the base of her head and cradled it as he would a newborn's. Her fragrance was subtle, but its spice and the scent of her skin filled his head as he inhaled it. Feeling her inexperience and shyness as his mouth consumed hers, he was both moved and heartened. He was almost certain she'd had no other man, and that was gratifying, but he knew that also meant she'd been alone all these years. Just like him.

China felt his arm encircle her and pull her against the wall of his chest, while his other hand moved from her head down her shoulder to rest on her ribs. Surely he would feel her heart thudding, even through her stays. As if she had no will of her own, she leaned into his embrace. At that, the kiss deepened, moist and hot, and she heard a low, urgent sound in his throat. His lips left hers and traveled over her cheek, to her temple, to a spot just below her ear, leaving a trail of soft, rich kisses, before returning to her mouth. His hand slid up from her ribs to the swell of her breast, supporting it for an infinite moment with a touch that was both weightless and demanding, burning like fire, wanting more—

China struggled out of his arms and leapt from the settee. "No. You won't do this," she said with a strangled voice that shook with panic, and fear of her own fervent reaction. "*We* won't do this." Agitated, she turned to run away.

"China, wait—" He tried to grasp her wrist, but she wrenched her arm out of his reach and hurried through the parlor. She heard his tread behind her. When he caught up with her and gripped her shoulders, a little cry escaped her, as if a trap had sprung, capturing her. The tulle lining in her gown's enormous puffed sleeves scratched her arms under his hands. He turned her around, his features etched with an intense, powerful longing. As little as she knew about men, for a lucid instant she sensed that it wasn't lust she saw in his eyes. That almost made things worse.

"God, I'm sorry, China. I didn't mean to scare—"

Her breath came in jerky spasms. "We are business partners," she reminded him, her hands trembling, her whole being trembling, "and that is what we will remain, Jake. That's all."

Jake leaned against the parlor doorjamb and watched her hurry down the hall to the stairs. Uttering a bitter curse, he pounded a tight fist against the wood. Then he went back to sit before the dying fire, elbows on his knees, head in his hands.

It took some sinuous maneuvering, but China managed to unhook her taffeta gown by herself. It was late and she didn't want to wake Gert to help—and who else was there to ask? Jake? She choked back a hysterical laugh. Her shaking hands didn't help matters either, as she stood with her back to the cheval glass, twisting to see over her shoulder. Free of the thing at last, she watched it fall in a midnight blue heap around her ankles. Snatching it from the floor, she draped it over the chaise longue. Then she hurried to remove her corset, swamped by a feeling of imminent suffocation from so many hours of confinement and the exertion of running up the stairs.

But no amount of maneuvering would take Jake's image from her mind. She sat at her dressing table to remove the pins from her black hair and paused to stare at the reflection of her still-flushed cheeks in the mirror. How on earth had she let him take her hand and kiss her and—

And, worst of all, even though it had been momentary, proud Miss China Sullivan had fallen prey to his charms, as so many other women had. She was just one more female to him. But the feel of his soft lips lingered in her palm . . . she slowly closed her fingers around it, remembering the potent sensation, the slight rasp of his beard on her skin, the sudden intake of her own breath. And the kiss that followed, his warm hand on her br—

Interrupting the thought, she impatiently released the gentle fist she'd made and scowled at herself in the glass. At least she had more sense than Althea Lambert; China would never allow Jake Chastaine and his hand-kissing tactic to fool her into believing he was any different from the irresponsible womanizer he'd always been.

She stood and changed into her nightgown, then climbed between the cold sheets of her bed and turned down her lamp. Although the night was quiet, the churning turmoil of her emotions sharpened her senses and made the likelihood of sleep remote. Every creak in the joints of the big house caught her attention, and the faraway lowing of a foghorn seemed louder than usual. When she closed her eyes, she could see only his face, fixed like a portrait on the inside of her lids. Opening them, the ceiling loomed above her, dressed in lacy shadows from the corner street lamp, like the shadows the alcove curtains had cast on Jake's strong features. Without thinking, she slowly raised her hand and pressed her palm to her lips.

Suddenly three soft raps sounded on her bedroom door. She lay frozen, holding the breath she'd inhaled, listening. She knew without doubt, without responding to the summons, who stood on the other side of that door. It was easy to complete the details of his likeness in her mind's eye: tall, slender, hair the color of summer wheat and old gold coins, long-lashed jade eyes. And, with a chill glimpse of destiny, she knew what might happen if she answered. So she waited tensely in the darkness, every muscle as tight as a banjo string, for the summoner to go away.

Finally she heard Jake's door close on the other side of the hall. Releasing the breath caught in her chest, she rolled over and punched the pillow under her head. After a moment she threw off the covers and padded silently to her door. She turned its key, not really sure if she was locking him out or locking herself in.

Chapter Eight

The next morning, Jake slouched down the back stairs to the kitchen, grumpy and taciturn. Before he reached the door, he detected the scent of hot biscuits and coffee. Aunt Gert hailed him as soon as she saw him, her ceaseless cheer blasting him like the noonday sun. The glare of it almost made him flinch.

"Well, here's our shipping baron now," she teased loudly from her post at the stove. "Did you have a good time at the party, Captain Chastaine?"

Jake grunted unintelligibly and snagged a buttermilk biscuit from the table, sidling around Susan Price to reach the blackberry preserves on the other side. Susan turned her unblinking pansy eyes on him—if he had been a more superstitious man, he would have sworn those eyes were trying to steal his immortal soul. He cut the biscuit in half and smeared the preserves on both surfaces, then mashed them back together to make an oozing sandwich.

"China looked so lovely in her dress, too—just like a princess. Didn't you think so, Jake?" Gert pressed on, wielding her cooking spoon like a scepter.

Offering a noncommittal noise similar to the last, Jake made a sour face and went to the stove to pour himself a cup of coffee. He felt Aunt Gert peering at him sharply, but he wouldn't meet her probing blue eyes.

"Well, I swear on Casey's bones," she said, invoking their old dog's memory "A body would think you and China had gone to a funeral last night, the way you two are acting. Pinched up as a pair of tight shoes, the both of you. You're mumping around, and she's upstairs complaining about a headache and asking for a breakfast tray in her room. Don't young people know anything about having fun anymore?"

It didn't seem to be a rhetorical question; she turned on Jake like a white-haired terrier who wasn't going to give up until she had an explanation. "Did you two have a difference?"

Jake nearly choked on his coffee. As fond as he was of Aunt Gert, he thought her mind usually had to struggle just to stay even with itself. But now and then she showed a flash of astuteness, and not always at the most convenient moment. An irritable directive for her to keep to her oatmeal pot sprang to mind, but he caught it before it slipped out.

Rather than answer a lot of questions and suffer through another meal with Susan Price's eyes boring into him, he turned and left the kitchen to return Cap's chair to the back parlor. He'd meant to do it last night, but after Dalton Williams arrived to deliver his speech, nothing that followed had been part of Jake's original plan for the evening.

He hadn't expected to feel the possessiveness toward China that had sprung to life despite his efforts to squelch it. He'd not intended to arrange to be alone with her, or to kiss her, especially after she'd so snippily forsworn him upstairs and left with a swish of her skirts.

He let his gaze turn to the alcove. The little nook was bright now, lit with feeble winter sun; it was no longer the intimate, shadowed corner of last night. Jake's only purpose had been to try to talk some sense into her about the Sailors Protective League, to make her understand the possible disaster brewing under the surface of her stubborn devotion. Of course, that had been a waste of time and breath. But she'd been there, mellowed with success and brandy, so beautiful it made him ache to look at her. He hadn't meant to touch her, to cover her mouth with his, but, well—damn it, how much was a man supposed to stand? Afterward, he tried to apologize; he knew he had frightened her, or insulted her, or both. But she would have none of it.

Still, he was certain that he'd felt her response, the way her breath quickened when he kissed her palm, the pounding of her heart under his hand for that brief instant before she pushed him away. And if he was honest with himself, he couldn't be altogether certain that another attempt at an apology had been the only thing on his mind when he knocked on her door half an hour later. The memory of her, so soft and fragrant and resting in his arms for that moment, had led him to her room and then kept him awake last night and deviled his sleep whenever he dozed off.

He muttered a vivid curse and hoisted the leather wingback to his shoulder. He couldn't understand it, he thought, carefully maneuvering around the other furniture and out to the hall. She'd taken Olin Meredith into her home, a cranky, profane old sea dog, and she worried and fussed over him like a mother. She also had Susan Price living there, a very odd, nearly destitute woman who gave Jake the creeps. Williams, a common sailor, China idolized as if he were one of the saints on the calendar. These were humble people; not a one of them had even a big toe on the bottom rung of the social ladder, so he couldn't accuse her of being a snob.

But Jake himself—he sometimes believed that if he were to stagger to the door, wounded and bleeding to death, China would order him to stay outside on the porch and die, and to do it quietly, too.

He carried the chair to the back parlor, carefully setting it down in the prints it had impressed into the worn carpet. Briefly, he sprawled in Cap's chair and stretched his legs out in front of him, feeling the cold surface of the hard-finished leather through his dungarees and shirt. Well, she could sulk in her room for the next month for all he cared, but he knew that wasn't really her way. She'd come out.

Whatever he had thought of China Sullivan in the last fourteen years—beautiful, spoiled, snooty—he'd never once thought of her as a coward. He knew she had courage. Lacking her brothers and her parents, she couldn't have managed all this time without it. He shifted on the hard leather, a twinge of guilt prodding him again.

Suddenly an idea came to him. There was one thing he could do that would ease his conscience, if not her resentment.

He pulled himself to his feet and went to get his coat. If he remembered correctly, his destination, the Western Union office, was on Third Street.

*   *   *

Jake was right, as far as it went. Gritty-eyed and cross from lack of sleep, China did decide to come out of her room later that morning, but not without some reluctance. After last night, she didn't want to speak to Jake, or see him, or have to sit at the same table with him.

With her taffeta costume put away in the closet, everyday life resumed and she dressed once more in a dun-colored skirt and plain blouse. It made her think of the fairy tale of Cinderella. Unfortunately, there was no handsome prince doggedly searching throughout the land for China, the one woman he wanted to share his life with. There was only Jake Chastaine, who plagued her thoughts and dreams, and who, aside from his rough handsomeness, was about as far from being a prince as a man could get.

She went to the mirror to braid her dark, curling hair, and raised tired brows at her reflection. There was a pale lavender smudge under each eye. Her life had been in turmoil since Jake had gotten here. He wouldn't trick her again with soft kisses, she promised herself, or those familiar, yearning looks he sometimes gave her that reached almost to her soul.

She wouldn't have to worry about it for long, anyway. After all, he would be leaving again in a few weeks. At that thought her hands, busy with the braid, fell still. Of course, that's why they'd had the dinner last night. That's what they were working toward—Jake's departure. Why, then, did she get a squeezing catch in her heart when she thought about it?

Shaking off the feeling, she tied the end of the plait with a narrow ribbon. Then she walked to her door and unlocked it, took a breath and turned the knob. Opening the door a crack, she peered into the hallway. From here, she could see that Jake's door was open. If he thought she would continue to provide maid service to him after last night—

She crept across the hall, quiet as a cat, her back flat against the wall. Poking her nose around his doorjamb, she looked into his room.

He wasn't there, and to her surprise, his bed was already made. Well—um, good, that was *good*, she told herself. She wouldn't have to look at the depression his blond head left in his pillows or touch the sheets that had laid against him all through the night. She would keep her distance from him as much as she could, without disrupting the family, and she wouldn't speak to him if she could avoid it.

If she could make herself avoid it.

That evening after dinner, the members of the Sullivan household, including Jake, drifted into the back parlor, as usual. The meal had been a dismal affair; a pervasive gloom hung over everything, even restraining Captain Meredith's salty volubility. China had pointedly ignored Jake and done her best to avoid the brief but intense looks he shot her from time to time. But she'd felt him sitting there, radiating an icy heat.

Aunt Gert had prattled on for a while about Mrs. Baker's lumbago, but eventually she gave up, as the near-silence at the table overtook her. In contrast, the normally reserved Susan Price roused herself from her passiveness. To tempt Jake's obviously thin appetite, she passed him every serving dish on the table until they all sat in a semicircle around his plate. The light from the chandelier created a soft halo on her fair hair, and her pale cheeks were suffused with color. In her muted voice, she coaxed him to eat. Watching this from beneath lowered lashes, China felt an unreasonable urge to tell Susan to shut up.

Now China loitered in the dining room, on the pretense of reorganizing the table linen drawers. She couldn't go to the back parlor with Jake sitting in there, long-legged and relaxed, the firelight emphasizing his eyes and full mouth, his fingers absently raking through his hair while he sat across the chess board from Cap.

China dragged her mind away from the mental picture and impatiently slammed the drawer she'd been sifting through. Annoyed that she, not Jake, was the exiled party, she left the dining room with the intention of going upstairs to her room.

In the evening quiet, Cap's voice boomed through the hall.

"Aye, sounds like you were in for a rough time of it, lad."

"It was the worst storm I ever sailed. It came up just like *that*." She heard the snap of fingers. "We lost three men that night. They disappeared so fast I never even saw their heads bobbing among the breakers. They were just—gone."

Jake's response made China stop in her tracks, and she edged toward the doorway to the back parlor. That voice, she thought, leaning against the wall, out of view. If she could just forget the sound of his voice. It drew her, tempted her. She had to fight the desire to go to him and rest her head on his knee while he told his story. To spend a thousand nights, ten thousand, in his arms, warm and safe, the worries of her life as light as thistledown . . .

As this mental image took detailed form, she pulled herself out of the daydream. Where in the world was her mind to consider such a thing? She pulled away and moved silently to the staircase. Climbing the steps to the second floor, she paused in the bathroom to look out the window at the carriage house. She did this several times each evening; if Dalton brought someone for her to tend, he would light the oil lamp and put it in the window.

She went to the glass and pushed the curtain aside. Beyond the black, winter-bare limbs of the trees, a single glowing flame illuminated the dark carriage house window.

China sighed and let the curtain drop. It would be another long night.

A woman was calling Jake back from the comfortable void into which he'd slipped sometime just east of midnight, and he resisted. Though it only whispered to him, it was a familiar voice, one that meant a lot to him. But right now he couldn't remember why. He put his arms around her and held her close, hoping that would soothe her, but she persisted.

"Jake! Jake, please."

He came awake then with a start and lurched up on his elbow to find China standing next to his bed. She held a candle, its feeble light illuminating a narrow circle around her.

China watched as Jake blinked at her owlishly, obviously trying to comprehend her presence. She'd almost regretted disturbing him as he lay asleep on his side, his arms wrapped around his pillow, hugging it to his chest with his cheek tucked against it. She'd stood there for a moment, just gazing at him. His face was smooth and relaxed, his breathing slow and deep. It was difficult to remember the promise she'd made to herself that morning, to ignore him and the dangerously soft feelings that were taking root in her heart.

Now she tried hard to disregard the distraction of his broad, muscled chest in front of her, and the way his biceps bulged, so she looked at his hair. But that was no better. His long golden hair was tousled, and once again she had to restrain herself to keep from putting a hand out to smooth it. He smelled warmly of sleep and linen sheets. Worst of all, she just knew he didn't have a stitch on under those blankets. A gentleman would wear a nightshirt. Of course, she recalled for the dozenth time, Jake was not a gentleman. But somehow that was becoming less of a liability.

"Whatsa matter?" he asked, disoriented. "What time is it?"

"It's just after two o'clock," she whispered.

He peered at her, and her dun-colored dress and white apron. "God, don't you ever sleep? Why are you prowling around at this hour?" he asked in a gravelly voice. He flopped over on his back and rubbed his eyes, then gave her an assessing, provocative look. "What are you doing in my room?"

Did he have to be so captivating, with his hair messed up and his face creased from the folds in the pillowcase? And why had she even noticed, in light of her emergency? "I didn't want to wake you, but I need your help. Please, Jake."

Some of her nervous urgency reached him. Something had happened, he decided, something serious enough to make her put aside their most recent dispute and seek him out. He turned his head to look at her again. "It must be bad if you've decided to start talking to me again. What's wrong?"

"Dalton brought a— a guest earlier tonight, just after dinner."

Jake recalled that China had disappeared after that tense half-hour in the dining room. He hadn't thought anything of it at the time. Clearly, when he wasn't paying attention, China could slip in and out with amazing deftness, which made it pretty hard to protect her. And since she'd been giving him the silent treatment, he couldn't begin to guess what she was doing. The Sailors Protective League, he reflected dourly, had been quiet lately. Now he realized where she'd gone and why, and irritation brought him to full wakefulness. No matter how many times he told himself to mind his own business and let her do as she pleased, it never worked. He came back up on his elbow.

"Damn it, China, why are you the one who has to help with this crusade? Haven't you figured out yet how much trouble Williams could land on your head?"

She scowled at him and automatically looked back over her shoulder. "Shhh! Keep your voice down! Can we argue about this later? There's a boy out in the carriage house, delirious and burning up with fever. He's young, but he's big, and I can't control him by myself. I need your help."

Jake stared at her a moment. "Oh, all right," he replied. He sat up and started to push the covers off. The dark blond hair on his chest continued down the front of his long torso to—

China gaped at him, wide-eyed, and jumped back. "*Wait* a minute!" she scolded. "Y-you don't have any clothes on."

He grinned at her suddenly. "No, I don't, and unless you want to see the whole picture, you'd better get out of here so I can put my pants on. I'll meet you in the hall in a minute."

She whirled and fled, her candle flame guttering in the resulting breeze, her face blazing hot. She waited a few feet down the hall and heard the clank of his belt buckle and, shortly, the sound of his boots crossing the floor. He came out of the room with both arms in his sweater sleeves and the rest of it bunched up across his shoulders. She tried not to stare at the line and contour of his lean frame before he slipped the fisherman's knit over his head and pulled it down. For a man who'd been roused from a deep slumber just a moment ago, he appeared amazingly alert. She supposed he was used to being awakened for emergencies at sea.

He took her elbow and they slipped quietly to the back stairs. "What happened to this man?" he whispered when they were away from the other bedrooms.

"Jake, he's not a man, he's just a boy. If he's older than thirteen or fourteen, I'd be surprised. Maybe he's just a runaway."

Jake snorted. If he was older than ten, he was no boy, in Jake's opinion. He'd commanded cabin boys who were eleven and twelve, and life at sea made them grow up fast. With muffled steps, they hurried down the staircase to the brightly lit kitchen. "All right, but why is he in the carriage house?" he asked.

China turned to grab a stack of towels from the

table. "Willie—that's his name, Willie Graham—
he told Dalton he was in the New Corner Saloon
afternoon before last. Alex Grant owns that one,
you know." The Grant family, including the ma-
triarch, Bridget, were notorious shanghaiers, with
boardinghouses and saloons in Astoria and Portland. "He thought knockout drops were put in his
beer but he managed to get away and hide in an
alley before they took effect. He's pretty big—
maybe that's why the drug took longer to work
and he was able to escape." She whisked a small
soup kettle off the stove, and Jake took it by the
handle for her. "In case he gets hungry," she
added.

"But eventually he passed out in that alley. He
was there all night, with the rain pouring down
on him. Dalton found him yesterday—at first he
thought Willie was dead. He wasn't, but then the
fever started and Dalton brought him here last
night."

"If he's as young as you think, he shouldn't
have been drinking in a saloon anyway. But I
guess I'm in no position to judge," Jake remarked
with faint amusement. Then he saw the fear and
compassion in her dark blue eyes when she
looked up at him, as though this young man's life
had been especially entrusted to her keeping. His
smile dwindled.

"Why did Williams leave you alone to handle
a job like this?" he asked tightly. "He gets the
glory and you—*we* get the work."

"No, that isn't true," she said, her expression
earnest. "It's not like that. Dalton asked me if I
wanted him to stay. I sent him home because I
thought I could manage. Willie wasn't delirious
then."

Jake gave her a skeptical look.

She hugged the towels in a tight grip. "I can't let him die, Jake. I just can't." Her voice was barely more than a whisper.

He studied her strained white face, her dark hair dragging loose from its braid, and the faint circles under her eyes. Her clothes were rumpled and the apron she wore was splotched with wet spots. What drove her like this? he wondered. Was it a need to prove something to Williams, to win or maintain his favor? Jake clenched his jaw at the thought. Whatever it was, she was determined. He supposed he didn't have any choice but to help her. She had no one else to turn to.

"All right," he agreed. "Let's go see what we can do."

When China opened the door to the carriage house apartment, a strong medicinal odor was the first thing Jake noticed. "Jesus, it smells like my old man's house," he grumbled.

"Oh, that's pennyroyal tea I'm brewing. I'm hoping we can get Willie to drink some, but when I tried to give him quinine for the fever, he thrashed around so much it was impossible." China put the door key back in her pocket and cast an anxious glance around the rough-walled apartment.

It had the look and smell of a sickroom: the low yellow light glowing from the single oil lamp on the table, the pungent scent of the tea, the air clammy from the steaming kettle, the rank stuffiness of an unwashed, fevered body. And it was hot in here; China had apparently built a big fire in the corner stove. Jake could feel the heat radiating from its cast-iron bulk.

She led the way to the bed, where he saw a tall young man, writhing and mumbling. Jake couldn't understand the words, but he detected an accent—British, he thought. He could see what stirred China's compassion. Willie probably *was* thirteen or fourteen and big for his age, but besides that, he had an angel's face—younger than his years, with the unnatural flush of fever. He'd flung off his blanket in his tossing, exposing a shirtless, pale upper torso. He was a scrawny kid with a thin chest that revealed every bone in his rib cage. Jake had seen lots of young sailors like him, but all of them had come aboard his ships voluntarily.

"They drugged him, huh?" Jake asked pensively.

China nodded. She took the soup kettle from him and set it on the table with her towels. "At least . . . at least he got away." She leaned over, feeling Willie's forehead with the back of her fingers. He jerked away from her touch and went on moaning. She shook her head, her expression set in worried lines. "But all those hours in the rain really did him in. He's still blazing like Hades."

Willie suddenly kicked a bare foot from the covers and Jake grasped the thin ankle to look at it. On the boy's bony instep was tattooed a pig. An amulet common to sailors, a pig placed on the foot or the knee was said to protect the wearer from drowning. Jake turned the foot for China's inspection. "Unless he needs a charm against drowning in the well, he's no runaway farm boy. He's a sailor, and it sounds to me like he's from Birmingham, or maybe Liverpool."

China gestured impatiently at the glass standing on the bedside table. It was half full of milky liquid. "That doesn't matter. I need to get this quinine into him, and I hope some tea." She perched on the edge of the mattress and picked up the glass, giving the cloudy contents a stir with the spoon that stood in it. Murmuring soothing encouragement to the fevered young seaman, she raised his dark, curly head and tried to tip the glass to his mouth. But with a spontaneous churning of arms and legs, he pushed her hand away and uttered a graphic epithet that stunned China, who, although no stranger to marine profanity, thanks to Cap, understood only part of what he'd said. Water and quinine soaked her apron front. She licked at the single drop on her lower lip and scowled at the remarkably bitter taste.

Jake pushed his sleeves up his forearms and glowered at Willie. "There won't be any more of that," he said. The frown over his green eyes was all the more ominous in the low light.

"Jake," China began sternly, sitting upright, "don't you hurt him. He doesn't know what he's doing, and he's only a boy."

"I'm not going to hurt him, but he doesn't need coddling, either. He needs the quinine. He glanced at China. He's been trained to follow orders."

"Graham, right? That's his last name?"

"Yes, but—"

He leaned over the bed, his thick hair falling forward, until his mouth was inches from Willie's ear. "Graham!" he shouted, startling both the patient and his nurse.

The effect was amazing. Willie bolted upright in the bed. "Sir!" He sounded almost lucid, but his wide brown eyes stared sightlessly.

"You can't yell at a sick person like that!" China whispered furiously. Jake silenced her with a look.

"Graham, I'm Captain Chastaine. Cook here expects you to take this medicine." China was aware that a ship's cook often doubled as the ship's doctor, but she raised her brows at her new title. Jake ignored her. "If you disobey, I'll clap your miserable, sorry hide in irons and lock you in the hold for the rest of the voyage. Then you and the rats can fight over the ship's biscuit and water we'll throw down to you. Is that clear?" His resonant voice was thunderous; it could carry in a gale.

China would have objected again, but even she was intimidated by Jake's absolute authority. She hated him in that moment as he stood next to the bed, a bullying, autocratic tyrant.

"Aye, sir!"

Jake nodded at her, satisfied. "All right, Cook. Graham will take his medicine now."

China glared at him venomously but said nothing. She mixed another dose, then pulled Willie back so that his head leaned against her shoulder while she poured the quinine into him. He shuddered at the foul taste, then turned his hot forehead against her neck.

"Mum," he mumbled in a tired youngster's voice, " 'ave yer come to take me 'ome?"

China clapped a hand over her mouth, struggling against the abrupt, gasping sob that climbed into her throat from her heart. He was so young, with no one to watch out for him or care for him. She put the empty glass back on the table and stroked his dark curls. Tears stung at her eyelids, but she kept her face tipped down so that Jake wouldn't see them. She cleared her aching throat to gain control of her voice.

"Hush, now, Willie," she crooned quietly. "Just rest so you can get well. I'm here ... I'm right here." For an endless time, she rocked the big child in her arms, his weight growing heavy against her as he slipped away into the troubled sleep of a fever patient. She was barely conscious of Jake, who leaned against the wall on the other side of the bed with his arms crossed over his chest, watching her.

Finally, his long shadow fell across her and Willie as he gently lifted the boy's shoulders from her embrace and eased him back down to the mattress, tucking the blankets around him. Then he held his hand out to her. She looked at his open palm extended to her, at the broad white scar that ran the width of it. Her gaze traveled from his hand up to his face, and she saw concern in his well-shaped features. The tyrant was gone, but the strength, the capable leader, remained.

"Come on," he said. "Let's sit at the table."

She put her hand in his and his fingers closed around it. She was exhausted, both physically and emotionally. That was why she gave in to his warm grip, she told herself, why she allowed him to pull her to her feet and lead her to the table.

"Damn, it's like a boiler room in here," he said, and raised the shade to unlock the window next to the table. He pushed it open a crack, and a breath of clean, cool air brushed her cheek, carrying the scent of the ocean.

A blue enamel pot sat on top of the stove. "Is there any coffee in that cupboard?" he asked, pointing to the cabinet on the wall.

She nodded dully, and he stood and rummaged through it, finding a can of Chase and Sanborn and two thick white crockery cups. He went about the business of making coffee with the kind of careless estimating that only a man would employ. Filling the pot at the sink, he dumped coffee into the water without benefit of spoon or measure. He looked into the pot, then shrugged and shook a little more in before he put it on the stove.

As she watched him, she saw a man who had centuries of mariners behind him. Not men who'd been taken against their will to serve on ships with unknown destinations. No, Jake Chastaine represented the breed of seafarer who had an understanding of and with the ocean that no landbound person could fully grasp. These were the men who became explorers and merchant captains, sailing the world on waters they thought of as their mothers, their lovers, their curses.

Taking the seat opposite her, he crossed his ankle over his knee while they waited for the coffee to boil. Beyond the window next to them, the night lay in stillness as the rest of the world found peace in sleep, or wept in despair, or made love in the dark silence.

China gazed at Willie again; for the time being, he rested quietly. She brushed at the strands of hair that, stirred by the faint breeze from the window, had escaped her braid and were tickling her face. "God, what must it be like to be so young and far from home, lost in a foreign country, with only strangers for company?" Her voice shook slightly with fatigue and the anguish hovering just within her control.

Jake glanced at the sleeping boy, then back at China's drawn, anxious face. She seemed very small and thin, sagging in the chair, and an unwanted flood of compassion washed over him. He could think of her as beautiful, tempting, or smart, even haughty and unapproachable, and be certain that it was only lust he felt stirring. But when he saw her like this, a tired, courageous fighter, struggling to save this boy's life, the feelings she kindled sprang from a different kind of ache: they came from his heart. And that scared him. Too many years lay between them, too many responsibilities. He had a different life now than he'd dreamed of at nineteen, when he'd watched her with frustration and anger.

Even so, he still wondered why she'd taken on a job like this. She wasn't trying to impress Dalton Williams, that was clear to him. Her commitment was genuine, her passion one that he couldn't understand. What had happened on those nights when there was no one to help her? And who would she turn to after he left with the *Katherine Kirkland*, on a course for the open sea and a crew that included boys no older than Willie? Suddenly a suspicion dawned on him, one that might explain all of this.

"China," he murmured.

She lifted her eyes to his. He reached across the small table to touch her hand where it rested on the painted wood, then stopped short, leaving a space of six inches between them. He drummed his fingers once, in sequence, his words hesitating at the back of his throat.

"What happened to Ryan?"

She looked at him with a mixture of horror and pain so acute he wished he could call back the question from the awkward silence where it hung. But it was out now. Her lips parted, but no words formed.

"Was he shanghaied out of Astoria?" he prodded gently.

China stared at her lap and raised a shaking hand to her forehead. She nodded finally, and he closed the gap between their hands. She didn't pull away, but swallowing hard, she said, "Four years ago. I never talk about it, Jake, and I'm not going to now. Please—" she drew a deep, shuddering breath, as though gathering strength to continue. "Please don't ask me anything more about it."

"Okay," he agreed softly. He tightened his hand around her fingers, then released them. "God, China, I really am sorry."

That was the answer, he realized. The reason everyone had acted so oddly that first morning at breakfast when he asked where Ryan was. The reason Willie Graham's troubles struck so close to China's heart. The reason for a lot of things. Ryan Sullivan, her little brother, had been stolen by the crimps. Jake had assumed he'd run away to sea— some boys did. He did some quick calculating. If Ryan had been gone for four years, he would have been ... Christ, he had only been thirteen years old when they took him. Somehow, that sounded very young when he applied it to the boy he'd known, not at all the age of a man. No wonder China was so upset about Willie.

"So many of them," China said at last. "They take so many." Her own voice sounded like little more than a strangled whisper to her ears. She felt tears rising again and, try though she might, she couldn't completely stop them. She dashed a hand across her eyes and looked away. "I don't usually fall apart like this. You'll have to excuse me."

When he didn't answer, she chanced a peek at him. His face was thoughtful as he considered her over the lamp flame. "Don't apologize. Sometimes

I think that women's hearts are all that save the world from going to hell, one boy at a time."

China suspected that he wasn't talking about Ryan, or even Willie, but her thoughts were interrupted when the coffeepot began to boil over. She rose to pull it off the heat, but Jake stood and motioned her back to her chair.

"I'll take care of it," he said and went to retrieve the heavy white cups.

She was content to let him. She was so heartsore and worn out, and thinking about Ryan only added to the strain. But she wasn't sorry she'd told him about her brother. Maybe it would make a difference to Jake now, make him see the league in a new light. She watched as he piled the cups, the sugar bowl, and two spoons into his arms. Then using one of her towels as protection, he grabbed the handle of the coffeepot. It was a luxury to have someone else take charge, even for a little while; she'd had the burden of responsibility for so many years.

He laid out a setting in front of her and poured the coffee. Lifting the cup to her mouth, she took a careful taste. It was scalding hot, heavy and black, a wicked brew intended for long nights.

Its taste must have shown on her face. Jake gave her a rueful look. "You might want to try it with sugar." Then he continued in the same quiet tone, "Do you remember that woman you saw me talking with that day outside the druggist's? Belinda?"

China's hand halted in mid-reach for the sugar bowl. Despite her zombielike fatigue, she felt a heat scorch her face that had nothing to do with the stove. She wasn't likely to forget that scene anytime soon, or how it made her feel. That woman had thrown herself into his arms and kissed him right there in front of God and the nation. Nor was China likely to forget the morning she made the mistake of bringing it up to him.

"I remember," she replied into her cup.

"I grew up with Belinda's husband, Roddy McGowen, on Tenth Street."

"Oh?" she replied faintly. She looked up at him again, the information causing a sudden flush of guilt that she was positive must show on her face. But, if Belinda had a husband, what was that China had seen between her and Jake? The embrace and the money?

Jake put his elbows on either side of his cup and hunched his shoulders. "She told me Roddy was shanghaied last summer. He was on his way home from his job at the cannery."

He had her full attention now, and she waited expectantly—for what she wasn't sure.

He lifted his cup and took a sip of the unadorned bitter brew he'd made. "I gave her money because she and her baby were sick and they needed medicine and food. She doesn't have any family here, but she wants to stay in Astoria so that Roddy will be able to find her when he comes back." He took a quick glance at Willie again, and closed one hand into a fist on the tabletop. "Look, I know shanghaiing isn't a good system, China. I never said it was. I'm not blind to this problem, or to what Williams is trying to do. I just wish you weren't taking the risks—oh, goddamn it, what's the use?" He ran his hands through his hair, his exasperation plain.

But she wasn't thinking about shanghaiing at that moment or about the Sailors Protective League. She was wrestling with the very guilty feeling that she'd been wrong to assume the worst about Jake and Belinda. It wasn't an easy thing to admit to herself, and she wasn't at all sure she wanted to admit it to him. She cast a sidelong glance at him.

"I didn't mean to, well, uh, you know after that dreadful scandal with poor Althea Lambert—"

Jake leaned back in his chair. "Oh, yes," he smiled without a trace of humor, "poor Althea, the ship chandler's daughter. Let me tell you the story about Althea Lambert." He hooked one arm over the back of his chair and began speaking with the voice of an impartial storyteller. The flame from the oil lamp highlighted the blond and red bristles in the beard that was beginning to shadow his face. China realized it had probably been almost a whole day since he last shaved.

"I'd been going into Lambert Brothers for years. Pop would send me there to buy equipment for the boat. When she was young, Althea used to sit at a desk behind the counter, doing her school-work. Later she started keeping the books, and sometimes, when her father and uncle were busy in the back or at the wharf, she'd wait on custom-ers. It seemed every time I went in there and Al-thea was alone, she needed help with something—a jar lid, a box on a high shelf, a heavy package. She used all her wiles, and she wasn't too clever about it. It was pretty obvious she was looking for a husband. Me, I guess. There might have been other men she tried to land, but I never heard about them."

Jake looked out the window into the yard, as if he were watching the scene play out against the moonlit landscape. "Well, I wasn't an idiot. I didn't jump at the bait she kept throwing in my face. She didn't give up, though. It got so bad, I hated going in there."

China couldn't help but raise her brows. This story didn't fit his reputation at all, but she tried to remain neutral as she listened. He went on.

"Finally, one day a couple of months before Quinn and I left, I went into Lambert's to buy rope. Althea was the only one there. She told me her father and her uncle would be gone for hours, and she asked me to go into the storeroom with her to, um, well— She said she loved me and wanted to marry me. Most of the men I knew would have gone with her, whether they liked her or not. But I told her no, there was someone else I cared about. That was probably my mistake. She flew into a rage. She said if I didn't marry her, she'd tell everyone that I'd taken advantage of her and that she was going to have a baby." He turned his eyes back to China and shrugged. "And that's what she did. Not too many people believed my side of the story. And for all I knew, she might have been pregnant by someone else, so hanging around to prove myself innocent may not have worked. It would have been a hell of a mess."

China remembered how she'd flinched the first time he'd said the word "pregnant," that day in the alcove. Now it seemed like a silly thing to be upset about. He was beginning to look tired, she thought, studying his well-formed face. Maybe Aunt Gert was right. Jake had never been an angel, but China realized that of all the qualities attributed to him over the years, she'd never heard him called a liar. She hadn't known Althea Lambert, but she'd known Jake.

"She left town, you know, three months after

you did. She went to Portland. The rumor was that there'd never been a baby." China refrained from adding that she'd believed the worst.

Jake nodded. "Pug Jennings told me. She isn't why I left Astoria. I'd planned to do that for a long time. But I guess it's a good thing I did. I might have found myself shackled to her." He shuddered. "That would have been hell on earth."

She believed what he told her, although she couldn't say why. And it felt good to sit here with him. She propped her chin on her hand, thinking of something he'd said earlier. China had never paid much attention, but she didn't remember Jake's name ever being linked to any one woman. Except Althea, of course. Sudden curiosity forced her tongue. "When you told Althea that you cared for someone else—did you make that up?"

He leaned forward slightly, his forearms crossed in front of him on the tabletop, and stared at her with a blank expression that revealed nothing. But China knew she'd been chastened for her nosiness just the same, and she dropped her gaze to the floor, her cheeks scorching.

Jake remained silent for a seemingly endless moment, then shifted in his chair and took out his watch. "It's almost four-thirty, China. I'd better walk you back to the house so you can get some rest."

"I can't leave Willie out here by himself," she protested, looking up again. "I'll have to give him more quinine in another hour or so."

"I'll stay with him. It would give Aunt Gert a real turn if you weren't in the house by breakfast time. She won't think it's so odd if I'm not there."

Reluctantly, China's opinion of Jake Chastaine crept up yet another notch. It was a tempting offer. She'd been up nearly twenty-four hours. "Well, if you're sure you want to—"

He stood and held his hand out to her again. "I'm sure." He smiled then. "Don't forget, I had a two-hour nap."

She let him help her to her feet. Her body felt like lead and her eyes burned. Even her clothes felt heavy. Standing so close to his tall, broad frame, she wished she could lean against him for just a moment, feel his arm around her, offering support. But of course that was an improper, fanciful desire. Exhaustion was addling her thoughts. She didn't know what excuse to use for having similar thoughts when she'd been well rested.

She walked to the bed to check on Willie again. He slept on and was still feverish under her touch, but not quite so much. "The quinine is helping," she said, turning back to Jake. "You only have to stay until seven o'clock. Dalton will be here then."

She thought a dour look crossed his face, but it happened so quickly she couldn't be sure.

"Well, come on, then," he said and steered her toward the door. "Everything is under control."

They walked across the back yard under a full moon that hung low in the western sky, its face veiled by gauzy clouds. At the back porch, he took her key from her and unlocked the door. The kitchen light fell across his hair and face. Yes, China thought, he was *very* handsome.

"Thank you, Jake, for everything," she whispered. "I couldn't have managed Willie without your help. I think he'll be all right."

Jake nodded. "You get some sleep." He looked into her eyes, then leaned forward and pressed a long kiss to her forehead. The very tenderness of it made her suck in her breath. She could feel the scratch of his beard on her skin, she could smell the wool in his sweater. It took all the willpower she had to keep from stepping closer and putting her arms around his waist.

When he straightened, she saw the dull wink of the little medallion he wore, and she reached for it.

"What is this, anyway?" she asked, trying to see it in the low light.

He looked down at it, then back up at her. His tired green eyes crinkled at the corners. "It's a Saint Nicholas medal. Every sailor needs protection against drowning, you know."

He smiled at her again, briefly touched her cheek in a kind of salute, and went back down the porch stairs and across the yard.

China watched until his shape disappeared under the trees, then she closed the back door. As she put out the light, she wondered if there was a charm to protect her heart from a blond, jade-eyed sailor.

Chapter Nine

The cramp in the back of Jake's neck brought him out of his doze. He'd been dreaming about China as she had looked that autumn morning seven years ago, standing on the dock as the *Pacific Star* was towed downriver. She was waving and calling, but the wind didn't carry her words to him.

"I can't hear you!" he shouted. *Dodging crewmen, he ran to the stern and leaned out over the taffrail, fighting a rising panic as she and the dock were left behind. The wind was icy and damp on his face, but sweat drenched his shirt. He knew he had to learn what she was saying; it could change the rest of his life.*

Then her voice was inside his head, soft, beseeching. "Jake, please come back. I love—"

His eyes snapped open and he looked around the room. A dream, it was a dream, he reminded himself. It had never happened.

He slumped in the same chair he'd occupied for hours, his feet propped on the end of Willie's bed, his arms crossed over his chest. The late-coming winter dawn was just beginning to reveal shapes in the yard beyond the window. Willie had been asleep most of the time, waking only briefly when Captain Chastaine held up his head and again ordered him to take his dose of quinine. The youth had asked about his mother, but he seemed satisfied when Jake told him she was just in the next room. He was doing better, Jake thought. He expected his fever to break this morning.

Jake rubbed his face. Then he slowly took down his feet and straightened his back—every muscle in his legs and shoulders was stiff. Standing, he looked at his mariner's watch. It chimed four bells as he opened it—just six o'clock. He put it back in his pocket and went to the stove to pour himself some more coffee, though it had acquired an acrid aroma from sitting on the heat for three hours.

Suddenly he heard a key in the lock. Damn it all, he smoldered, he'd told China to get some rest. Now she was back, less than two hours after he'd sent her inside. He strode toward the door as it swung open, prepared to deliver a short, effective lecture, and found himself face to face with Dalton Williams.

The atmosphere was immediately charged with bristling tension as the two men assessed each other.

Jake spoke first. "You're early." He stood out of the way to let Williams in. "China said you'd be here at seven."

He brought the cold morning in on his big pea coat. "What are you doing here, Chastaine?" Walking to the narrow bed, he looked at the sleeping Willie. "Hunting for crewmen?"

Jake tightened the muscles in his back, no longer feeling the ache. He already stood a head taller than Williams; the flexion pulled him up a bit more.

"You've got a hell of a nerve to ask me that, Williams, when you came here on Saturday night, uninvited, to get handouts from *my* guests. That was quite a performance you gave them—I thought the ladies were going to swoon from it." He couldn't keep the derision out of his voice.

"China invited me to her home. I didn't need your permission," he reminded Jake, then sent him a look of cold blue suspicion. "You seem to know why I'm here, but I haven't heard your explanation yet."

Goddamn the high-handed son of a bitch, Jake swore to himself. "After you dumped the responsibility for this sick boy on China, she needed help. And at two this morning, I was the one she asked, since there was no one else. He was delirious and flopping around like a tuna on a gaff. I sent her inside a while ago because she's worn out."

Williams face reflected surprise before he apparently conquered it. "I asked her if she wanted me to stay, but she didn't. She said she could manage."

"Don't apologize to me," Jake snapped. He pulled his chair back to the table and sat down. "Save it for her. She has no business being involved with this, anyway." He gestured at Willie. "If you want to risk your own neck, that's fine, but letting a woman take that same risk isn't what I'd call noble."

Williams walked to the table and sat across from him, tipping the chair back against the wall. He regarded Jake speculatively, then shrugged, shifting his coat. "The way I see it, there wasn't much honor in accusing that same woman of sharing a berth with me."

Jake felt the veins stand out in his neck. God, China had told Williams about that? Apparently she felt close enough to this man to confide in him. That same knife-edged pain, swift and keen, whipped through him, the pain he felt whenever he considered China and Williams in the same thought. He hoped his face didn't look as red as it felt. "You're right. It was a damned lousy thing to say to her, and I'm the first one to admit that I was wrong to do it." He leaned toward the former seaman. "But it didn't put her life in danger."

Williams maintained his silence for a long moment and held his gaze steady on Jake, who merely stared back. The very faintest of smiles appeared at the corners of his mouth, but there was no humor in his cobalt eyes. "Have you ever been shanghaied, Captain?" he inquired softly.

Jake shook his head once and took a sip of the burned coffee.

"Twenty-seven men were taken from Astoria the same night I was. We were dumped in the hold of the *Cecille*. Some had been drugged, some had been hit over the head. There were boys no older than him—" he nodded toward Willie, "men my age, a poor old bastard in his sixties. And one six-and-half-foot wooden cigar store Indian that had been wrapped in a tarp and sold for fifty dollars as a passed-out drunk." The smile grew infinitesimally.

Jake had heard of episodes similar to that of the wooden Indian. He was once told about twenty poisoned men who were shanghaied. They had been sold after they mistakenly broke into an undertaker's cellar and drank formaldehyde from barrels they'd believed to contain rum. The crimp had collected seven hundred dollars for delivering a crew of men he knew were dead.

Williams resumed his story, that thin smile still

in place. "I came to belowdecks about fifteen miles out. Of course, the ship's articles had been signed, but not by any of us. It was dark in the hold, and it stank like a cholera ward in a Calcutta hospital. The old-timer, he had rheumatism so bad, I figured they'd feed him to the sharks straight off. Some of the young ones were sniffling for their mamas, a couple of them were plotting escape. Other men grieved over wives and children left behind. There were sailors, like me, who were sold out by boardinghouse landlords, or whores, or bartenders. Some of the landlubbers were seasick. Nearly all the others were sick from the bad liquor they'd been given, or the knockout drops, or having their heads whacked. There was one boy who didn't complain, though, because he never woke up. He'd been on his way home from school—that's what his friend told me, one who was with him when they were taken. That boy was all right. But the unconscious one ... the sailor runners hit his head so hard they cracked it." Williams drew a deep breath, but he didn't surrender his eye contact with Jake.

"I held that boy's broken skull in my hands. I could feel the bones shift under his scalp like a smashed eggshell. He died in my arms before dawn. Another man died, from alcohol poisoning, I think. There was no decent funeral, no shrouds from the sailmaker, no service; they were pitched over the starboard side after dark. In the end, though, the rest of us were in the same spot: we all owed two months' pay for the privilege of being kidnapped to that ship."

Jake sighed. As much as he disliked Dalton Williams, he didn't doubt for a moment that he was sincere in his campaign. "Look, I'm not saying that I don't understand why you started the Sailors Protective League. China is the one I'm worried about. I can't make her seriously see the danger she's in." He told Williams about the conversation he'd overheard at the Blue Mermaid his first night in port.

"I know," Williams replied calmly. "She told me about that, too."

Jake frowned at him. He struggled to keep his temper in check, but his voice rose sharply. "Well, for God's sake, tell her to give this up! She'd listen to you."

The other man shook his head, his mouth turned down. "No. She has her reasons for working with the league. I need her help, and we've kept this carriage house a secret. Besides, she's a smart woman and she's old enough to make her own decisions."

For just an instant, Jake had the eerie sense of falling backward through seven years to a conversation he'd had with China about Quinn. She'd asked for his help, and he'd given her essentially the same answers that Williams was giving him now.

And there wasn't a thing Jake could do about it. She *was* smart, but she was also as obstinate a woman as he'd ever met, and naively fearless.

He looked out the window. The sun was up. He had to meet with Peter Hollis at his cannery in a couple of hours, and right now he probably looked like hell. He stood and went to look at Willie. The boy was coming around.

"Gorblimey," Willie gasped in weak horror, recognizing the fierce Captain Chastaine standing over him. "Captain, sir. I didn't mean to sleep through my watch, sir." Sweat had plastered his hair to his head. He tried to sit up, but Jake pushed him back down against the pillow and smiled at him.

"Take it easy, Graham. You don't have to get up. Mr. Williams here is going to stay with you now." He stood aside so the boy could see the man who had rescued him from the alley.

"Oh—aye," Willie replied in confusion, obviously trying to make sense of the strange, yet familiar, face and the surroundings.

"One thing before I go, though, Graham," Jake said. He fixed the tall, gangly young sailor with a stern look. "You stay out of saloons until you get a little older. Drinking might stunt your growth."

During the next few days, China's path rarely crossed Jake's. Willie Graham recovered quickly, and after he no longer required her care she began spending more time working with Dalton on the boardinghouse project. He was glad for the help. The need for a safe, decent shelter for sailors was more important than ever. With the money they'd collected, and other donations that were beginning to come in, Dalton began the repairs needed on the dilapidated old house he'd told her about. The formidable task of making it liveable commenced, and China rolled up her sleeves to tackle the job.

Dalton gave Willie a corner in the parlor to sleep in and made him China's assistant. The lad, obviously moony about his former nurse, tripped over himself to do her bidding. She found his sighing infatuation both irksome and touching.

Aside from the project at hand, China had another motive. She hoped that by losing herself in the work, she could squelch the impossible, futile attachment forming in her heart for Jake Chastaine.

As she scrubbed at the grimy wainscoting in the boardinghouse dining room, again and again her mind returned to the night in the alcove when he'd kissed her. It was impossible to deny that she'd liked it, the way her heart had galloped, partly from fear, but mostly because of the way it felt.

Jake's mouth pressed into her palm. Consuming her mouth. Hot against her throat. His touch, gentle and yet demanding. She interrupted the memory with no little irritation and plunged her rag into the bucket of suds at her feet.

When she stopped to consider it, she was astounded by this turn of events. As recently as two months ago, if she'd been told that she would someday develop a crush on Jake (and that's *all* it was, she was certain of that), she'd have been outraged. Even now, she couldn't say what sort of relationship theirs was. They weren't friends, exactly, but at some point during the last few weeks, she'd stopped hating him.

No matter how hard she worked, at night she would lie in her bed watching the shadows cast on her walls by the bare tree limbs outside, imagining that she heard his soft tap on her door.

She no longer bothered to tell herself to stop thinking about him or to remember that Quinn was gone because of him. No such mental scolding worked. The only thing she could do was stay away from him. But she couldn't say that she felt better for it.

China had felt alone many times in these last few years, but she'd never truly been lonely. Until Jake had arrived.

Jake spent his days in business meetings. His

three original contacts—Stanhope, Buchanan, and Hollis—had referred him to competitors and associates, all interested in shipping their goods on the *Katherine Kirkland*. Many of them also congratulated Jake for taking a stand against shanghaiing. He was somewhat chagrined to realize that word of Dalton Williams's presence at the dinner had worked in his favor. He supposed he should be grateful, but he couldn't muster an ounce of gratitude for Williams, although there was a perverse satisfaction to be had from the situation. Fortunately, China's name never came up during these conversations, and he was careful not to mention her.

Aside from that issue, Jake had a cargo lined up that included flour, grain, canned fish, and lumber, all destined for various points between Portland and Bombay.

Now he stood on Monroe Tewey's dock, watching while Monroe's crew caulked his ship's seams with oakum. They pushed the tar-soaked jute into each joint, singing a chantey as they worked. He could smell it, pungent and grassy. She'd been scraped—her hull was smooth again—and when the caulking was finished, she would get a coat of tar. The rare bright sun on this early March morning shimmered along her rigging. Everyone he had talked to who'd seen the *Katherine* remarked on her grace and beauty, and he was proud of her.

It wouldn't be long now before she was back in the water. He missed the sensation of his hand on her wheel, making her respond to his touch. He could almost feel the rise and fall of her deck under him, hear the sigh of her timbers as she sliced through the swells, her full sails gleaming white under a tropical sky. He knew her, what to give her, what to expect from her.

But more often these days his mind turned to a woman from whom he never knew what to expect. It could be exasperating, this uncertainty, but it had an appeal that he felt pulling at his thoughts and the course of his future, luring them away from the sea like a magnet on a compass needle.

And that frightened him more than anything else.

One evening, when China was in the kitchen making tea for Susan and herself, Jake came in from outside. He'd missed dinner again; that had happened so often lately that he'd told Gert not to bother putting a plate in the oven for him anymore. China hadn't been alone with him, or seen much of him at all, since the night he helped her take care of Willie, more than a week earlier. She'd begun to suspect that he was avoiding her. The appalling truth of the matter was that she missed him, and though she chided herself for the thought, she let her eyes rest on him, taking in every detail of his lean, broad frame, like a blind person who had just regained her sight.

He smiled. "You're exactly the one I wanted to see. Come out to the back yard." He took her shawl from its hook by the stove and, draping it over her shoulders, grasped her hand.

She pulled her arm away. "Back yard? I really don't have time—"

"Yes, you do. Come on, China, come outside. I want to show you something."

His expression was so open and appealing, she couldn't tell him no again. "All right," she relented, abandoning the teapot on the table.

He nodded, apparently satisfied, and took her hand in his to lead her down the back steps to the yard. It was a mild, clear night, rare at this time of year. He stopped on the path between the house and the gazebo. The wind rustled the tree branches, raising the scent of fir needles.

"Look," he murmured, pointing at the sky.

China looked. "I don't see anything," she said, very aware of him.

"You have to keep watching," he said, and somehow his arm was around her shoulders. From the river, she heard the far-off clanging of a buoy, growing louder, then softer with the shifting wind.

She craned her neck to scan the sky—searching for what, she couldn't imagine. But she found nothing, and she was beginning to feel a little uncomfortable, like he'd tricked her somehow. He was too close, and she fit into the shelter of his arm too easily.

"Jake, this is silly. I'm going back to—"

"There!" he said, pointing again. "See?"

And China saw a bright star fly across the velvet night, as though it had escaped its moorings in the heavens. "Yes," she breathed, spellbound. She kept her eyes trained on the stars, looking for movement, and she realized that they sprinkled the dark sky, leaving luminous trails as they went. "Oh, Jake, it's beautiful. I've never seen anything like it."

"You should see it on the ocean. The sky is so much bigger out there, without trees or mountains or buildings to get in the way. In good weather, sometimes I'd string my hammock on deck and lie there, watching the stars rain down." There was a sound in his voice of wonder and admiration.

"I hope they don't all fall tonight," she said, her

head tipped back against his arm. "So there'll be some left to look at."

Jake chuckled. Her remark was sweetly child-like, making him think of the young girl she might have once been. He couldn't say for sure; it was a side she had not shown to him. She'd usually made a point of avoiding him.

But this week he'd been dodging her. It tied his insides in knots to look at her and know he couldn't touch her, to watch her wearing herself out with that damned boardinghouse and be unable to help her. To lie awake at night, edgy and tense, knowing that across the hall she slept. Twice he'd actually gotten up, intending to sneak into her room just to sit at the end of her bed and watch her sleep. What a brainless thing to do. Luckily, as soon as he closed his hand on her doorknob, cold and metallic to the touch, he regained his wits. No woman had ever put as many crazy ideas in his head as China Sullivan had.

But tonight he'd glanced up at the sky on his way to the back door and seen the star shower. And he'd wanted to share it with her. Now it felt like the most natural thing in the world to stand here with her, warm and protected in the curve of his arm. Then he recalled his original reason for seeking her out this evening. He reached into his pocket, withdrew two pieces of paper, and offered them to her.

"Here, I have something for you."

"What is it?" she asked, pulling away. Faint light from the kitchen window reflected dimly off the paper. China's face was only a silhouette in the darkness.

"This," he replied, holding up an oblong shape, "is a check for your share of the cargo I've gotten for the *Katherine Kirkland*—less the price of one dress. It's drawn on Astoria National Bank, and the money is there for you. This—" he extended the other slip "—is Quinn's address in San Francisco."

China reached for that one first, slowly, her hand suspended in midair. "Quinn's address," she repeated faintly, her fingers closing on it. "How did you get it?"

She saw the subtle lift of his shoulders, bulky with the covering of his heavy coat. "It wasn't too hard. I wired a couple of people and had them check around." He nodded at the paper in her hand. "Anyway, now you know where your brother is."

China wasn't sure if she should be glad for his consideration. It only further eroded her crumbling defenses against a perilous tenderness coming to life within her. A tenderness that made her want to reach out in the darkness to touch his face, bury her face against his neck, feel the kiss of his warm mouth on hers. "I—well, thank you," she said, her voice trembling slightly. Fighting the desire to act on her feelings, she took a deep breath, then folded the check with Quinn's address to tuck into her skirt pocket.

When Jake had envisioned China's reaction to these tokens, she'd been pleased and his conscience had weighed less heavily. She'd blamed him for her brother's absence, and now he'd given her a way to reach him. She'd made a point of letting him know that the family was strapped for cash, and he'd found a way to help her. But all he heard from her was a bored sigh and a halfhearted acknowledgment. Damn it, could he do nothing that satisfied her? And why in the hell should he care if she was pleased anyway? There were women in other places waiting for him to come into port. Beautiful women who had cried when he left their beds and had promised him such vividly described physical pleasure if he'd return, that the thought of it had made him ache before the ship had cleared the harbor. What kind of idiot was he to keep trying to please this one cold, stubborn female?

Yet even as he asked himself these questions, he suggested, "Let's watch the stars for a while."

"Oh, I don't think—maybe we shouldn't . . ." China's voice trailed off and she shivered in her thin shawl, not entirely from the night air. *No, no—Jake, don't do this—*

But Jake ignored her halting protest as though she hadn't spoken. "Here, you can wear this and we'll sit on the back porch." He took off his coat and put it around her shoulders. The very weight of it made it seem like the pockets were full of sand. But it was warm inside from his own body heat and she burrowed into it, surrounded by the scent of him that affected her like a philtre. She found it impossible to refuse.

He led her up the back steps and settled her on the long, weathered bench that had been there since they were children. He sank down next to her, leaving about a foot of space between them. Sitting low on his spine, he stretched his long legs out in front of him and crossed his ankles. A square of light from the kitchen door window fell over them and threw his clean, well-formed profile into sharp relief.

China cast sidelong glances at him, studying his straight nose and wide brow, the long muscles in his forearms below his rolled-up shirtsleeves, the line of his throat above his open collar. The damp air didn't seem to bother him as he sat next to her, loose-limbed, contemplating the stars with a mariner's eye.

"Are you going to write to Quinn?" he asked, bridging the silence. With a long index finger, he traced the edge of her billowing apron where it rested between them on the weathered boards of the bench. "To tell him about your father?"

She wasn't sure how to answer. Now that Quinn's whereabouts were no longer a mystery, China was less certain than ever how she felt about her brother. Jake may have taken him away from the family, but there was no good reason why he'd never contacted her in all these years. Even Jake was surprised that he hadn't written.

"I don't suppose it would matter to Quinn, one way or another. The Captain was like a stranger to all of us. Maybe it was harder on him, growing up with no father, I mean. That's why I swore I'd never marry a sailor. I wanted my husband to be at home, to know his children." She pulled the edges of his coat around herself.

Jake was oddly silent, and she thought of something her brother had once told her.

"Quinn used to say that your father wanted you to marry a fisherman's daughter and settle down," she said.

He uttered a single, gruff chuckle, letting his eyes rest on a constellation overhead. "Oh, yeah, he did. But that wasn't what I wanted. We argued about it a lot. Christ, we battled about nearly everything I did or wanted to do."

China pressed on. She wasn't sure she really wanted to know, but she couldn't stop the next question. "If you never had—um, a *friendship* with

Althea Lambert, uh—was there ever a special one? Were you ever in love?"

When Jake didn't respond, she turned to look at him. He hadn't answered the last time she asked about this either. He sat up and shrugged, obviously uncomfortable with the question. He toyed with his watch chain, and even though his head was tipped down, she could see the scarlet flushing his face and ears. He behaved as though she'd asked him if his bladder was full.

Jake was indeed uncomfortable. In the society in which he'd grown up, men didn't discuss love. It wasn't mentioned between sweethearts, husbands and wives, or fathers and their children. It was a very personal subject. On Tenth Street, if a woman asked her husband if he loved her, she was likely to hear, "Well, I married you, didn't I?"

Just when China was wondering if he would answer, Jake glanced at her with a strangely bittersweet smile. Then he leaned back against the wall and looked away, crossing his arms over his stomach. "It was a long time ago." He spoke the words softly, as if summoning a fragile, cherished memory. China felt a sudden, painful stirring of envy for that woman, whoever she may have been.

He was silent for a moment, then he nodded to himself as if in confirmation. "Yeah, there was someone once, but it was one-sided. I'd watched her for years, waiting for the right chance to say something to her. But there was a big class difference between us, and the chance never came. I was just a kid who grew up on the docks, and she was a lady from a wealthy family. I knew she didn't like me much, and that made it harder." Absently, he raked his fingers through his pale hair. "She never would have guessed how I felt about her, and where I come from—well, men don't talk about that stuff anyway." China saw his face flush again slightly. "So I went to Otto Herrmann's and bought her a gold filigreed box that came from France. I thought it might do the talking for me. But when it came to giving it to her, I didn't have the guts to face her. So I gave a quarter to one of the kids on my street to deliver the package. Then I paid him a dollar to take her roses every week for a month." He lifted his eyes to connect with hers. "It was dumb, I guess. I'd hoped she'd realize I was the one who sent them." His faint smile was lopsided. "She never did."

China gaped at him, stunned. No, it wasn't possible. "Y-you gave me that box? And the roses?" Her voice was just a shaky whisper. "*You?*"

He nodded, his expression watchful.

"But—but, there was a note with it—"

" 'To the sweetest flower in Astoria,' " he mumbled. "I couldn't sign my name to something like that. I didn't have the nerve."

That was the line written on the note she'd found inside the potpourri box. She'd never told anyone what it had said. But Jake could have found that out somehow, she thought wildly, unable to comprehend the truth that she faced. Maybe Quinn had gotten into her desk and read it and told Jake about it.

"I guess you've never looked at the underside of that box," he said.

She shook her head, eyes wide, like a person who'd just undergone a horrifying shock. In that instant, she couldn't have supplied her own name if asked.

"You should."

"Wh-why?"

"In the center you'll see where I had Mr. Herrmann engrave a tiny heart with two sets of initials inside it. *JC* and *CS*."

China continued to stare at him. He had to be making it up—he had to, because she didn't want it to be true. She didn't want to be in love with Jake Chastaine, and if he was telling the truth, the fate of her heart was sealed. She'd resisted it every day since he'd come back. Everything about loving him was wrong for her. He mocked the way of life she'd held so dear, he was dangerous, and too tall and hard-muscled for gentility. Delicate coffee cups and stemware looked incongruous in his big hands.

And, oh, God, worst of all, he'd be leaving very soon, gone away to sea again. A tremendous weight of feelings for him lay on her heart and if she gave in to it, she would be crushed by it when he was gone. She clenched her hands inside the long sleeves of his coat, her heart pounding like a hammer.

Jake looked at China, and saw her shock and disbelief. A tired bitterness washed through him. At the time, he'd been afraid to tell her the gold box was from him. Now, all these years later, her reaction was every bit as bad as he'd expected then. The pain of it was just as sharp.

Better that he'd kept his mouth shut and let her go on believing that Zachary Stowe had bought the damned thing for her. Like a fool, he'd revealed everything, his heart and how he'd felt about her. Attempting a salvation of his self-esteem, he reiterated, "Like I said, it was a long time ago."

But it was obvious that she still saw him with the same eyes as she had then. One corner of his mouth turned down. He had to change that, he vowed to himself. He had to make her recognize him for the man he was, or he would forever be lost to himself. Scalding anger and mangled pride churned in his belly.

China felt Jake's big hand close on her wrist. He hauled her roughly to his lap. He held her in one arm, and when she struggled to get away, he put a leg over her knees so she couldn't stand up. She squirmed in his arms, trying to escape, but her strength was no match for his. She couldn't touch her feet to porch flooring, and she felt suspended, vulnerable.

"Let me go this instant!" she said, gasping for air.

"China, look at me." His voice was low and jagged, demanding attention. He put his hand on the back of her head, and his fingers sank into her dark hair, forcing her to face him. She lifted her gaze to meet his. Just inches away, his eyes were like two hot green coals, burning into her in the low light. Was it rage she saw, or lust, or pain? She didn't know, but it was too frightening to watch, and she quickly looked away.

"Jake, let me go." Anguish and fear reduced her voice to a quavering whimper. She pressed her hands against his chest.

"Look at me, damn it!" he insisted, and shook her once. His fingers tightened in her hair, and he pulled her head back a bit farther. She could hear his breath coming as fast as hers, harsh and shaky, ruffling the fine strands of hair on her forehead.

As soon as their eyes met again, he made an inarticulate, frustrated sound, and his lips came rushing down on hers, while his arm pulled her closer. She braced for violence, but instead his touch was fevered, soft and urgent. His tongue, slick and intent, forced her lips apart to gain access to the inside of her mouth. He was trembling—she could feel it, separate from her own shivering. Beneath this tender assault, her resistance wavered. Finally, she slid her hands from the wall of his chest to loop her arms around his neck, and she was kissing him back.

Jake had shut out nearly all coherent thought, acting mainly on instinct and need. He released China's knees and turned her toward him, letting her feel the evidence of his arousal against her hip. Freeing her hair, he dropped his hand to the lapels of his coat where they overlapped down the front of her torso. He reached between the layers of wool, seeking the soft warmth of her breast. Her nipple immediately responded beneath his touch. Dragging his mouth away from hers, he pushed open the coat to press a kiss on the hardened bud through the thin fabric of her blouse and chemise, wetting it with his tongue.

She called his name, low and throaty. "Jake, please—we can't do this," she said helplessly. "I'm angry at you." But her words lacked conviction, and even as she protested, her hand came to rest lightly on the smooth nape of his neck under his hair. "I don't like you."

He held her more tightly, and put swift, soft kisses on her temple and her throat, then buried his lips against her breast. "I'm going to change your mind," he growled.

Heaven help her, she knew he already had.

With a muttered curse, he grappled with the tiny buttons on her blouse, popping one of them off in his impatience. He pulled the fabric aside to reach her bare skin, exposing it to the night air.

Goose bumps rippled over her body in waves. She felt his breath, ragged and warm between her breasts. When his hot, moist mouth closed on her nipple with a suckling pressure, China couldn't stifle the moan that rose in her throat. This was insane, she told herself. *She* was insane to lie here in Jake Chastaine's arms and let him do these things to her. No man had ever touched her like this. But she couldn't have stopped him any more than she could have held back the ocean with a broom.

Jake inhaled her dark, spicy scent as it floated to him from the warm folds of her clothes. He felt like he'd never made love before, as though twenty-eight years of pent-up desire and longing were to be satisfied at last by the soft, fragrant woman in his arms. He could feel her heart beating like a bird's just beneath his mouth, and every time she squirmed, the heavy ache in his groin intensified. But while he told himself he should let her go, that it was wrong to take her in his anger and loneliness, he thought about spiriting her away to the bed in the carriage house.

His face was bent to her soft flesh, his hand restlessly stroking her hip, when she abruptly stiffened in his arms and sprang to her feet. Startled by her sudden movement, he looked up at her.

"What's—"

But she wasn't looking at him. He followed the path of her gaze to the pale, stricken countenance of Susan Price, who stared at them through the window in the kitchen door. China gripped the edges of Jake's coat and closed them over the gaping front of her blouse. She pushed at her hair, which had worked free of its pins and hung down her back in long, black skeins.

"Jesus Christ," Jake ground out, seeing the woman. He jumped up, stepping in front of China to shield her from Susan's prying eyes, and scowled back at her. She whirled and ran from the room, her steps vibrating faintly through the porch flooring.

For a moment, China thought she might faint. She took a deep breath and waited for the sickening giddiness to pass. The hypnotic spell of falling stars and Jake's lips that had robbed her of good sense was replaced by scorching disgrace. She slipped out of his coat and shoved it at him. With shaking hands she hastily fastened her blouse, her fingers faltering at the gap left by the missing button. Then she looked down at the wet mark he'd left over her breast. The night breeze chilled the spot, making her nipple pucker again. A low, dry sob escaped her. She wrapped her shawl tightly across her chest.

Unable to look at him, she reached for the doorknob.

He clutched arm. "China, don't go—"

She turned to face him then and gestured at the bench sitting under the square of light. "Why? So you can shame me in front of the rest of the family? I think one of them was enough. You accomplished what you set out to do."

Jake dropped his hand from her arm, guilt dousing the fire that raged through him. Though she whispered, her voice lashed him like a whip. Her face was chalky in the dim light, framed by her dark hair.

"God, China, you don't really think I—how the hell did I know she'd come to the window?"

"Good night, Captain Chastaine," she choked, and sped inside.

Jake sat heavily on the bench again, and pushed his hair off his forehead, his coat in his arms. An odd sense of grief welled up in his chest, as though he'd lost something. He supposed he had. Whatever skimpy respect he'd gained from China had just slipped away because he'd wanted so badly to touch her, to hold her to him. And thanks to a whim of fate and bad timing, he'd succeeded only in humiliating her.

Damn that crazy Susan Price, he thought.

Chapter Ten

China couldn't sleep. She listened to every creak, every groan, waiting for the sound of footsteps going to the room across the hall. Sometime near three o'clock, after hours of tossing, she climbed from her rumpled bed to huddle on the little sofa in front of her fireplace. Her hair was twisted into a curly snarl around her head, and she grabbed a hairbrush from the table beside her to work out the tangles. Throwing a shawl around her shoulders, she tucked her feet inside her nightgown and watched the flames burn down to crimson embers.

She thought of the scene that had taken place on the back porch because she could think of nothing else: Jake, full of an angry passion, an irresistible maleness, holding her against his wide shoulder and igniting senses she hadn't dreamed she possessed, edging her toward complete abandon. Then, Susan's stunned face looming over them in the window, seeing, well, *everything*.

China didn't know where Jake had gone and she told herself she didn't care, considering the position he'd put her in. Didn't that prove he wasn't the man for her? As if she needed it proved to her.

Skulking like a wretched coward, she'd hurried

directly upstairs after leaving him, scared to death she would meet Aunt Gert in the hall or, worse, Susan Price. Would she tell what she had witnessed? China couldn't begin to guess what the widow might do. But one thing was certain—in Susan's expression she'd seen the look of a woman jilted. It didn't make any sense. Despite his reputation, even China didn't believe that Jake had been trifling with Susan. She gave him the creeps. There was no other way to think of it; China had seen his reaction herself a number of times.

It was like a nightmare, she fretted, abandoning her hairbrush and rubbing her forehead. Still, those endless seconds of humiliation had been pinpricks beside the one feeling that, above any other, Jake had aroused while she sat in his powerful arms. That feeling had been security. She'd felt safe with him, protected, and that was something she hadn't known in years. Of all people, that he should be the one to give her that sensation—well, there was simply no accounting for it. But to have a sample of such shelter, only to know it couldn't last, was torment.

And the potpourri box? Jake claimed to have given it to her. She could confirm what he'd told her—she simply wasn't sure she wanted to. Three times tonight she'd gone to the desk drawer where she stored her keepsakes. Inside, jumbled together with old letters, postcards, and ribbons, there reposed two notes—the one Quinn had left on her pillow the morning he'd gone and the one she had always assumed was from Zachary Stowe. If Jake had given her the gift, his handwriting would be on both notes. But she hadn't been able to make herself open the drawer.

Well, nothing was as bad as not knowing, she

told herself. With strength of purpose, she went to her desk and lit a candle, its flame casting long shadows on the walls. This time, she allowed her hand to hesitate on the drawer handle for only a moment before pulling it toward her.

A dry, papery smell drifted up to her as she sifted through the contents, old valentines edged with scraps of yellowing lace, a gull feather that she'd found on the front doorstep two days after Ryan had been taken, a bumpy pearl she'd discovered in an oyster from the fish market. Finally she found what she sought. She withdrew the two notes and, sinking to the hassock next to her, carefully unfolded them and smoothed them over her lap.

Drawing the candle a bit closer, she first examined Jake's scribbled signature on Quinn's letter. It was carelessly, hurriedly written. She'd always resented seeing his name at the bottom of the page, and had wondered why he'd bothered. Then she studied the note that had been tucked inside the gold filigreed box.

To the sweetest flower in Astoria.

The words were meticulously formed, and China could envision the note's author practicing the short line many times on scrap paper before committing it at last to this piece of vellum. But for that very reason, she couldn't absolutely determine whether Jake had written this or not. It was as painfully neat as an example in a Spencerian penmanship book. She sighed and refolded the letters. After working up her courage to look at them, she still didn't have the answer she sought.

The only other way to verify Jake's story was

to do as he'd suggested—look at the bottom of the box. Tomorrow. Maybe.

Beyond the warmth of her room, China became aware that in the last six hours the weather had changed. The wind had picked up, pushing ahead of it a hard rain that beat on the windows. It was a fierce, cruel night, not one to be out in. She turned her ear in the direction of the hall for a moment, not really expecting to hear anything. Then, rising from her seat, she padded to her door. After a second's hesitation, she opened it a crack and peeked out. The oil lamp at the window burned like a candent sentinel, a solitary beacon to light the night.

Jake's door was open and the room was dark.

China knew without looking that he wasn't there, or anywhere in the house. She closed her door again with a quiet click and leaned her head against the jam, her heart as heavy as a rock.

After China had run into the house, Jake stormed down to the Blue Mermaid in a restless fury, with the express intention of getting stinking drunk and buying the entire night from one of Pug's saloon girls. Who needed her? he thought, as he neared the Astor Street saloon. What did he want with a snippy female who made him feel like a— a— Oh, God, sometimes she made him feel like a wharf rat, but other times she gave him looks that stirred his heart and his hunger. That was the woman who had kissed him back tonight, who had clung to him with her arms around his neck.

Jake found Pug behind the bar and stated his wishes in very direct terms.

"We got just what you want, Jacob," Pug

grinned at him from his riser behind the bar. "Go find a table and I'll send Matilde to you. That girl could make every man buried in Hillside Cemetery stand at attention." He pushed a whiskey bottle and a glass across the counter.

Jake threaded his way around customers and spittoons to a seat at a dim corner table. A moment later, a voluptuous woman approached, her breasts nearly bursting from the top of her tight green satin dress. She sashayed to him and wedged herself between his legs. The oversweet fragrance of violets accompanied her.

"I'm Matilde, honey. Pug told me to take good care of you because you're a special friend," she purred, and looked him over with an experienced eye. Reaching out a dimpled hand, she flipped her fingers through his hair. "I see what he means. I like those goldy locks. I'd love to pleasure you, and I've got the whole night to do it." She took one step forward and pressed her thigh against his crotch.

Jake sat back in his chair and considered her, trying to look beyond her ink black hair. He'd always avoided physical entanglements with black-haired women, especially prostitutes. It was stupid, but they made him feel unfaithful to . . .

Matilde leaned forward then and replaced the touch of her thigh with her hand, lifting a brow at what she found beneath the denim.

"Hmm, it feels like you need a lot of woman to help you with this," she said, offering a professional assessment. "And, honey, I'm a lot of woman."

She was a lot of everything, Jake thought: huge white breasts, big hazel eyes, pouty rouged lips, heavy perfume, coarse black hair. In fact, she was too much. He'd been months at sea and hadn't shared a woman's bed since New Orleans, but he felt his desire fizzle away like a spent match.

He downed a shot of whiskey. Then he straightened in his chair to reach his front pants pocket. He flipped a five-dollar tip into her hand. "Matilde, it's not that I don't appreciate the suggestion. But I've got other things on my mind tonight."

Catching the coin, Matilde laughed in genuine amusement, her bosom quivering like aspic. "Believe me, Captain, I'm not the least bit interested in men's minds." She chuckled again and turned to walk away. "Except maybe to make them lose them."

Jake rested his forehead on the heel of his hand and poured another drink as he watched Matilde's green satin hips sway up to a logger at the bar. She twined herself around him like a tree snake. He almost laughed.

He didn't want just any woman, Jake realized with weary resignation. It wouldn't have mattered if Matilde had been a redhead or a blonde. He wanted China. And like the irrepressible urge to touch a tongue to an aching tooth, he couldn't stop himself from reviewing their brief moments together in the dark of the porch. The sweaty, noisy, beer-soaked saloon fell away as he recalled her black hair tumbling across his arm like a crushed-velvet drape, her fine-boned gracefulness, the unbelievable softness of her skin, her instant response to his touch, the faint, spiced wood scent of her, the taste of her—

Oh, damn it to hell, he groaned inwardly. The whiskey wasn't helping, and unless he drank himself senseless, the memory of China wasn't going to fade. Neither would the eerie specter of Susan Price's face staring at him through that window. He drained his glass and threw a coin on the table.

Back outside on Astor Street, he glanced up and saw clouds blowing in from the Pacific, hiding the wonder of falling stars. He'd have to move fast if he wanted to make it to Monroe's repair yard before the sky opened.

As he left behind the chaotic din of jangling pianos, raucous laughter, and the confused babble of languages common in a seaport town, he knew peace was just a few minutes away. He was going to sleep with his ship tonight, the one woman he knew who would ask nothing of him.

In the morning, Jake still hadn't returned when China left her room to go to the league boarding-house. She walked to the hall window to turn down the lamp, then paused in his doorway. The bed that he now made himself hadn't been slept in. Misery swelled like a bubble in her chest.

Well, she was simply going to stop worrying about him; he was a grown man, he'd sailed the world. And he'd put her in a highly compromising position that she didn't want to consider too closely in the light of day. Her face burned every time she thought about it.

When she reached the hall downstairs, she heard Aunt Gert in the kitchen, breakfast pans rattling. China didn't think she could endure sitting at the same table with Susan so soon after the incident last night. She supposed it was more cowardice on her part, but she couldn't help it. Heaven knew how long Susan had stood there, watching them.

"Aunt Gert, don't bother fixing anything for

me," she said from the kitchen door. "I've got an errand to run. I'll eat later."

Gert turned to look at her, then shook her spoon in glowering vexation. "Seems nobody in this house eats at a regular time anymore, except Cap and me. Jake is never here for dinner, and now he's out God-knows-where, you're off doing some other business, Susan hasn't come down. I don't know why I bother!"

"Oh, dear, I am sorry," China commiserated, meeting her aunt at the stove. "I'll tell you what. I'll cook dinner all next week and give you the evenings off."

"Hmph," Gert groused, and turned back to her fried potatoes, using her apron for a potholder on the handle.

"Won't that help a little?" she appealed.

"Well—I guess." She saw a shadow of a grin on her aunt's face, her easy, good nature returning.

China patted her arm and went to the hall for her cloak. Then she heard, "But if things don't return to normal around here, I'm going to go cook for people who appreciate it."

What was normal? China had begun to wonder. She put on her cloak and let herself out the back door to slip away down the wet morning street to the boardinghouse. Preoccupied and fretful, she barely noticed that the trees were starting to bud and that the crocuses poked tender green blades from the tidy flower beds in her neighbors' yards.

She pressed her bag to her side reassuringly. She carried Jake's check with her, intending to go to the bank later in the morning. At least she had some money now, more than she'd hoped for, and she remembered seeing a good dining room table at a secondhand shop. They needed one for the boardinghouse; maybe she'd be able to provide it.

The big, ramshackle house came into view on the next block. Harbor House, they'd decided to call it. China shook her head at its appearance. It still needed a lot of work, but she and Dalton were making progress. Three stories tall, with a lovely wide veranda on the second floor, the once elegant residence sat high on its corner lot, the white paint worn down to bare wood in some places. The shrubbery in the yard encroached on the walk and completely covered two of the main-floor windows. Other windows were boarded up, and they knew the roof leaked.

But inside, with Willie's help and that of a few sailors who owed Dalton their freedom, things had taken shape. They'd cleared away years of junk and unsalvageable furniture left by the previous occupant (thereby dislocating the rats that had settled in the emptiness), washed and painted walls, and scrubbed floors. Dalton, using his most persuasive rhetoric, had managed to acquire donations of decent used furniture, a few beds, and dishes. The place wasn't luxurious, but it was a good start.

China slowly made her way up the walk, following the wide path Willie had hacked out of the jungle of rhododendron, arborvitae, and straggling, overgrown grass. She mentally composed a list of jobs that needed doing in the yard. It had been a low priority, but they couldn't let this go forever—the house looked terrible outside, and with spring coming it would only get worse.

Just as she reached the bottom front step, the door swung open and Dalton walked out to the porch to meet her. Dressed in dungarees and a gray chambray shirt, he was smiling as he put his hand under her elbow and waved her through the door.

"Come and see what Peter Hollis sent over," he said. China could hear the excitement in his voice. He led her to the parlor and pointed at a forest green sofa and matching chair.

"Peter sent them? Dalton, they look brand-new!" she said, surprised by this show of generosity.

"Not new, but rebuilt. The upholstery shop just delivered them."

And Jake had told her it was a mistake to talk to people about the league, she thought. Well, they'd proven him wrong. It had been the best thing she and Dalton could have done. So many had come forth because of that one Saturday evening, to make this house possible.

From somewhere upstairs she heard a muffled pounding and looked up at the ceiling.

"Oh, that's Willie nailing door molding back on. I never would've guessed that boy had such a talent for carpentry."

"I'd bet Willie didn't either," she replied drily. Dalton had a forceful personality, and he knew how to get work out of people. "Do you suppose he might have a talent for chopping back that thicket in front of the house? It really looks terrible."

Dalton nodded in agreement. "I'll set him to the task this afternoon."

She told him of her plans to buy the dining room table, and he positively beamed. A usually intent man, single-minded in his purpose, he was smiling more these days.

He surprised her even more when he took her hands in his and danced her across the bare, water-stained floor. Her skirts flared around her ankles, and she whooped with laughter. "Dalton, I've never seen you so happy!"

"You bet I'm happy. This is going to work, China," he laughed too, triumphantly, his cobalt eyes lit with a zealous fire. He twirled her again. "Harbor House is actually going to work. It's *real*. But I couldn't have done it without you." He stopped abruptly, breathless and grinning. Then he looked into her eyes, his expression growing more serious, and suddenly took her face in his hands and kissed her.

Dalton's scent was different from Jake's. That was the first thing China noticed. And he was shorter and more slightly built. It wasn't an unpleasant experience, but aside from her surprise, she didn't have that funny sensation in the pit of her stomach that she got when Jake kissed her. Nor was there that hopeless feeling of surrender that made her want to wind her arms around Jake's neck and stroke his hair, while he pulled her hips against his.

Dalton withdrew, a bit self-conscious, and smiled at her again. Then he began pacing around her on the hardwood floor, his features at once animated and thoughtful, his hands linked behind his back.

"We work well together, you and I," he said, then gestured around the room. "Look at everything we've done. Think of the lives we've saved. We make a good team."

She sat on the new sofa and ran her hands over the fresh upholstery, watching him stride the width of the room. He had a new idea brewing.

She could almost see it taking shape as he stared at the floor, his brow furrowed in thought. "You did most of the work, you know," she said.

He shook his head adamantly. "No, I didn't. It's been equal—like a partnership. You took as many risks, struggled just as hard. And you know better than anyone else how important our cause is." He tapped his chin speculatively. "I've been thinking about Portland ... their shanghaiing problem is even worse than Astoria's. I haven't had much time to give to it, but once this house is running smoothly, I'd like to go to Portland and see what can be done." He shifted his gaze to her. "Will you come with me?"

China was puzzled. "How could I help in Portland when I live here?"

His pacing brought him around to stand in front of her. "We'd have to move there together." He dropped to one knee in front of her and took her hand, enthusiasm radiating from him. "Marry me, China, and we'll go to Portland and continue our work with the Sailors Protective League. Think of the good we could do, the men we could save from the crimps."

Marry him! China stared at him, vaguely conscious that her mouth was open slightly. "Wh—why, Dalton, I—uh—"

He was on his feet again, plotting a strategy, while he circled the sofa. "It's well known that the Grants are just as active in Portland as they are here. And Jim Turk works in both towns too."

He went on with this verbal review of the facts as he knew them, acting as though his stunning proposal was merely one more element thrown into the mix. Marry Dalton Williams?

His voice faded to a hum in the back of her

mind as China forced her churning thoughts to slow for a moment, at least enough to let her consider the situation. If she became his wife, it would get her away from Astoria and its memories, good and bad. She had tremendous respect and admiration for Dalton—he had a great passion for his work. She was positive that he respected her, too, although she knew without being told that he didn't love her.

Nor did she feel the fervent depth of emotion for him that she did for Jake, but maybe that was just as well. She and Jake certainly had no future together. After all, he'd be leaving, probably within the next week or so. At that thought, she dropped her gaze to the piping on the sofa cushion, and a surge of regret rushed through her, making her eyes sting.

"—and I don't expect you to answer right now," Dalton was saying. "But will you think about it, China?"

Realizing that he'd asked a question, she looked up at him again and gave him a shaky smile. "Yes, of course I will," she replied, standing. "For now, though, I'd better go see about that table." She'd meant to spend the day working in the kitchen, but now she wanted to get away so she could think.

Dalton nodded, all business. "Ask them if they can deliver it this afternoon. I'll be here until three o'clock, and I'd like to see it." He walked her to the door, his attitude toward her no different than it had ever been: respectful, polite, slightly distracted.

The hammering continued from the second floor. "Willie's going to be sorry he missed you," he teased.

China wasn't. Dealing with the calf-eyed young

sailor was more than she could manage in her present state of mind. But she smiled anyway. "Poor Willie. I feel sorry for him sometimes. It isn't much fun to be in love alone."

Chapter Eleven

The sky had turned leaden by the time China started for home, and a preliminary drizzle was falling. The odors of the canneries and sawmills were held close to the streets by the low-hung clouds. With no distraction but her damp skirts, her gaze wandered to the mist-shrouded river on her far right, and she let her mind shift to Dalton's proposal.

She was very fond of Dalton Williams, though she'd thought of him mainly as a champion, a hero, all this time. Now she was forced to consider him as a man.

Four years ago she wouldn't have given even a minute to contemplating such a marriage. A union between herself and a man of unknown parentage, who'd grown up in doorways and alleys? It would have been utterly unthinkable. But she had to admit that he was surprisingly well-spoken and well-mannered, despite those beginnings.

Still, they had nothing in common except the Sailors Protective League. Without that, what lay between them? Not love, or tenderness. Not even the hazy outline of a shared history, such as she and Jake had. Mutual respect? Yes, but again, that tied back to the league.

She crossed a muddy street, automatically raising her hem as she went, her train of thought intact. Those things she craved from marriage—intimacy of spirit and companionship—she imagined she wouldn't have them with Dalton. She supposed she might learn to love him—a lot of women learned to love husbands after the wedding, even in more well-favored matches. But she and Dalton would always be two isolated individuals, fond of each other but sharing only their work, a living space, and a last name. She suspected that would be enough for Dalton. For herself, she wasn't as certain.

When China was half a block from home, the drizzle became a full-fledged downpour, and she lifted her heavy skirt to dash to the front porch. Letting herself in, she stood in the entry and took off her wet shoes, hat, and cloak, then put them on the hall tree.

"Aunt Gert?" she called. "I'm back." Hearing no response, she was about to walk down to the kitchen when her attention caught on a metallic gleam in the front parlor. She paused in the doorway, looking at it, then advanced slowly into the room. Her stockinged footsteps were silent on the deep carpet as they carried her to the small cherry table near the fireplace. She stood before it, looking at the gold filigreed box, then extended her hand. Her fingertips brushed the cool porcelain lid, and she hesitated.

Do you really want to know? she asked herself. What she found on the underside of that box could change her mind, her heart, her life.

Yes, she wanted to know. She *had* to know. She picked up the box and carried it to the alcove, where the light was better. The texture of the gold wire was rough under her fingers, the whispered scent of old roses still detectable. Quickly, before her courage failed her, she turned it over and stared at the bottom.

Her legs suddenly nerveless, she drew a deep, shuddering breath. She felt behind her for the settee and sank to the buttoned cushion, unable to take her eyes off the shiny gold surface in her hand.

There, engraved with a jeweler's delicate skill, was a small heart that contained the initials CS and JC.

She pressed the box to her breast and fought the torrent of emotion that tightened her throat. Jake *had* loved her, for years, apparently, and she'd been oblivious to it. That was why he'd signed Quinn's note. Maybe it had been the reason why, sometimes when she would turn suddenly, she'd catch him watching her.

And Zachary Stowe? He fell still lower in China's regard. He had claimed responsibility for the gift, and with well-acted, self-effacing bashfulness. All the while an audacious fisherman's son, with a heart that held unsuspected tenderness, had watched from the background, hoping she would realize the truth.

With shattering insight, China realized that she had been the "someone else" Jake told Althea Lambert he cared for. And, as he'd so specifically pointed out last night, it had all happened a long time ago. She bowed her head and pressed the filigreed box to her lips, miserably aware of one thing: Jake Chastaine no longer loved her.

But she was falling in love with him.

It was late afternoon when Jake finally returned to China's house, grubby, bristle-faced, and tired.

He'd slept fitfully in his unheated bunk on the *Katherine Kirkland* last night. Then he'd spent the day in the rain, overseeing some of the final repairs. Tomorrow, he would go to the Blue Mermaid and leave the message his crew awaited—to report to the ship in three days. He expected her to be loaded and ready to sail in a week's time.

As he trudged to the back porch stairs, he glanced at the bench where, for a few moments with China, he had let pride and lust rule his head. It was a good thing his days in Astoria were numbered. He wouldn't be able to continue living under this roof with her, wanting her despite the lifetime of difference between them and hating himself for it.

But what he wanted right now was a bath and a razor. Absently, he rubbed his hand over the rough stubble on his jaw. He could soak in the tub for a while and be finished in time for dinner, providing he didn't fall asleep in the hot water. Aunt Gert probably wouldn't be expecting him; he hadn't been home for dinner lately. Maybe it wasn't too late—she could throw a little extra in the pot for him.

But when he let himself in the back door, instead of finding Aunt Gert and the aroma of her cooking, he stepped into an empty, dusk-darkened kitchen. It was five-thirty and the stove was cold; not a pot or pan sat on its black surface. One of Gert Farrell's qualities that he'd always counted on was her consistency. When he'd left Astoria, knowing that she was here with China and Ryan had given him a small measure of comfort. Now, looking at the deserted kitchen, something felt wrong to Jake.

He walked through the silent hall down to the

back parlor, the only lighted room on the first floor. Captain Meredith dozed by the fireplace in his wingback chair, alone. He approached the old sailor.

"Cap," he said, and lightly tugged at his sleeve.

The old man jumped, then looked up at Jake and took a snuffling breath. "Jesus, lad, you gave me a turn."

Jake took the chair opposite him. "Sorry," he smiled, raising his voice a bit to be heard. "Do you know where Mrs. Farrell is? Or China?"

"Oh, aye. They've both gone looking for that wispy little Mrs. Price. They said they've not seen her since last night."

Jake frowned. "Wasn't she at breakfast?"

Cap shook his head, reaching for his cold meerschaum pipe on the table next to him. "No, and neither was Missy." He pointed the stem at Jake with a gnarled hand. "Things have been pretty stirred up since you got here, boy. You've got these women all dithery, most especially the widow."

He looked away from Cap's shrewd raisin eyes. He was more observant than Jake had supposed, perhaps more so than himself. He'd never really wanted to think about why Susan followed him with that hollow, haunted gaze. He'd only known he didn't like it.

"I don't mean to say that I think you've been trifling with her. I know where your interest lies, and it isn't with a faded slip of a woman like Mrs. Price. She's kind of thin and watery, not strong like Missy."

Jake raised his eyes again, feeling a flush creep up his throat.

Cap clamped the pipe stem between his teeth

and sucked on it, making a wet, bubbling noise. "She's an odd one, a bit like a ghost ship—all mist and gauzy sails, with no one at the helm. But I expect she heard something, or saw something that fouled her lines. And now she's run away from it, because that's all she can do." He made a careful scrutiny of Jake. "Seems everyone had a rough night. You look like hell yourself."

Jake resisted the urge to fidget in his chair. Cap was hitting a little too close to the truth for his comfort, from every direction. He felt vaguely guilty without good reason. "Aw, hell, Cap. I'll bet I haven't said more than a hundred words to Susan Price."

Cap only nodded. A pocket of hot pitch burst in the fireplace, creating a shower of sparks.

Jake glanced at the window. It was getting dark out. "Do you know where they went, China and Aunt Gert, I mean? I don't like the idea of them being out this late."

"They'll be back soon enough," the old man replied confidently. "I don't care so much about dinner being late, but I want my medicine."

Jake made a face and stood. "What's in that stuff anyone could want?"

Cap's eyes twinkled. "Alcohol, mostly."

Jake laughed.

Just then he heard the front door open, followed by the sound of feminine voices. He stepped out into the hall.

"Oh, Jake," Gert began, hand-wringing anxiety in her voice. "I'm so glad *you're* here. Susan is missing and we can't find her anywhere. We need to tell the police."

He heard Aunt Gert, but he saw only China. His eyes locked with hers, and a dozen things he might have told her flashed through his mind. Personal things that had nothing to do with this time or place. Feelings that he wished he could act upon.

But China spoke first, her hands folded at her chest like a supplicant. She was pale, and her jawline looked sharper than usual. "We searched all the places she usually goes, but—Jake, please, will you help me find her? I feel ... I feel responsible for her. You understand, don't you?"

He understood. If something happened to Susan Price because of what she'd learned last night, China would never forgive herself. It didn't matter that theirs had been the actions of two adults, accountable only to themselves and their own hearts. He nodded, but stopped himself from touching her face. Instead he showed her his dirty hands. "Just let me wash up a little and change my shirt. I'll be down in five minutes."

Out of habit, Jake went to the back stairs, and took the steps two at a time. As he neared the second floor, he paused, hearing a strange, colorless sound echo faintly through the stairwell above him. Listening, he thought it might be a cat's-paw, airy and weightless, sighing around the walls of the attic. But after a moment, he realized it wasn't the wind; this had a melodic quality, like singing.

Passing the second floor, he continued slowly up the spiral staircase toward the attic. It grew darker as he climbed, and he reached into his pocket for a match. Striking it with his thumbnail, he held it cupped in his hand. When he reached the musty attic, the song took more definite shape and Jake recognized it as an old, sweet Scots ballad about the whalers of Tarwaithe.

The person singing it, in a childlike, ethereal chant, was Susan Price. Her high, clear notes ricocheted off the walls of the unfinished barnlike room, intensifying the echo.

She sat next to the window on the bottom step of the circular tower staircase, staring intently at the river. The corner was illuminated by the oil lamp at her feet. Jake shook out the remains of his match and approached her cautiously. She didn't seem to notice his presence and he didn't want to startle her. His experience with this kind of problem was sorely limited, he had no idea how she would react upon seeing him. The one thing instinct told him to do was speak quietly.

"Hello, Susan," he murmured.

She turned to look at him, her light hair tumbled wildly around her shoulders. A smile of welcome and pathetic joy lit her face. "Oh, Edwin," she said. "You're home at last."

China paced in the entry, waiting for Jake. She had sent Aunt Gert, always inept in emergencies, to the kitchen to put together a hasty dinner. Listening to Gert's wailing panic had made it difficult to control her own fears.

The instant she'd asked for Jake's help, China had felt better. He might not know where to find Susan, but his strength and confidence, his very presence, were reassuring.

Still, the minutes ticked by and he did not return. China glanced out the window. Twilight was about to give way to full darkness, and the idea of a woman, especially one as unworldly as Susan, wandering Astoria's nighttime streets only increased her distress. Sighing, she marched toward the stairs to see what had become of Jake.

But when she reached the second floor, she couldn't find him. He wasn't in his room and he wasn't in the bathroom. After calling him and walking the length of the hall runner to check behind every closed door, she determined he wasn't up here.

"Well, for God's sake," she said aloud, increasingly uneasy. Was everybody in the house disappearing, one by one? She was about to go back downstairs, thinking she'd missed him somehow, when she heard the ceiling creak overhead, as though someone had taken a step. The noise brought her up sharply.

She went to the back stairwell, the only way to the attic, and listened. Though it came to her as a low, droning murmur, she couldn't mistake the sound of Jake's voice. Then she heard a female reply. She grabbed a candle from the linen closet and, lighting it, tiptoed up the steps.

Jake felt the hair on the back of his neck rise as Susan regarded him with huge pansy eyes that showed almost no color save the black of her pupils. Making no sudden moves, he retrieved an old stool from the corner and sat down in front of her. He did his best to ignore the icy chills that flew down his spine at her unearthly expression.

"What are you doing up here, Susan? China has been looking everywhere for you."

She smiled at him. "I come up here every day to watch for your ship. I knew you'd come home. That's why China keeps the lamp in the hall window. So you'd see it and come back."

At her mention of the lamp, Jake swallowed. "Susan—," he began, but she rushed on, as though afraid of what he'd say if given the chance.

"See?" she said, holding out a locket. "I've kept your photograph here, close to my heart. I've never forgotten you, Edwin."

From the corner of his eye, Jake detected movement and felt, rather than saw, China lingering in the doorway, quiet as a cat. He silently complimented her for figuring out they were here; he felt as if he might need a witness.

Susan opened her locket's hinged face to show him a picture of Edwin Price. He'd had a good face, a strong one, but he'd borne no particular physical resemblance to Jake, except that his hair was nearly identical in color.

Jake groped for something to say that would make her see reason. Only one possibility came to him. He hunched forward on the stool, his elbows on his knees, his hands laced between them. "When I was six years old, I lost my mother." He sighed and dropped his gaze to the floor, wondering if there was any point in opening this wound. But when he glanced up at her, she seemed to be listening, so he went on. "Nearly everyone in Astoria thinks she died. But she didn't. She just picked up and left town."

In the shadow of the doorway, China felt her eyes widen at this revelation, and with great effort she quelled a surprised gasp. But she jostled the candle in her fist and felt hot wax splash on her fingers.

"Well, being so young, I didn't understand how she could do that. And, God, I missed her something awful. So I used to pretend that she was just gone for a while—you know, visiting friends in Seaside or in Olney—and then she'd be home. But eventually I had to face the truth: she wasn't coming back. I never saw her again." Jake leaned forward and put one hand on Susan's arm and the other flat to his chest. "I'm not your husband, Susan. I'm John Jacob Chastaine. Edwin Price drowned at sea, and he isn't coming home either."

China bit her lower lip, hard, to keep her eyes from welling up.

Susan stared at Jake. "But—"

He just shook his head again. "No."

She turned away then and rested her head against the window. There was nothing to see now but the lights along the waterfront. Time dangled in the silence. "I know," she replied finally, choking the words out. "It was so hard to lose him. I just didn't want it to be true, s-so I told myself that it wasn't. When you came—you don't really look much like him, but you reminded me of him. I thought maybe . . ." She spoke against the glass, misting it with her words.

Jake drew a deep breath and glanced at China, subtly motioning her forward.

China left the doorway and approached slowly, not sure how to proceed. "Susan, dear, will you come downstairs now? Aunt Gert will fix you soup and a toddy."

Susan kept her face turned to the window. Her voice sounded like an old woman's, tired, defeated. "Can I have it in my room?"

"Of course you can. That sounds like a wonderful treat." China came closer and touched her shoulder. Susan rose from the step and buried her face against China's neck, apparently unable to face Jake. China flashed him a look of unspoken gratitude and mimed that he should go downstairs himself.

Jake watched the two women leave, then sat on

the stool again for a moment, as weary as he'd ever been in his life.

When China walked into the kitchen an hour later with Susan's tray, Jake was sitting at the table, cleaned up and combed. He'd carelessly slung his big frame on one of the chairs, and the gaslight reflected off his thick, pale hair, casting shadows under his jade eyes and across the bones of his strong hands. The remnants of Aunt Gert's thrown-together meal of soup and a sandwich lay before him on the tablecloth.

Seeing him there, looking tired but still painfully attractive, made her pause. And tired though *she* was, the sight of him, long-boned and lean-muscled, retained the power to bring a heat to her face.

"How is she?" he asked. There was no question who he meant.

"I gave her a sleeping powder. Maybe she'll feel better tomorrow." She shook her head worriedly. "I hope so, anyway." Taking the tray to the sink, she felt like she'd packed more trays to more people than she could count.

"I want to thank you for what you did upstairs, Jake," she said, turning to face him. "I know that Susan is a bit—well, a little odd, I guess."

Jake arched a brow at her understatement.

"All right, I suppose she's quite odd. I didn't realize how much trouble she was in. But I don't think she was always like this. And I know what it's like to wait for someone, wondering when he'll be back. When there's no body to bury, it's harder to accept the death."

He stood and walked over to her, putting a hand under her elbow. "Come on, sit down," he said. "I'll get your dinner." He guided her to the table.

She sent him a flimsy smile. "Are you going to get even with me for those first few meals I gave you?"

He went to the stove, where the soup kettle simmered. He chuckled. "I should, but I'm going to let you off easy tonight."

She eased herself into a chair, glad for the chance to sit. He ladled the soup into a bowl and set it before her. Then he brought a part of a chicken and a loaf of bread to the table and began cutting slices. He seemed easy and familiar with the task; the slices were uniform, and he even cut off the bread crusts.

China watched, fascinated, as he assembled a sandwich for her, as nice as any restaurant's.

He noted her interest and smiled. "Surprised, huh? When I went to sea, I spent a year or so in the galley. Ship's cooks are pretty tough; you get it right or they'll boil *you* for dinner."

China thought of the things that had recently passed between them and around them—the night on the back porch, the potpourri box, the emergency with Susan, the story about his mother. All this painted a picture of a complex man with many layers. A man who veered sharply from the insensitive, truant hell-raiser she'd believed him to be. He had altered her concept of him again and again in the last two and a half months.

"But I'd learned my way around a kitchen pretty well before that. Who do you suppose did the cooking when I lived on Tenth Street with Pop?"

"I never thought about it, I guess," she said, tasting the soup.

"Your old cook, Edna, and Aunt Gert showed me a few things," he said, grabbing an orange from the pantry. He brought it back to the table and pierced the rind with the edge of a spoon, releasing its fragrance. "The rest I picked up along the way. I can roast a turkey, make a stew, bake a cake."

She thought of him as a youngster, trying to manage on his own, with only Aunt Gert for female input, and her heart contracted a little. She'd lost her own mother when she was young, but she'd grown up with a loving family around her. As far as she knew, Jake and his father had always been at odds.

"Was it true, what you told Susan about your mother?" she inquired softly. She looked at him as he sat across from her, stripping off the orange peel, stripping away her last defenses. His big hands were dexterous and, she remembered, surprisingly gentle.

He breathed a slight sigh. "Yeah."

"Do you know where she is?"

He held an orange section out to her on his open hand, and she took it, putting it in her mouth. Silence stretched between them. Finally he said, "You know how it makes you feel to talk about Ryan?"

She looked up from her plate and saw his eyes darken. Nodding, she let the subject drop. The more she learned about him, the less she knew, it seemed.

He leaned back in his chair and pulled off two more orange sections. One he put on her plate and one he bit in half. "The *Katherine Kirkland* is going back into the water in two days. I'll be moving my gear back to my quarters then."

China put down her soup spoon, suddenly no longer hungry. "When does she sail?"

"In a week." He leveled a watchful gaze on her, as though waiting for her response.

A week. What could she say? Good? Two months ago she would have danced on the kitchen table to hear such news. Of course, everything had changed. But to admit it, to let him know that she cared, now, when his love for her had long since died—that was out of the question. Afraid that almost anything she said would betray her heart, she let her gaze fall on the fine planes of his face and maintained her silence.

Jake gave her the last orange slice and pushed his chair back to stand up. One corner of his mouth turned down in a mocking smile. "I thought you'd want to know."

Chapter Twelve

Late the next afternoon, China sat in the front parlor alcove, looking at the underside of her gold filigreed box. She ran her fingertips over the engraving, feeling the slight depressions that formed the initials. Jake had been out most of the day on business, and despite her best efforts to keep busy, there had been moments like this one, when she could only mope around. China rested her chin on her hand and looked out at the forest of masts lined up in the harbor. Really, it was for the best that he was going. Life would finally resume its normal pace and cadence after the *Katherine Kirkland* upped anchor.

And now that Harbor House was nearly ready to open, perhaps . . . perhaps she might give more consideration to Dalton's proposal. After all, as she'd told herself before, she had great respect for him, and she was fond of him. Maybe Portland would be interesting, too. It would mean leaving the family for a time, but certainly she and Dalton would come back.

Susan had lingered in her room all day, saying she was too tired to come out. She might improve, though, once Jake was gone. Oh, yes, everything would be better.

China glanced at the engraved initials again. If

Jake's leaving would solve so many problems, why did the prospect of his absence make her feel so horrible?

Just then she heard Cap's awkward, cane-supported gait on the front steps, and she went to the front door to let him in. Back from his daily afternoon walk, he was out of breath and even more red-faced than usual, as though he'd been chased to the porch by the doomed phantom ship, the *Flying Dutchman.*

"Cap! Are you all right?"

"There's big doings, Missy, big doings. Looks like there might be an honest-to-God riot brewing over at that boardinghouse you've been working on."

"What!" she exclaimed.

He nodded and stumped to the chair that sat in the hall between the front and back parlors. Taking off his cap, he fanned his face, ruffling his thin hair. "Aye. Seems one of those goddamned crimpers stole a man last night and dumped him on a ship that lay at anchor at Clatsop Spit. Came first light, he jumped overboard and tried to swim to a fishing boat nearby. He didn't make it." He reached into his pocket and produced a big red handkerchief to blow his nose with a honking *blat.*

"You mean he drowned?" she asked.

"That he did, Missy. He sank like a bag full of rocks."

"God in heaven! Then what?"

Though his face was no longer as florid, he still hadn't quite caught his breath. "How about a drop of brandy before I tell you the rest? I'm stove in."

She hurried to the liquor cabinet in the front

parlor and brought him a glass and the brandy bottle.

"Bless your good Irish soul, Missy," he said, and poured a measure down his throat in one gulp. Thus fortified, he continued. "The fishing boat skipper was able to recover the body. He brought it in and reported the death. I guess the dead man was one of the Finn lads from Uniontown. With a wife and two little ones left behind." He held his glass out to her, which she dutifully refilled, and he took another drink. "When the word got around—and it didn't take long, believe me—that Williams fella got some townsfolk together to march to the mayor's office to protest."

"Dalton Williams?" she said, aghast.

"Aye. They were ranting and raving 'No more shanghaiing, no more shanghaiing.' But some sailor-runners tried to stop them. When I started for home, Williams was piloting his group to the boardinghouse, and the sailor-runners were on their heels."

"Didn't anyone call for the police?" she asked, tempted to take a drink of the brandy herself.

Cap unbuttoned his coat with stiff fingers and felt around in his pockets for the meerschaum. "Even if they did, you know it would do nary a bit of good. The law tends to look the other way when it comes to shanghaiing, the lousy bastards."

Yes, she thought, and that was why the Sailors Protective League was formed. Well, there was nothing to do but go to Dalton. Of course he was capable, but she couldn't stand by and let him face this alone, not after all they'd been through together for the league.

She put the brandy bottle in his hand. "Here,

Cap. Why don't you go out to the kitchen and get yourself some hot coffee to make a toddy? That'll warm your bones."

"Oh, trying to sidetrack me, eh?" He gave her a sharp look. "You're a pretty smart woman, Missy, but I'm not so old and feeble that I don't know my barnacles from my binnacles. And if you're thinking of going to that boardinghouse, you're letting yourself in for a peck of trouble, I can tell you."

China affected what she believed to be an innocent expression, then averted her eyes from his probing gaze. "Don't worry about me, Cap. You know I'd never do anything so dumb. Besides, I have Susan to look after."

"Aye, well—" He sounded unconvinced but apparently was willing to let it drop. He rubbed his hand over his jaw and looked at the brandy bottle. "Maybe a toddy would be just the thing to cure what ails." With considerable effort, he hoisted himself out of the chair and took a couple of hobbling steps toward the kitchen. Then he turned and looked back at her. "I can give you but one bit of advice, Missy: keep your head down and your ass covered. It's not as much fun, but you'll live longer."

China raced toward Harbor House with no particular plan of action in mind; it was simply her duty to be there. Her low heels rumbled hollowly over the plank sidewalk, and she pressed a hand to the ache developing in her side.

But when she caught sight of the mob in the street up ahead, she slowed her headlong rush, pulling her cloak tighter. The odor of stove oil reached her nose. With daylight waning, several in the crowd carried blazing torches, their smoky flames gleaming brightly against the darkening sky. She felt the anger emanating from them, and as she cautiously drew closer, she saw that the people in the street were merely an overflow of those who were crammed into the front yard. A low, angry buzz ran through them, but their attention was focused on the front of the house. She recognized the impassioned, stentorian voice of Dalton Williams, carried on the wind currents.

China sidled around to the front yard, hovering on the fringes of the throng. Front windows that had previously been hidden behind the shrubbery were now visible. Apparently Willie had made good progress with the yard work. From her place in the back, she couldn't see much except Dalton's head as he paced back and forth on the porch.

". . . wife and two children who'll never see him again. This man had his whole life ahead of him, but it was cut short by the greed of men in expensive suits, to whom a man's life means nothing—*nothing*—and by politicians who allow this kidnapping and murder to continue!"

China detected a powerful, frank edge of emotion in his voice that surprised her. A thrilling, forthright speaker, Dalton had never resorted to theatrics to win an audience's sympathy, and she wondered why he was doing it now. But then, as if to answer her question, the crowd shifted just enough to reveal the cause of his reaction. On the porch flooring at his feet lay the gray, lifeless form of a man, obviously the drowning victim. The Finn had a full head of thick blond hair that, upon first glance, made China's heart turn over in her chest.

She stepped up on a nearby carriage block to get a better view.

Dalton stopped pacing and raked a hand through his hair. "We'll never make sense of Frans Hakkala's pointless death. But, by God, let him not have died in vain. Raise your voices to make the politicians hear you, the judges, the police. Save your sons and your brothers, and the hearts of your women. Because the crimps are out there—right now, tonight, tomorrow. In broad daylight and in the night's darkest hour. And next time they may come for you!" He leaned over and spoke a few words to the two men closest to the edge of the porch, and put a consoling hand on the shoulder of each of them. Then they climbed the steps and lifted the blanket-wrapped body to bear it away.

A respectful silence descended upon the crowd as a path opened for the pallbearers. From the other edge of the group, a malevolent voice rang out, "You'd better sleep with one eye open, Williams, because *you* could be next."

China whipped her head around toward the direction of the speaker, but could see nothing. Almost immediately after, a brick arced across the yard, smashing a front window.

The mob's angry buzz grew to a deafening roar of fury, and the mass erupted into total confusion, violent and frightening. Which were friends and which were foes was impossible to ascertain in the chaos. China hadn't envisioned a scene like this. She knew she ought to stay out of the way, but when she saw that brick and heard the glass shatter, she jumped forward, outraged. How dare these mindless, uncaring barbarians damage Harbor House, the object of painstaking work and worry? They were completely out of control, attacking like wild animals that had picked up a blood scent. She saw, and heard, an axe handle swing down upon the head of a man standing far too close to her, making a sickening pulpy thump, like a broken watermelon.

She tried to fight her way through the crowd to Dalton but was pushed back again and again. In the falling twilight, the torches glittered around her, bobbing like gargantuan fireflies. Over the shouting and swearing, she heard more glass breaking. Finally, miraculously, Dalton saw her and struggled against the tide to reach her.

"China," he shouted over the din, "you shouldn't have come. This has gotten out of hand."

"But the house—they'll destroy it."

They became separated again by the surge of the crowd that wedged between them and widened the breach. Fearing not only for the house, but also for their safety, she tried to find her way to the edge of the pandemonium. But with the darkness and the moving sea of humanity surrounding her, she was losing her sense of direction. Her hair tumbled down around her shoulders, flying free from its pins.

Suddenly China felt a hand grab her arm, and she swung around, ready to wrestle free from whoever held her, by whatever means it took. She turned and saw Jake, his jaw tight. The orange torch flames reflected in his narrowed eyes and gleamed on his blond hair.

"I might have known I'd find you here!" he shouted over the noise, fury in every line of his face. "Did that goddamned jackass Williams bring you down here? Is he trying to get you both killed?"

China would have challenged his remarks, but things were moving around her so quickly that she felt as if she was being sucked into the whirlpool of the shouting, angry mob. Real terror began to envelop her, and she was grateful for his strength beside her. That feeling of safety that she'd known before with him returned now.

Jake put his arm around her shoulders and pulled her to him protectively while he looked up to scan the nearby crowd for Dalton. When he spotted him, he shouted for him in a voice trained to carry over the roar of a gale. "Williams! Over here!"

Dalton plowed a path to them. "Did you come down to join the party?" he snapped at Jake. The three of them were pushed together by the swarming pack as it lunged and fell back.

Jake glanced behind him when someone bumped him, nearly knocking him over. He turned back to Dalton, his expression venomous. China felt certain that if he could have gained enough room in the tightly packed mass, he would have pulled his fist back and smashed Dalton's face.

"This is no place for China. You take her home," Jake ordered, raising his voice over the surrounding roar. "I'm going to my ship to keep an eye on her. God knows what you've started with this flashy stunt."

"Look, Chastaine," Dalton started, bristling at Jake's commanding tone. "I'm not one of your hands that you can—"

"Get her out of here, *right now*, mister."

"Stop it, both of you!" China demanded.

Ignoring the press of bodies around them, the

two men stared at each other in a fierce battle of wills, rage in their eyes. Finally, Dalton grabbed China's hand and pulled her out of Jake's embrace.

"Jake," she called, "aren't you coming with us?"

But as soon as a gulf opened between them, the mob rushed in like the ocean into a tidal pool. China lost sight of Jake, and Dalton maneuvered them down the street.

"You can't just leave!" she said. "Don't sacrifice everything we've worked for just to see me home."

"We're doing what he wanted," Dalton answered as he elbowed a man out of his way. "I have to get you away from here. And I'm coming right back."

As he pulled her from the brawl, China twisted around, trying to see over her shoulder. "Dalton, Jake could be killed," she declared.

"Not Chastaine," he said. "He knows how to take care of himself."

They trudged over the sidewalk, and China saw frightened faces at the windows of the houses they passed. She was rattled herself and wished she could sit down for a minute to get the strength back in her legs.

All the while, Dalton kept up a steady, intent monologue, thinking aloud more than speaking to her. He seemed exhilarated by the energy and anger of the people they'd left at the boarding-house, and his mind raced forward with plans.

"A few more demonstrations like this and they'll have to take us seriously. I just need to keep these people incited—Christ, I hope that a poor chump's death isn't the only thing that will budge them from their apathetic asses. If the *Astorian* prints a story about this—"

Distracted, he kept her hand in a hard grip and dragged her along as though she were a child. When they neared the house, China looked up at the second-floor hall window and saw that it was dark. She hadn't had a chance to light the lamp before she left.

Dalton took her as far as the front steps. "Well, I've got to go back. I can't leave Harbor House alone. Anything could happen. And those people need a leader."

"Those *people* are trying to tear the house down!" she emphasized, trying to tuck up her hair.

He shook his head. "No, it wasn't one of our group who threw the brick. It was one of Turk's men."

She put a hand on his arm, horrified. "You mean they were there too? Dalton, please be careful. You could be hurt, or arrested, or—"

"Arrested," he said, seizing upon the word. His cobalt eyes gleamed speculatively. "That might have some value. I'll have to give some thought to that."

"I don't think that would be a good idea—"

He leaned forward suddenly and pecked her cheek. "Thanks, China. You shouldn't have come tonight, but I'm glad you did."

He trotted down the steps, and she watched him as he ran under the gaslight on the corner. Then he disappeared into the night.

China sat at the kitchen table, then rose and went to the back door for what seemed like the hundredth time since Dalton had dropped her off.

The yard was silent and dark except for the whisper of rain falling on the trees. The wall clock marked the time. Ten forty-five. It had been hours since she last saw Jake, just before he was engulfed by the flood of insane humanity swirling around him. Had he escaped that morass and made it back to his ship? Worry and dread had her listening to every creak the house made, wondering if she heard footfalls on the back steps.

She scolded herself for not having enough courage to go down to his ship at the waterfront to see if he was safe.

Just as she sat down again, she heard a key scraping in the lock. She jumped out of her chair and flew to open the back door. When she saw Jake standing on the porch, she bit back a cry of horror.

"Oh, God, Jake," she exclaimed, pulling him into the kitchen when she thought he might topple over. Wet and dirty, his heavy blond hair was darkened by water and blood in a gory mix that ran down his face in thin streams. Sometime during this endless night he'd lost his coat, and he stood before her in a torn, rain-soaked shirt and dungarees. His clothes smelled of smoke, and his face was sooty. He lifted his eyes to look at her with an expression of silent appeal and such utter exhaustion that she hoped she could control the tears that threatened to make her voice shaky. She thought her heart would break just to look at him.

"What happened?" she asked in a spare whisper. Not waiting for an answer, she grabbed a towel and pressed it to his face, trying to mop up the blood and rainwater to determine the extent of his injuries. She took his hand and held it on the towel, then turned to reach for her shawl. "I'm going for the doctor."

He sank into a chair and closed a hand on her skirt to stop her. "No, don't go. I was going to go back to the *Katherine Kirkland*, but I wanted to see you—uh, so you could fix this. I'll be all right."

"But you're hurt," she said.

"Please, China. You can take care of it."

She hesitated, but maybe he was right. She really didn't want to leave him anyway. "Okay," she agreed. Then, eyeing him for a moment, she went to the pantry and brought back a bottle and a glass. "Here, drink this."

"Thank you," Jake whispered and uncorked the whiskey bottle, not bothering with the glass. He tipped his head back and tossed a swallow down his throat.

China gave him a questioning look. He nodded and she moved closer, letting him clutch her skirt in his fist again while she examined his scalp. The significance of this wasn't lost on her. Jake was a natural leader, accustomed to being in command. She'd never known him to show any apprehension or weakness. To hold on to her skirt like a child was a kind of surrender for him.

The one wound she found looked to be just a nasty gash, but she'd have to get him washed off to see what other damage had been done.

"How did this happen?" she asked, gently probing his head, feeling for swelling.

He touched a careful hand to his scalp and looked at the blood on his fingertips. "I don't know for certain. A lot of angry, yelling people were in the street, with all kinds of weapons. Well, you saw what it was like. At least no one was shot, I don't think. After a while I couldn't tell who was fighting who. I'm not sure they could, either. There was a fire," he said wearily, then took another drink. "I can't say how it started. But the boardinghouse caught first, then the next two houses. I knew I had to stay."

China stared at him. "Is it gone? The boarding-house, I mean?"

He shook his head. "Williams and I managed to keep it under control until the fire department got there. There's some damage, but it can be fixed."

Relieved, she looked into his tired eyes. "Thank you, Jake. I—I know how you feel about the league and—well, thank you." She resumed sifting through his hair, searching for other wounds. "Um, how was it that you found me there?"

She felt him flinch when she touched a tender spot on his scalp. "I was at the Blue Mermaid when I heard about the riot. News like that travels fast. I figured you might be foolish enough to jump into the thick of it, and I was right."

"Oh," she murmured, not entirely displeased, despite his unflattering observation. "Do you think you're hurt anywhere else?"

He reached up and stopped her hands, pulling them away to hold between both of his own. Through the soot and blood, she saw his earnest expression. "China, listen to me. You've got to stop working with Williams. Next time it could be *your* house that burns. And it wouldn't be just you who got hurt. Think of Aunt Gert and Cap and Mrs. Price. Think of having no place to live at all."

China bit her lower lip, his words painting a hideous picture in her mind. She could imagine yellow-orange tongues of flame licking out through every heat-shattered window, the roof crashing in, the family trapped. But then she thought of that poor man this afternoon who had drowned trying to escape the slavery that had been imposed on him.

Right now, though, none of that mattered. She had to take care of Jake.

"We can talk about that later. Do you think you can climb the stairs?" she asked. "We need to clean you up."

After a moment he gathered what strength he had left and hoisted himself out of the chair. Too tired to stand straight, he seemed shorter than usual to her. He put his arm around her waist as if it was the most natural thing in the world, and she led them up the back stairs. That arm at her waist became heavier with each step they took until they reached the second floor.

China steered him into the bathroom and sat him down on a low upholstered bench. "You can take a bath after I look at your head, but I need to wash your hair now so I can see what I'm doing. If I push this bench to the tub for you to sit on, do you think you can manage it?"

He made a face of some kind; it was hard to tell through the soot. "I guess," he replied. He stood and she moved the bench. He reached for his shirt buttons with hands that looked as heavy as lead and were no more effective. Finally China nudged them aside and opened the buttons. She moved behind him and stripped off his wet, bloody shirt, the sleeves turning inside out as they peeled away from his muscled arms and shoulders. The chain holding his Saint Nicholas medal winked at the back of his neck in the gaslight.

She tossed the ruined garment into the corner and, pulling a towel from the towel bar, pointed him toward the tub. "All right, come sit down over here and—" His bare, muscled arms came into full view and she stopped dead, her breath suddenly gone from her lungs. She put a hand to her throat as she stared at his left bicep. Jake turned to look at her and followed her gaze to what she'd found.

It was a tattoo. Not so odd—lots of sailors had tattoos of all kinds of things. Sweethearts' and wives' names, nude women, hearts, serpents, anchors, crucifixes to guarantee last rites in case of fatal illness or accident. But Jake's tattoo was nothing like those. This was a personal talisman that he carried with him, apparently in hopes that it, in turn, would eventually carry him back to Astoria.

The needle of the tattoo artist, in thousands of punctures, had driven black ink under Jake's skin to draw an accurate reproduction of the lamp in the hall window. It was encircled by the words LIGHT THE LAMP FOR ME.

China lifted her eyes to meet Jake's. He moved away self-consciously and slumped on the bench with his back to her, his head down. She heard him sigh, then he spoke. His usually smooth, rich voice sounded tired and papery, as though he recounted an ancient tale.

"It was that first trip out. We'd been around the Horn twice, counting both voyages, and we anchored in San Francisco. We were so glad to be back in America, and Quinn wanted to celebrate. So we went ashore and stopped in a lot of dockside bars. After a while, we were three sheets to the wind and the fourth one shaking. Quinn found, um, a lady to keep him company, so I left him to walk the waterfront and clear my head."

He shivered and China saw goose bumps rise on the broad plane of his back. She wanted to cover him with the towel, but something about the sound of his voice stopped her.

He went on. "I walked for a long time and it got pretty late. It was way past midnight by the time I decided to start back for the ship. The streets were quiet, and even a lot of the saloons had closed up. I felt, I don't know, lost or something that night, like I didn't have a home anywhere in the world. All those dark windows ... Then up ahead I saw a window with a light in it, and I thought about your lamp, like I had every day since the morning we left. But this light turned out to be in a tattoo parlor. I walked in and drew a picture of what I wanted. When I walked out, I had this." He turned his head and looked down at the tattoo.

China stared at the shadows under his shoulder blades, curved and shaped with muscle. With the benefit of hindsight, she was beginning to regret very much that he'd ever left. Maybe all of their lives would have been different if he and Quinn had stayed. Maybe if Jake had spoken up, if she'd known how he felt ...

He shivered again, making the gold hair on his arms stand erect, and this time she stepped forward to drape the towel over one of his shoulders. She perched on the high edge of the tub next to him, but he kept his eyes on the floor. The soot on his face muted his expression. Much as she wanted to sit here, just to be near him, she knew he was cold and she had to tend his wounds. She stood and pulled an enameled pitcher from the corner cupboard, then filled it under the taps.

"Here, let's clean you off," she said quietly, and eased his head forward. She gave him a bar of castile soap to wash his face. Then she poured the warm water through his grimy hair and gently lathered it with the soap. He leaned his arms on the rolled edge of the tub, dropping his forehead to rest on them. His Saint Nicholas medal clanked against the porcelain. She felt the stiff, tight muscles in his neck. Pulling his chain aside, she kneaded his neck and shoulders, using the warm lather to smooth her firm strokes. He uttered a wordless sound of relief.

Tired and hurt though he was, she felt a deep sense of intimacy as she touched him, and a foolish, distressing desire to kiss his arm where it bore the tattoo of her lamp.

She moved her hands higher to massage his head lightly. The suds were gray with soot, except in two places, where they were tinged faintly pink as well. "Jake," she murmured. "Why did you leave Astoria? I didn't know how you felt, or what you thought. Couldn't you have tried to tell me?"

He lifted his head to look at her, his expression hard and cynical. She felt color creep into her cheeks. "Oh, sure," he said. "You could barely stand to be at the same dinner table with me. And you were busy with your tea parties and that little pimple, Zach Stowe."

Maybe that was true. If he'd stayed, would her opinion of him have been magically transformed? After all, seven years earlier, she had believed she

would marry Zachary Stowe, and Jake Chastaine
had been just one of Quinn's stray-dog friends.

How could she have been so damnably blind?
So wrong about *everything*? It made her heart ache
to listen to him talk about his love for her in the
past tense, as a thing now obsolete that had never
had a chance to really live.

He let his head drop again, and continued, "Besides, I did try to tell you. With that gold box. I
guess it was my fault for not having the guts to
sign my name on the note." He lifted his shoulders in a kind of reclining shrug. "But it's just
as well that you didn't know. It wouldn't have
worked, you and me. Pop was probably right
about that."

She reached for the pitcher to rinse his hair,
pouring water slowly through the clean, pale
strands. She noticed that underneath, where the
sun hadn't touched it, his hair was the same sandy
color it had been when he was a boy. Lifting the
towel off his shoulder, she blotted the dripping
mass.

"Your father said that? You talked about me?"
She put the stopper in the tub drain and turned
on the taps. Then she picked up some cotton
wool and got the bottle of witch hazel from
the cupboard.

Jake paused a moment, as though searching his
memory for the words. "Yeah. Pop told me to stay
with my own kind where I belonged, and away
from you. A highborn lady would do me no good,
he said. I didn't want to believe him—Christ, we
had some fights about it. But I suppose he knew
what he was talking about."

"Good heavens, why? I've never met your father." China was annoyed to learn that she'd been

the topic of a heated debate over a reason she'd known nothing about, then judged and condemned. She stood behind him, carefully dabbing at gashes on his scalp with the antiseptic. They'd stopped bleeding, but at one point she heard Jake's hissing intake of breath when she touched a tender spot.

"Does the name Bedford mean anything to you?" he asked.

"Yes, they're a wealthy Portland family. I met them once when they visited Astoria, but I was just a girl at the time."

His shoulders drooped ever so slightly. "Years ago they used to spend their summers here. Dr. Bedford would take a house for his wife and daughters, then come down on the weekends."

One of the daughters was a rebellious free-thinker. She loved to sneak away from her boring, ladylike sisters to walk along the docks and watch the fishing boats come in. That was how she met twenty-three-year-old Ethan Chastaine.

"Her name was Lily and she had a big crush on Pop. She'd be there, waiting on the dock every afternoon when his boat came in, pretty as a flower with her big straw hat and summer dresses. She'd tag after him, refusing to go home, pestering him with a thousand questions. He tried to convince her that he wasn't the one for her, that she ought to find a man from her own world. Lily wouldn't hear of it. She was nineteen, old enough to know what she wanted. And she wanted him. It didn't matter to her that he was a fisherman, she said. She loved him so much she'd be happy anywhere they lived, even in a shanty on Tenth Street."

China sat on the edge of the tub again, facing Jake, to tend a cut near his hairline. He made two fists against his knees, and his eyes looked like green ice as he stared up at her.

"Well, Pop was only a man, and a young one at that. She was too hard to resist and at the end of summer they eloped across the river to Ilwaco."

China let her hands fall and stared at him.

He nodded. "Lily Bedford was my mother."

That, thought China, explained Jake's blond good looks. The Bedfords were very attractive people, and his ancestry showed in the shape of his head, the symmetry of his frame and muscles, the fine bones of his face.

"Do you remember much about her?" she asked softly.

He gave her a familiar lopsided smile, one she was beginning to realize covered a lot of hurt. "She was beautiful, I think. She had light hair and blue eyes." He tipped his head back to consider her. "They were dark blue, like yours. But mostly I remember that she always seemed sad."

The cocky impudence that China had always associated with Jake was absent, and in the void she found a man plagued with self-doubts.

"Life on Tenth Street isn't easy for any woman," he went on, speaking as though to himself. "But for her, someone used to comfort and plenty, I guess even love couldn't overcome the emptiness. I can still remember her sitting on our front porch in a rocking chair, watching the river go by for hours at a time." He stared unseeing at the water flowing from the tap. "Then one day I woke up and she was gone."

Gone to the angels? six-year-old Jake had asked his father. Like the mother of one of the neighbor boys, a few doors down? No, he'd been told, she'd gone to Portland. Jake couldn't conceive that his mother would leave them. So he made up the story he told Susan Price, for himself and others: his mother was away visiting friends, but she'd be back. His father had taken the story a step further, telling their neighbors and friends that his wife had died while visiting relatives. His pride hadn't permitted him the luxury of the truth.

Ethan Chastaine became a bitter man and a humorless, argumentative father. "He told me I was wasting my time chasing after a rich girl. Back then, I thought that if I went to sea and made something of myself, maybe that rich girl would look at me differently." Jake rubbed his forehead in a kind of weary gesture. "But she told me I'd never be welcome in her home again. So then I had no reason to stay—if I had, I think Pop and I would've killed each other, and I probably would've had to marry Althea Lambert."

China felt her throat tighten as she listened to him, and she cleared it, trying to ease the aching constriction. "But Jake, you dragged my brother with you. We had so little family. You may have had no mother. I had no *parents*, even before my father drowned."

His head came up at her words, and he briefly touched a hand to her arm. Water droplets fell on his bare shoulders from his hair, catching the light like crystals. "China, Quinn was my best friend. He was like a brother to me, too. But I knew him for what he was—bored and a little selfish. Most of all, he was a hellion. We got along because we were alike. You must know that. He wasn't like those prinking boys who came to your parties. And after that day in the alcove with you, I practically begged him not to ship out with me. I told him his family needed him. But I couldn't change his mind."

For a frozen moment, she could see Jake running against the backdrop of her memory, young, tall, and spare-fleshed, with Quinn loping along beside him, the summer sun gleaming off their two heads, one sandy blond, the other black as midnight.

Her heart grew heavier in her chest by the minute. She felt as though she were living some Shakespearean tragedy of misunderstood intentions, words not spoken, opportunities lost forever.

China reached for the taps to turn off the water. The room was hot and damp with steam. She turned to face him again, crossing her arms over her chest to keep from putting her hand to his cheek.

"So, now I know why you left. Why did you return to Astoria after all this time? You could have found a cargo for your ship anywhere in the world."

He leaned over and trailed his hand in the bath water. His words came with difficulty. "Yeah, I could've. But when I got the *Katherine Kirkland,* I had to come back to prove that I'd succeeded—to Pop, to everyone who thought I was just a guttersnipe and could never be anything else. That ship, owning her has gotten me something I never had here before—I have respect. Not a lot, but enough. From Pop, although he'd rather die than admit it, from the men I'm doing business with, from some of the people who expected me to fail." He raised his eyes to hers and leaned forward slightly, his words emphatic. "I like that, China. It feels *good.* And there isn't much in the world I'd trade for it."

She regarded him as he sat before her, strong and broad-chested, with a sense of honor and loyalty that she had never suspected. Before, when she'd looked at him, she'd merely seen the ways in which they were different. If only she had seen the ways that they were the same, before their lives had diverged. But she hadn't, and the chance to alter their course was long lost.

She rose from her seat on the edge of the tub. "I'm glad you got what you wanted, Jake. Are you going back to your ship tonight?"

He stood too and looked at his watch. "It's almost midnight. If it's okay with you, can I stay here tonight? I'll be out of your way before breakfast."

Out of her way, out of her life. It was too late now to let him know how she felt. Too late for almost everything. She glanced at him one more time, taking in the quintessence of everything he was. The chances were good that he'd never be back. He belonged to another woman now, the *Katherine Kirkland*. And China had to begin sealing him away in a corner of her heart that she'd not open again.

"You're welcome to stay. After all, your rent is paid through the end of the month." She went to the door and paused, letting her eyes touch briefly on his left arm. "I don't suppose you had anything to eat."

"Not here, I didn't," he said. "I guess I'm *really* late for dinner tonight."

She smiled ruefully. "If you're hungry, I can find something for you in the kitchen before I go to bed. It won't be fancy, but it'll help."

"That would be great, China. Thanks." As polite as two strangers, she thought.

China walked out, pulling the bathroom door closed behind her. On her way downstairs, she tried to block out the look she'd seen on his face, the familiar crooked smile.

Chapter Thirteen

The bathroom door latched, and Jake stripped off his filthy, wet dungarees and gratefully immersed himself in the hot water. He uttered a low groan as it covered his shoulders and he stretched out his legs to the end of the tub. The heat flowed over him and sank into his aching muscles, loosening them. He'd miss this tub after he left; two feet deep and over five feet long, it was a far cry from washing in sea water. But that was the least of his worries.

He hadn't meant to come back here tonight. His wounds weren't mortal. But after the fire and the raging confusion at the boardinghouse, he had to make sure China was safe. He couldn't trust Dalton Williams to put her welfare above that of the Sailors Protective League. Williams was so ready to sacrifice himself that he probably would think nothing of sacrificing her as well.

Luckily, his first and second mates had returned to the *Katherine Kirkland*, so his ship wasn't sitting in the water unguarded. But there'd been no one to look after China.

And after he sailed in a few days, Jake pondered for the hundredth time, what might happen to her then?

He dipped his hands in the hot water to splash

his face. It wouldn't be like the last time he'd left, he swore to himself, lathering a washcloth. It couldn't be. Sometimes he'd wondered if missing her hadn't been the reason he'd been so seasick those first few weeks.

Just sitting here with her tonight stirred up a lot of old dreams he'd rather had remained asleep. God, while he'd talked about his mother, it had taken every bit of self-control he had to keep from hiding his face against her breast, to inhale her fragrance, to shut out the rest of the world and its problems. She made him want to protect her. But Cap was right—China was strong, and her strength offered shelter to him too. That was a feeling he'd never had from a woman before. At least, not since he was six years old.

Tomorrow . . . tomorrow it would end when he moved back to the *Katherine.*

Jake started, his eyelids snapping open. He must have dozed off for a while—the bath water was cool and his goose bumps were coming back. He hauled himself out of the tub and grabbed a towel to dry off with, then tried to wrap it around himself. It was kind of small and the ends didn't overlap enough to tuck them in, but he couldn't find the one China had used on his hair. He struggled with the skimpy thing and gave up, gripping the terry cloth with one hand. What the hell, he only needed to wear it to get to his room. He combed his hair back with his fingers. It felt good to be clean again, and he was curiously energized after the nap.

Just then he heard a faint tapping on the door. Goddamn it, if that was Susan Price—

"Jake?" China called softly. "I left a sandwich

and a piece of pie for you on the kitchen table. If you're all right, I'll be going to bed now—"

Tying the two corners of the towel over his hip, he strode to the door and pulled it open. China stood there, wearing a nightgown, a wrapper, and a surprised expression.

China gaped at Jake in his state of near nakedness. It seemed like he'd wound a hand towel around himself, for all the covering it provided. It was just long enough to cover the gist of him, and the side of one firm-muscled buttock was exposed. There was no part of him to decently let her gaze stray to, except his face. And somehow the unmistakable desire she saw in his eyes made that most difficult of all. She recognized it easily; it was the same look she had seen two nights earlier on the back porch.

She glanced down at her own attire, an aged nightgown that had been washed so many times, the fabric was translucent, betraying her nipples as shadowy smudges beneath. Her hands flew to the edges of the wrapper, pulling them together.

"Oh! I didn't expect you to open the door. There's a sandwich—uh," she glanced over her shoulder toward the stairs, "you know, on the kitchen table." Good Lord, she was babbling like an idiot. She had to get away. "Well, good night."

She turned to dash down to her bedroom, but his hand closed on her elbow before she could escape.

"China."

He asked a dozen things in murmuring her name with a voice both resonant and intimate, none of them could she answer with words. She kept her face averted and closed her eyes, praying briefly, for what she wasn't sure. Strength of will, maybe? Or better yet, that he would suddenly be stricken ugly and undesirable.

"China." Once more, and he gently pulled her toward him, nearer to his embrace. She braved a look to see if her silent prayer had been answered. But no. Still tall and unutterably male, he had a presence that vibrated with a tangible energy. Everything female in her struggled to respond to him, and she fought the treacherous urge. If she gave in to her feelings, it would only be that much harder on her when he left.

"No, Jake, you won't do this to me again—" She heard the anguish in her own voice.

His arms closed around her. Rigid and barely yielding, she put one hand flat to his sternum, intending it to be a barrier between them. But under her palm she felt the soft, dark blond hair that she knew reached from his chest to a place that disappeared beneath the line of the towel. His heartbeat, strong and vital, pulsed beneath her fingertips. Her resolve wavered.

China was so tense, she imagined she felt like an ironing board. Maybe he'd lose interest and let her go. Instead he rubbed one hand up and down her back, under the fall of her curls. "I just want to hold you," he whispered.

She wasn't naive enough to believe that was *all* he wanted. He was a man of powerful appetites— hadn't he demonstrated that on the back porch? She stiffened her spine, trying to pull away. But her determination to remain aloof faded still further when she looked up into the long-lashed jade eyes. The heat, the yearning she saw there stopped her flight.

"Hold me?" she parroted, mesmerized.

"And kiss you," he added, lowering his head

to hers to capture her lips. His mouth was demanding as it moved over hers, evoking sensations she tried hard to ignore. She heard his breath quicken, and her own with it.

He broke the kiss for an instant. "And touch you."

The hand that had stroked her back came forward to rest just under her arm, not quite brushing the side of her breast.

When he freed her lips, he enfolded her against himself, pressing her forehead to his collarbone. Oh, God, there was an infinite comfort in being held in Jake's arms, a sense that this was where she belonged. His skin was warm and damp from his bath; she could feel it through her thin nightclothes. He smelled faintly of castile soap, and the witch hazel she'd dabbed on his scalp. He felt too good to let go of. This was heaven, it was hell.

And when he's gone? Ruined, you'll be ruined if you do this, her nagging conscience whispered again. But what was she saving herself for? The answer stood before her, wrapped in a towel that was too short for him. She'd saved herself for Jake. It was baffling, but no other man had seemed so right for her. Now he was asking for her, and she had no will to do anything but yield.

She turned and rested her cheek against his shoulder. "Oh, damn it, Jake," she breathed with quiet despair, and allowed her hands to slide from his chest around his ribs to his back.

That uncharacteristic curse was all Jake needed to hear from China, because behind it, he knew, was her surrender. "It'll be okay," he said against her ear. Maybe he'd reassured her; he felt some of the tension leave her. He swept her up into his arms and bore her down the hall, away from possible prying eyes, to his room. She was small and delicate and trembling, with her face tucked against his neck.

He sat her on his big bed and walked to the fireplace, holding a lighted match to the paper and wood he'd laid that morning.

China watched him as he rose again. Illuminated by the flames, he looked like a young, beautiful pagan god in his loincloth, his small gold medallion shining on its chain. He approached slowly, and sat down a foot away from her, the mattress sagging under his weight.

He reached for her hand and lifted it to his mouth, letting his eyes drift closed. Honoring it with a kiss, he touched the center of her palm with his tongue. China jumped, and pulled her hand away as though electrified.

Jake gave her a questioning look, and inched a little closer.

"I guess—" she said, feeling a little foolish, "I'm just . . . oh, just—"

"Just what, honey?" he asked so gently, she felt stricken. Why couldn't it have always been this way? she despaired. Why had fate chosen this last moment to make him kind, to strip off her blinders and let her see the man he really was?

"I-I'm scared," she admitted in a small voice.

He smiled at her and took her hand again, resting it on his knee. "So am I."

"You are?" she asked, surprised. Jake knew everything, he'd been everywhere, he'd lived a sailor's life. He must have had lots of women. "But you've done this before," she faltered a bit, embarrassed. "You have, well, experience."

"I've *never* done this," he said, putting his arm around her.

"Why, Jake Chastaine, I can hardly believe that!" she challenged, momentarily forgetting her fear. "Are you going to sit there and tell—"

"I've never made love with you before." Tucking her more securely in his embrace, he kissed her temple, her cheek, the outer corner of her eye. His lips were full, warm.

"Oh," she breathed. She gulped a bit, hearing him put into words what they were going to do. *Ruined, you'll be ruined if you do this,* her nagging conscience whispered. But what was she saving herself for?

Jake *was* scared. China Sullivan, the regal, unapproachable princess he'd watched from his youth, now sat in his arms ready to give him her virginity. Sometimes she'd made him so angry back then, he'd lain awake at night and pictured a scene like this. Except that in his imagination she'd squirmed beneath him, aflame with desire, sobbing and begging, while he tormented her by withholding what she needed. He felt a little guilty for that now. It hadn't really given him much pleasure then, either. Just a monumental ache in his groin that wouldn't quit.

The ache was back, but tonight would be different. It had been months since he'd had a woman. And an eternity, it seemed, since he'd actually made love. The women he'd known in the last few years had been more interested in the number of times and ways he could satisfy them.

But China would need slow tenderness, and, given the circumstances, that might not be easy for him. The scent and feel of her ignited flames in him that licked through his body like Saint Elmo's fire. Yet no matter how he burned, he had to remember that this was her first time. He closed the remaining gap between them and took her face between his hands to kiss her.

China felt the soft rasp of his beard against her chin as his lips claimed hers again, hungrier this time. By intuition, or perhaps from her brief experience with him, she let her lower jaw relax. His tongue, warm and slick, invaded her mouth to explore the satiny recesses.

Ending the kiss, he stood and pulled her to her feet. He tucked her long black curls behind her shoulders, then nuzzled her neck. It gave her a funny shivery feeling.

Slowly, Jake lifted his palm from her waist and slid it along her ribs, where it rested just below the swell of her breast. "It's so good to hold you," he murmured, drawing her against the length of him with one arm. Letting his hands slide behind her, he gripped her buttocks to pull her to his hips. Once the contact was made, he rocked against her flat belly, and a groan worked its way up his throat.

China felt his swollen hardness. This time, without layers of skirt and petticoat and denim between them, it was all the more obvious. Downright frightening. Last-minute panic flooded through her, and she struggled to free herself from his embrace.

They stared at each other, their breathing labored.

"If you want to change your mind, that's all right." His voice took on a strained, gritty sound. "But if you're going to, you'd better do it right now and go to your room. Otherwise, I don't think I'll be able to stand it."

China glanced at the door on the shadowed side

of the room, then fearfully scanned the alarming bulge in his scanty towel and contemplated escape.

He caught her look. "Yeah, I want you bad, and it's no secret."

Was this wrong, what they were doing? she asked herself again. Would she be sorry? Very probably. She let her gaze travel upward to his face. A slight frown creased his brow. Even though it was cool in the room, a fine sheen of perspiration dotted his hairline. He returned her scrutiny, waiting tensely.

In frustration, Jake took her into his arms again. "We were meant for this, China, from the day we were born," he breathed harshly in her ear. "You know we were. Tell me that you know it."

Yes, she knew it, and suddenly it was as though she'd always known it. There was no argument she could muster. No further objection she could voice to herself. When he left Astoria, well, so be it. They would have this night.

All those years, she'd seen him come and go from the house, and she'd felt his eyes on her, though she pretended otherwise. And she'd watched him, too, telling herself that the rude, cocky fisherman's son was not even worth acknowledging. She realized now she'd told herself that because when she had looked at him, she felt a frightening, indefinable pull. The differences of backgrounds and beginnings that lay between them, none of that mattered. Because what Jake said was true: they were meant for this.

And because, God help her, she was hopelessly in love with him.

"Tell me, damn it!" he insisted. His voice was severe—angry, but his touch was tender as he dragged his wide palm from her waist, over her ribs, to gently support her breast. Then, with impatient swiftness, he unbuttoned the front of her nightgown to reach her bare flesh. China's breath stopped when he brushed his fingers over her nipple. She felt it tighten in response.

"I know it," came her whisper. "From the day we were born ..."

Satisfied with her answer, Jake buried his mouth against her throat and pulled her tightly to him. "Then I'm going to make love to you."

"Yes," she agreed dreamily, and he laid a line of kisses along her shoulder.

To enhance his suit, he pushed aside the fabric of her gown and bent to place moist, soft kisses on her breast. She sighed and put her hand on the nape of his neck. Her flesh was unbearably smooth and full under his lips, and he had to remind himself of his resolve to make this right for her. No small task when what he really wanted was to push her down on the mattress and ruck up her nightgown to claim the warm center of her.

Instead he slipped his hands inside the thin garment to slide it and the wrapper off her shoulders and let them drift to the floor.

"Oh, Jake, don't—" Lowering her face, she tried to cover herself with her arms.

"Hush, now," he soothed. "I want to look at you." He lifted her hands and held them wide, taking in the splendor of her.

In the fire's glow, her skin was the color of rich cream. She made him think of the tales he'd heard about mermaids trapped on land to become sailors' wives. Heavy black curls that tumbled to her waist. Full, lush breasts with dusky coral nipples. A dark triangle at the juncture of her thighs. Awestruck, he swallowed hard, resisting the impulse to kneel at her feet in adoration. She was even sweeter than he'd imagined.

"God, China, you're the most beautiful woman I've ever seen."

China felt dreadfully self-conscious, standing before him without her clothes. But his praise sounded so honest, she relaxed a little.

Jake put one of her hands on the knot he'd tied at his hip, and looked meaningfully into her eyes.

"Come on, honey," he urged again, "don't be afraid."

Her fingers fell on his warm skin and lingered, motionless. She hadn't thought she'd have to *do* anything. She'd supposed her role was to let Jake do what he would. After all, she had no experience in this.

But then he dipped his mouth to her breast again. When his lips tugged on her nipple with light, sucking pressure, a quiet moan escaped her. She arched against him, nearly standing on tiptoe. A fire started in her that shot arrows through her abdomen, melting her from the inside out. If Jake hadn't been holding her, she might have toppled over backward. Almost reflexively, she groped for the knot.

Jake straightened and stood motionless while she untied his towel. Briefly, she held the fabric, then let it fall between them. She cast a timid glance at his aroused body, limned by firelight. But before she could give it much thought, Jake reached for her hand and closed her fingers around himself. The feel of him was a surprise: hot, smooth, rigid. She tried to draw back, but with his hand closed over hers, she couldn't. The action of her fingers pulling over his flesh seemed only to inflame him.

"Jesus Christ," he groaned. He tipped his head back and briefly shut his eyes, sucking in a rough, hitching breath. "Do that again."

"You mean this?"

He nodded, and she continued for a few moments, her shyness fading. She delighted in his restless response. It gave her a sense of power, of allure. Finally he pulled her hand away.

His quest became more urgent. He bore her to the mattress and laid her on her back as his mouth moved over her. Laying his body down next to her, he put kisses on her throat and ears and breasts. He felt so fiery to her touch, she wondered if he had a fever. Then she realized her own skin was just as warm.

A confusion of painfully intense sensations coursed through her, as though she were delirious. She saw Jake hovering above her on his elbow, his pale hair gleaming in the firelight as he lowered his head to tease her other nipple. She felt his breath coming fast as it fanned her skin.

When he moved his hand past her rib cage, down her flat stomach and over her thighs, she was overtaken by a breathless urgency she'd never known before. A tightness, a heaviness rode low in her belly, spreading out and down, until it began a liquid, pulsing ache.

Jake pressed the heel of his hand on that ache, once, and heard her inhale sharply. He reached for her again, this time with gentle, searching fingertips that delved her exquisitely sensitized flesh. When he found the most sensitive point of all, wet and swollen, she gasped and arched against his hand.

"Oh, God, China," Jake whispered hoarsely upon finding her so near to readiness. Full and heavy, his own desire escalated to a grinding need. He caressed her throbbing, slippery flesh with rapid strokes.

Instinctively, China put out a searching hand and found the febrile, hard length of him trapped against her thigh. When she tried to wrap her fingers around him, his breath caught and he nudged her hand away.

"Better not, honey. I won't last."

China didn't know what that meant, but she was certain she would lose her mind from this tender agony he inflicted upon her. It only grew worse as the seconds passed. She writhed under his touch, moaning. Somewhere in the corner of her mind came the thought that her behavior was distinctly unladylike, but she couldn't help it.

If only he'd stop. If only he'd never stop. She uttered a desperate, choked request that had no real form.

"Jake, please . . ." She pressed her face against his chest. His heart thundered under her ear.

But he heard her cry for help. He pulled her beneath him and covered her body with his own. His weight, bearing down on her, was comforting.

"China, honey, open your legs to me," he said with a shaky whisper. "I'll try to be careful."

With what, she wondered distractedly. He coaxed her thighs apart, and the sweet torment she'd felt was replaced by a blunt, painful pressure as he slowly thrust into her. She made a wordless noise of protest in her throat.

"I'm sorry," Jake murmured with regret. Then he smothered her cry with a kiss, and pushed through with one firm stroke. He sank into the warm tightness of her with a deep, groaning sigh.

Jolted from her passion, China froze, surprised

and disappointed by the pain, every muscle rigid. Grabbing handfuls of the bedding, she squirmed against the mattress, attempting to separate herself from the hurt.

"Try to relax and hold still," he urged, kissing the tears at the corners of her eyes. "It'll be better in a minute."

How could it be? she wondered, disillusioned.

But then Jake began moving inside her, slowly. A careful thrust forward. A gentle retreat. Again. And again. Like the ebb and flow of the ocean. As China's body adjusted to accommodate him, the pain dwindled and heat flared once more, with double the intensity. She arched against him, meeting his thrusts in a rhythm that was inborn, set by ancient instincts.

And for this instant in time, they left the lonely isolation of being two individuals to become one, together.

Releasing the sheets wadded in her fists, she looped her arms around his sweat-damp back. She lifted her hips to him as a kind of offering, so that he could somehow satisfy this ferocious, aching need that threatened to consume her.

In response, his strokes came faster and harder. The throbbing between her legs escalated to an extreme that was almost painful.

"Oh, God," she moaned. "Jake . . . Jake—"

"Let it come, honey," he whispered raggedly. "It's what you need . . . what we both need."

He wrapped one arm under her waist and plunged deeper into her until suddenly, China felt as though the mattress had dropped out from beneath her. Only Jake held her at this breathless, silent, quivering brink.

Then she tumbled into an abyss where wave

after wave of hot spasms wracked her body, the muscles clamping down in swift contractions of excruciating pleasure. She heard her own voice but didn't know if she formed words.

Jake reared high over her on arms that trembled, his head up, his breathing labored. His thrusts were short and hard, striving for relief. China looked up at him, at the sweat gleaming on the column of his throat, at the pained expression on his face.

From deep in his chest a sound rose, half groan, half sob, as if a goal of comfort and solace, long sought, was finally found. His body convulsed in rapid pulsations and she felt the scalding heat of him pour into her.

Consumed, he let his head drop between his shoulders, then he lowered himself to lie on top of her, sweat-soaked and panting into the pillow. She thought she heard him say her name, but she wasn't certain. When his breathing quieted, he slowly rolled to his back and took her with him, settling her against his side.

Her limbs were comfortably languorous, and lifting her hand to his chest was an effort.

He looked down at her with heavy-lidded eyes. "Are you okay?" he asked, kissing her forehead.

"Yes," she whispered, her heart aching with love for him. "What about you?"

His lids closed and his mouth turned up in a smile of sated exhaustion. He reached for her hand and pressed it to his lips. "I'm fine. As a matter of fact, can't remember the last time I was so fine."

China expected the regret to settle in, a cold, aching knot in her stomach, but she supposed that might not be until tomorrow. For now, she was content to lie here with Jake.

He would be leaving soon, on a voyage that would take months and months. After that . . .

She glanced at his tattoo in the dying firelight. This talisman had brought him home once.

Maybe it would work again.

A ruddy glow was all that remained of the fire, and cold crept into the room with stealthy progress. Outside, wind and rain beat against the windows with a muffled sound. China slept, her head pillowed on Jake's shoulder, one soft breast flattened against his ribs. The quilts were pulled up around her so that only her face was visible in the near-darkness. He gently began to ease his arm out from beneath her so he could tend the fire, but in her sleep, China made a little noise of complaint.

"Shhh," he comforted. "Go back to sleep, honey."

She turned her face toward his chest. He lay back and contented himself with tucking them in more snugly, creating a pocket of warmth in the big bed.

The scent of her, wood and spice, and his own satisfied desire, came to him. She was his now, whether she knew it or not, whether he wanted it or not, no matter what separate paths their lives would take tomorrow. They'd left a mark on each other's souls as indelible as the tattoo on his arm, and he would regret it.

It had been one thing to hanker for her—what had that been? A desire to conquer her? Not a very noble ambition, though he admitted to himself that it was possible. Lust? Definitely.

But there was one more aspect, an emotion that he'd doggedly ignored. It had sat within him, trying to make its small voice heard, for years. Then tonight, at the instant he'd joined his body to hers, it had come storming to the fore with a silent scream.

When Jake had taken China, he'd lost himself.

He lifted his hand to cradle the back of her head and pressed his cheek to her forehead. With his other hand, he gently rubbed her back, feeling with his fingertips each vertebra under her soft skin. In response, she stirred briefly and burrowed against him, tangling her legs with his, seeking warmth and closeness.

When the *Katherine* sailed, he would be gone for a long time, but maybe, just maybe, he'd have a reason to come home to Astoria. Yesterday he wouldn't have thought so. It would be easier if she cared for him. But, still, now, a glimmer of hope stirred in his heart.

Gathering her to the shelter of his arms, he kissed her temple and waited until her breathing resumed the slow, even rhythm of sleep. Then he sighed and, certain that she would not hear, whispered into the dark of the night.

"I wish you loved me, too."

What *was* that sound? China nestled against Jake's warm, bare body, trying to shut out the faraway voice dragging her back to wakefulness. Not yet, she prayed. She didn't want the night to end yet.

He was asleep on his side and she wrapped her arm around his waist, tucking her head between her pillow and his back. Groggily, he reached behind and patted her hip.

God, there it was again. Someone was pounding on the front door, too.

"Captain!"

Beside her, an electrified jolt ran through Jake's body, and he sat up in the darkness as though he had springs in his back. "Huh? When?"

"Captain Chastaine!" Coming from outside, it was a young man's voice. Sleepy though she was, China detected an urgency that made her uneasy.

Jake bounded out of bed and went to the window that overlooked the front yard. Lifting the sash, he stuck his head out. From the color of the sky that framed his naked silhouette, China saw that it was just before dawn.

"I'm Captain Chastaine. What do you want?" he called down in a lowered voice.

"Captain, Mr. Tewey said you better come quick! Your ship is on fire!"

China heard the sound of footsteps running away, a muffled splashing on the wet street.

"What a minute!" he yelled after the messenger. But apparently, he was gone.

"Holy Christ," Jake said hollowly. He turned and groped through the dark to the night table, almost knocking it over when he bumped into it. He fumbled around on its surface and suddenly a match flared. His face was a ghastly gray-white, etched with what she recognized as hideous fear. He lit the bedside lamp with a hand that shook ever so slightly.

Stunned and momentarily paralyzed, China could only clutch the sheet to her bosom and stare at him. "Jake—my God—your ship—"

But he didn't even favor her with a glance. He stalked to the dresser and yanked open drawers, putting on the first clothes his hands fell on. Every movement was tense and jerky. His breathing had a harsh, rasping sound.

"I'm coming with you," China said, scooting to the edge of the mattress.

He looked up from the task of lacing his boots, and arrested her with a flinty, merciless glare. She recoiled at the emotion she saw in his eyes. It was so intense, she couldn't give it just a single name.

"No, you're not," he ordered hoarsely. "I don't have time to worry about looking after you, too."

"But—"

He strode to the bedroom door and turned back to her. "I don't want you there, China." Then he was gone, his steps reverberating through the hall, down the stairs.

China looked around herself, at the bed she'd shared so briefly with him, where she'd given him her body and her heart. He could try to shut her out, but she wasn't about to let him face this emergency alone. She might not be able to help fight the fire, but she could be there to give her support—*something*.

She threw off the covers and gathered up her discarded nightclothes. She couldn't let them be apart at this horrible moment.

Chapter Fourteen

Jake pounded down the center of the pre-dawn street, straight through the puddles left by the night's rain. Soaked to the knees, he barely felt his wet wool pants slapping heavily against his legs. He had no coat, but he was sweating through his shirt. His heart hammered so fast in his chest, he couldn't detect its separate beats. A sharp-clawed cramp dug into his side. He braced it with his hand and kept running. He had to get to the wharf before too much damage occurred. He'd had experience with a shipboard fire; the tricky part was keeping it contained. If it spread too far, he'd be back in the repair yard for weeks.

But before Jake reached the waterfront, his fear began to escalate. The low clouds in the western sky glowed faintly, ominously red. The blaze would have to be huge to be seen from here. Now and then, the smell of smoke and burning tar drifted to him on the shifting wind. He ran faster.

When he reached Monroe's dock, he ground to a stop on the wooden planking, appalled by the lurid spectacle ahead. The waterfront stood in bright relief, as though lighted by an August sunset. Gasping for breath, his side aching, he gaped in horror at the enormous fireball in the Columbia River that was his ship. It looked as though the ceiling of hell had cracked open and reached up through the water to envelop her.

The *Katherine Kirkland* was completely, hopelessly engulfed in boiling yellow and white flames, and drifting slowly downriver. He realized she must have been cut loose to prevent the fire from spreading to the wharf. Now the current carried her toward the ocean like a Viking's funeral pyre. The tar he'd ordered for her hull created an oily black smoke that hovered over her like a death shroud. He could hear the roaring noise of the inferno, and even here, where he stood, waves of dull heat reached him.

Sweating and lightheaded, he gripped the bollard next to him with a shaking hand.

The *Katherine*'s masts burned from the deck to their heads, their cross-pieces making them look like leafless trees. Bits of canvas sail fluttered up toward the sky, carried on hot drafts and glowing crimson, then wafted down to the black water.

Through the blinding white translucence of the burning hull planks, the frames of her skeleton were darkly visible. Suddenly, her foremast gave a creaking groan and crashed heavily to the deck in a raging blizzard of hot sparks.

Dying. His ship was burning to death, taking with her the past four years of his life and the future he'd planned so carefully. And there wasn't a single goddamned thing he could do about it but watch. Horrible, aching grief welled up inside him, bitter and dark.

Jake tightened his hold on the bollard and leaned over the edge of the dock and vomited. The roiling water below seemed to spin in a dizzying vortex, and he briefly feared he'd lose his balance and fall in. Finally he drew a shaky breath and straightened, as weary as an old man.

Farther down the dock he saw a small knot of spectators, and he made his way toward them. One of them, Monroe Tewey, broke away and met him.

"It's a hell of a thing, Jake, a hell of a thing." Monroe's eternal toothpick darted from one side of his mouth to the other.

"Do—" Jake's voice came out as a croak and he cleared his throat. "Do you know how it happened?"

Monroe nodded, rubbing his short, grizzled hair. "It was the crimps that did this, five or six of them, and they had it in for you personal. My boy saw them leave your ship with your two crewmen. Knocked out they was, and those bastards dumped them in a dinghy. I guess they'll wake up on some other ship. Then the crimps poured gallons of kerosene over the *Katherine* from stem to stern and threw a torch on her. One of them said something about this being your reward for helping the Sailors Protective League last night."

Biting, ironic laughter formed in Jake's chest and sat there, itching at the back of his throat. All this time he'd worried that China was the one in danger, that the crimps would retaliate against her. Big hero that he was, he'd jumped into the fray at Harbor House to save both her hide and her precious boardinghouse.

Monroe took up the rest of the story. "My boy ran to get me right away, but with all that kerosene she went fast, Jake. By the time we got back here, she was burning so hot I couldn't do nothing but cut her lines. Otherwise, the whole wharf would have gone up. She was a real beauty." The man shook his head, and looked at the flaming wreck on which he'd so recently worked. "It's a hell of a thing," he muttered again, with obvious regret. Then he added in a louder voice, "We've got coffee over here, if you want some."

Jake jammed his hands in his pants pockets and gazed at the *Katherine,* saying nothing. After a moment Monroe gripped Jake's shoulder, then left him in silence and returned to the group farther down the dock. Jake felt their eyes on him, but he didn't acknowledge them. He couldn't do anything but witness the death of his ship.

That was how China found Jake a few minutes later. A gray dawn was just breaking, but the clouds overhead concealed most of the light.

As she neared him, she stared openmouthed at the burning hulk in the river, aghast at the magnitude of the destruction. She'd supposed that one of the holds had caught fire, but this—oh, God, this was complete obliteration. She'd never seen anything like it.

In the odd half-light she approached Jake, but he continued to watch the blaze, his expression blank. His face still eerily lacked color. He didn't look at her. He didn't move.

"Jake?" He appeared so disconnected, she began to wonder if he was aware of her presence.

Only his mouth moved. "You weren't supposed to come here. I told you not to." Then he turned his head to regard her with eyes that froze the blood in her veins. "But when did you ever listen to me?"

"I-I didn't want you to be alone with this. I wanted to help." Her voice reflected the way she felt—uncertain, frightened.

"Help!" He laughed then, and the empty, humorless sound of it made goose bumps rise on her scalp and neck. His teeth gleamed white. "Help." He shook his head and laughed again until tears came to his eyes.

She knew he didn't love her, but even the tenderness and affection that had radiated from him a few hours earlier were gone. She gestured feebly at the warped, charred mass of oak that burned on in the river. "Well, yes, now I see that—"

He glanced at the onlookers, then gripped her elbow and hauled her farther down the dock. China tripped over a coil of rope and he jerked on her arm to keep her upright. Leading her to a wall of crates that gave them some privacy, he released her.

"What more could you do?" he demanded. "Light the match for the sons of bitches who doused her with lamp oil?"

His voice quavered and she looked up into his face. She saw raw grief and rage there. She saw indictment.

"What are you talking about?" she asked, her heart beating heavily in her chest. She tried to back away, but he clutched her shoulders in a tight hold that made them ache.

"You wouldn't listen to me when I told you the kind of trouble you could stir up." He shook her slightly. "Why did you hang on to that damned crusade of yours, like a dog with a bone? China, those bastards burned my ship! They set fire to her because they saw me last night at the sailors' boardinghouse. And I was there because I was trying to protect *you*." Even as he shouted at her, tears coursed down his face, catching on the gold and red stubble of his beard, but he seemed not to notice. He pressed his forehead hard to her shoulder for an instant, and a single, enraged sob escaped him. Then he pushed her away, regaining some control. "They even took the two crewmen who were standing watch."

Contrition swamped her. She had believed that only she and Dalton were at risk. Yes, it was dangerous work, but the danger had been just to her. Or so she'd thought. Behind her, a high-pitched moan echoed across the water, sounding for all the world like a banshee's wail. She glanced back at the remains of the *Katherine Kirkland* and saw she was beginning to break up.

China turned back to him. Her own voice shook and was hardly more a whisper. "Oh, God, Jake, I'm so sorry. None of this was supposed to happen. You weren't even supposed to know about the league." She twisted her hands in the ends of her shawl, her words gaining volume. "But that day you saw me with Dalton, you assumed such horrible things. I wish I'd been strong enough to let you believe whatever you wanted. I wasn't."

Jake sighed and pulled out the tail of his shirt to wipe his face. How long was that incident going to hang over his head? he wondered. He'd been wrong to make the accusation, but her offended pride was nothing compared to his current catastrophe. His stomach was still a little jumpy, but otherwise he felt dead inside. All of his emotions, save howling anger, were draining away, leaving him hollow.

"Maybe it wasn't supposed to happen, but it did! Jesus, China, did you really think your enemies would let you thumb your nose at them without getting even somehow?" He strode back and forth in front of the crates. "How did you get mixed up with Williams in the first place?" In the gloomy dawn, she looked pale and frightened. Right now, he didn't care.

"I told you how. He formed the Sailors Protective League and I wanted to work with him," she hedged.

"Oh, so he just came to your door one day and asked you, a woman he didn't know, to take strange men into your carriage house and nurse them back to health. And you agreed."

"Well, no, not exactly."

He stopped pacing and gripped her chin. "Well, just how was it, exactly? Goddamn it, I have a right to know why my ship is burning up out there in the harbor!"

China glared up into his bloodshot eyes, and pushed his hand away. She hated him for forcing her to open this wound. "I met Dalton the day he came to tell me that he'd been shanghaied with my brother. But the crimps didn't just steal Ryan. They smashed his skull. Dalton held him in his arms while he d-died. He wanted me to know so I could stop worrying about him."

The information stunned Jake. "Ryan is dead?" He thought back to that conversation he'd had with Williams the morning they sat with Willie Graham. "Why the hell didn't you tell me before now?"

"Because until last night, when you helped with the fire at the boardinghouse, you *didn't* have the right to know." China tipped her face down, trying to hide her tears, but it was no use.

"Who told you that? Dalton?" he scorned.

She looked at him again, her shaky voice adamant. "No, Jake. I know you don't like him. But I'm grateful to him because he came all the way back to Astoria to tell me what happened to Ryan. I was never really certain. I only knew that he left for school one morning and never came home. For two years, every time someone came up the walk, I'd run to see if it was him. Sometimes at night I'd imagine that I heard him at the front door, and I'd hurry downstairs to look." Her voice broke and a sob crept up her throat, almost overtaking her ability to speak. "I-I should have guessed he was gone. Two days after he disappeared, I opened the front door and found a seagull sitting on the porch."

"Jesus," Jake said, automatically touching his Saint Nicholas medal. Among seafarers it was a commonly held belief that gulls were the souls of unshriven sailors who had drowned at sea.

China pulled in a steadying breath. "Dalton took care of Ryan so he wouldn't be alone at the end. H-he died so . . . horribly. When he told me about the league, I offered the carriage house because I felt I owed it to him, and because it was the right thing to do. You did the right thing, too, last night."

"And this is what it got me," Jake said with weary reflection.

Finally, the tears that she'd successfully pushed down so many times before came to her now in hard, gasping sobs. The losses were too great for her to bear with a brave front.

He put his hand on the back of her head and drew her face to his shoulder, but it was the action of a stranger. He was tense and distant, and she sensed in him an aloofness, a rejection. It felt so familiar, she almost expected to look in his eyes and see a cocky, rude insolence. God, how that hurt. China loved him with the full measure of her heart, and remorse over the loss of his ship sat like a millstone on her conscience. There was so much pain in their history—so many misunderstandings, so many things left unsaid.

He dropped his supporting hand from her head, forcing her to stand upright and alone. He lifted his gaze to follow the *Katherine*. Caught in the main current, her hull was far downriver now, leaving a trail of smoking debris in her wake.

"What about all the agreements you set up with your shippers? Will you be able to make other arrangements for them?" she asked quietly. The feeling of separation was stronger than ever.

Jake crossed his arms over his chest. His voice was low, bitter. "No. I'm finished, ruined. Insurance will cover this loss, but—" he shrugged "—any respect I gained from these people is going up in smoke with her. They'll think I'm just a wharf rat after all, irresponsible, unlucky."

"I don't believe that, Jake," she argued. "No one can blame you for this. Besides, a lot of those businessmen are opposed to shanghaiing. They even gave us money for Harbor House."

He shook his head, having none of it. "It's one thing to give a few dollars to a charity. It makes people look good and feel good. But business— that's different. After this kind of trouble, they wouldn't want to leave their cargo in the warehouse where it could be destroyed if the crimps decide to come back."

Jake pushed away from the crates and lifted a hand to touch her cheek. He let his eyes look upon her face one more time, just as he'd looked upon the *Katherine*.

He could blame China, or Dalton Williams, or the crimps for what had happened here this morning. He could tip his face up to scream at heaven, curse fate, and wonder why he'd been singled out for disaster.

Yet, when he came right down to it, the fault lay with him. It grated on his soul to admit that Pop had been right, but there it was in front of him. Jake knew now he'd been a fool to think he could rise above the life he'd been born to. To earn respectability and the hand of a lady. And his punishment for trying was the death of his dream.

He didn't expect to see China again, except perhaps to pass her on the street. Where he was headed, she would never find herself.

"I'll come by the house later to get my gear," he said, dropping his hand.

"Why? Where are you going?" China asked, sick with foreboding. His mask of aloofness slipped for a moment, showing her a man who was lost and defeated. She'd never realized until this moment how much of his dauntless self-confidence had been merely a front.

A humorless smile touched the corners of his mouth. "I'm going back where I belong. Back to my father's house on Tenth Street."

China dragged uphill toward home, alone. The sun was higher now, but the sky remained gloomy, appropriate to the events of the morning.

She'd watched Jake walk away from her on the dock, resignation stooping his wide shoulders. The years of her life had been riddled with losses: her parents, Ryan, and what she now recognized as Quinn's desertion. But none of them had touched her with this razor-edged heartache.

Because no matter how good her reasons had been for working with Dalton, she knew she bore the responsibility for the destruction of Jake's ship. No, she hadn't lit the match. But she'd put him in the position of being perceived as a league sympathizer, and that had made him a target for revenge. And now she also bore the responsibility of somehow making it right for him.

She passed a yard with a perimeter of still dormant rosebushes. Into her mind crept the memory of a rowdy, complex blond youth. He'd gotten into fights, cast insolent looks at her, and honored her with a poetic tribute and armloads of roses. She and Jake could never be together; she knew he wouldn't be able to forgive her for what had happened to his ship. Their one night of sweet tenderness was all they'd ever have.

When she reached the house, she let herself in the side door and crept upstairs. Thank God the rest of the house had slept through the earlier racket. At least she didn't have to make any explanations about where she'd been. She simply wasn't up to talking about it.

She stopped in the doorway of Jake's room and looked at the big bed, with its sheets and blankets flung back. His towel was still on the floor. Oh, the fires he'd summoned in her last night in that bed. It brought a flush to her cheeks to think about it, and an overwhelming sadness.

She walked in and sat on the mattress, gently pressing her hand to the indentation in his pillow. If he'd merely sailed away, she would have felt the same longing, but they might have parted on better terms. She drew a deep, jerky breath, and scalding tears blurred her vision. There might have been hope . . .

She couldn't bear to see him so defeated. But how could she fix it? She couldn't snap her fingers and make another ship materialize to transport that cargo.

Her head came up suddenly as an idea occurred to her. No, she couldn't make a ship materialize, but she knew one man who might be able to rescue them from this crisis. But would he? Yes, if he knew Jake was in trouble. She dashed a hand across her eyes and sat a little straighter. Elements of a plan began to form in her mind. This just might work.

She jumped up and went to her own room, straight to the desk where she'd put Quinn's address. Finding it, she glanced at Jake's handwriting on the paper and pressed the note to her bosom.

She'd help Jake if she could—even if it meant helping him right out of her life.

China stood at the counter in the Western Union office composing the wire to Quinn. She'd been working on it for a half hour but still struggled with the words. She had to deliver a lot of information in a couple of persuasive lines to a man she didn't even know anymore. It wasn't easy. Surrounded by the litter of false starts, she crumpled another page she'd been writing on. She glanced up at the clerk, who raised his brow slightly at the wads of paper around her. Finally, she decided on the direct approach.

JAKE CHASTAINE NEEDS A SHIP IN ASTORIA FOR CARGO TRANSPORT. SITUATION DIRE. WIRE BACK RESPONSE. CHINA SULLIVAN

She supposed she didn't need to add her last

name. But it had been so many years since she'd had any contact with Quinn, she felt as though she might need to prod his memory.

After she paid the clerk and the message was sent, China walked to Harbor House. In contrast with the evening before, the street was quiet, but evidence of the conflict remained. The road was a muddy bog, churned and rutted, probably from the fire engine and horses' hooves. Pieces of wood, old handkerchiefs, buttons, broken bottles, even a single shoe, were scattered and ground into the mud.

Rounding the corner, she saw that the yard's jungle of shrubbery and tall grass was flattened in some places, scorched in others. Then she realized that what had been the dining room window was now a gaping, blackened hole. On the front porch Dalton Williams was pulling off charred siding with a claw hammer.

When he saw China, he lowered the hammer and came forward to hand her up the steps. He looked exhausted, unshaven and grubby, which oddly served to make his cobalt gaze even more piercing.

"Dalton, I'm so glad you're safe." Through the broken window she saw a couple of men she didn't recognize working inside.

"The scurvy bast—they tried to burn us out, but we're still here. And after the fire department got here, the rioters started drifting away." He tipped his head to look into her eyes. "You look like you didn't get much more rest than I did," he remarked, but not unkindly.

China glanced quickly at the planking under her feet, self-conscious. If her lack of sleep showed on her face, was the reason for it also written there?

But Dalton went on, apparently unsuspecting. He gestured at the burned corner of the house. "I know you're worried, but try not to lose any more sleep over this. It's a hell of a mess in there— we've got water soaking into the flooring and I think your table is a loss. But we can fix this." He hooked the hammer under another ruined board.

The smell of wet, incinerated wood was strong out here. What must it be like inside? And had anything else in town burned last night?

This thought brought her back to the main reason for her visit. She looked at Dalton's dirty, tired face, trying to guess what his reaction might be to her request.

"Dalton, I need to ask a favor of you."

He lowered the hammer again and dragged his forearm across his smudged, sweating brow. "You know I'll help if I can. What is it?"

She laced her gloved fingers together. "Early this morning the crimps set fire to Jake's ship."

The faintest of smiles touched the corners of his mouth. But she'd seen that expression before, and she knew it didn't stem from amusement or joy. He'd told her once that sometimes, when really bad things happened, the only way to talk about them was to smile. It hurt too much otherwise.

"Jesus God," he muttered. "Was that the red glow toward the west?"

China nodded. "There's nothing left. I watched it myself. She burned to the waterline and broke up downriver."

He winced and shook his head, then began plying his hammer again. "I feel bad for that barkentine. I saw her—she looked like a good sailer. It's a wasteful loss of a good ship."

"Yes, well, it's just about ruined Jake. Everything important to him was tied up in that ship," she swallowed before going on, "and—and I feel like we should do something for him."

He glared at her, and the look was so intense she took a step back. "Do something for him! What the hell for? If he had his way, the league would be as dead as his ship."

Dalton Williams could be very intimidating when provoked, but China stiffened her back and scraped up the courage to face him. "You know that isn't true, Dalton. He just isn't as . . . *earnest* about it as we are. Now he's in trouble. I only want you to ask two or three of the men here to stand watch at the warehouse for a few nights. In case the crimps come back before I can get this sorted out."

Dalton yanked viciously on the blackened window frame. "I can't believe you're asking for this. I told you weeks ago, if Chastaine doesn't support us, he's an enemy. He's used shanghaied crews before, and as long as he sails under wind power, he'll use them again." He pushed on, forestalling her next comment. "Yeah, I know he claimed he paid them well and saw to their welfare. I may not keep him out of the water, but I'll be damned if I'm going to help put him back in."

China's forbearance began to fray. The last twenty-four hours had been fraught with emotionally charged events—the riot and the boarding-house fire, her sweet, brief interlude with Jake, and the scene on the dock. "Dalton, you owe this to Jake," she insisted, her voice low. "Didn't he help you control this fire last night?"

He turned to look at her and raised his brows, apparently surprised by her attitude. "He just happened to be here because he was looking for you."

"What difference does it make? He stayed to help. And because of that, the crimps believe he's involved with the league too. Not only that, but when you come down to it, if it hadn't been for Jake's business dinner, we might not have had enough money to open Harbor House."

Dalton hooked a thumb in his pocket and rested his weight on one hip. Clearly, he was mulling this over with no great enthusiasm.

"Damn it, China . . ." He pushed a hand through his sooty hair.

"You owe this to me, too, Dalton. I've never asked for anything, and I've carried my share of this load. Now I could talk to these men myself, but it would mean more coming from you. Jake did the right thing for the league. I think you're a big enough person to put aside your personal feelings to do the right thing for Jake."

He sighed, then harpooned her with a speculative blue-green gaze that suddenly made her feel transparent. It was as though he'd detected the difference between the innocent she'd been yesterday and the woman she'd become during the night. And the reason for that difference. His voice dropped to a confidential tone that would reach no other ears. "For Jake, huh? China, have you given any thought to what we talked about the other day? About going to Portland, I mean?"

She wandered to the end of the porch. It was strewn with chunks of blackened cinder that crunched beneath her shoes. She turned to look at him. "The league means a lot to you, doesn't it?"

An ardent gleam lit his eyes. "Sure it does. People are really beginning to listen to us. After last night, they're going to start demanding that something be done about shanghaiing in Astoria. Nothing else is as important to me." He paused here, then stumbled, "Well, of course, you—we—"

China shook her head, smiling slightly. "No, Dalton, not me, or even we. You're married to the league. It's your passion, your darling, I suppose. It will always come first in your heart, and that's good. The work is crucial and it needs someone with single-minded dedication. But . . . I know I'd need to be more to my husband than just his assistant."

She wondered why she had no trouble being candid with Dalton, yet couldn't voice her feelings to Jake. Perhaps it was because with Jake, she stood to lose so much more by revealing her heart.

Dalton approached her and started to reach for her arm, then let his hand drop. "China, China! That isn't how I see you. We're equals, a good team. I need your courage and your ideas." He lowered his eyes for an instant. "I know our backgrounds are miles apart—"

She almost laughed. Backgrounds. They'd once been so very important. She knew he didn't understand what she meant.

History was dotted with restless, fire-eyed men like Dalton. They spearheaded revolutions, willing to sacrifice everything for their convictions, moving through the shadows to expose corruption and oppression. They led righteous, ragtag armies to victory, they died on battlefields and had songs sung about them.

Dalton Williams was a martyr to his cause, and nowhere in his life did the role of husband fit.

"Our backgrounds aren't the problem, Dalton. And you can always have my ideas. They're yours as long as you can use them. But I can't marry you, as fond as I am of you, as much as I respect you. If I ever marry, it will be to a man who needs my *heart*."

He watched her, then simply nodded. His silence was his reply, and she knew her point had reached him.

"Now," she continued softly. "Will you ask three of the men here to stand watch at that warehouse for the next few nights?"

He gazed at her for a long moment, obviously struggling between his wish to deny Jake and his desire to please her.

"Okay." He exhaled. "Not for Chastaine. But for you."

When China got home, she pulled off her gloves and cloak and put them on the hall tree. She wished she could go to her room and lie down to shut out all the feelings besieging her—anxiety, grief, fatigue.

A jumble of questions whirled in her mind. Would Quinn wire her? She didn't even know if he was in San Francisco. He could be on a voyage somewhere. And where had Jake gone after he'd left her? She knew he was old enough to take care of himself, but she couldn't help but worry about him.

Passing the back parlor, she saw Aunt Gert sitting at the marble-topped table, her white head bent over her calling cards. China ambled in and dropped tiredly to the sofa.

Gert glanced at her over her spectacles, then went back to the task. "Jake was here an hour ago," she said, pulling out a misfiled card. "He took all of his belongings and left. He didn't look very good."

So he'd gone already, China lamented. "Did he tell you what happened this morning?" she asked quietly.

Gert nodded and leveled a vaguely accusing frown on her. "He did. Do you think it was fair to involve him in your business with that sailors league?"

China sat up, suddenly defensive. "Is that what he said? *I* didn't involve him. He took it upon himself to look for me last night at Harbor House."

"Well, heavens above, child, what did you expect him to do, let you risk your neck in a riot? You've taken lots of chances over the last two years, but that was probably the most dangerous. And it put him in danger, too."

The last two years? China had allowed herself to be openly associated with the league only a few weeks earlier at the dinner party. No one else besides Dalton knew what she'd been doing. "I thought the league was a worthwhile charity—"

Gert plowed on with mild vexation, as though China hadn't spoken. "And I'll tell you, I held my breath every time you went out to the carriage house. Why, anything could have happened to you. When Jake got here, I was glad to see that he figured out what you were doing and started watching out for you."

"You knew about the carriage house?" China stared at her aunt, her jaw agape.

"Of course I did. I know more than you think about what goes on around here."

China was astounded. "You never said anything . . ."

"There wasn't any point. You're as stubborn as Quinn, in your own way. Besides, dangerous as it was, I thought taking care of those men might make you feel a little better about Ryan." Aunt Gert tapped a stack of cards on the tabletop and put them in their box.

She had believed herself to be so clever, thinking that her dotty aunt was completely unaware of her activities. She was beginning to doubt everything she'd been certain of even just yesterday.

"How did you find out?" she asked, feeling curiously breathless.

"I had a talk with Dalton Williams one day when I went out back looking for my old iron kettle. You can well imagine my surprise when I found him out there patching up an injured sailor. We'd met, of course, the day he came to tell us about your brother. But that didn't explain what he was doing there that afternoon, and I demanded that he tell me." She fanned the edges of the next batch of cards. "When he balked, I threatened to send for the police and have him arrested for trespassing. He talked, all right. But he asked me not to trouble you with it—he said you had enough to worry about."

Dalton had never mentioned it either. "Does anyone else in the house know about this?" China murmured.

"Certainly not! When have I ever been a talebearer? I'm sure Susan doesn't know much of anything, truth be told. And Cap, well, that dear old dickens, he's not one to mince words, or to keep his opinions to himself." This last observation brought a secret smile and a blush of color to Gert's thin face. She dropped her gaze to a cherub-laden card on the cool marble table.

Despite the surprises being flung at her, China didn't miss this last one, and her brows rose at Gert's modest blush. Aunt Gert and Captain Meredith? Ever since Jake had arrived, China had been so preoccupied with her own worries, it seemed she'd lost track of the daily doings of the household.

"You and Cap?" she sputtered.

"He's winked at me a few times, and I won't deny he's caught my attention. Think we're too old, do you?" Gert challenged.

China sighed and massaged her forehead. "No, but it wouldn't matter what I think anyway. I've been wrong about so many things, Aunt Gert. I thought I wanted my old life back, but then when those people came for dinner, I realized how boring and shallow they are."

The older woman wagged a finger at her. "Some are, but not all of them."

"I'd always believed that Jake was no good," China continued. "That he was immoral and irresponsible, that he had no honor."

"And that wasn't true either, was it?"

China's voice dropped to a near-whisper. "No. I was wrong about that too."

Gert reached over and patted her hand. "You can't be certain of what's in a person's heart just because of where he was born. You have to take each person you meet as an individual. Jake is no saint. But he's ten times the man that Zachary Stowe will ever be." Gert gave her a patient smile. "Don't be too hard on yourself, dear. At least you learned from your mistakes."

She had, but China feared that she'd learned it all too late.

*   *   *

Late that afternoon, a young man in a billed cap and a dark coat pedaled his bicycle up the steep hill to the biggest house in Astoria. He carried with him a telegram addressed to the lady of that house, Miss China Sullivan. The young man had transcribed the wire himself, turning meaningless dots and dashes into an intelligible message that read:

WILL ARRIVE ASTORIA IN SEVEN DAYS
WITH SHIP AND FULL CREW STOP
TELL JAKE AND FAMILY STOP
QUINN SULLIVAN

China stood at the open front door and held the telegram in shaking hands.

She glanced up at the receding messenger, who was now just a dark image at the far end of the street.

Tell Jake and family.

She wasn't ready to kill the fatted calf just yet, although the tone of Quinn's unadorned directive suggested that he felt it was in order. But he was coming. At least he was coming.

Tomorrow morning she would set the second part of her plan in motion, and it would be the riskiest thing she'd yet dared.

Chapter Fifteen

"It was terrible news, China," Peter Hollis said, shaking his head. "The crimps don't fear the law, and apparently they have no need to. It's got to stop. I didn't see the fire myself, but I've talked with others who saw the flames from as far away as Main Street. I suppose Captain Chastaine is busy trying to sort it all out."

China sat across from Peter in his office at Pacific Maid Packing Company. He was the last of Jake's shippers that she needed to speak with. So far she'd convinced all but one of them to wait for Quinn's ship. Some had required the collateral she offered. The others had waived that right.

She smoothed her grape faille skirt. "That's exactly it, Peter. Jake is occupied, and since he and I are partners in this venture, I'm trying to help with the details." She explained that her brother was on his way from San Francisco to provide transport.

"Mr. Buchanan, Mr. Stanhope, Mr. Boyer, the Fields brothers—they've all agreed to let their merchandise stand in the warehouse until Quinn arrives. It will mean only a week's delay."

Peter leaned back in his chair, pensively rubbing his bearded cheek with the backs of his well-tended fingers. "I don't know. It sounds risky.

Chastaine is on the crimps' blacklist now; they may not be finished with him yet. In a fire, tin cans explode, their labels burn off. It would rain canned salmon all over the waterfront." He shuddered at the picture.

China remembered that the night of the dinner party, Peter had shown the most trepidation when Dalton spoke of battling shanghaiing. Even as a youngster, he'd been fretful and cautious. She wasn't particularly surprised that he hesitated now.

"Dalton Williams is providing three men to stand guard at the warehouse," she countered.

"I don't mean to dampen your enthusiasm, China. And believe me, I certainly appreciate your efforts. But the guard could conceivably be overpowered. That cargo is worth a lot of money to this cannery. I probably shouldn't mention this, but—well, we just couldn't afford a loss like that. As a matter of fact, my father is trying to sell his bar piloting business to generate capital for Pacific Maid. I'm afraid I'll have to decline your offer and pull our cargo out of there."

China suppressed a sigh and looked directly into Peter's bland face. "Perhaps you'd feel more comfortable if some kind of collateral secured our agreement."

Peter leaned forward, suddenly curious again. "Collateral? What did you have in mind?"

"My home."

He sat up straighter. His brows nearly reached his receding hairline.

Such a young man to be losing his hair, she thought irrelevantly.

"Excuse m-me?" he stumbled.

She'd already done this three times today, but

that didn't make it any easier. Her hands grew icy in her gloves. "If your cargo is damaged before it's loaded or if you lose money because of the delay, you will be reimbursed. That's a guarantee. And I'm offering my house as security."

Peter fidgeted in his chair and began straightening the items on his scarred oak desk. "This hardly seems—" his hand strayed to the inkwell, then over to the blotter. "—I don't know. A lady's home—" He pushed a stack of papers away, then pulled them back. Clearly he was unsettled by her offer.

"Trust me, Peter. I wouldn't make such a proposal if I had any doubts about the safety of your merchandise." She hoped she sounded more confident than she felt. The truth was, anything could go wrong, and if she lost the house to pay these men, the family could be on the street. But Jake had no confidence left at all, and she was mostly to blame. She gathered her remaining courage and smiled at Peter Hollis. "But if you agree, I'll be happy to have the contract drawn up."

He studied her for a moment, then shook his head. "No. I'll leave my salmon in your warehouse until Quinn gets here. But I think I can manage without collateral."

China quietly released the breath she held. "Good, then. We'll be in touch when Quinn arrives."

Peter escorted her to the door, and China left feeling triumphant.

She turned for home, tired but pleased with what she'd accomplished. She had no practical business experience beyond collecting rent money from her boarders and stalling creditors. To make up for it, she'd taken advantage of the scanty remains of her social standing. She still knew many of the people Jake had courted, and that fact, combined with the dinner party, had helped her gain access to these men's offices. And once inside, she found she was able to win their confidence.

The sun rode low on the western horizon as China neared her street, and the shadows grew long. This morning, before she set out on this round of calls, she'd sent a message to Jake at his father's house, asking him to meet her at the house tonight around six so they could discuss all of this. There was just enough time to get something to eat and wash her face before he arrived. She yearned to see him, to be in the same room with him again, if only for a little while. Maybe if he knew she wanted to help him, he'd feel more kindly toward her.

Just as she climbed the front steps, Aunt Gert, Susan, and Cap came tumbling out the front door.

"Oh, hello, dear," Aunt Gert said, somewhat breathlessly. "We had an early dinner. I left a plate for you in the oven."

"Wait! Where are you going?"

"No time to talk now, Missy. See you when we get back." Cap stumped along behind the two women, and they all headed down the twilight street toward town.

"Well, for heaven's sake," China exclaimed, watching them hurry away. The three of them looked like a funny little family, with Cap and Gert as the white-haired, elderly parents and Susan Price as their daughter. China wondered briefly where they were going, but Jake was uppermost in her thoughts, crowding out her curiosity. Her feeling of isolation was stronger than ever.

She made her way to the kitchen, found her dinner, and sat at the table to eat by herself. She thought of the nights Jake had eaten in here alone, when she'd bothered to put something aside for him, and she suffered a pang of conscience.

After eating, she washed her face, repinned her hair, and hurried downstairs to the alcove to wait for Jake. Surely he would be here. So much was at stake; he couldn't just walk away from everything he'd worked for.

But the minutes ticked on. The house was too quiet. Suddenly her mind jumped ahead to the coming years, and she imagined being alone here, with no one. Aunt Gert and Cap gone, Susan gone. She shivered. If it hadn't been for them, she would be in the house all by herself now, a lonely spinster with nothing. She smiled a little sadly.

That crazy Miss Sullivan, she lives up there in her big house with her lamp. A little touched, you know. They say someone broke her heart and she never got over it. Sometimes she walks down to the river and sits there by the hour, like she's waiting for her love to come home.

The clock chimed and China shook herself out of her maudlin, fanciful woolgathering. It was seven-thirty. She looked out the window again for what seemed like the hundredth time, but no tall blond figure approached. The alcove was dark and China finally realized Jake wouldn't be coming. She rose from the settee, fighting the disappointment weighing on her. Didn't he realize how important this was?

If he thought he could ignore her, he'd learn tomorrow that she was not so easily dispensed with.

* * *

Tenth Street. China glanced up at the street sign. She had never been here in her life. She'd never had a reason to be here. But now she did. Under the early-morning sun, she looked at the shabby little row houses ahead, bleached by weather and apathy to silver-gray. There was not a breath of difference between them in the way they were constructed and they had no yards. Rather, the variations were marked by their small porches: a straggling flower box here, an old chair there. And by the front windows, some with frail lace curtains, others with shades, still others with cardboard over broken panes. The smell of frying onions and fish floated to her, mixed in with the odors of the pilings underneath the street and the smoke from cook stoves.

She wasn't positive which house belonged to Ethan Chastaine, and she didn't have an address. But she'd once heard Aunt Gert say it was at the end of the row, on the edge of the river, and Jake had mentioned a rocking chair. Nervous and uncertain, China took a fortifying breath and set her feet in motion.

On her left, two thin dogs waged a snarling dispute over a bone. Farther ahead on her right, a haggard-looking woman beat a balding rug that she'd hung over her porch railing. Her front door was open and from within China heard the high-pitched, frenzied shrieking of a sick child. As she passed, the woman cast a distrustful, almost hostile glance at her.

China felt very conspicuous, an unwelcome outsider. She tried not to gawk at her surroundings. But while she couldn't imagine deserting her own child, she began to understand a little of Lily Bedford's despair. For a young woman like Lily, raised in luxury and never lacking for anything, the hopeless reality of a place like this could certainly have plunged her into the kind of melancholy Jake said had overtaken his mother.

China continued to the end of the narrow street. Two houses remained, one on each side. The one on her right looked abandoned; all of its windows were broken and an air of desolation hung around it. On the front porch of the other, an ancient fisherman with gnarled, arthritic hands sat mending his nets.

She had apparently missed Jake's house somehow. She glanced around for the woman who'd been beating the rug, intending to ask directions. But she was gone. Except for the old fisherman the street was deserted. Well, there was no one else to ask. China tugged on the hem of her short jacket and approached his porch.

She cleared her throat. "Excuse me, I'm looking for—" The man looked up from his work, and she halted in midsentence, her mouth dropping open. She was confronted by a pair of green eyes so painfully familiar, her words remained trapped in her throat. They surveyed each other, Ethan Chastaine and China Sullivan, assessing, curious, wary.

There were strong similarities between father and son, and differences, too, that she knew must have come from Lily Bedford. China recognized Jake's wide brow and the growth pattern of his beard in the silver bristles on his father's face. But his long, straight nose and full mouth must have been a Bedford trait, along with his light hair.

"I know who you're lookin' for," Ethan said with thinly veiled suspicion. His voice was the rumbling ghost of Jake's. "And I know who you are. But I'm wonderin' what you want with my boy."

"Jake and I have something important to discuss, Mr. Chastaine. Do you know where I might find him?" she asked, bristling at his rudeness. Her voice didn't shake, but her insides felt like jelly. She closed her gloved hands into fists, trying to conquer her fear. She felt at a tremendous disadvantage, standing down here in the street while he presided from the rocker on the porch, like a dilapidated Neptune on his throne. "It's very important that I talk with him. I sent him a note asking him to visit me last evening." She let her gaze rest pointedly on his seamed face. "Perhaps he didn't receive it."

The shuttle in Ethan's hand flashed in the morning sun as it wove in and out of the net. "He got it. He was busy."

Irritation and stress erupted in her. "This isn't a social call, Mr. Chastaine. Jake's future, and mine, are at stake. He entered into a business agreement with me, and I need to talk to him about it. Now, sir, will you please tell me where he is?"

He gave her a hard stare, as though trying to decide if he would tell her. Finally he jerked his head in the direction of the front door. "He's inside, but don't expect him to do no handsprings when he sees you." He gave her a sly, fleeting grin. "He had a late night, if you know what I mean. Jacob always did catch the ladies' attention."

China felt the blood rise to her face, and the sickening hollow feeling in her stomach only grew worse at his implication. Of course, why would Jake feel that he owed her any allegiance now?

"Well, go on in, if that's what you want," Ethan grumped, gathering his net out of the path to the door.

"Thank you," China replied stiffly. She approached the step and leaned over to push the net aside more to avoid walking on it.

"Damn it, girl," he snapped, grabbing it away from her, "don't be puttin' your hands on that. Don't you know it's bad luck for a woman to touch fishin' nets? I've got enough grief with this rheumatism keeping me on shore. I don't need a woman fiddlin' with my nets so I can't catch nothin' at all!"

It took all of China's fortitude to keep from running away, away from Ethan Chastaine and this place, which looked dismal and gray even under the spring sun. But with a poise summoned from deep within her, she merely tipped her head. She walked to the door and grasped the knob. Pausing for a heartbeat, she turned it and walked in. She tried to latch the door behind her, but it didn't catch.

The heavy smell of liniment was the first thing she noticed. She looked around, but it wasn't until her eyes adjusted to the dim room that she noticed a sagging, threadbare sofa against one wall. Sprawled out there she saw Jake, the inside crook of his elbow over his eyes. The stubble on his jaw looked like it had been growing for a couple of days. His shirt was unbuttoned and gaping open, revealing the dark blond hair she knew was so soft to the touch. The rhythmic rise and fall of his chest told her he slept.

That strong chest where she'd pressed her cheek while he made love to her.

His dungarees hung low on his hips, seeming to catch on the sharp bones of his pelvis. China let her eyes roam over him, from the pale hair spilling out behind his head, to that chest, down his flat stomach and his long legs, bent at the knees over the end of the battered sofa. She'd never doubted for a moment that he turned women's heads. Had she really lain beside this man only two nights ago and given him her soul as well as her body? And, oh, God, had he lain beside some other woman last night? She pressed her hand to her mouth, waiting for the burning sting behind her eyelids to subside.

Forcing herself to remember why she'd come, she approached uncertainly and watched him another moment, hoping he'd wake up on his own. But that prospect was unlikely. A whiskey bottle, corked but half empty, was wedged between his hip and one of the cushions. Standing this close to him, she could detect the vague odor of alcohol overriding the liniment smell in the room.

"Jake," she called softly.

He didn't stir.

"Wake up," she called again.

He lifted his arm away from his eyes, but they didn't open. He rolled toward her and blindly reached out to pat her leg. "Go back to sleep, China," he mumbled.

She realized where his sleep-fogged mind believed they were, and her cheeks grew warm again. "Jake," she said and nudged his arm. "Please. I need to talk to you."

His eyes snapped open, and he sat up so suddenly that China took a step back. Seeing her, he groaned.

Her heart contracted. He looked terrible. The only color in his face was in his eyes. They were bloodshot and red-rimmed, and purple shadows lurked beneath his lower lashes.

Jake looked up at China, then slowly dropped his head to grip it tenderly between his two hands. "What are you doing here? You aren't back to help, are you?" he asked, feeling as though these might be his last words on this earth. The noise bounced around in his skull like a ricocheting bullet. He was miserably queasy, making the everlasting stink of the liniment even harder to take. He didn't want to see China anyway, but especially not if he looked as bad as he felt. And that was a distinct possibility.

"You're drunk," she charged.

"Not anymore," he muttered.

"But you've been drinking. A lot."

"You sound surprised." He couldn't see her face—he was looking at the floor between his feet. But he heard that pinched-up sound in her voice, the one she'd used when she first saw him back in January. "The crew and I had a little wake for the *Katherine* at the Blue Mermaid."

She grasped the bottle by the neck and pulled it out for his inspection. "I guess this just followed you home." He took the bottle from her and set it on the floor. "May I have a few minutes out of your busy schedule, please?"

He carefully glanced up at her again, his eyes aching with the movement. She stood before him in the midst of this hovel, nicely dressed, wearing a hat and gloves, tensely gripping her bag. Her hair was pinned up, and her sapphire eyes glared at him in his defeat. The beautiful princess now saw where he came from, and at his worst. The humiliation combined with the hangover made him wish he could crawl away and die.

"Yeah, sure," he sighed. Then he gestured listlessly at a straight-backed chair next to the sofa. "Have a seat."

China perched on the edge of the chair and studied Jake, very conscious that his father was listening to their every word just beyond the partly open door. She was tempted to make an issue of his present condition, but when she came right down to it, who was she to judge him? The means she'd chosen to cope with losing Ryan had put them in this predicament, whether she had intended it or not.

"I met with our shipping customers yesterday," she began.

His head came up sharply at this. He winced at the movement. "Well, you've been busy, haven't you? I was going to talk to them tomorrow, to tell them our deals are off. As if they don't already know. And what do you mean, *our* shipping customers? What did you say to them?"

She related the conversations she'd had with Peter Hollis and the others, omitting the details of collateral and Dalton's initial refusal to help. "Except for Quincy Johnson, I got everyone to agree to keep their goods in the warehouse."

"Really? And what am I supposed to do with the stuff, China? *Swim* all that flour and salmon and lumber around the world on my back? In case you've forgotten, I don't have a ship."

She struggled with his sarcastic hostility. "Quinn will be here in less than a week with a ship, Jake."

Jake could hardly believe what he was hearing. He closed his eyes for an instant and swallowed. "Christ, does the money mean that much to you?" he asked hoarsely.

China wasn't sure what reaction she'd expected from him, but it hadn't been this. She stared at him, hurt, insulted. "No, not the money! You don't know—"

He frowned at her. "What I know is that you wouldn't write to Quinn to tell him his own father is dead, but when you saw the dollars slipping away, you didn't waste a minute getting him up here. Well, maybe your brother can handle this. Unless Williams arranges to burn Quinn's ship, too."

China jumped to her feet, quivering with indignation. "I did *not* do it because of the money."

"No? Why, then?"

"I have my reasons!"

"What reasons?" he insisted, rising from the sofa and leaning toward her.

"What difference does it make?"

"I want to know why you're doing this!" He towered over her, his face inches from hers.

"May God curse me for a fool, I'm doing it for you! So you can go with Quinn, back to San Francisco, back to sea. Because you love it," she blurted angrily, then her voice trailed away. "And because I love *you* . . ."

A heavy silence hung between them for a moment, broken only by the sound of their harsh breathing and the braying of a far-off steam horn.

Jake stared at her, shaken to the marrow of his bones. She might not have confessed to trying to gain anything for herself. But he'd expected to make her admit she wanted to raise cash for the Sailors Protective League.

Instead, she'd said she loved him. Now? When he'd been brought to his knees? He'd never had the courage to tell her how he felt. He sure as hell couldn't do it now. Three days ago he would have done almost anything to hear her utter those words. Three days ago. It might as well have been three years.

"I don't want you to love me, China," he said, his voice hard. "It's too late."

Too late. China saw the look of dread her words had brought to Jake's ashen face. Obviously, her admission was the last thing he wanted to hear. Of course it was, she thought bitterly. What an awkward burden to be the object of unwanted adoration.

When he finally spoke, he sounded older than his father. "You wasted your time with those meetings. I don't want to have anything more to do with ships or shipping. This," he said, waving his arm around, "this is where I belong. When I tried to rise above it, I got slapped back down. The fire yesterday morning, that was the last straw."

The echo of desolation in his words tore at her heart, but his self-pity annoyed her. "So you're going to sit here and drink every night and make me handle *your* agreements by myself?"

He fidgeted uncomfortably, his head pounding like a hammer on a rock. "No one asked you to get involved in this."

"Then who was that man who offered to make me his partner if I would arrange a business dinner for him?" she demanded incredulously.

He had the grace to look embarrassed. "That

didn't make you responsible for seeing this through," he mumbled.

Suddenly the front door swung open, and Ethan Chastaine limped into the room. He was a larger man than China had originally thought, probably as tall as his son if his rheumatism had allowed him to stand upright.

"Is this girl tellin' the truth, Jacob? Did you give your word to people?"

"Jesus, Pop," Jake sighed, pushing his hand through his hair. "How long have you been listening out there?"

"Long enough. If you promised to ship that cargo, and you don't, you're not the man you've been tellin' me you are." He turned to look at China, and it seemed that his expression was a little less hostile than when they first spoke. "You say your brother's on his way?"

She could only nod in response to his question. Ethan was not the least bit ashamed to admit that he had eavesdropped on their conversation. He must have heard everything, even her personal feelings.

He turned back to Jake. "Then I think you know what you have to do. You'd best see to it." He shuffled to his chair in the corner and lowered himself into it with a loud grunt.

Jake scowled at his father, then tugged on China's sleeve and led her to the small porch. He shut the door behind them. In this light, he looked worse than ever. He squinted painfully against the bright sun.

"Jake," she said quietly, "you can't stay here. It won't be good for you. You were meant to be at sea, in command." Even as she said the words, she mourned the truth of them. He would never be content with a job on land.

Jake leaned against the porch railing and gazed at the closed door, then back at the river. He knew she was right. He and Pop would be at each other's throats in no time, and then what? Would he go to Peter Hollis, hat in hand, and ask him for a job in his cannery? Or maybe to Douglas Buchanan for a job in his flour mill? He seriously thought he'd rather be dead than endure a life like that.

And what about this woman who claimed to love him? He couldn't bear the pain of thinking about that now. He risked a look at her face. She would always be his beautiful fairy tale princess—distant and unattainable, like a mirage that never grew closer no matter how long he sailed toward it. Fate had decreed that when it allowed those crimps to burn the *Katherine*. She'd been his pathway to China; she'd given him the confidence to try to win her heart. Now he could muster only enough courage to send her away. There could be nothing between them because *he* had nothing, and he didn't deserve a woman like China Sullivan. He felt less of a man than he had when he'd left seven years ago.

He wished that just once more before he left he could hold her in that big bed, protected by the shelter of the night. But it couldn't be. The best he could hope for was to carry the rich memories of their union with him for the rest of his days.

"Go home, China," he said. "I'll look for my razor and get cleaned up. Then I'll go see those shippers about the details."

She nodded, glancing at him with those sapphire eyes. "All right."

"China?"

She turned.

"Thanks."

"I thought you wanted me to work on the fishing boat with you, Pop. That's what you've always said." Jake stood in the tiny parlor and rummaged in his sea bag, searching for his shaving brush.

"I know I did. Jacob, will you stop rootin' around in that damned duffel bag? Come over here so I can see you without cranin' my neck like a pelican."

He pulled a low stool over and sat in front of his father. He wasn't comfortable with this; it made him feel like a child.

Ethan shook his head and looked around the room, at the drab walls. He spoke with difficulty, the words coming from a heart that held its secrets tightly. "We've never seen eye to eye about much of anything, you and me. I wanted you here, to settle down and accept what you had, to stop pining for something else. It didn't matter much if you was happy—a body can't expect to be happy. But even when you was a boy, runnin' wild with Quinn Sullivan and those other kids, I knew you wanted to get away from here. And first chance you got, you left. You were like your mama that way." He absently rubbed one of his aching knees. "And now you don't belong here no more. Quinn's sister is right—and smarter than I thought." He sounded disappointed with his discovery.

"Quinn's sister," he repeated to himself.

"Don't look so down in the lip about this," Ethan said. "You care about her, don't you?"

Jake automatically glanced away. "Yeah," he muttered, "but, damn it, she's so stubborn. She wouldn't listen to me about anything, and that got us into a hell of a mess."

Ethan put his hand on Jake's shoulder, surprising him. He looked up into his father's lined face and swallowed hard at what he saw there.

"Jacob, sometimes it's the people you love who disappoint you the most. You just have to let it go and love them anyway."

China dragged through the next couple of days. Jake didn't come to the house, but time and again she stood in the bedroom doorway across the hall from hers and looked in. She'd remade his bed and straightened the room so that it looked as though he was still using it. Finally, realizing that she was just making herself miserable, with a knot in her throat she stripped the sheets and blankets and closed the door for the last time.

On top of that, though she was a woman who prided herself on being in control of her emotions, now she often found herself on the verge of tears.

At meals she tried to resume the routine and pattern the family had known before Jake had come to them, but nothing was the same. Though he no longer lived in the house, his presence was still felt, and his place at the table had assumed nearly the importance that Ryan's held.

Conversation buzzed around the riot and the loss of the *Katherine Kirkland*, but she couldn't join in. And Susan was no more talkative than before, but at least she never mentioned her lost husband now.

China's sense of alienation was sharpened one afternoon when Cap summoned her to the back parlor to tell her that he would be leaving.

"Oh, Cap, why?" she asked, truly distressed. "Is it something we've done, or not done? Where will you go?" She sat stiffly on the edge of the old sofa next to his chair. He leaned over to give her knee a clumsy pat with his gnarled hand.

He peered at her face, growing alarmed when he noticed her eyes welling up. "Now, Missy, don't take on so. I'm not going far. Dalton Williams wants to go to Portland, and he needs someone to watch that boardinghouse."

She groped in her apron pocket for her handkerchief. "But Cap," she sniffed, hating her weepiness, "don't you like it here anymore?"

He poked a toothpick into the cold bowl of his meerschaum. "It hasn't a thing to do with that, not a thing. But since you two got that place going, I've stopped by in the afternoons to trade yarns with some of the men there." He quirked a bushy white brow at her. "You can't say it made your little heart beat faster to listen to stories about my sailing days. The lad was a good audience, and he understood what I was talking about, but he's gone now." He put the pipe back in his mouth.

She couldn't help but smile at him. He was a dear old soul, the closest thing to a father she'd ever had. "What about Aunt Gert? I'll bet she doesn't think this is a great idea."

"Oh, aye, she's good with it. I expect she'll be coming down to cook for us sometimes. It's just a few blocks over, you know."

"When will you go?"

"This week, I'd say. Dalton has the repairs

going pretty good, and he's all afire to tell the politicians in Portland how wrong they are to ignore shanghaiing." He gave her a fond glance. "I'll miss you, girl, but I want to spend some time with old tars like me, and I won't be denying it. A man likes to think that his life is still worth talking about, even if he's looking at its sunset."

Chapter Sixteen

Just two mornings later, China answered the front bell and found Dalton at the door. He was shaved and combed and dressed in his usual pea coat and dungarees. In his left hand he gripped a battered valise. No one could accuse him of using league funds for his own advantage, she reflected wryly.

He stepped into the entry and set the valise on the floor, looking uncomfortable, as he always did when in her house. "I'm on my way to catch the boat to Portland," he said.

"Cap told me you were going this week," she said, feeling awkward as well. It seemed odd to be saying good-bye to him; they'd seen each other at least twice a week for more than two years and had spent many long, anxious hours in the carriage house.

He nodded. "I don't know how long I'll be gone—it could be months. I'm glad the old guy is going to stand in for me."

China smiled. "I think he just wants an audience for his yarn spinning. I'm going to miss him around here." She gazed fondly at his plain face. No one would guess from looking at it the noble soul that lay beneath. "I'm going to miss you too."

A man always self-possessed, he suddenly

flushed. He glanced at the runner under his boots, then back up at her. "We did good work together, you and I. We didn't save them all, but we were able to help a few. There are men at home with their families right now because of that."

"That matters more than anything," she agreed. "I'm pleased with what we accomplished—the boardinghouse, making people listen."

Impulsively, he reached for her hands and held them in his own. "China, are you sure you won't change your mind and come with me? I, well, I guess I can't give you grand romance. I don't think it's in me. But I'd respect you, and honor you, and be proud to call you my wife."

"Oh, Dalton," she whispered. She looked at his intense cobalt eyes and squeezed his hands, touched by his modest eloquence. Some women married and never had the simple things that he offered. They should have been enough for her, and maybe they would have been, if he were Jake. But he wasn't. "I *am* honored that you have asked. But it wouldn't be fair to either of us if I said yes."

"It's Chastaine, isn't it?" he asked quietly.

She nodded, feeling her throat tighten. As strong as her love was, she wasn't surprised he'd detected it. "You'll write to me, won't you? And visit once in a while?"

The corners of his mouth lifted with a familiar, faint smile. "As soon as I'm settled, I'll send you my address. And I have to come back and check on you and Harbor House."

He leaned forward and pressed a warm, lingering kiss to her forehead and cheek. She felt his sigh ruffle her lashes. Then he released her hands and picked up his valise.

She watched as he opened the door and walked

down the steps. "Please be careful," she called
after him.

He turned to look at her from the sidewalk, and
gave her a little salute. "For you, anything."

China stood on the porch and kept her eyes on
him until he was too far away to see. "God go
with you, Dalton Williams," she murmured.

Late that afternoon China stood in the pantry,
gathering potatoes in her apron for dinner. Aunt
Gert had gone with Cap to help him set up
housekeeping at Harbor House, and Susan had
trailed along with her. She wondered sometimes
what Susan had been like before Edwin's death.
Had she been vivacious and outgoing? It seemed
unlikely, but China suspected they would never
know. She guessed that the dim, shadowy person
who inhabited Susan's form was the only one
they'd ever see.

Her hands were full when a knock sounded at
the back door. She'd told Cap he could have the
leather chair if he could find a man at the house
to pick it up. Muttering under her breath, she supposed he'd sent someone already. Cap wouldn't
want to be without his chair, not even for one
night.

She gripped the corners of her apron in one
hand to make a sling for the potatoes and went
to answer the knock. Expecting to find a burly
sailor or two, she didn't bother to peek around
the gingham curtain. But when she opened the
door, her jaw dropped and shock rippled through
her like a lightning bolt.

On the back porch stood a tall, good-looking
man with midnight black hair and eyes the color
of a summer sky. Her throat closed suddenly, and

she swallowed again and again, trying to make it function.

"Quinn?" she gasped, her voice hardly working. "Quinn!"

He gave her a crooked smile, and the ends of the apron slipped from her nerveless fingers. Potatoes bounced on her feet and out the door onto the back porch where his duffel bag sat.

"Does this mean you're glad to see me, China?" he laughed, showing off his broad white grin. He held his arms open and she threw herself into his embrace with an incoherent cry.

"Damn you, Quinn!" she sobbed helplessly while she clung to him. He tightened his arms around her enough to lift her feet off the flooring and brought her into the kitchen.

"It's okay, China, don't cry," he urged, putting her down.

She backed up and gave him a hard slug in the arm. "No, it's not okay! Where have you been all these years? Why didn't you ever write so I'd know if you were alive or dead?"

He winced. "Jake told me you're pretty angry about it."

"You've seen Jake?" she demanded, searching her pocket for a handkerchief. "When did you get in?"

"Early this morning. I ran into him at the wharf, or I would have been here sooner. I had to get the details about what we'd be shipping. We started taking on cargo just after twelve today."

"W-when are you leaving?" she asked, fearing the answer.

"Noon tomorrow."

"Oh, Quinn," she lamented, her voice quivering again, and she sank into a kitchen chair.

"It can't be helped. But we have tonight to catch up." He sat down opposite her. "Jake said some serious things have happened around here, but he wouldn't tell me what. He said I should hear about them from you."

He had the same seasoned look Jake had: harder-edged, with a few lines around his eyes, more muscled, a lot more mature than the boy who'd run away.

She couldn't take her eyes off him. "I'm glad to see you, but I'm so furious with you, I'm not sure you have the right to know." Then grudgingly she added, "Still I suppose it wouldn't be right if I didn't tell you what's become of us."

She began by telling him of their father's death. This he listened to without much reaction. She could understand that. She might as well have been reporting the death of a long-ago neighbor. None of them had been close to the Captain.

But when she told him that their father had died broke, forcing her to sell off furniture and take in boarders to support herself and Gert, his impassive mask fractured just a bit.

Then she told him about Ryan. She'd suppressed it for so long, she didn't know how to begin. She looked at him sitting across the table from her, and thought, of an original family of five people, she and Quinn were the only two left. She began haltingly, but as she progressed her words gained power. And her brother leaned forward in his chair to listen, a crease deepening between his brows. She spoke of the anguish and worry, the agony of not knowing what had happened to Ryan, the two years of silence that were finally ended by Dalton Williams.

She looked directly at Quinn, unwilling to cushion the blow of her words. She wasn't going to make this easy for him. Two pairs of blue eyes stayed riveted on each other. "When I learned the truth, it was worse than I'd dreamed. Ryan died in the hold of the *Cecille*, about thirty miles out of Astoria. The crimps had crushed his skull when they hit him over the head. Dalton held him until he was . . . gone. Our brother was thirteen years old, Quinn. Only thirteen."

He stared at her, saying nothing. But she saw the horror written in his eyes, and the guilt. The muscles in his throat worked. The color had drained out of his face.

"China, God, I'm sorry. I know that doesn't help, but—" He shook his head, as though trying to assimilate what she'd told him. "I can't believe it, I just can't believe it. Ryan—he was only a little boy the last time I saw him. I thought he'd be here. I brought him a present . . ."

China could almost feel sorry for him, receiving shock after shock in the space of ten minutes. Almost.

She clasped her cold hands around her handkerchief and rested them on the table. The obvious question remained, but she hadn't a clue to the answer.

"Quinn, you would never tell me why you wanted to leave Astoria. Then one morning I woke up and found your note, and you were gone. I think you owe me an answer. For years I blamed Jake and hated him for it, because I couldn't bring myself to blame you. But I know now that he really didn't have much to do with it. And all this time without a word from you— God, what a selfish, heartless thing to do! Did you hate us so much?"

He left his chair and sank to one knee next to her. "No! Don't ever think that! I just felt like I was suffocating here. I had to get away."

"That's the same thing you told me then," she charged with some impatience, looking at his upturned face. "It's not very enlightening."

He put his hand on his chest, and his expression was earnest. "China—those parties and lunches you used to have, they were fine for you. But I didn't want a life like that. I had always wished for a father who was here, but I'm like him, and I understood how he felt. I wanted to journey the world, to fight storms and sail clear waters. I tried to explain it to you." He glanced at the floor. "I guess I didn't do a very good job. Anyway, when Jake said he was leaving, I begged him to let me go too. He wanted me to stay here and look after you. I always figured he was sweet on you."

Her brother, apparently, hadn't been wrong about that. "But, Quinn, to just sneak away like that? Without even saying good-bye?" she said.

"It was a rotten, cowardly thing to do, and I've cursed myself for it more times than I can count. Back then, I knew there'd be a big scene if I gave you any warning that I was going. You were so set against it when I tried to talk to you about it. So I wrote the note and left it on your pillow."

"Why didn't you ever write after that?" Her voice was barely more than an anguished whisper. "Even once? Couldn't you have at least told me you were safe? I never knew where to find you until Jake gave me your address."

"I wrote lots of letters, from every ocean I sailed." He turned away. "I just never sent them. And the more time that passed, the harder it became to think of what to say to make you forgive me. Eventually I gave up. Anyway, I thought you'd have married Zach Stowe by now."

Yes, didn't everyone? China thought. Jake was right. Her brother had been spoiled and selfish. She just hadn't let herself see it. But, besides Aunt Gert, he was the only family she had, and she still loved him.

"At least I can help you now. This is my chance to make things right," he said, taking her hand in his. She heard the rough emotion in his voice. "You won't have to worry about boarders or debts anymore. I'll see to that. And I'll be back more often. I promise."

Tentatively, she reached out and put her hand on his dark hair. He rested his forehead on her knee.

"I'm glad you're here, even for just a day," she admitted. "It's not good to feel like you have no one in the world. Believe me, I know."

When Aunt Gert returned from Harbor House, the boisterous, emotional reunion continued through dinner. Quinn had gifts for all of them, beautiful things from faraway lands. Susan, unaccustomed to such activity and noise, sat wide-eyed as she witnessed the tears and the laughter. China noted with affection that he even managed to coax the woman out of her shell when he presented her with a lovely mother-of-pearl fan.

But eventually the hour grew late, and her brother announced that it was time he headed back to his ship, the *Aurora*.

"Oh, Quinn, you have to stay here tonight. We haven't seen you in so long," Gert declared. "You can stay in your father's old room."

He pushed his chair away from the table and

rubbed his full stomach. "I can't this time. Since Jake's got the crimps stirred up like a school of dogfish sharks, I'll feel better if I'm with the *Aurora* tonight. My shareholders would probably appreciate it, too."

After he was gone, China climbed the stairs with leaden feet to go to bed. She paused before the lamp, its flame glowing softly in the night, casting shadows on the wall. Was it just a silly superstition, this ritual of the lamp? she asked herself despondently. It was intended to guide loved ones home. But she'd lost far more people than she'd gained: her father, her brothers, her friend, and now her love.

She went to her room and closed the door, wondering when it would stop hurting, when this terrible yearning for Jake would end. And as she blew out the candle next to her bed, she knew she would carry it with her all of her days.

Early the next morning, China had just finished the breakfast dishes when Jake appeared at the back door. She hadn't seen him in days, and it took all her willpower to keep from flinging herself into his arms as she had Quinn's. But she'd already revealed her heart in that horrible weak moment at his father's house. That had been bad enough. She couldn't bear to see him get the awkward, squirmy look again that told her he didn't reciprocate her feelings.

"Hi," he said tentatively. She was glad to see that he'd replaced his lost coat. He looked much better than he had the last time she'd seen him, more rested, more handsome, more endearing. "Can I come in for a minute?"

"Of course," she said, with a cool composure

that surprised her. She smoothed her hands over her skirt, trying to steady the tremor he'd started in them. He walked in, tall and wide at the shoulder, filling the kitchen with his presence. The instant he passed her, she detected his familiar, distinctly male scent of soap and fresh air and salt. Oh, Jake, Jake, she thought, how have we come to this?

He turned to look at her, and jammed his hands in his pockets. She'd once regarded that habit as an annoying trait, but she had come to realize that it signified his uncertainty.

"I wanted to stop off and say good-bye," he said. "I guess Quinn told you we're leaving at noon."

She nodded. "I was sorry he couldn't stay longer, but," she shrugged, "he promises he'll visit more often and write once in a while." She smiled in spite of herself. "I'm a little skeptical, but hopeful."

He smiled back. "Cap came down to the dock to give us his blessing. I think he wishes he was going with us. I do too, sort of. I like that old guy."

"Oh, he'll have plenty to do," she replied. "He's gone to live at Harbor House now, and he'll be busy keeping that place in line."

He rested his jade eyes on her. "Are you going to keep working with the league?"

She fiddled with the waistband of her apron. The league had been such a sore point between them. "Probably not as much. We accomplished what we set out to do with the boardinghouse, and Dalton has gone to Portland. I admit the campaign sometimes seems futile, with politicians and police bribed to look the other way." She drew a breath and dared to gaze at his eyes. "We did a lot of good, but the cost was high." She expected him to agree vehemently, bitterly.

Instead, he only nodded, letting her off the hook. "I know steam is going to replace sail eventually. And when steam takes over, shanghaiing will end. Those ships need skilled crews, and they can't be bought in dockside saloons." He paused. "Maybe it'll be for the best, but I'll be sorry to see it happen. There's real beauty in a ship flying ahead of the wind, her canvas full and white under the sun."

With a sense of desolation, it occurred to her that no matter what had transpired between them, what intimacy they had shared, ultimately the sea had won that which she herself had only dreamed of: his devotion.

Jake stepped closer and lifted his hand to touch her arm, then didn't. "I want to thank you for helping me save those shipping contracts. If it hadn't been for you, I would have let them go— I wasn't thinking straight after . . . for a while."

He let his gaze skim over her, resting softly here and there, on a dark curl, on the curve of her cheek, her pale throat, the fullness of her breast, her small waist. He had to carry these fragile pictures away with him so that he could summon her memory when he needed it—during the deepest hour of the night, or in moments of doubt or worry or loneliness, when his soul would long for her. When he could comfort himself with the knowledge that she had come to love him. Even if it had been for just a while. Even if they would never be together.

China cringed when she saw Jake take out his watch.

"Well," he sighed, "I've got to be going. We still have work to do before we cast off."

It hadn't been long enough, she railed inside. Only three months, the blink of an eye in a person's life. She wanted to scream and weep and bar the door. Instead, she looked up at his jade green eyes and asked, "Will you write once in a while? To let us know how you are?"

"I'll write," he said hoarsely.

She put her hand on his coat sleeve, where she knew the tattoo lay under his clothes. "Maybe you'll get a chance to visit again someday?" she posed with a shaky voice.

Jake cleared his throat. "Maybe." And for the space of a breath he thought that if, this very minute, she asked him to stay, to give up every other dream he'd ever had, he'd do it, and gladly. Even if it meant working in a cannery for the rest of his life. If he could come home at night to hold her and protect her and let her shelter him, it would be worth the drudgery.

But the moment passed and the request didn't come. Of course it didn't. He'd already told her it was too late.

An awkward silence stretched between them. Finally Jake took China into his arms one last, urgent time. The wool nap of his new coat prickled against her cheek. He bent his head down to hers.

"Take care of yourself, honey," he whispered. "God, I wish things could have been different."

She felt his lips on her temple and she lifted her face to his. When his mouth covered hers she responded with hungry desperation. Heartache, piercing and cruel, flooded her in waves. She clung to him tightly and wrapped her arms around his slender waist inside his coat. Inhaling his scent, she tried to commit to memory the feel of his lips on hers, the rush of his breathing, the small anguished noise that sounded in his throat.

Finally, he disentangled her arms and brought both of her hands to his mouth for a final kiss.

"Quinn asked me to give you this, too," he said, and pressed another kiss to her cheek. Then he reached inside his coat and produced an envelope. "Read this after we've gone, okay?"

She took it from him, feeling the rough linen texture of the paper under her fingertips. She glanced down and recognized Jake's firm pen strokes where he'd written her name. She couldn't speak; her throat was too constricted.

Suddenly he seized her by the back of her neck and brought her mouth hard against his lips once more. Then he turned and strode to the door, pulling it open. She stumbled after him.

"Good-bye, China," he choked and pounded down the stairs.

She took two running steps out to the porch and watched him hurry down the path that led to the front of the house. Turning, she thundered through the kitchen and down the hall to the front parlor. Over the blue Persian rug she sped to the alcove windows in time to see him run down the sidewalk, past the house, and on toward the waterfront.

Then he was gone.

"Good-bye, Jake."

A bubble of sorrow swelled under her heart, making her breath short. She turned from the windows and dropped to the settee, seeing the letter she still clutched in a death grip. He'd said to wait until after twelve to read it, but, dear God, what did it matter now, when her heart was breaking?

She turned the envelope over in shaking hands and carefully opened the flap. Inside was a single sheet of heavy cream paper, creased once, bearing the same bold ink strokes as the envelope.

Unfolding the note, she read the two short lines he'd written then clapped her hand over her mouth to muffle the sob that rose from her throat.

> To the sweetest flower in Astoria
> I love you
> John Jacob Chastaine

"I appreciate your confidence, Hollis. Considering everything that's happened, I would have understood if you'd decided to cancel our agreement," Jake said, backing up to let a husky stevedore pass. The docks teemed with activity under the spring sky; horses and wagons, screeching gulls, the noisy chug of steam-powered winches, shouting longshoremen, and merchants all jostled together, raising a familiar racket and making the rough planking vibrate beneath their feet.

On his way home for lunch, Peter Hollis had come down to look at the *Aurora*, the steel-hulled bark that would carry his canned salmon. His timing couldn't have been worse as far as Jake was concerned. He'd felt empty and numb after leaving China; he didn't want to talk to anyone. But he obliged Peter by giving him a tour. The *Aurora* hadn't the grace of the *Katherine Kirkland*, or her beauty of design, but she certainly appeared seaworthy and she would get the job done.

"I admit I had some reservations," Peter conceded after they returned to the dock. "Pacific Maid Packing has been on a bit of shaky ground financially. When my father finds a buyer for his bar piloting business, the capital will make a big difference to the cannery." He nodded toward the steam tug tying up to the *Aurora* to tow her over the Columbia River bar. "Till then, we can't afford to lose a sizable cargo in a fire. Quinn and his ship wouldn't have been much help if he had gotten here and found there was no warehouse. So I was ready to tell China we'd have to withdraw—until she offered that collateral. If she was willing to risk her home, I knew she must have a lot of faith in you, and it gave me confidence. Of course, I didn't hold her to the offer, although I understand a couple of your other shippers did."

Jake stared speechlessly at the mild-looking Peter Hollis. He turned a poker face on the man, but he was reeling from the information. China had pledged her home, the only material thing she had left, to save his business and his dignity. He shuddered inside; if he had failed her or stuck with his original plan to stay on Tenth Street—

"Ah, here comes your third partner now," Hollis remarked, as Quinn joined them. "I was just telling Chastaine that your sister was able to convince me to wait for your ship when she offered her home as security against any loss. It was a pretty bold thing to do."

Quinn flashed a private, angry look at Jake, but said only, "China's got a lot of courage, that's for sure." Then to Jake, "We've only got a few minutes before we cast off."

Hollis bade them farewell and good luck, and left to get his lunch.

After he was gone, Quinn turned to Jake and

gripped his forearm. "Did you ask China to use the house for collateral with those men?" he demanded, suspicion in his voice.

Glaring at him, Jake yanked his arm free and responded in a low voice, "I can't believe you're asking me that, Quinn. The first time I heard anything about it was just now. Besides, don't you think it's a little late to start playing the protective brother?"

Quinn's own expression turned both sheepish and rueful. "Hell, I'm sorry. She must have pretty strong feelings for you to wire me for help and to risk the house. What happened between you two? No offense, but I always thought she could barely stand you. Jesus, she could barely stand either of us."

Jake gave him a black look. "Look, Quinn, I really don't want to talk about this."

"Whatever you say," Quinn shrugged with a knowing look.

They stood at the starboard rail, watching the crew of the *Aurora* swarm over her, making last-minute gear and rigging checks. When a boy who reminded Jake of Willie Graham came to report a problem in one of the holds, Quinn left to investigate.

Jake leaned his elbows on the rail, not really seeing the swarming bustle on the dock. What he saw instead was a red-shingled roof on the distant hillside. It had been the first thing he looked for three months earlier, when he'd sailed into Astoria on the *Katherine Kirkland.*

Oh, hadn't he been full of piss and vinegar then, so proud of himself, ready to show Pop and everyone else what a big man he'd become. But most especially he'd wanted to prove it to the woman who lived under that red roof.

And now he was sailing away again, with less than he'd had when he'd gotten here. His ship was a litter of broken black cinders that had washed up on the Columbia's banks between here and Point Adams. He'd lost everything that mattered—the *Katherine* and the woman he'd thought to win. His stomach clenched into a tight knot that felt like a fist.

Some men went to sea because they were running away, or they wanted adventure, or they sought, as he once had, to make their fortunes. He was leaving this time because he had nowhere else to go. The sun fell across his back, but he was oddly chilled by the thought. It had always been enough before, he and the ocean. Maybe because he'd hoped it wouldn't be forever . . .

Quinn had solved whatever problem had been brought to him, and now he rejoined Jake at the rail.

"We're all set," he said, and signaled the first mate.

The shouted order to raise the gangway and cast off brought Jake back hard to the present. He turned to take one last look at Astoria and the red roof on the hillside. When he would see them again only God knew.

Suddenly a curious sight caught his gaze—a solitary female figure standing on the dock amid the sweating, swearing laborers and cargo. Her lavender skirt was a conspicuous spot of delicate color. The brisk spring breeze lifted her hair from her shoulders, and she pulled her shawl close around herself. Jake was hurtled back to a gray dawn seven years earlier, when this same woman had come down to the waterfront. The memory of her, waving frantically, vulnerable and alone, growing smaller and smaller as their ship left her behind, had visited him in dreams many times since. And he'd suffered an aching emptiness in his soul that, in all these years, would not be filled.

"Not again," he vowed aloud. "Not again, damn it!" He turned to China's brother, fear and urgency driving him. "Quinn, order the gangplank dropped!"

Quinn turned to look at him. "What the hell are you—"

"*Give the goddamned order!*" Jake shouted. He gripped Quinn's lapels, his heart hammering against the base of his throat. "I'm not going to leave her again!"

"Okay, okay," Quinn said, and ordered the gangplank lowered again. Obviously baffled, he followed Jake's riveted gaze and saw his sister standing on the dock.

Jake ran aft and waited impatiently for the crewmen to obey, then flung open the gangway and scrambled down the ramp.

"China!" he roared.

Immobilized, China stared at Jake, tall and blond against the backdrop of the *Aurora*, unable to believe her eyes as he pounded over the planking toward her. He ran in front of a moving horse, causing the animal to rear and the driver to swear mightily at Jake, but he didn't slow down. He dodged crates and barrels, nearly mowing down a man pushing a wheelbarrow. Nearing her, he opened his arms and her paralysis fell away.

"Jake!" With a sobbing cry, she sprang forward into his embrace.

They rained a hundred frantic kisses on each

other and babbled each other's names again and
again, while curious bystanders turned to look
at them.

"I'm sorry, Jake, I read your note right after you
left. I know you said not to, and I know you said
I don't listen but—"

"Shh, it's okay, it's okay. If it brought you down
here, I'm glad you didn't listen." He pressed her
head to his shoulder and stroked her hair. His
breath came in harsh gasps.

Finally he took her face between his big hands.
They were cold, and she felt the slight tremor in
them. He tipped his head back and glanced at
the sky. Swamped with the jumble of emotions
coursing through him, he knew what he wanted
to tell her, but could he make himself say the
words? They'd been stuck in his heart for years,
never traveling as far as his throat. Writing them
had been easier.

"I need you in my life, China. I need you to
come home to, to be with." He bent his head to
hers. "I want to hold you in the night, to give you
a place with me that's safe and quiet, where we
can close out the rest of the world."

China held her breath, enraptured by his words.
This was what Dalton, as dear as he was, could
never have given her. She closed her eyes, feeling
the brush of his lips against her ear.

"When I came back three months ago, it was to
see *you*. To see if you were all right. To see if you
were married. If you had been, I think I would
have killed that weasely little bastard, Zach
Stowe."

"Why, Jake, why?" China urged, employing his
own pressure tactics.

"Well, because . . ." he stumbled to a halt.

She would hear him say it. "Tell me why any of it mattered!"

"Because I love you!" He pressed his lips to her forehead and intoned more gently, "God, how I love you." Once he'd said the words, it was as though the fetters fell away from his heart, and it gave up its long-held secrets. "Since I was fourteen years old, since that day you tried to bandage my hand. I just didn't know what it was. I tried a hundred times and as many ways to forget you. I never could do it. You're in my blood, in my soul, you're etched on my arm."

"Oh, Jake," she whispered.

"I want you to be mine. Will you marry me, China?" he asked. The expression on his face was tense, expectant.

She'd sworn she would never marry a sailor and spend her life the way her mother had, alone and waiting. But she realized she'd spent the last seven years waiting for a man with honor, waiting for Jake Chastaine.

"Yes, I will, yes," she said. She held his hands in hers and looked up into his jade eyes. "I love you too much to lose you. If a few days or weeks at a time is all we—"

He crushed her to him in a fierce embrace. "Then we'll do it today, this afternoon before the ship leaves."

"But can we do that?" she asked. "Who will we find? I don't think Father Gibney—"

"Father Gibney is going to have to work it out later. I'm not going to take the chance of having something coming between us again. We're getting married this afternoon at the courthouse."

"But—will we have no wedding night?" she murmured, suddenly shy.

"You don't understand, honey. I'm not leaving you," he pledged. "I'm not leaving Astoria. But Quinn has to go this afternoon, and I want him to give the bride away."

"Jake, really? You're giving up the sea? What will you do?" Her love for him increased with each thing he told her.

He pushed her hair back from her forehead, grazing her skin with his fingertips. "I heard about a little bar piloting business that's for sale here. It might be a good way to spend the insurance money from the *Katherine*. I think she would approve." His green eyes darkened as he looked at her. "But I'll figure that out tomorrow. Tonight, though, you're my chief concern. We'll have another wedding night, don't you worry."

"Another?" she puzzled.

He gave her a bashful look. "Well, I kind of figured the first time I made love to you was our wedding night. I told you I loved you that night, too."

"No, you didn't," she protested, pulling back. "I would have remembered."

He put his arm around her shoulders, and they began walking back toward the *Aurora*. "I waited until you were asleep."

China turned her face drowsily against her husband's wide chest, wrapped in dreams and contentment. She felt his hand stroke her bare hip. Dusk had fallen over this part of the world, washing the room in grays and pinks. They lay in her bed, having been too impatient when they got here to bother with making up the big bed across the hall.

The hasty civil ceremony at the courthouse had

lacked the pomp of a big church wedding. But to China, nothing could have been more romantic. Of course, Aunt Gert had sobbed like a paid mourner at a funeral. Even Cap, who'd come along with Gert, had sniffled loudly, swearing he was as proud as if China were his own daughter. The sentiment had caught at China's heart, until she saw him pull one of her embroidered linen napkins from his pocket to blow his nose.

Remembering the scene, a little huff of laughter escaped her, ruffling the hair on Jake's chest.

"What?" he murmured, lengthening the sweep of his strokes to include her back.

"I was just thinking about this afternoon, and Cap with my good linen napkin. I'd wondered why they kept disappearing. And did you see the look on Quinn's face when you told him to come ashore to be your best man? I thought he was going to have apoplexy."

"Huh, *I* thought he was going to shoot me. When you were picking out your ring from Herrmann's display case, he asked me if you're pregnant."

She gasped and rose on one arm, clutching the sheet to her breasts and pushing her hair back to look at him. "My *brother* said that? How nice of him!"

Jake smiled at her from the pillows, his white teeth showing in the low light. "Oh, it's okay, China. Don't get your garters in a knot," he cajoled, running his forefinger along the tops of her breasts where the sheet didn't reach. "I guess you can't blame him. It all happened so fast—the wedding, seeing him off afterward. This morning he thought I was going to San Francisco with him. So did I."

"I'm glad you didn't go," she said, letting her eyes wander over the beauty of him: his jade eyes and wheat blond hair, the muscled chest and strong arms, the narrow hips and long legs. The insolent fisherman's son who had kissed her that day in the alcove, the boy she'd cast adrift to wander the world, had come back to her a man. The engulfing love and tenderness she felt for him were emotions she had never expected to realize.

"I'm glad you stopped me," he said. Pulling her back down to him on the mattress, he laid a line of kisses over her neck and shoulder. He lifted away the sheet to expose her breasts, bending his head to press a kiss between them, over her heart. She wriggled luxuriously against the bedding, then she caught sight of his tattoo.

"Jake, wait a minute," she said, putting her hand on his hair.

"Uh-uh," he replied, continuing his exploration of her flesh with soft, fluttery kisses.

She slid out from under his mouth. "Jake, this will only take a second, and it's important. It can't wait."

"What's the matter?" he asked, clearly puzzled.

China slipped into her wrapper and tied the sash, pulling her long hair out from the collar.

"You don't need to worry about that," he said, pointing at her covering. "With Aunt Gert and Susan staying at Harbor House, you can run through the halls naked if you want. What are you doing, anyway?"

"Stay put, I'll be right back." She pulled open the door and stepped out into the hall.

Of course he didn't stay put. She heard his bare feet pad across the hardwood floor behind her and stop in the doorway.

China approached the lamp at the window and removed its glass shade. Finding a match in the box on the table, she struck its red sulphur head and it flared to life.

"For all men gone to sea," she began, touching the lighted match to the wick.

After she said the prayer, she returned to the crook of her husband's arm, and they watched the lamp for a moment, glowing in the dark of the new evening. A beacon for the living and in memory of the lost, so that all may find their way home.

Just as Jake Chastaine had.